Ransom

Also by Daniel Silva

An Inside Job
A Death in Cornwall
The Collector
Portrait of an Unknown Woman
The Cellist
The Order
The New Girl
The Other Woman
House of Spies
The Black Widow
The English Spy
The Heist
The English Girl
The Fallen Angel
Portrait of a Spy
The Rembrandt Affair
The Defector
Moscow Rules
The Secret Servant
The Messenger
Prince of Fire
A Death in Vienna
The Confessor
The English Assassin
The Kill Artist
The Marching Season
The Mark of the Assassin
The Unlikely Spy

DANIEL Silva

Ransom

A NOVEL

HARPER
An Imprint of HarperCollinsPublishers

hc.com

FIRST EDITION

Library of Congress Cataloging-in-Publication Data has been applied for.

ISBN 978-0-06-338422-4

Printed in the United States of America

26 27 28 29 30 LBC 5 4 3 2 1

As always, for my wife, Jamie, and

my children, Lily and Nicholas

And who can know the truth about motive?
Sometimes I think not even the villain himself.

—P. D. James, *The Black Tower*

Cast of Characters

Gabriel Allon	Art conservator, retired spy
Chiara Zolli	Tiepolo Restoration Company
Irene and Raphael Allon	Children of Gabriel Allon and Chiara Zolli
Ingrid Johansen	Professional thief, computer hacker
Alice Winter	British socialite
Edward Knight	British billionaire
Liam Higgins	Personal assistant, Edward Knight
Phoebe Chadwick	International relief worker
Sophie Maxwell	London lawyer
Ella Burns	London banker
Julian Isherwood	London art dealer
Sarah Bancroft	London art dealer, former CIA operative
Christopher Keller	Field agent, Secret Intelligence Service
Oliver Dimbleby	London art dealer

Niles Dunham	Curator, National Gallery
Jeremy Crabbe	Bonhams, London
Simon Mendenhall	Christie's, London
Amelia March	*ARTnews* magazine
Timothy Peel	Devon and Cornwall Police
Elenore Tremayne	Devon and Cornwall Police
Douglas Chapel	London Metropolitan Police
Eva Aragón	Policía Nacional
Peter Hoffmann	Bank Josef Bänzinger & Co.
Karl Gruber	Austrian dog owner
Dr. Rutger Timmerman	The Secret Sharer
Dmitri Savin	Russian oligarch
Graham Seymour	Director general, Secret Intelligence Service
Nigel Whitcombe	Secret Intelligence Service
Parish	Caretaker, Wormwood Cottage
Miss Coventry	Cook, Wormwood Cottage
Jonathan Lancaster	British prime minister

Geoffrey Sloane	Chief of staff, 10 Downing Street
Larry the Cat	Chief mouser, 10 Downing Street
Lars Mortensen	Director general, Danish PET
Kalla Eriksen	Danish prime minister
Anton de Graaf	Director general, Dutch AIVD
Amanda Wallace	Director general, MI5
Miles Kent	Deputy director, MI5
Yuri Ivanov	GRU Unit 29155
Zoya Danilova	GRU Unit 29155
Valery Fedorov	GRU Unit 29155
Samantha Cooke	London *Telegraph*
Charlotte Rose	Wickham House staff

Part One

Proof of Life

1

Ibiza

Most years it was Phoebe Chadwick who got the ball rolling, usually in late January, when the weather was at its gloomiest and the streetlamp outside the window of her Bloomsbury office burned for days on end without a break. Phoebe was a senior project coordinator for a respected but perpetually underfunded international relief organization. Her work, while rewarding, left her forever short of financial resources herself. Her three closest friends all had piles of money. Sophie Maxwell worked for a Magic Circle law firm, and Ella Burns did something dubious in the City. Beautiful Alice Winter got her money the old-fashioned way. Alice had married it.

It was not the way they had planned it when they were at Cambridge. Back then, when they were afire with youthful zeal, they swore they would avoid the trappings of wealth and material comfort. They were going to put their costly educations to good use, help others, make a difference. Only Phoebe, after earning a prestigious first in global economics, had lived up to her word. Sophie had planned to be a human rights lawyer but ended up looking after the interests of corporations instead, including Ella's appalling bank. And Alice? She was going to be a crusading journalist, perhaps write a novel or two, but all that changed when she met Edward. Now she was a boldface name in *Tatler*. The it girl.

They had taken another vow before leaving Cambridge, that every summer they would spend a week together somewhere delightful with no spouses or offspring or significant others present, just the four of them. That promise they had somehow managed to keep, though it was Phoebe who inevitably saw to the planning. She shouldered this burden with the blessing of the others. If she could organize an airlift of food and medicine into Darfur, they reckoned, she could arrange something as ordinary as a weeklong stay in the South of France.

They had holidayed there twice, first in Saint-Tropez, then, two summers later, in the Luberon, in the same yellow villa where they had filmed that movie. They had done Venice and Tuscany, of course, and no fewer than three Greek islands. Looking for a change of pace, they had spent a week cycling across Switzerland, a dreadful mistake. Patagonia had been spectacular but exhausting, the yoga retreat in the Himalayas an unmitigated disaster. So disastrous, in fact, that Phoebe feared the trip might be their last. This year had to be perfect; otherwise they might drift apart. Alice was already floating away, held aloft by Edward's billions. Text messages went unanswered for days, phone calls went straight to voicemail. Even Ella, who was closest to Alice, sometimes had trouble reaching her. Phoebe had all but given up trying.

Her work intruded—an outbreak of severe famine in the Central African Republic—and it was officially spring before she had a spare moment to think about the trip. After considering and rejecting several options, she settled on Iceland. Yes, it was cold there in June, but there were glaciers and volcanoes to explore, and the spa at the Blue Lagoon was to die for, or so Phoebe had been reliably informed. She made preliminary inquiries, drafted a proposed itinerary, and forwarded it to the others in a group text. Sophie was game, but

Ella groaned. The ever-delinquent Alice waited ten long days before responding. She did so with a call to Phoebe's mobile. Her voice sounded postcoital.

"Sorry, darling Phoebe, but I'm afraid dreary Iceland simply won't do. We're going somewhere very warm and obscenely glamorous. But don't worry, I'll take care of everything."

"What do you mean?"

"I *mean*, Pheebs, that this year's trip is on me."

"I can't possibly allow you to pay for my holiday."

"Trust me, I'm not."

Alice refused to divulge their destination or offer any description beyond her original *very warm and obscenely glamorous*. Phoebe packed accordingly and, as instructed, presented herself at the London City Airport Jet Center at 4:00 P.M. on the second Friday of June. Accompanied by Sophie and Ella, she boarded a waiting Bombardier Challenger 605. Alice was seated in the passenger cabin, one golden leg crossed suggestively over the other. She looked as though she were returning from a holiday rather than embarking on one.

"Where are you taking us?" asked Phoebe as she accepted a glass of champagne from the cabin attendant.

"Definitely not Iceland," replied Alice. "Good heavens, Pheebs! What on earth were you thinking?"

Their destination turned out to be a Bond-villain fortress of glass and stone perched atop a cliff on the northern coast of Ibiza. There were six bedrooms, three adjoining sitting rooms, a media room, a game room, a hotel-style fitness center and spa, and a staff of four, including a chef from one of the hottest restaurants in Paris. At the base of the cliff, reached by a treacherous footpath, was a rocky cove with water the color of lapis lazuli. Evidently the cove had a name—Cala something or other. When spoken by Alice it sounded like the most exotic place in the world.

Their schedule, to the extent they had one, revolved around the consumption of food and alcohol. Lunches were lengthy wine-soaked affairs served on the shaded terrace. They passed the late afternoons poolside or dozing in their rooms—Phoebe's was the size of her flat in Notting Hill—and at half past nine each evening they drove to dinner in an open-top Mercedes Cabriolet. Alice always paid the bill with that flashy black credit card of hers. Then she would drag them to a nightclub for a few hours of ear-shattering music and dancing. Inevitably they would run into a member of her crowd from London. She posted selfies on her many social media feeds. Her legion of followers swooned with envy.

By Tuesday morning Phoebe needed a vacation from her vacation—and perhaps from Alice as well. She slept late, then logged on to the villa's Wi-Fi network and returned a few emails. It was approaching one in the afternoon by the time she went in search of the others. Sophie and Ella were waging war on the red clay tennis court. Alice was stretched topless on the sunbaked tiles at the edge of the pool, one foot dangling in the water, so beautiful she scarcely looked real.

Phoebe sat down on a chaise longue and drew a book from her bag. Alice stirred, took note of Phoebe's presence, and closed her eyes again. "What are you looking at?" she asked.

"Your breasts, if you must know."

"Lovely, aren't they?"

"Scrumptious."

"They can be yours for twenty-five thousand quid."

"I dare you to post a photo of them online."

"Tempting, but Edward might not approve." Alice turned onto her stomach as though suddenly self-conscious and raised a hand to her brow. "What are you reading?"

Phoebe showed her the cover. It was an old P. D. James mystery.

"The killer is Julius Court," said Alice. "Apparently he was in business with some rather awful people from Marseilles. Heroin, I believe. He leaps to his death from the cliff near Toynton Grange after shooting Dalgliesh in the shoulder."

Phoebe set aside the book with a sigh. "When are you going to write yours?"

"My novel? I haven't a spare minute," replied Alice without a trace of irony. "Besides, what would I write about?"

"A girl named Alice Winter."

"Who would want to read a book about me?"

"Everyone, I imagine."

She rolled those liquid blue eyes of hers. "It can be a crashing bore, you know."

"The Royal Enclosure at Ascot?"

"All of it, Pheebs. It's the same bloody crowd night after night with a slightly different seating arrangement. Your life is far more interesting than mine." Lowering her voice, she added, "All you need now is a husband."

"Are we going to have this conversation again?"

"You'll be forty soon."

"I realize that."

Phoebe was the oldest of the foursome and thus would be the first to cross the dreaded threshold. She was also the only one yet to wed. Sophie and Ella were married to equally successful men and both had the requisite two children, though Ella was carrying on a torrid affair with a man from a rival bank. Alice had Edward, of course, but they were childless. At moments like this, Phoebe thought it was for the best. Alice would make a terrible mother.

"Are you still seeing what's-his-name?" she asked drowsily.

"Jean-Marc?" He was a doctor from Médecins Sans Frontières whom Phoebe had met in Sierra Leone. For two years they had been involved in an on-again, off-again relationship. Phoebe informed Alice that she and Jean-Marc were currently off-again.

"Perhaps I can introduce you to someone."

"I doubt any of your posh friends would have much interest in someone like me."

"It wouldn't hurt if you occasionally tried to enjoy yourself." Alice trailed a fingertip over the surface of the pool. "Incredible, isn't it?"

"This house?"

"It's a *finca*, Pheebs."

"It must have cost a fortune."

"Must've," agreed Alice, and rolled onto her back. Phoebe read her P. D. James novel for a few minutes more but soon lost interest. Alice had spoiled the ending.

Phoebe had read not long ago that "The Second Coming" was the twentieth century's most frequently quoted poem, especially the bit about things falling apart. Yeats had been writing about a world in crisis, an approaching age of disorder, but Phoebe thought his prophetic words could be applied to long-standing friendships as well. Eventually the center cannot hold. Sooner or later some revelation is at hand. For Phoebe it occurred that evening when she attempted to pay the check at a pricey beachside restaurant on the eastern side of the island. Alice, who had drunk more wine than usual, placed her black credit card on the tray with a crooked smirk and said, "Don't be ridiculous, Pheebs." Then she extended an arm and snapped a selfie. The flash of the phone's camera was like a lightning strike.

Ordinarily Phoebe overlooked Alice's childish social media habit, but not tonight. She too had drunk an extra glass of albariño with dinner. The time had come for an intervention.

"Must you always do that?" she asked.

"You wouldn't understand, Pheebs."

"Who would?"

"It's about personal branding."

"Sounds painful."

Alice's gaze was as pitiless as the sun. "Fuck you, Pheebs."

Things went from bad to worse later that evening at a nightclub appropriately called Precipice. Phoebe declared it atrocious, and Alice predictably took offense. What followed was their worst quarrel since the night Phoebe had nearly pushed Alice off the Magdalen Bridge. The row intensified during the drive back to the villa and concluded with slammed bedroom doors and a final exchange of vulgarities. Sophie the lawyer attempted to negotiate a settlement, but Ella, perhaps sensing a break was inevitable, kept to a safe distance. Phoebe had no doubt that Ella had already chosen sides.

Morning brought a brief truce, but only because Alice left the villa to do a bit of sightseeing, or so she said. It was early evening when she finally returned. She brushed past Phoebe as though she were invisible and went to her room to dress for dinner. Sophie engaged in a few minutes of shuttle diplomacy to determine whether a rapprochement was possible, but Alice made it clear she had no interest in making peace. Phoebe defused the situation by announcing that she would be dining alone at the villa. The chef made her coq au vin, which she consumed while reading the rest of her novel. The perfect evening was spoiled by the photograph that appeared on Alice's Instagram account shortly before midnight. The caption might have read *Fuck you, Pheebs.*

The thought of spending another three days trapped in a villa with a resentful Alice held little appeal. One of them had to go. Because Alice had insisted on paying for everything, Phoebe was the logical choice. She spent a final night in her luxurious room, and in the morning, while the others were still sleeping, she took a taxi to the airport. Her flight to London departed at midday. As the plane gained altitude over the northern coast of the island, she spotted golden Alice lying on the tiny beach of Cala something or other. Then the plane plunged into a cloud and Alice was gone.

2

Devon

If anyone was to blame for what happened next it was Julian Isherwood, a respected dealer of Italian and Dutch Old Master paintings and éminence grise of the London art world, a portion of which convened each afternoon at the bar of Wiltons to celebrate their triumphs or, as was more frequently the case, drown their sorrows. During one such gathering—it might have been early May, though the precise date was of little consequence—Julian lent his ear to Niles Dunham, a learned curator from the National Gallery known for his infallible eye and unfailingly pleasant demeanor. On the afternoon in question, however, Niles was uncharacteristically cross.

"My Botticelli exhibition," he explained.

"The one you've spent six months planning?"

"Yes, that one, Julie. My esteemed director has decided to cancel it."

"Sir Avery has something against Botticelli?"

"Sir Avery has no money."

"Deplorable," declared Julian.

"A sad state of affairs," agreed Niles.

But such was life in Britain in the age of austerity. Faced with soaring budget deficits and shrinking tax receipts, His Majesty's Government had slashed funding for the arts to the bone, leaving

London's great museums to fend for themselves. A recent renovation of the National Portrait Gallery had been carried out almost entirely with private donations. Small museums in the shires were hanging on by their fingernails.

"Is there no chance he might reconsider?" asked Julian.

"None whatsoever. As far as Sir Avery is concerned the case is closed."

"And what if you were to raise the funds yourself?"

Niles cast a despairing glance down the crowded bar toward tubby Oliver Dimbleby, a thoroughly disreputable dealer from Bury Street. "I'd rather spend an evening discussing Oliver's latest sexual conquests than go hat in hand to wealthy donors."

And there the affair might have ended, with a Botticelli exhibition that was not to be, had Julian not resolved to take matters into his own hands. He broached the subject with his partner, a brilliant American named Sarah Bancroft, and Sarah encouraged the endeavor, though she was confident it would come to nothing. Still, it might provide Julian with a project to occupy his copious amounts of spare time. These days his contribution to the management of Isherwood Fine Arts was largely ceremonial. He rarely set foot in the gallery before noon, and by one o'clock he was sitting down to lunch at one of London's better tables, usually with female company. The bar at Wiltons was typically the final stop of his busy day. Sarah's as well.

But how to go about raising the millions of pounds required for the exhibition? Julian supposed he could call in a few favors and twist the odd arm, but like Niles Dunham he recoiled at the very thought. Better to throw a fundraiser, he decided. But not some stodgy affair with lukewarm prosecco and wilted canapés. It would have to be something splashy and perhaps a touch over the top, the art world bash of the season. He had a venue in mind, a grand estate near the sea in Devon owned by a longtime client. Much to Julian's delight, the client agreed to host the event and foot the bill for the food and drink. All that remained was a bit of eye candy, an art world celebrity who would move the needle and draw a crowd. Sarah already had someone in mind. Julian thought it a marvelous idea, as did Niles Dunham.

"The question is, will he agree to do it?"

"Could be a tough sell," admitted Julian.

"I hear he bought a cottage out in Cornwall."

"Gwennap Head, to be precise."

"Cornwall is rather close to Devon, you know. Right next door, in fact."

"Don't worry, Niles. I'll be sure to include that in my pitch."

In the end it was Sarah who made the request. As expected it was met with considerable resistance, but she nevertheless managed to break down his defenses. As for the format, she suggested a heavily scripted interview with a friendly reporter. He reminded her that there was no such thing.

"What about Amelia March of *ARTnews*?"

"I'd feel better if you handled it."

"I couldn't possibly."

"You used to work as an undercover operative for the Central Intelligence Agency. Something tells me you can impersonate a journalist for a few minutes."

And with that the deal was done. Sarah and Julian drew up the guest list, and the invitations went out. They included the name of the event's star attraction, all but eliminating the possibility of a last-minute cancellation. He left his cottage near Gwennap Head at four in the afternoon on the third Saturday in June and, accompanied by his beautiful Italian-born wife, set off for Devon. He was confident that one way or another he was making a dreadful mistake. As the saying went, no good deed goes unpunished, especially where his old friend Julian Isherwood was concerned.

What's the worst possible thing that could happen tonight?"

"The world might come to an end."

"Short of that," said Chiara.

Gabriel considered his answer. "I suppose one of the valets could scratch my new Range Rover."

He had taken delivery of the vehicle the previous afternoon. His young daughter, an aspiring climate militant, was appalled by his decision to purchase a petrol-powered behemoth rather than something small and green. He had rationalized his decision by pointing out that for nine months each year the Allon family resided in an apartment overlooking the Grand Canal in Venice, where they utilized public transport or moved about the city on foot. Furthermore their newly renovated Cornish summer cottage was fitted with solar panels that provided most of their electricity. All things being equal, Gabriel was as carbon-neutral as a man could be.

"I was referring to your appearance at this evening's gala," said Chiara.

"I just know I'm going to regret it."

"You might actually enjoy yourself, you know."

"Impossible."

"Try, darling. Give the audience a glimpse behind the curtain."

"At what?"

"The real Gabriel Allon."

"Can you imagine?"

"It would definitely be a night to remember."

The real Gabriel Allon was now regarded as the world's finest restorer of Italian Renaissance paintings, a distinction bestowed upon him after his recent restoration of a newly discovered portrait by Leonardo da Vinci. But he had spent most of his career living and working under an assumed identity created for him by an intelligence service headquartered in Tel Aviv. Julian Isherwood had been complicit in his decades-long deception, and Sarah Bancroft had been one of his most effective weapons. Sarah knew all of his dirty secrets. And for better or worse, Gabriel knew hers.

He cast a sideways glance toward Chiara, who was examining her appearance in the vanity mirror. Her hair was dark and riotous, with shimmering highlights of auburn and chestnut. Her eyes were the color of caramel and flecked with gold. The strapless evening gown she wore left little to the imagination.

"You should probably return your eyes to the road," she said. "Otherwise you might have an accident."

"Don't think it hasn't crossed my mind."

Chiara recited the imaginary headline. "Renowned art conservator injured on the A30."

"Slightly injured, thank goodness. But regrettably he was forced to cancel his appearance at a gala fundraiser at Wickham House."

"Was the conservator's wife injured?"

"Not a scratch."

"Leaving her capable of nursing the conservator back to health?"

"I'm afraid so."

"Physical therapy?"

"Several hours a day."

Chiara raised the visor. "Poor you."

"Is this the sort of thing I should talk about tonight?"

"Your boundless sexual needs? Probably not."

"What about the time I killed that dirty bomber outside the gates of Downing Street? Or the time Sarah shot that Moscow Center assassin in Zurich? I think the audience might find that interesting."

"I suppose you could tell them about Zizi al-Bakari."

"What about Ivan Kharkov?"

"I'd leave Ivan out of it," said Chiara. "Ivan was a real downer."

And then there was the night he had killed the second-in-command of the PLO in front of his wife and children in Tunis. Or the night a bomb exploded beneath his car in Vienna—the night that was different from all others. But all that was in his past now. He was no longer Israel's angel of vengeance, he was the director of the paintings department at the Tiepolo Restoration Company, the most prominent such enterprise in Venice. Chiara was the firm's general manager. Which meant that, for all intents and purposes, Gabriel worked for his wife.

He headed southward toward the sea along a series of narrow B-roads, through Bridge End and Bantham Cross and South Milton, and slowed to a stop at an imposing stone gate at the stroke of 7:00 P.M. A line of luxury motorcars stretched along the gravel drive, at the end of which stood stately Wickham House, originally built in 1681 by a member of the House of Commons, currently owned by Edward Knight, a billionaire real estate baron and collector of Old Master paintings.

An attendant in a royal blue windcheater directed Gabriel toward an empty space on the green lawn. He pulled on his suit jacket and escorted Chiara toward the entrance of the manor house. Her stiletto-heeled pumps added ten problematic centimeters to her already statuesque frame. She gave him a downward glance.

"Well?" she asked.

"Something tells me you're going to be the center of attention this evening."

"No chance of that, darling. Wait until you get a look at our host's wife."

"And how shall I refer to her? Lady Knight?"

"Winter," replied Chiara. "Her name is Alice Winter."

3

Wickham House

The London art world and its mistress had descended on Edward Knight's grand terrace. Gabriel plucked two glasses from a passing tray, champagne for Chiara, sparkling water for himself, and searched the crowd for a familiar face. After a moment he spotted Julian Isherwood tilted precariously against the balustrade, chatting with Niles Dunham. He took Chiara by the hand and started toward them, but Amelia March appeared seemingly out of nowhere and blocked their path. Gabriel was surprised to see her. He had been assured the event would be closed to the press.

"What are you doing here?" he asked.

"I was invited."

"By whom?"

"Tonight's hostess."

"Where is she?" asked Chiara. "I'd love to meet her."

"So would I, but Alice has yet to make an appearance. Neither has her husband, for that matter." Amelia drew a reporter's notebook from her handbag. "Might I trouble you for a quote, Mr. Allon?"

"On what particular subject?"

"Your presence here this evening."

"My remarks are entirely off the record. And if you so much as print a single word of them in your magazine, you will lose a very valuable source."

Amelia went in search of other prey, and an enormous man with snow-white hair and a crimson nose took her place. "You're him," he blared, pumping Gabriel's hand. "I'm Montagu, by the way."

"What do you do, Mr. Montagu?"

"It's Lord Montagu, if you must know. And I don't do much at all." He turned to Chiara. "Is this lovely creature your wife?"

"My bodyguard, actually."

"Dangerous business, art restoration?"

"It can be."

His lordship beckoned her ladyship, who brought along two other couples, and soon Gabriel was surrounded and under siege. At last he felt the soft touch of a female hand and, turning, found himself gazing into the flawless face of Sarah Bancroft. She looked ravishing in her black cocktail dress.

Gabriel kissed the proffered cheek. "Did your husband let you out of the house dressed like that?"

"He's out of town."

"Not again."

"I'm afraid so."

Sarah's husband worked for a clandestine department of the Secret Intelligence Service that carried out politically sensitive black operations. Service regulations forbade him from discussing any aspect of his work with his American wife. She never knew where he was, when he was coming home, or when he might be leaving again.

She escorted Gabriel and Chiara across the terrace and into the warm embrace of Julian Isherwood. He looked at the glass in Gabriel's hand with an expression of mock horror.

"Sparkling water?"

"I have to keep my wits about me for the interview."

"Nonsense, petal. Have a glass of the Bollinger instead. I think you'll find it's a performance-enhancing drug."

Niles Dunham hailed a waiter and exchanged Gabriel's mineral water for a glass of champagne. "I can't thank you enough for agreeing to do this," he said. "Needless to say, I am forever in your debt."

"Other way around, Niles."

"I have something for you, if you're interested."

"If you could afford my services, we wouldn't have to hold this fundraiser. Besides, I'm booked for at least a year."

"Who's first?"

"I am," said Sarah. "A lovely Grand Canal scene by Bellotto."

Niles rolled his eyes.

"You disapprove of Bellotto?"

"Chocolate box."

"Nonsense."

A murmur went through the crowd, and heads began to turn.

"Is that Alice?" asked Chiara.

"No such luck," replied Gabriel.

It was only Olivia Watson, the former fashion model who now ran a wildly successful contemporary art gallery in King Street. Gabriel knew Olivia's dirty secrets too.

"Bitch," whispered Sarah over her drink.

"Now, now," said Gabriel.

"Did I miss something?" asked Niles.

"Long story," replied Julian, his tone cautionary.

A chime sounded, summoning the guests to dinner.

"Saved by the bell," said Gabriel.

Sarah frowned. "Unless the lovely Ms. Watson and I happen to be seated at the same table."

Niles leaned close to Gabriel. "Do tell."

"Sarah's husband once had a brief but passionate affair with the lovely Miss Watson."

"You'll pay for that," breathed Sarah.

"Is there anything else I should know?" asked Niles.

It was Chiara who answered. "Sarah was once madly in love with my husband."

"Well, well," said Niles. "The plot thickens."

They joined the procession from the terrace into the cavernous great hall. A dozen large paintings adorned its walls, mainly French baroque and neoclassical. The place cards were arranged in alphabetical order along a lengthy rectangular table. Gabriel and Chiara were seated at table one, Sarah at table two. Olivia Watson, after locating her place card, headed for the nether regions of the vast chamber.

"Crisis averted," said Chiara.

"For now," replied Gabriel.

Table one had nine place settings instead of ten. Gabriel was seated between the heiress of a brewing dynasty and a well-preserved countess from Kent. The countess, while grasping Gabriel's hand, appraised him with no small amount of surprise.

"I thought you would be taller," she announced.

"I hope you're not disappointed."

"I'm sure you're the one who's disappointed, Mr. Allon. After all, you have to sit next to a septuagenarian noblewoman instead of the marvelous Alice Winter."

"Have you seen her?"

"Not yet. Apparently she's running late for her own party."

Gabriel glanced across the candlelit table toward the empty chair next to Chiara. "So is her husband, it seems."

"Know him?" asked the countess.

"Can't say I do."

"He's terribly rich." She lowered her voice. "Much richer than the heiress to your left."

"What does he do, exactly?"

"I believe he buys and sells property."

"Sounds fascinating."

"Evidently he owns most of Sussex."

"I never realized Sussex was for sale."

"Everything is for sale in Britain these days, Mr. Allon."

The waitstaff appeared with the first course, and a plate was laid in front of Edward Knight's empty chair. He appeared a moment later, a tall, lean figure of perhaps sixty with a handsome sun-bronzed face and a shock of gray hair that hung over the collar of his costly but carelessly worn suit. Unlike every other man in the room he was tieless, neckwear being optional for those of limitless resources. With apologies for his lateness, he sat down and introduced himself to Chiara. They exchanged a few words, then Edward Knight met Gabriel's gaze across the table and nodded once in greeting.

"Good of him to finally grace us with his presence," said the countess beneath her breath. "But he seems to have misplaced his wife."

"I wonder where she could be."

The countess tucked into her smoked salmon. "Don't worry, Mr. Allon. I'm sure Alice will turn up sooner or later."

Not five minutes after taking his seat, Edward Knight drew a mobile phone from the breast pocket of his suit jacket and raised the device to his ear, eliciting a quiet *tut-tut* of rebuke from the countess. The conversation was brief and, in Gabriel's opinion, unpleasant, for it cast a shadow that lingered on Knight's face for some time after. As the waitstaff were clearing away the first course, an underling appeared at his elbow, a sleek and slender creature, late thirties, perhaps, with fashion-model features and a head of coiffed and gelled blond hair. He whispered something into Knight's ear, and the wealthy businessman was suddenly on his feet. "Forgive me," he said to no one in particular, "but I'm afraid my wife has taken ill." And with that he was gone again.

"Poor Alice," said the countess. "I do hope it's nothing serious."

Edward Knight did not return for the main course—it was rack of lamb served with a gorgeous Pomerol—or for the remarks by Sir Avery Ramsay, the National Gallery's director. The event, he announced, had raised nearly ten million pounds, more than sufficient to fund the most important Botticelli exhibition in a generation. Niles Dunham delivered a mercifully brief lecture about the artist and his work before introducing Gabriel and Sarah. For forty-five minutes they held the audience in their thrall. Sarah never once strayed from her prepared questions, but Gabriel went much further than he had intended. Chiara watched his performance as though wondering which carefully hidden secret he would reveal next. Three tables away, Amelia March scribbled in her notebook without cease.

The interview concluded with a time-lapse video of Gabriel's restoration of *Portrait of a Young Woman* by Leonardo da Vinci, made from the still photographs he had taken at the conclusion of each day's work. The first image showed the painting in a fully stripped state, the last in its current condition. The audience rose to its feet and roared its approval. Gabriel, as he stepped from the stage, felt as though the weight of the world had been lifted from his shoulders. It was, he thought, long overdue.

Amelia March accosted him first. "You were brilliant," she declared.

"How accurate are your notes?"

"Verbatim in places."

"In that case, print whatever you like," said Gabriel, and started across the crowded room toward Chiara. Reaching her proved a challenge, for at every turn there was another hand to shake, another compliment to accept. She waited until they were back in the Range Rover and bound for Cornwall to deliver her review.

"It was definitely a night to remember."

"The real Gabriel Allon?"

"And then some."

"A shame about Alice, though."

"Yes," said Chiara. "She really did throw a lovely party."

4

Gwennap Head

To call the Allon residence at Gwennap Head a cottage was a misnomer. In truth it was a substantial nineteenth-century farmhouse set upon fifteen of the most picturesque acres in the southwest of England. Adjacent to the main dwelling, reached by a flagstone walk, was a refurbished outbuilding that Gabriel had converted into his studio. Its floor-to-ceiling windows gazed across a meadow of purple thrift and red fescue. The towering lighthouse atop Wolf Rock, so named for the howling sound of its deadly gales, shone nine miles out to sea.

On the morning after the Wickham House fundraiser, he set off along Cornwall's famed Coast Path toward Penzance, a rucksack over one shoulder, Irene and Raphael at his side. For twenty minutes, as they made their way along the sea cliffs, he was subjected to a litany of complaints regarding one Cecily Newton, the delightful, mild-mannered Cornish girl from Sennen Cove who had looked after the children the previous evening.

"She was mean to us," insisted Irene.

"Was she really?"

"Cruel, even."

"I rather doubt that. In fact, it sounds to me as though you're upset that you weren't invited to the fundraiser."

"It wasn't nice to leave us at home alone."

"You weren't alone, you were with Cecily. But please speak English while we're in Cornwall."

"Why?"

"Because it's quite possible that you will attend university here in England, and you have to learn to speak English without such a pronounced Italian accent."

"We'll speak English only if you promise never to leave us with Cecily again."

"I shall make no such commitment."

"Then Raphael and I shall continue to speak in Italian," huffed Irene. "With our pronounced Venetian accents."

The children marched along the footpath at a stoic clip, trying gamely to keep pace with their father, but they began to tire as they approached the Tater Du Lighthouse. Chiara met them at Lamorna Cove, and they had a bite to eat at the little beach café. Gabriel checked the *ARTnews* website and saw that Amelia March had posted her story about the fundraiser. It took nearly two minutes for the article to download. They were in the middle of a cellular dead zone, one of several along the Cornish coast, including one at Gwennap Head.

"Well?" asked Chiara.

"The real Gabriel Allon," he replied. "In his own words."

"And yet the world didn't come to an end."

"We'll see about that."

Chiara and the children headed back to the cottage in the Range Rover, and Gabriel, alone, made the six-mile trek to Penzance Harbor, where he took delivery of a new Beneteau sailboat. The vessel was thirty feet in length and nine feet across the beam, smaller than the Bavaria 42 he kept in Venice but large enough to accommodate a family of four comfortably. He ran it across Mount's Bay on the prevailing southwesterly wind and was back in Penzance in time for dinner. Chiara and the children met him at a quayside restaurant called the Boatshed. Irene and Raphael, after reviewing the menu, placed their orders in English.

"How did you manage that?" Gabriel asked Chiara quietly.

"I threatened them, darling. How else?"

The children spoke only English for the remainder of dinner and over breakfast the following morning, which dawned cloudy and cold. Gabriel read a book by the fire until eleven o'clock, when he spotted a white transit van bumping up the property's long drive. Inside, entombed in a protective wooden coffin, was *View of the Grand Canal with the Rialto Bridge*, oil on canvas, 136 by 242 centimeters, by the eighteenth-century urban landscape painter Bernardo Bellotto. Gabriel disassembled the crate, then, with Chiara's help, secured the enormous painting to a pair of Italian-made studio easels.

He pointed toward the terra-cotta palazzo on the left side of the canvas. "Your *other* home," he said. "The one I'm still paying for."

"Lovely, isn't it?"

"Quite. But I'm afraid it needs a bit of work."

"And the rest of the painting?"

"I won't know until I strip it."

"How long do you suppose it will take?"

"Suffice to say," replied Gabriel, "I won't be spending much time aboard my new sailboat."

In the lexicon of art conservation, to strip a painting meant removing the dirty varnish and the overpainting of previous restorations. It was a mind-numbing task that involved cleaning the surface of the canvas with hand-fashioned swabs of cotton wool dipped in a carefully calibrated solution of acetone, methyl proxitol, and mineral spirits. Most conservators were trained in basic chemistry, but Gabriel, who had no formal education, relied on instinct and experience when preparing his solvent. The mixture had to be strong enough to dissolve the unwanted material but not so strong that it damaged the underlying painting. Each swab could clean about a square inch of the surface before it became too soiled to use. Then Gabriel had to fashion a new swab and start again.

By early evening he had cleaned the facade of the terra-cotta palazzo and the two gondolas moored along the landing. He took a break for dinner, worked late into the evening, and was back in his studio before Chiara and the children had awakened. The skies poured with rain all morning, but by midday the sun was shining brightly and the wind was blowing fifteen to twenty. Deserving of a break, or so he assured himself, he sailed the Beneteau out to Wolf Rock, then, after rounding the lighthouse, returned to Penzance.

He adhered to a similar schedule on Wednesday and Thursday—toil at the canvas in the morning, take to the sea in the afternoon—but on Friday he became so engrossed in his work that he lost track of time. At two fifteen, as he was removing the dirty varnish from Bellotto's rendering of the Rialto Bridge, he became aware of a motorcar advancing up the drive. It was an unusual sight; the cottage was isolated, and a prominently displayed sign at the entrance read PRIVATE. Also unusual was the vehicle itself. It was a Rolls-Royce saloon model, silver and midnight blue in color. The car eased sedately to a stop outside Gabriel's studio, and the engine died. Then, into the crystalline Cornish sunlight, stepped none other than Edward Knight.

He was dressed for a day in the countryside in a zippered pullover, corduroy trousers, and stylish chukka boots. Spotting Gabriel emerging from his studio, he flung an arm into the air as though hailing a taxi.

"Allon," he called out genially. "I hope I'm not intruding on your work."

"As a matter of fact, you are," said Gabriel with a smile. "Mind telling me how you managed to find my house?"

"You're the famous spy. You tell me."

"You either searched the property records, or you asked Julian Isherwood. I'm betting it was the latter."

"He assured me that you wouldn't mind if I dropped by." Knight surveyed the cottage with a practiced eye. "What a lovely place you have here. Very charming indeed."

"It's not exactly Wickham House, but we're quite fond of it."

Knight glanced toward the entrance of Gabriel's studio. "Do you allow visitors?"

"Never."

"Julian seemed to think you would make an exception in my case."

"Did he?"

"I'm interested in acquiring the Bellotto," explained Knight. "Julian said you would allow me to have a look at it."

"He didn't mention it."

"It must have slipped his mind." Knight took out a mobile phone. "We can ring him, if you like."

Gabriel planned to place the call himself, though not in the presence of Edward Knight. He did not know why the billionaire real estate investor had driven himself to deepest Cornwall, but he suspected it had little to do with *View of the Grand Canal with the Rialto Bridge* by Bernardo Bellotto.

Together they headed up the flagstone walk and through the open door of the studio. The painting was awash in the searing white light of two halogen lamps. Knight planted himself before it, hands on his hips, elbows splayed.

"Extraordinary, don't you think?"

"It would certainly be a worthy addition to your collection."

"How much do you suppose it's worth?"

"Julian would know better. I'm only a conservator."

"Come now, Allon. Modesty doesn't suit you."

He gave it a moment of thought. "*View of Verona with the Ponte delle Navi* fetched ten and a half at auction not long ago. I think this painting is better."

"How much better?"

"It might go for as much as twelve."

"And what would be your share of the proceeds?"

"You don't expect me to answer that, do you?"

"Ten percent?" persisted Edward Knight.

"More like five."

"And if the painting went for twenty million?"

"You would be vastly overpaying."

Knight set off on a slow tour of the studio, pausing at Gabriel's stainless-steel trolley. "The tools of your trade. One of them, at least."

"I only have one trade these days."

"You don't expect me to believe that, do you?"

"Believe what you like, Mr. Knight."

"I believe you still find time to dabble in your old line of work." Knight returned to his original position before the canvas and folded his arms in thought. "And what if I required your services, Allon? How much would it cost me?"

"That depends on the size, condition, and approximate value of the work in question."

"She's five feet ten inches tall and worth an extraordinary amount of money."

"Your wife?"

Edward Knight nodded gravely.

"Current condition?" asked Gabriel.

"Gone," answered Knight. "Vanished without a trace."

5

Land's End

Gabriel pulled on a pair of Wellington boots and led Edward Knight across the flower-strewn meadow to the Coast Path. After a moment's deliberation they headed north, past the National Coastwatch Institution observation point, around a pair of rocky coves, toward Land's End. Knight, seemingly oblivious to the beauty of his surroundings, was describing a piece of real estate, a lavish home on the northern coast of Ibiza, a *finca* in the lexicon of the island, rentable for the princely sum of two hundred and fifty thousand euros a week during the summer high season. He had arranged for his wife and three old friends from Cambridge to stay at the property the previous week. It was, he explained, something of an annual ritual.

"They were supposed to return in time for Alice to attend the fundraiser. But around eleven o'clock on Saturday morning, the pilot of my private plane informed me that Alice and her friends had not yet arrived at the airport. To be perfectly honest, I wasn't terribly alarmed. Alice has many admirable qualities, but punctuality isn't one of them."

"You rang her, I assume?"

"Yes, of course."

"And?"

The call went straight to voicemail, so Knight phoned one of the three women who had accompanied Alice to Ibiza, a lawyer named Sophie Maxwell who practiced at the same Magic Circle firm that represented Knight's company. Sophie informed him that she had not seen or heard from Alice since late the previous morning.

"Why didn't she tell you earlier?"

"You're a man of the world, Allon. Do I really need to explain why one of Alice's oldest and closest friends might have neglected to tell me that my wife had failed to return to her rented villa on Ibiza the previous evening?"

"She suspected that Alice was with another man?"

Knight made no reply.

"Is it possible?"

"That beautiful Alice has run off with her dashing young lover? I rather doubt it."

"Does she have one?"

"Rumors about affairs have surfaced in the less reputable press from time to time, but Alice has always denied it."

"Do you believe her?"

"Not entirely."

"But you've never pursued the matter?"

He batted away the suggestion. "I'm a busy man, Allon."

It was not quite a denial. "What happened next?" asked Gabriel.

"I instructed Sophie Maxwell to telephone the Spanish authorities. Evidently they weren't terribly concerned either. It won't surprise you to learn that British tourists aren't always on their best behavior when they visit Ibiza."

"But your wife is no ordinary tourist."

"I made that point when I rang the commissioner of the Policía Nacional. He assured me that he would commence an island-wide search for Alice at once. He rang me with the results while I was having dinner with you and your wife at the fundraiser."

"There was no sign of her?"

"Not a trace. With the exception of her rental car," added Knight. "The police found it at the bottom of a ravine about three kilometers from the villa. I slipped out of Wickham House during your interview with Ms. Bancroft and flew to Ibiza that very night."

He remained on the island, he continued, for the next seventy-two hours, monitoring the search for his wife. At Knight's insistence it was conducted with discretion, with no statements to the press or requests for assistance from the public. It turned up nothing other than a single Hermès sandal, which was found lying on the beach of a small cove.

"Who confirmed the sandal was Alice's?"

"It was Ella Burns."

"And what does Ella do?"

"She works for HSBC."

"And the fourth member of the party?"

"Phoebe Chadwick."

"Banker or barrister?" asked Gabriel.

"International relief worker. She left Ibiza the day before Alice's disappearance and returned to London on a commercial flight."

"Any particular reason?"

"Apparently she and Alice had a row for the ages at dinner one evening."

"About what?"

"Alice has millions of followers on social media, and she tends to them assiduously. Phoebe disapproves. She's not terribly fond of me either," said Knight. "But that is neither here nor there."

The footpath bore them up the slope of a gentle rise to the Land's End Hotel. Knight announced that he was in need of refreshment, so they went inside and were seated at a window table in the restaurant. Gabriel, a regular patron of the establishment, ordered the Cornish cream tea for two.

"How very English of you," remarked Knight.

"When in Rome."

Knight smiled in spite of himself. "I suppose you're wondering what any of this has to do with you."

"The thought crossed my mind."

"The Spanish authorities are at a loss to explain my wife's disappearance. Frankly they strike me as totally incompetent."

"In my experience they're rather good at what they do."

"You operated in Spain in your previous life?"

"Next question, Mr. Knight."

"I was wondering," he said, "whether you might agree to serve as my representative in this matter."

"Representative?"

"Adviser, consultant, specialist—you choose the word, Allon."

"How about hired gun?"

"That's two words," said Knight. "And I'm hoping a gun won't be necessary."

"If you want my advice, you should allow the Spanish police to go public."

"Can you imagine the spectacle? Alice's disappearance would become an international sensation. In my opinion this matter needs to be handled quietly by an experienced professional." Knight paused, then added, "Someone like you."

"Surely you have a security consultant on your payroll."

"I use a firm in Mayfair. It's quite small, very exclusive. Most of its employees are former MI5 and SAS officers. They provide me with bodyguards when I require them and conduct discreet inquiries on my behalf."

"And what did your exclusive Mayfair security firm have to say about me?"

"I didn't bother with a background check, Allon. Your reputation precedes you."

"If that were the case, you wouldn't have bothered to come all the way to Cornwall."

A look of desperation appeared on Edward Knight's face. "I came here because I have nowhere else to turn. Will you at least travel to Ibiza and have a look around? I'll make it well worth your while."

"I don't want your money."

"I suppose there's a first time for everything, after all." The waitress appeared with their order. Knight added milk to his tea and gave it a single violent stir. "As you might imagine, I'm not used to hearing the word *no*."

"I haven't actually uttered it yet."

Knight laid the spoon upon his saucer.

"I assume the Spanish police have attempted to locate Alice's mobile phone."

"Without success," replied Knight.

"What about her credit cards?"

"There's been no activity since last Friday afternoon."

"Anything unusual?"

"She made a five-hundred-euro purchase at the Louis Vuitton boutique near the marina."

"I didn't realize it was possible to spend only five hundred euros at Louis Vuitton."

"It was a cotton ballcap."

"And the police are certain that Alice was the one who purchased it?"

Knight nodded. "I've seen the surveillance video. After leaving the boutique, she walked to a nearby ATM machine and withdrew two thousand euros in cash."

"That's a rather large sum of money."

"Not where Alice is concerned."

"It might well explain why she's missing."

"A robbery gone wrong? The police put forward the same theory."

"Was she wearing jewelry?"

"A wristwatch, rings, bracelets, and a necklace, all extremely valuable. Even so, she would have handed over everything to a thief without a second thought."

"No sentimental value?"

"Alice isn't the sentimental type."

Edward Knight didn't strike Gabriel as the sentimental type either. "You can't keep her disappearance a secret forever. Someone is bound to notice she's missing."

"All the more reason I would like you to leave for Ibiza as soon as possible. But don't worry about your travel arrangements. My personal assistant will see to everything. Liam Higgins is his name. You might have noticed him at dinner the other night."

"I'm sorry," said Gabriel, "but I haven't the time. I promised Julian that I would finish the Bellotto by the end of the summer."

Knight produced his phone and dialed. It took four attempts before the call finally went through. "Good afternoon, Ms. Bancroft. Edward Knight here. Listen, I just had a look at the Bellotto, and I absolutely must have it. How does twenty million sound?"

The connection failed before Sarah could reply. Knight put away his phone with a frown. "The cell service is dreadful out here. How do you possibly manage?"

Gabriel contemplated the blue sea. "Just fine, Mr. Knight."

6

Gwennap Head

They saw to the logistics during the long walk back to Gwennap Head. Edward Knight wanted his newly minted representative to leave for Ibiza immediately, but Gabriel insisted he required twenty-four hours to put his affairs in order. With any luck, he added, the situation might resolve itself by then. Knight, while disappointed, agreed to the delay. His private executive helicopter, he said, would be waiting at Land's End Airport at two the following afternoon. It would deliver Gabriel to Luton, where he would board the company Bombardier for the flight to Ibiza. Liam Higgins would arrange first-class lodgings at the Ibiza Gran Hotel. Knight would inform the commissioner of the Policía Nacional of Gabriel's pending arrival.

Next they discussed communications. Knight wanted the number for Gabriel's private mobile phone. Gabriel replied that Knight could reach him through the good offices of Isherwood Fine Arts.

"It's too unwieldy," he protested.

"I'm sure you'll find Sarah Bancroft most accommodating."

"Is it true she used to work for the CIA?"

"Wherever did you hear a thing like that?"

"The London art world is rather small, Allon." They had arrived back at the cottage. Edward Knight opened the door of his Rolls. "I insist on being kept abreast of your every move."

"You won't hear from me until I have something concrete."

"Are you forgetting the price that I paid for the Bellotto?"

"You haven't paid anything yet."

"I'll transfer the money to the gallery's account at Barclays first thing in the morning." Knight glanced toward the entrance of the cottage. Chiara stood in the open doorway, arms folded, an inscrutable expression on her face. "I suppose you'll have to tell her everything."

"There are no secrets between us."

"You're a very lucky man, Allon."

Knight slid behind the wheel of the Rolls and started the engine. Gabriel waited until the car had passed through the security gate, then turned and set off across the drive. It was all Julian's fault, he would tell his wife. It usually was.

And how exactly are you supposed to find her?"

"I have a terrible feeling I won't."

"She's dead, you mean?"

"It sounds as though the Spanish authorities are leaning in that direction."

Gabriel was seated atop a stool in the kitchen, watching Chiara prepare dinner. On the counter before him was a laptop computer and a platter of bruschetta topped with creamy polenta and caramelized mushrooms. They paired well with the wine he was drinking, a perfectly reasonable Sancerre he had picked up at the Morrisons in Long Rock.

Chiara refilled his glass. "You realize, I hope, that your new friend Edward Knight may know more about his wife's disappearance than he's telling you."

“Much more,” agreed Gabriel.

“And yet you know nothing about him.”

“That’s not quite true.” Gabriel indicated the laptop. “It says here that Knight cracked the top one hundred on the Times Rich List this year for the first time, with an estimated net worth of two point three billion pounds. A remarkable achievement, given the fact that his divorce from wife number one cost him nearly a billion.”

“I suppose Alice was to blame.”

“Boys will be boys.”

“How did they meet?”

“Alice was working as a freelance journalist at the time. Edward granted her a rare interview.”

“Rather unprofessional on her part, don’t you think?”

“These things happen,” lamented Gabriel with a sigh.

Chiara spooned a mixture of ricotta and leeks onto a sheet of freshly made pasta dough. “And how, precisely, did Edward Knight earn his billions?”

“As far as I can tell, he’s never built an actual building in his life. He simply buys existing commercial and residential properties and rents them out.”

“He’s a glorified landlord—is that what you’re saying?”

“Glorified being the key word,” added Gabriel. “The Knight Group owns a large portion of Sussex, several office buildings in the City of London, and huge tracts of housing in places like Notting Hill, Shepherd’s Bush, and Battersea. And those are the properties we know about. Knight’s business is notoriously opaque. He’s fond of anonymous shell companies and brass plate trusts, which allow him to conceal the true scale of his empire.”

“So he could be much richer than *The Times* suggests?”

“He didn’t bat an eye at dropping twenty million on the Bellotto.”

"A million of which will flow to you?"

"Upon completion of the restoration," said Gabriel sheepishly.

Chiara set aside the bowl of ravioli filling and took up her phone. Her thumbnails clicked against the screen.

"May I ask what you're doing?"

"Reviewing Alice's social media feeds." She shook her head slowly in dismay. "One wonders how she found the time for all this. It's really quite juvenile."

"I post, therefore I am."

Chiara turned the phone in Gabriel's direction. On the screen was a photograph of a suntanned Alice Winter flanked by two thirty-something women. They were seated at a beachside restaurant on Ibiza.

"Sophie Maxwell and Ella Burns," said Gabriel. "Her classmates from Cambridge."

Chiara swiped to another photograph. "And this, I assume, is Phoebe Chadwick?"

Gabriel nodded.

"Interesting, don't you think? Phoebe Chadwick leaves Ibiza in a huff, and a day later Alice vanishes."

"Are you suggesting that a relief coordinator from a respected global aid organization somehow engineered the disappearance of one of her closest friends?"

Chiara dragged a forefinger across the screen and showed Gabriel a new photograph. "What about him?"

It was Edward Knight, his arm around the slender waist of his attractive young wife. He wore the expression of a man who did not like to have his picture taken.

"He has a rather airtight alibi," Gabriel pointed out. "After all, he was sitting next to you when he learned that his wife's rental car had been discovered."

"So he says." Chiara laid a second sheet of pasta atop the first and began slicing perfect squares of ravioli with a daggerlike knife. "For the record, I couldn't hear a thing that assistant of his whispered into his ear."

"You don't really think he had something to do with his wife's disappearance?"

"The husband of a murdered wife is always the leading suspect."

"She isn't a murder victim yet. And if Edward Knight were somehow connected to his wife's disappearance, the last person in the world he would ask to find her is me."

"You *are* quite good at finding things," said Chiara. "Lost Leonardos, ancient temples, even the odd terrorist."

"You forget to mention trouble."

"That too. Which is why you should tell Edward Knight to hire another investigator."

"The twenty million he spent on the Bellotto would indicate he has his heart set on me."

"At least have a look under Knight's fingernails before you go running off to Ibiza," said Chiara. "You're liable to find something unpleasant."

"And how am I supposed to do that?"

"Why don't you phone one of your many friends in the British government?"

"You can be certain that Edward Knight has friends in HMG too."

"What about your friend from the Devon and Cornwall Police? He might know something."

Gabriel plunged a bruschetta into the ravioli filling and devoured it in a single bite.

"Must you?" asked Chiara.

"I dip," replied Gabriel. "Therefore I am."

7

Gunwalloe

Gabriel waited until morning to pack a bag. He left it in the entrance hall of the cottage, then made the hour-long drive around Mount's Bay to Gunwalloe, a tiny hamlet on the western side of the Lizard Peninsula. He parked the Range Rover along the stretch of road that passed for the village high street—it had neither a name nor a numeric designation—and purchased the London papers at the Corner Market, which wasn't on a corner at all. Next door was one of Cornwall's better bakeries. The proprietor, a spherical woman named Vera Hobbs, greeted him warmly.

"And what brings you back to Gunwalloe, Mr. Allon?"

"A craving for one of your famous Cornish pasties."

"What a coincidence. Your old friend told me the same thing." Her eyes settled briefly on the man sitting alone at a table against the window. His name was Timothy Peel. He wore a dark suit of moderate quality and an open-necked dress shirt. There was no mistaking him for anything other than what he was, a detective for the Devon and Cornwall Police. "You're not in any trouble, I hope."

"None beyond the usual, Vera."

"Devil," she whispered.

"I've been called worse."

"Not by me, Mr. Allon. I always adored you. Even when you were pretending to be that rather unpleasant Italian fellow. His name escapes me."

"Me too," quipped Gabriel.

Vera Hobbs plucked a square of tissue paper from the dispenser. "Beef, chicken, or veggie, my long-lost love?"

"How's the chicken today?"

"I'm offended you would ask."

"And might I trouble you for a cup of tea as well?"

"For you, my prince, it would be no trouble at all. Have a seat. I won't be but a minute."

Gabriel turned away from the counter and sat down with Timothy Peel. The detective had the face of Michelangelo's David and looked younger than his thirty-six years. He consulted his wristwatch at length, as though to indicate that Gabriel was late, then directed a policeman's wary gaze toward the luxury sport-utility vehicle parked on the opposite side of the road.

"Nice sled," he remarked. "Almost as nice as your new sailboat."

"Am I the target of an investigation, DS Peel?"

"I'm a detective inspector now, remember?" Peel had received the promotion for his role in the apprehension of a serial killer whom the newspapers had christened the Chopper. Never mind that it was Gabriel who had put two and two together. "And no, Mr. Allon, you are not the target of an investigation."

"I'm relieved to hear that. But how did you know about the Beneteau?"

"I was investigating a robbery at a shop in Wharf Road, and a lovely new sailing vessel in the harbor caught my eye. Naturally I was curious as to the identity of its owner."

"Don't you need a court order for that sort of thing?"

"My inquiry was unofficial in nature."

"Who ratted me out?"

"It was Ronnie Mills."

President of the local sailing club and keeper of the hard-to-come-by moorings in Penzance Harbor. "And did Ronnie Mills allow you to board my vessel?"

"He might have."

Gabriel frowned. "I have another tip for you, DI Peel. It concerns the identity of the burglar who broke into that shop in Wharf Road."

"Ronnie's alibi checks out."

Vera Hobbs appeared with Gabriel's order.

"Breakfast of champions," said Peel.

"Cornish champions, at least," added Gabriel, and sliced into the flaky crust of the pasty.

"Chicken," said Peel disapprovingly. "Always the chicken."

"You have something against chicken, Timothy?"

"I'm quite fond of it, actually. But you might try the beef on occasion."

"I do."

"In all the years I've known you, I have never once seen you eat a beef pasty."

Timothy Peel had been all of eleven years of age when Gabriel first made his acquaintance. They had lived next door to one another in the Lizard town of Port Navas. Peel was the neglected son of divorced parents, and Gabriel was the reclusive foreign gentleman who spent his nights restoring paintings and his days sailing the Helford River on a lovingly restored wooden ketch. He had bequeathed the boat to Peel when his old service called him out of retirement, thus the new Beneteau.

He poured a few ounces of milk into his cup and added the hot tea. Timothy Peel sighed. "Tea first, Mr. Allon. Then the milk."

"It is a scientific fact that milk first produces a superior cup of tea."

Peel took out a detective's notebook. "Shall we? I haven't got all day."

"By all means. I wouldn't want to keep you from your appointed rounds."

"This conversation never happened. Are we clear?" Peel opened the notebook. "Your friend Edward Knight has no criminal record whatsoever. He has, however, been the target of numerous investigations by His Majesty's Revenue and Customs regarding his payment of taxes, or lack thereof."

"I'm shocked to hear that."

"As was I," added Peel archly.

"What about Wickham House?"

"He paid sixty million for it—in cash, by the way. The owner of record is the Knight Group Limited."

"Does he own any other properties in our little corner of Britain?"

"A shopping center in Plymouth and another one in Exeter. He also owns a large tract of land along the North Devon coast."

"What about Alice?"

"I'm not sure whether anyone owns her."

"I was referring to run-ins with the authorities."

"Two arrests," said Peel. "Both while she was a student at Cambridge."

"For what?"

"Political protests. The Iraq War, Palestine, the usual. She should have been arrested a third time, but the DI handling the case was overruled by his chief constable."

"When did the incident occur?"

"Four months ago. The night of February the twelfth, to be precise."

"In Devon?"

Peel nodded.

"And the officer who wasn't allowed to bring charges?"

"Detective Inspector Timothy Peel."

I assume it wasn't a political protest."

"An automobile accident. Her third, as it turned out. She wrapped her Aston Martin roadster around a tree about a mile from Wickham House."

"I spent last evening reading everything I could find online about Alice Winter, and there was nothing about a serious road accident."

"That's because no record of the accident exists."

"How is that possible?"

"I'm getting to that, Mr. Allon."

The accident, Peel continued, occurred at approximately two fifteen in the morning, but it would be nearly an hour before another motorist happened upon the scene. Alice, semiconscious and disoriented, was taken by ambulance to the A&E ward at Devon and Exeter Hospital and treated for a concussion, a scalp laceration, and two fractured ribs. Peel had been working a late-night stakeout in Perceval Road—a major drug case involving four of Exeter's finest—and headed over to the hospital to take charge of the inquiry. He arrived to find a dazed and bruised Alice Winter resting comfortably in a private room, accompanied by her husband and his barrister. She was in no condition to answer questions, so Peel posed them to her husband instead. They were polite in tone, nothing confrontational or accusatory. Namely he wanted to know what a wealthy socialite like Alice Winter was doing behind the wheel of an automobile at two o'clock in the morning.

"And the answer?"

"She was on her way back to London, or so Edward Knight claimed."

Peel then attempted to ascertain why that was the case. At which point Knight's barrister declared that his client would be answering no further questions.

"Sounds to me as though the barrister and his client were hiding something."

"Nothing gets by you, does it?"

"What could it have been?"

"Why does any woman leave her twelve-bedroom manor house in the middle of the night?"

"They must have been quarreling."

"That was my distinct impression. The question is, what were they quarreling about?"

Peel decided not to press the matter—Knight, after all, had not been in the vehicle at the time of the accident—so he went to have a quiet word with the physician who had treated Alice, a courtly chap called Dr. Rajiv Singh.

"And what do you suppose the good doctor told me?"

"That Alice had been under the influence at the time of the accident."

Peel nodded. "That was his suspicion."

Over the strenuous objections of Edward Knight and his lawyer, a uniformed PC administered a field breathalyzer test at half past six that morning, some four hours after the accident. It indicated that Alice was slightly below the legal drink-drive limit of thirty-five micrograms of alcohol per one hundred micrograms of breath.

"Which meant she was probably *over* the limit at the time of the accident," said Gabriel.

"One would think," agreed Peel. "But higher authority instructed me not to pursue the matter further."

"What happened to the records?"

"Expunged. It was as if it never happened." Peel closed his detective's notebook. "Why are you so interested in Edward Knight?"

"I'm restoring a painting he intends to purchase."

"And?"

"Let it go, Timothy."

Peel took up his phone and typed. "Isn't that strange," he said after a moment. "It's been a week since Alice's last post on Instagram." He set aside the phone. "Missing, is she?"

"Did I say that?"

"Didn't have to." There was a brief silence. "Anyone looking for her?"

"The Spanish police."

"You're going to help them?"

"Something like that."

"Theory of the case?"

"Haven't got one."

"Gone astray?" suggested Peel.

"Maybe."

"Dead?"

"Could be."

"That leaves one other possibility."

"I suppose it does," agreed Gabriel, and finished the last of his chicken pasty.

8

Cornwall–Ibiza

"Are they ever going to speak to me again?"

"Only in their Venetian-accented Italian."

"It's come to that, has it?"

"A showdown," said Chiara.

She was behind the wheel of the Range Rover. Irene and Raphael were in the back seat, long-faced, mute.

"I should have walked to the airport," said Gabriel.

"In those clothes?"

He was wearing a sport jacket, gabardine trousers, and suede derby footwear. "I'm flying private and staying at the Ibiza Gran."

"How will you possibly manage?"

Chiara sped past a collection of stone outbuildings belonging to their neighbor, a sheep farmer called Twigg. The road was scarcely wide enough to accommodate the Range Rover, and lined on both sides by dense hedgerows.

"Don't you think you should slow down a tad?"

"I wouldn't want you to miss your flight." She turned onto the B3315. It was two lanes instead of one. "What do you suppose would have happened to me if I smashed your lovely new Range Rover into a tree?"

"Fortunately there are no trees on this road."

"And what if I had been drinking?" asked Chiara. "Do you think the Devon and Cornwall Police would have looked the other way?"

"I do have a considerable amount of sway with them, but I wouldn't have used it. Driving under the influence is a serious infraction. A definite no-no."

"I would have been forbidden to drive a motorcar in the United Kingdom for several years."

"At the very least. But it's also possible that you might have been barred from entering the country."

"An undesirable foreigner?"

Gabriel laid a hand along her thigh. "I wouldn't go that far."

"So why did the police turn a blind eye to Alice's vehicular misdeeds?"

"It might have something to do with the fact she's married to one of the richest men in Britain."

"Billionaires get to play by different rules?"

"Haven't you figured that out by now?"

She removed Gabriel's hand. "For the moment, I'm more interested in why Alice got behind the wheel of that car in the first place."

"Timothy was under the impression there had been a domestic disturbance."

"I wonder what it could have been."

"Perhaps Edward heard a rumor about his wife and another man."

"What did he expect when he married a girl like Alice Winter?"

"Wedded bliss and monogamy, I imagine."

"Their relationship began with an extramarital affair," Chiara pointed out.

"So did ours."

"There were extenuating circumstances."

"I'm sure Edward told himself the same thing."

A helicopter appeared before them, traveling east to west across the cloudless sky. It sank toward the green Cornish horizon and vanished from view.

Chiara glanced at her wristwatch. "Right on time."

She turned onto the A30 and followed it to the old Quaker burial ground. Land's End Airport was a mile to the north. They arrived to find the helicopter resting on the tarmac, rotor blades drooping. It was a Sikorsky executive model, sleek and black. The cabin door hung open, held by a man wearing dark trousers and a white shirt with epaulets on his shoulders.

"Be sure to write," remarked Chiara.

"I'll be back in a day or two."

"Where have I heard that before?"

Gabriel kissed Chiara and his two silent children, then, bag in hand, headed into the little wooden terminal building. Liam Higgins, Edward Knight's personal assistant, was waiting inside, immaculately attired in an overly fitted suit that lent him the appearance of a hotel concierge. He offered Gabriel a pale, manicured hand.

"Good afternoon, Mr. Allon. Follow me, please."

Together they crossed the apron and boarded the Sikorsky. Higgins settled into the leather chair on the port side of the cabin, Gabriel on the starboard. "Just so there's no misunderstanding," he said as the helicopter lifted from the tarmac, "I work alone."

"Don't worry, Mr. Allon. So do I."

"In that case, why are you here?"

"A bit of housekeeping, that's all."

On the floor of the cabin were a pair of attaché cases, black in color, identical in shape and size. Higgins opened one, removed a file folder, and handed it to Gabriel. Inside was a printout of Alice

Winter's credit card charges during her brief stay on Ibiza. It ran to several pages—restaurants, bars, nightclubs, a pharmacy, a hair salon, the Louis Vuitton boutique near the marina. The last transaction was a twelve-euro charge for parking. The time was 2:56 P.M.

"Is this the only card she used?"

"None of her other credit cards show any sign of activity." Higgins handed over another file. "Those are the emails and text messages she sent and received while she was on Ibiza and for the week preceding the trip. You can see her social media posts for yourself."

"How did you access her data?"

"Her personal computer at Wickham House."

"And if I wanted to see her emails and text messages for, say, the previous six months?"

"You would have to take that up with Mr. Knight."

Higgins returned the attaché case to the floor, then handed the second case to Gabriel. Inside were bundles of newly minted hundred-euro banknotes.

"What am I supposed to do with this?"

"I believe the Americans call it walking-around money. Use it as you see fit."

"How much is there?"

"A half million. Any money left over is yours to keep."

Gabriel closed the attaché case. The housekeeping, it seemed, had reached its end. At length he asked, "How long have you been working for him?"

"Mr. Knight?" Higgins made a show of thought. "It's been four years now."

"And before that?"

"I served as the personal assistant to another successful businessman."

"Anyone I know?"

"I doubt it," said Higgins, and picked a fleck of imaginary lint from the sleeve of his jacket.

Gabriel gazed out his window at the green Cornish countryside below. To be continued, he thought.

It was Gabriel's abiding fear that Edward Knight's factotum planned to accompany him on the flight to Ibiza. He passed the two-and-a-half-hour journey in solitude, though, without so much as a cabin attendant to see to his needs. Alice Winter's emails, text messages, and credit card charges served as his reading material. A quick tally revealed that she had managed to spend more than fifty thousand euros during the six days she spent on Ibiza, all while receiving and dispatching text messages at an astonishing rate. She was especially prolific during the small hours, was disdainful of punctuation, and fond of profanity and puerile three-letter abbreviations. She messaged her husband sparingly, as though conscious of not bothering him with trivial matters. There was nothing in the exchanges to indicate tension in their marriage. Nor did Gabriel notice anything to suggest that Alice was involved in an extramarital affair. But then these were only her iMessage texts. Unfaithful spouses, like spies and terrorists, tended to do their communicating via encrypted or clandestine means.

It was a few minutes after seven o'clock when Edward Knight's Bombardier plopped onto the runway at Ibiza Airport. Higgins had arranged for a car to take Gabriel to his hotel, a modern edifice overlooking a bone-white boulevard lined with palm trees. While crossing the crowded lobby he was gripped by an unshakable sense that he was being watched. The young woman at reception, after inspecting his passport, handed him a room key and a telephone message. It was from a certain Inspector Aragón of the Policía Nacional.

"Perhaps I should find another hotel," said Gabriel.

The receptionist raised an eyebrow. "Is it serious?"

"Could be."

"In that case, Señor Allon, you should probably hide out here. We'll take good care of you."

He asked the receptionist to dial the inspector's number. She complied with the request and handed him the receiver of her landline phone. Placing it to his ear, he heard the lethargic pulse of the Spanish ringback tone. He also heard, from somewhere in the cavernous lobby, the simultaneous bleating of a mobile phone. The bleating ceased at once, as did the ringback tone.

He returned the receiver to the receptionist and headed upstairs to his suite. It had a comfortable sitting room and a private terrace with a small infinity pool. He placed most of the cash in the room safe and left the rest in the attaché case, which he concealed in the drawer of the credenza. The phone on the writing desk rang as he was hanging his clothing in the closet. It was his friend from reception, informing him that Inspector Aragón was waiting for him downstairs in the lobby.

Leaving his room, he engaged the privacy light and wedged a tiny slip of paper into the doorjamb—a telltale, in the lexicon of his previous trade. As the elevator carriage descended he produced a quick mental sketch of the Spanish detective awaiting him in the lobby. Dark suit, formfitting white pullover, ash-blond hair, fair skin, thirty-five at most. The shoes were low-heeled pumps, functional but stylish. Not the sort of footwear worn by most Spanish cops. Not at all what Gabriel had been expecting.

9

Ibiza Gran Hotel

Are you carrying a gun, Señor Allon?"

"Should I be?"

She slipped a forefinger beneath the left lapel of Gabriel's jacket and had a look for herself. Then she searched the right side and ran a hand discreetly over the small of his back.

"Don't you want to check for an ankle holster?"

"You don't strike me as the type." She extended her hand in greeting. "I'm Inspector Eva Aragón of the Policía Nacional."

"So I gathered."

They sat down at a table in the lobby bar, and the inspector, after engaging the waiter in a few pleasantries, ordered *café solo* for them both. Her eyes were restless and a peculiar shade of blue-gray. She wore no jewelry other than a digital wristwatch, and her nails were trimmed short like a boy's. Her left hand appeared slightly swollen. There was an abrasion on one of her knuckles.

"First time in Spain?" she asked.

"You tell me," replied Gabriel.

"You flew into Madrid a couple of years ago using a passport bearing the name Gabriel Allon. A surveillance team from our domestic security service attempted to follow you, but you gave them the slip in Salamanca. They were wondering what you were doing there."

"I was visiting a friend."

"Friend have a name?"

Gabriel decided there was no harm in answering truthfully. "Magdalena Navarro."

"The painter?"

"Very impressive."

She ignored the backhanded compliment. "How do you know her?"

"Some other time, Inspector."

She reached into her handbag and withdrew a thick file. "For the record, this is all highly unusual. If it were anyone but you, I would have refused."

"I'm flattered."

"So easily?" Smiling, she placed the file on the table. "Where would you like me to begin?"

"I've always found it helpful to begin at the beginning."

"But which beginning, Señor Allon?" She opened the file. "There are so many from which to choose."

Inspector Eva Aragón chose as her starting point the victim's last day on the island, though even this was problematic, she added, because the Policía Nacional had yet to determine conclusively that Alice Winter was in fact a victim of a crime or that she was no longer on Ibiza. Interviews with her friends Sophie Maxwell and Ella Burns had established that she left her rented villa late Friday morning to do a bit of shopping. Neither woman was able to recall the exact time of her departure, but she drove past a security camera in the nearby town of Sant Miquel at 11:28 A.M. She arrived in Ibiza Town shortly before noon and, after leaving her Mercedes in a public car park, had coffee and *torrijas* at a café on the Vara de Rey. From there she window-shopped her way eastward to the marina, then stopped for a spritzer and tapas at Calma. Leaving the restaurant, she popped into Dolce & Gabbana and Dior before heading to Louis Vuitton, where she purchased a cotton ballcap.

"Price available upon request," remarked Inspector Aragón.

"I'm told there's video."

She laid a still image of the transaction on the table. Alice was handing her credit card to the saleswoman. She was wearing a white blouse, white capri pants, flat-soled Hermès sandals, and a great deal of jewelry. She was, thought Gabriel, a robbery waiting to happen.

"Her husband says she withdrew two thousand euros from a nearby ATM machine."

The detective slid a second photograph onto the tabletop. It had been snapped by the ATM's camera. Alice, in sunglasses and her new Vuitton cap, was almost unrecognizable.

"Where did she go next?"

"The car park where she left the Mercedes. She departed—"

"At 2:56 P.M.," Gabriel interjected. "The twelve-euro fee is her last known charge."

Inspector Aragón handed over another photograph, a rented Mercedes convertible lying capsized at the bottom of a rocky ravine. "We cannot say for certain how it ended up there. It's an isolated stretch of road, very steep and narrow, lots of switchbacks and dangerous curves."

"She has a rather dubious driving record."

"She wouldn't have been the first tourist to drive off that road. But our working theory is that she was targeted by professional thieves."

"Any suspects?"

"The usual."

"Translation?"

"We have a few homegrown criminal gangs on our enchanted little island, but the real pros come from elsewhere, just like the tourists. French, Albanians, Turks, even Italians."

"What sort of Italians?"

"We had a crew from Naples last summer. They arrived on a chartered yacht and stole everything they could lay their hands on. Wristwatches, mainly. Mobile phones too. There's a huge market for smartphones in Shanghai. They get cleaned up, repackaged, and sold as new devices. It's a multibillion-euro industry."

"When was the last time a thief killed someone over a phone or a wristwatch?"

"It's rare, Señor Allon, but it happens. Especially when the victim decides to stand her ground."

"Alice's husband seems to think she would have handed over her valuables without hesitation."

"Perhaps Alice's husband doesn't know his wife as well as he thinks he does."

Gabriel asked whether any blood had been found in the car. Inspector Aragón replied with a shake of her head.

"That would suggest she wasn't behind the wheel when the car plunged into that ravine."

"The Policía cannot say that with certainty, but that is our suspicion."

"What *can* the Policía say?"

"That one week after her disappearance, the whereabouts of Alice Winter remain unknown. With each passing day the odds of finding her alive are dwindling. Or dead, for that matter," she added.

"Is there still an active search?"

"It grows less active by the day. We've checked every square meter of the surrounding woods. There's no body."

"Perhaps you should be looking for a grave instead."

"It's not so easy to dig a hole in the soil of Ibiza, Señor Allon. Not if one is in a hurry. It's far more likely that they disposed of the body at sea."

"Which would explain the sandal you found."

"It might."

Gabriel gathered up the photos. "I'd like to see the ravine where you found the car. And we should probably have a look at the villa as well."

"It will be getting dark soon. I'll take you in the morning."

"Not tomorrow," said Gabriel. "Now, please."

"If it were anyone but you," said the detective, and rose reluctantly to her feet.

10

Sant Miquel

Her car was an unmarked Citroën. She drove it very fast, with the swollen hand balanced atop the wheel.

"What happened?" asked Gabriel.

"I'm sorry?"

He indicated the damaged appendage.

"A suspect foolishly tried to resist arrest."

"And so you hit him?"

"Several times." With a sideways glance she added, "I'm a black belt."

"Which discipline?"

"Karate."

"Unsightly but effective."

"Are you a martial artist?"

"No," lied Gabriel. "I'm a real artist."

"What do you do in your spare time?"

"I search for missing British socialites. They don't give you a belt for that sort of thing." They were hurtling along Ibiza's main north–south highway. The terrain around them was parched and brown. It reminded Gabriel of the valley of his youth. "And what was the poor chap's crime?" he asked.

"The man I hit? He was dealing drugs in the nightclubs."

"Isn't that why people come to Ibiza in the first place? To take drugs in nightclubs?"

"Some," she admitted. "For better or worse, we are the party capital of Europe."

"Surely you're not from here."

"The north," she answered.

"Aragón?"

"As a matter of fact, yes. An old Moorish village called Alquézar."

"What brought you to Ibiza?"

"A man, if you must know."

"Is he still around?"

"Thank goodness, no."

"You didn't strike him, I hope."

"I definitely thought about it." She navigated a busy traffic circle. "And what about you, Señor Allon? Tell me something about yourself."

"Just type my name into the little white box. It will tell you everything you need to know."

"Trust me, I did. You've lived a remarkable life. But how did you get mixed up with Edward Knight?"

"Friend of a friend," replied Gabriel vaguely.

"What do you think of him?"

"I'm more interested in your opinion."

"He seemed unusually calm and collected, given the circumstances. I suppose that's what they mean by a stiff upper lip."

The highway narrowed to two lanes and carried them past vineyards and olive groves to the town of Sant Miquel. The modular white apartment buildings were rose-colored in the dying twilight. Inspector Aragón pointed out a café where a few locals were drinking Estrella Galicia at a table in the street.

"The CCTV camera that photographed Alice's car on Friday morning is over the doorway of that bar."

"Did she pass by here again on Friday afternoon?"

"At three fifteen," replied the detective.

Beyond the town loomed a bony ridge of hills. Inspector Aragón expertly handled the hairpin turns without once lifting her foot from the throttle. Finally she applied the brakes and rolled to a stop along a stretch of road no wider than the hedgerow-lined lanes of Cornwall. On the left side of the road was a retaining wall of sun-bleached stone. On the right, the passenger side, was a deep ravine.

She opened the boot of the Citroën and from inside removed a torch and two emergency roadside triangles bearing the emblem of the Policía Nacional. She placed one triangle behind the car and the other in front, then offered the torch to Gabriel.

"After you," she said.

He peered into the ravine. The bottom, if there was one, was in shadow. "You don't happen to have a length of rope, do you?"

"Policía detectives don't carry rope, Señor Allon."

He removed his sport jacket and tossed it into the back of the car. Then, after first switching on the torch, he stepped hesitantly from the verge and began his descent. The ground beneath him was rocky and unstable. He crept forward, fencerlike, with the torch in his outstretched right hand and his left extended behind him for balance. He was aware of Inspector Eva Aragón behind him, moving with the silent surefootedness of a deer.

"Didn't I read somewhere that you were a mountain climber?" she asked.

"You have me mistaken for someone else. I only paint mountains."

"Perhaps I should lead the way after all. At the rate you're going, we'll miss dinner."

"I thought you Spaniards ate at midnight."

"My point exactly."

Gabriel maintained his present rate of descent, and gradually the steep hillside gave way to flatter ground.

"That's far enough," said Inspector Aragón. "This is where the car came to rest."

At the edge of a coppice of juniper and Aleppo pine, noted Gabriel. He played the beam of the torch over the rocky soil, then lifted his gaze toward the pair of winking red triangles on the road above.

"There's no way she could have survived a crash like that. Not in an open-top car."

"Unlikely," agreed the Spanish policewoman. "Someone must have rolled it into the ravine."

"The thieves?"

She pursed her lips thoughtfully, then nodded.

"And where do you suppose Alice was at the time?"

"Another vehicle, I imagine."

"Go on, Inspector."

"Alice and her friends didn't exactly keep a low profile while they were here. They stayed in the most expensive home on the island, ate in the best restaurants, and partied at the hottest nightclubs. To make matters worse, Alice was constantly posting photos of herself on social media."

"Isn't that de rigueur these days?"

"I suppose. But a crew of professional thieves was bound to notice that the wife of a British billionaire was staying on the island with three female friends and no bodyguards."

"How did it go down?"

"Somehow they forced her to a stop. If I had to guess, they overtook her after she left Sant Miquel and were lying in wait when she arrived up there. They stuck a gun in her face and told her to hand over her purse and her valuables. Rather than comply with their demands she resisted."

"Things got physical?"

"These hoods have short fuses."

"Then what?"

"They forced her into their vehicle, and the situation went from bad to worse. Alice is desperate now. She's fighting as though her life depends on it. Flailing, kicking, gouging with her nails. The thieves subdue her, and what was once a simple robbery is now aggravated assault and battery. At this point the only way to get out from under a long prison sentence is to make Alice disappear."

"Not bad," said Gabriel. "But it's all based on guesswork and supposition."

"Not entirely," replied the inspector.

"The Hermès sandal?"

She nodded.

"Where is the cove where it was found?"

"On the eastern side of the island."

"And the villa where they were staying?"

She pointed to the north. "Just over that hill."

He directed the beam of the torch toward the steep slope of the ravine. "A shame about that rope," he said, and started to climb.

They loaded the emergency triangles into the boot of the Citroën and followed the serpentine road to the summit of the ridge. The sea appeared, stretching like a bolt of black silk toward the distant Spanish mainland. The last light of dusk had faded, the first stars had appeared. A ferry was approaching Ibiza from Valencia; a colossal cruise ship festooned with lights was heaving its way toward Barcelona. Sailing vessels and motor yachts dozed at anchor along the coastline.

The road turned inland and the sea vanished from view. They sped past a noisy restaurant, a small hotel, and a colony of whitewashed villas. The property at the end of the road was hidden behind walls of stone. Security lights flared automatically as Inspector Aragón pulled up at the entrance. She typed an eight-digit passcode into the keypad and the gate swung slowly open.

"This is still an active crime scene, by the way."

"Don't worry," replied Gabriel. "It won't be my first."

She headed up the drive, past manicured trees and hedges, past a red clay tennis court, and slowed to a stop at the entrance of the villa. There was another keypad next to the door. She entered the same eight-digit code and led Gabriel inside.

The interior lights were motion activated. They pulled on crime scene gloves and shoe covers in the entrance hall and padded silently across the marble floor, into an enormous great room. The furnishings were contemporary and costly—southern European chic. Beyond a retractable wall of glass was a sweeping terrace, and beyond the terrace lay the sea. There was not another residence in sight. It was as if they had Ibiza to themselves.

"Who owns this place?" asked Gabriel.

"An anonymous shell corporation. The identity of the real owner is a matter of considerable speculation on the island."

Gabriel contemplated the meritless abstract canvas adorning one of the room's walls. "Let us say for argument's sake that Alice Winter's fatal encounter with your as yet unidentified thieves took place at approximately half past three on Friday afternoon."

"Three-twenty-five, I'd say."

"And yet her friends Sophie Maxwell and Ella Burns didn't report her missing until the following day."

"At 12:37 P.M. Ibiza time."

"Did you ask them why they waited?"

"Several times." She pointed toward a seating area. "In this very room."

"And?"

"They said their friend Alice had a wild side, and they weren't worried when she didn't come home that night."

"Were you satisfied with their explanation?"

"I wouldn't put it that way. But I was confident they had nothing to do with their friend's disappearance, especially after my colleagues found the car."

"At approximately eight o'clock that evening?"

"More like seven fifteen. My superiors delivered the bad news to Edward Knight in Britain and then ordered me to seal the room where his wife had been staying."

"I'd like to see it, please."

"Not a chance, Señor Allon."

"And if I were to ask nicely?"

The door was defaced with a large X of crime scene tape, but inside the bed was immaculately made and nothing was out of place. "The maid straightened up after Alice left the property on Friday morning," Inspector Aragón explained. "This is the way I found it on Saturday afternoon."

Lying on the bedside table was a novel by Ian McEwan. Gabriel opened it to the page marked and read the first line. *Within the half hour Briony would commit her crime . . .* He closed the book and returned it to its original place.

"Where are the rest of her things?"

She led him into the bathroom suite. Atop the vanity was a formidable array of cosmetics and creams and other beauty supplies. Gabriel unzipped a leather tote and found a small pharmacy of pain relievers, allergy medication, antidepressants, and sleeping tablets. In a matching jewelry case were two wristwatches, a double strand of pearls, diamond earrings, and a gold-and-diamond bracelet. In the drawers of the vanity were swimsuits, undergarments, pullovers, shorts, fitness attire, all bearing designer labels. The rest of her clothing was hanging in the walk-in closet. Displayed on the top shelf was a selection of hats. A broad-brimmed straw sun hat, a stylish fedora, a navy blue baseball-style cap by Prada.

"Why do you suppose she needed another one?" asked Gabriel.

"That one's a Prada. It also happens to be blue."

"And?"

"The hat she bought at Louis Vuitton was white."

"How many baseball caps does one woman need?"

"I'm afraid you're asking the wrong woman." She led him out of the bedroom suite and locked the door behind them. Outside, they pulled off the gloves and shoe covers and climbed into the Citroën. "Have you cracked the case?"

"Not quite. But I'm getting there."

"Let's hear it."

"The disappearance of Alice Winter had nothing at all to do with robbery."

"What happened to her?"

"Perhaps it went something like this . . ."

11

Ibiza Town

She took him to a traditional Catalonian restaurant near the walls of Ibiza Town's ancient center and over tapas and a bottle of Majorcan red offered a forceful rebuttal to his theory of the case—that Alice Winter, wife of the billionaire real estate investor Edward Knight, had been kidnapped. The theory's most glaring flaw, she said, was the lack of any demand for money on the part of Alice's supposed abductors. After all, the inspector added, such demands were the central element of any kidnap-for-ransom scheme.

"You've handled a lot of kidnap cases, have you?"

"Only one."

"Did it involve a demand for ransom?"

She shook her head.

"So you're something of an expert—is that what you're saying?"

The inspector regarded him across the table, the light of a candle playing in her peculiar blue-gray eyes. The floor of the restaurant was rough stone, the ceiling vaulted. She had to raise her voice to be heard over the multilingual din of the well-lubricated evening crowd.

"And what about you, Señor Allon? Have you handled kidnapping cases before?"

He offered a noncommittal shrug in reply.

"But you consider yourself to be an expert nonetheless?"

"A battle-scarred veteran," he suggested.

"You have a rather large one on the left side of your chest." She paused, then added, "I noticed it while I was searching you."

"It's the entry wound. The exit wound is a damn sight worse."

"That incident in Washington?"

He made no reply.

"Did it change you?" she asked.

"Almost dying? A great deal."

"How so?"

"Misguided Spanish policewomen don't annoy me nearly as much as they used to."

Inspector Aragón spooned paella onto Gabriel's plate. "How do you explain the lack of a ransom demand?"

"Kidnap-for-ransom cases are a test of will between the loved ones of the victim and the kidnappers themselves. Each side is always looking for an advantage, leverage that can be brought to bear. At the moment, Alice's abductors are holding all the cards."

"It's been eight days since her disappearance. How long do your kidnappers intend to wait?"

"Long enough to convince Edward Knight that his wife might be dead. That way, when the time comes to ask for money, he'll pay anything to get her back."

She added some of the paella to her plate. "It's not so easy, you know, caring for a hostage."

"That's correct. The hostage has to be given food and water and taken to the toilet, all while blindfolded. Eventually the kidnappers begin to get worn down, anxious. That's the time to strike a deal."

"A woman like Alice Winter would be worth a great deal of money. But you have absolutely no evidence to support your theory that she has been kidnapped. Therefore I would advise you not to raise it with your client."

"Don't worry, I have no intention of mentioning any of this to Edward Knight."

"What *are* you going to tell him?"

"That I'm confident you will soon find his wife. With my help, of course."

"What makes you think I need your help?"

"Let's not spoil an otherwise pleasant evening."

"And if I accept your offer? What would be our first move?"

"We're going to reconstruct Alice Winter's movements during the seven days she spent on the island. The restaurants where she dined, the nightclubs where she danced, the boutiques where she shopped. And then we're going to review every minute of surveillance video we can lay our hands on."

"This might come as a surprise to you, Señor Allon, but I've already done that."

"And what did you discover?"

"Absolutely nothing of value."

"That's because you were looking for thieves instead of kidnappers."

"And how do kidnappers look?"

"That depends on the kidnapper. I have a feeling that Alice's were of the highly professional variety. And they would have been watching her from the minute she and her friends arrived on Ibiza."

Inspector Aragón refilled his glass with the Majorcan wine. "Unless, of course, there were no kidnappers."

Eva Aragón met Gabriel at nine the following morning at Calma, the popular harborside restaurant where Alice Winter had taken her last meal on Ibiza. The manager, a put-upon Spaniard called Rodrigo, escorted them to a cramped office next to the kitchen and with a heavy sigh sat down behind a computer.

"The same date and time?" he asked.

The inspector nodded.

"The video hasn't changed, you know."

"Just get on with it, Rodrigo."

He tapped a few keys, and a shot of the restaurant's open-air dining room appeared on the screen. The inspector pointed toward the woman sitting alone at a sunlit table at the edge of the pier.

"There's our girl."

"Surprise, surprise," said the restaurant manager beneath his breath.

"May I see her arrival?" asked Gabriel.

Rodrigo displayed the feed from the camera at the restaurant's entrance and rewound the video at three times the normal speed. A moment later Alice shuffled backward across the screen. Then Rodrigo clicked the PLAY icon, and she approached the entrance at an unhurried pace, a bag over one shoulder.

"Did she have a reservation?"

"No."

"Table for one?"

Rodrigo nodded.

A middle-aged couple entered the restaurant next, followed by a pair of dark-haired men in their thirties. Gabriel snapped a photograph of the two men with his mobile phone, then said, "May I see the dining room again, please?"

Rodrigo switched the feed and adjusted the time stamp. Alice Winter sat alone at her waterside table, phone in hand, arm extended. The photo would appear on Instagram at 2:17 P.M. *My last day on*

Ibiza . . . It would be her last post as well. She left the restaurant twelve minutes later. No one followed her.

They headed next to La Casita, scene of Alice's quarrel with her friend Phoebe Chadwick, then to La Plaza, where Winter and party had been three in number rather than their usual four. At neither establishment did Gabriel notice anything unusual in the surveillance video. The same was true of every other restaurant where the women had dined during their stay on the island, including La Gaia, the Michelin-starred eatery in Gabriel's hotel.

After a break for lunch—it was a quick slice of pizza rather than the traditional Spanish midday feast—Gabriel and Inspector Aragón set off for Ibiza's world-renowned nightclubs. The largest were multilevel venues that could accommodate thousands of revelers. Even so, Gabriel had no trouble spotting Alice amid the flashing lights and pulsating bodies; she was the sort of woman who stood out in a crowd. Not surprisingly she was the subject of no small amount of male attention. Gabriel studied the faces of the men who lingered too long in her presence, and those who appeared to watch her from afar. At a club called Amnesia she threw a drink into the face of a handsome young man who tried to pull her onto the dance floor. At Pancha, reputedly Ibiza's most glamorous nightclub, a surveillance camera spotted her entering a private room.

"Who else was in there?" asked Gabriel.

"According to Sophie Maxwell and Ella Burns, they were some of Alice's friends from London. The kind of friends with a lot of money."

"I don't suppose you know their names."

"They're in the case file."

Alice remained in the private room for twenty minutes. She left Pancha at 3:22 A.M., accompanied by her three friends from Cambridge. Gabriel didn't bother to photograph the spaced-out kids who followed them out the door.

"Seen enough?" asked the inspector.

"Actually I haven't seen a thing."

"How about some coffee? I know just the place."

It was the little café on the Vara de Rey where Alice had stopped on the day of her disappearance. There was no video to review—it wasn't that sort of place—and the waitress on duty hadn't been working on the morning of Alice's visit. The *café solo*, however, was perfect. Gabriel drank his first cup and immediately ordered a second.

"Is there nowhere else she went while she was on the island?"

"She left the villa for a few hours the morning after she had the argument with her friend Phoebe. Said she was going to do a bit of sightseeing."

"Does Alice Winter strike you as the sort of woman who enjoys seeing the sights?"

"Not really."

Gabriel drew his phone and checked Alice's Instagram account. She had posted twice that day. One was a photograph of three friends enjoying dinner at La Plaza restaurant. Ten hours earlier, at 12:17 P.M., she had posted a photo of a towering rock formation off the Ibizan coast.

"Es Vedrà," explained Inspector Aragón. "Home of sirens and sea nymphs, if you believe the legends."

"Do you know where Alice was standing when she took it?"

"Sure, Señor Allon. I think I might."

12

Cala d'Hort

The popular swimming cove known as Cala d'Hort lay on the western side of the island, a drive of thirty minutes from Ibiza Town. Inspector Aragón slid the Citroën into an empty space in the car park, then, after removing her shoes, set off across the beach. Gabriel followed after her in his sport jacket and suede footwear, much to the bemusement of two young women stretched seminude upon the sand. At the water's edge he drew his phone and snapped a photograph of the jagged rock formation rising like a weathered gravestone from the flat waters of the Balearic Sea. Then he compared it to the photo taken by Alice Winter two days before her disappearance.

"It's exactly the same," said the inspector. "It was definitely taken from this beach."

"It wasn't, actually." Gabriel pointed toward the restaurant at the far end of the cove. "It was taken right over there."

It was nearly six o'clock, the lull between lunch and dinner, and only two tables were occupied. The barman was thirty or so, with a shaved head, pierced ears, and tattooed arms.

Gabriel handed the man his phone. "Do you recognize her? She was here about a week and a half ago."

The barman gave the photo a cursory glance. "Sorry, my friend."

Inspector Aragón laid her credentials on the bar. "How about now?"

"On second thought," said the barman, "she looks familiar."

"She's British," replied the inspector. "She would have been driving a flashy Mercedes convertible."

"Was she alone?"

"You tell me."

"She was alone when she arrived, but she met someone."

"Who?"

"A guy who was hanging out on the beach. It looked to me as though they were surprised to see one another."

Gabriel reclaimed his phone. "How did it happen?"

"She noticed him walking past the restaurant and waved to him." The barman shrugged. "Just one of those things."

"Did she call out his name?"

"She might have. But I don't remember what it was."

"How did he look?"

"Tall, thin, decent shape."

"What about his face?"

"He was wearing a hat and sunglasses." The barman pointed toward the distant end of the open-air seating area. "They were sitting at that table over there."

"Did anyone else get a better look at him?" asked Inspector Aragón.

"Mariella."

"Their waitress?"

The barman nodded.

"Mariella what?"

"Cruz."

"And where can we find Mariella Cruz?"

"She's off today."

"That's not what I asked you."

The barman folded his arms. "You can find Mariella in San Rafael."

"Great," said Inspector Aragón. "Where in San Rafael?"

The problem, she explained, was one of supply and demand. Mass tourism on Ibiza had driven up the demand for low-wage seasonal workers, and yet the supply of affordable housing had dwindled, replaced by multimillion-euro estates owned by superrich foreigners. The monthly rent on the inspector's small apartment in Ibiza Town was twenty-five hundred a month, which devoured most of her modest government salary. Still, she considered herself fortunate. Many of the island's essential workers—its firefighters and teachers, its nurses and ambulance drivers—had no choice but to commute from the mainland each day.

"Needless to say, a dishwasher or hotel maid can't afford to spend sixty or seventy hard-earned euros on airfare. The lucky ones live in one-bedroom apartments with ten other roommates."

"And the ones who aren't so lucky?"

"You'll see when we get to San Rafael."

It was located in the center of the island astride the highway that connected Ibiza Town to the port of Sant Antoni. On the northern side of the town, just beyond the football pitch, was a makeshift village of tents, shanties, and caravans.

"Welcome to the other side of paradise, Señor Allon. The owner of the land rents the plots for four hundred euros a month. He charges another hundred a month for water and electricity."

"He must be doing very well for himself."

"Too well, if you ask me."

Gabriel climbed out of the car and accompanied the detective into the encampment. Shanties of plywood and corrugated metal, crude tarpaulin tents, worn-out cars and rusted caravans—the other side of paradise indeed. At the center of the camp was a dusty common area with four portable lavatories and a single water tap. Two young boys were kicking a ball about, watched over by an exhausted-looking woman of perhaps thirty. Inspector Aragón addressed the woman in Spanish, and she shook her head in reply. Then, after having a look at the inspector's credentials, she pointed toward the encampment's western boundary.

It was there they found Mariella Cruz. She was seated on a folding beach chair outside an aged French-made caravan. She wore a cotton tank top and shorts and a pair of soiled trainers. Her hair was nearly black, as were her eyes. They settled first on Inspector Aragón.

"I've been expecting you." She glanced at Gabriel. "You too, Señor. But I'm afraid my colleague Ramón didn't catch your name."

"Did he tell you why we wanted to see you?"

"He said it had something to do with the Englishwoman who sat at one of my tables a few days ago."

Mariella Cruz had not risen from her folding chair or offered her hand in greeting. Perhaps, thought Gabriel, she regarded herself as an untouchable. She seemed to sense his discomfort.

"It's not so bad here, Señor No-Name. Much better than my last place."

"And where was that?"

"A garage in Santa Eulària. I shared it with six other girls. No water, no electricity, no toilet." She shrugged. "Heaven on earth."

"And before that?"

"Long story. And very boring."

Gabriel handed Mariella Cruz his mobile phone. "Do you remember her?"

She lowered her eyes toward the screen. "The Brits all start to look the same after a while, but this one I remember. Hard not to."

"What about her friend from the beach?"

"I really didn't get a good look at him."

"Was he British as well?"

"He spoke perfect English, but he had a slight accent. It might have been German."

"How old was he?"

"Maybe forty."

"Hair color?"

"Sort of blond, but it was hard to tell because of the hat. For all I know, he was bald on top."

"Wedding band?"

"I didn't notice. But he was wearing a nice watch. A Rolex Daytona, the platinum model." Her eyes settled once more on Inspector Aragón. "Don't you have any questions?"

"Any plans for the rest of the evening?"

"A long soak in my Jacuzzi," she quipped. "And then dinner at a fancy restaurant."

"Put on some proper clothes, Mariella. You're coming with us."

It was a ten-minute drive from San Rafael to the Policía Nacional headquarters. The inspector placed Mariella Cruz in an interview room and escorted Gabriel to her cramped office. There she rang a colleague who dealt with matters related to immigration and passport control and instructed him to prepare a list of all German, Austrian, and Swiss males who had visited the island the previous week. At Gabriel's suggestion she added Dutch males to the request, as well as those from Denmark, Norway, and Sweden.

"How soon?" asked the colleague.

"Tonight."

"Impossible."

"Anything is possible," said the inspector.

The Policía's headquarters were located in a drab quarter of Ibiza Town but within walking distance of a glittering waterfront promenade. With a flash of her credentials, Inspector Aragón secured a coveted table at El Principe, where they plied Mariella Cruz with some of the finest food and drink the island had to offer. It was approaching half past ten when the inspector's phone rang. Gabriel paid the bill with Edward Knight's cash, and they hurried back to the Policía HQ.

At any given time during Ibiza's high season there are nearly one million tourists on the island. A significant portion are German citizens, drawn by the warm weather and discount air fares. During the second week of June there were more than ten thousand. Some fifteen hundred were German males between the ages of thirty and fifty. Mariella Cruz sat at Inspector Aragón's desk, head in her hands, eyes fixed dully on the computer monitor, as passport photos came and went. Only a handful warranted more than a second or two of scrutiny. The last appeared on the screen shortly after midnight: Gerhardt Zimmer, forty-eight years of age, from Frankfurt.

"No," she murmured. "Not even close."

The list of Austrian males was mercifully shorter. Mariella dispensed with them quickly, then turned her attention to the male visitors from Switzerland. The twenty-second entry on the list was Peter Hoffmann, thirty-nine years of age, 188 centimeters in height, born in Zurich. He had a full head of straw-colored hair and a fine-boned, cleanly shaved face.

Mariella Cruz stared intently at the screen. "That's him."

"Are you sure?" asked Gabriel.

"Definitely. No doubt about it."

Gabriel drew his phone, searched the name Peter Hoffmann, and was buried beneath an avalanche of results. He added the words *Zurich* and *Switzerland*, and the number of results shrank considerably. One was an asset manager at Bank Josef Bänzinger & Co. Gabriel clicked on the link and saw a photograph of the same man, though this time he was wearing a pair of rimless spectacles.

He showed the photo to Inspector Aragón. "He did his graduate work at the London School of Economics."

"Which would explain his perfect English."

"It would," agreed Gabriel.

"And before that?"

"University of Cambridge."

"Which would explain how he knows Alice Winter."

So it would appear, thought Gabriel. He snapped a photo of Peter Hoffmann's passport, then looked at Mariella Cruz.

"Who left the restaurant first?"

She delivered her answer to the computer screen. "He did."

"Where did he go?"

"Back to the beach."

"Was he with anyone?"

"I didn't notice."

"And what about the Englishwoman?"

"She stayed for another ten minutes or so, then left."

"How did she pay the bill?"

"Cash," she answered. "No tip."

They stopped at the Ibiza Gran Hotel long enough for Gabriel to remove a substantial sum of cash from his room safe. During the drive back to San Rafael he slipped the money unobserved into Mariella Cruz's worn handbag. Inspector Aragón escorted her through the darkness of the encampment to her caravan. Then she returned to the Citroën and they started back to Ibiza Town.

"How much did you give her?" she asked.

"A standard bundle of hundred-euro banknotes."

"Ten thousand euros?"

"Very impressive, Inspector."

"And very generous on your part."

"I wish that were the case, but the money wasn't mine."

Gabriel's phone pulsed with an incoming text. It was from Sarah Bancroft in London. Her message was two sentences in length. Gabriel's reply was briefer still. He tapped SEND and gripped the phone tightly in his hand. Gazing absently out his window he asked, "Who was the victim?"

"I'm sorry?"

"In your one and only abduction case."

"A child," replied Inspector Aragón after a silence.

"How old?"

"Eleven."

"Boy or girl?"

"What do you think?"

Girl . . .

"And what went wrong?" asked Gabriel.

"Everything."

"He killed her?"

"He raped her for a few days. Then he killed her and threw her body into a river up in the Pyrenees. She was eleven, Señor Allon. Eleven."

"Did you get him?"

"Eventually. And guess how many other girls he had killed?"

"I'd rather not."

"Six," she answered. "And those are the ones we're sure about."

Gabriel was silent.

"Do you have children?" she asked.

"A boy and a girl."

"How old are they?"

"Eleven."

Another silence, longer than the first. "It's time for you to face facts, Señor Allon. Alice Winter wasn't kidnapped, she was murdered."

"With all due respect, you're mistaken. Alice was definitely abducted."

"How can you be so certain?"

"Because her kidnappers just made contact with her husband."

13

Berkeley Square

The headquarters of the Knight Group were located in Berkeley Square in Mayfair. Gabriel arrived there late the following morning, having flown to London from Ibiza aboard the company Bombardier Challenger. Liam Higgins met him in the lobby and escorted him upstairs. Two blue-suited security men stood guard in the elevator foyer, and two more were posted outside the glass-enclosed conference room where Edward Knight, a cigarette in one hand, was anxiously pacing the carpeted floor. He ceased his wanderings long enough to take note of Gabriel's presence.

He stabbed out the cigarette in an overflowing ashtray. "Forgive me. A dreadful habit, I know. I used to burn through two packs a day. It was Alice who convinced me to quit."

"How did she do that?"

"She said she wouldn't marry me if I didn't."

Knight lit another cigarette and exchanged a look with Higgins, who handed Gabriel a single sheet of paper. It was a printout of an email that had been sent to a general inquiries address listed on the Knight Group's website. It was long on threats but short on specifics. There was no demand for ransom—that, the kidnappers said, would come later. They wanted Knight to send a phone number they could use for the opening round of communication. Any attempt to pinpoint their whereabouts would result in the death of the hostage.

Gabriel read the email a second time, then slid it onto the conference table. Knight was contemplating him through a fogbank of cigarette smoke.

"I have to say, Allon, you don't look terribly surprised."

"I'm not."

"Truth be told, I was relieved when it arrived. If nothing else, at least I know Alice is alive."

"Which is exactly the way the kidnappers want you to feel. Try not to give them the satisfaction."

"I'll give them anything they want." Edward Knight lowered himself into the leather chair at the head of the table. His ragged appearance notwithstanding, it conferred upon him a sense of authority. "I want this matter resolved quickly, Allon. If it's a few million they want, they can have it."

"You should prepare yourself for a demand that runs into the tens of millions, if not higher. Furthermore, ransom negotiations are never quick."

"My security firm told me the same thing. They offered to provide me with an experienced kidnap-and-ransom specialist to handle the negotiations. I told them I didn't need one. After all," said Knight, "I have you."

Gabriel went to the credenza and drew himself a cup of coffee from the pump-action thermos. He should have told Edward Knight to find someone else, should have walked out the door. The image of a woman alone in a darkened room, her hands bound by tape, a bag over her head, would not let him.

"I'll need an apartment, somewhere quiet with not too much foot traffic. I'll also need phones. A half dozen should do." He shot a glance at Higgins. "And plenty of spare SIM cards."

"What else?" asked Knight.

"A guarantee."

"What sort of guarantee?"

"That neither you nor your friends from your exclusive Mayfair security firm will interfere with the negotiations."

"You have my word."

"Then we should probably reply to their email." Gabriel sat down next to Knight. "Use the landline number for this office."

Higgins placed a laptop on the table. Knight nudged it toward Gabriel. "Perhaps you should do it, Allon. At this point, I don't think I'm capable."

The original email was displayed on the screen. Knight recited the direct number for the conference room extension, and Gabriel entered it into the reply and reached for the touchpad.

"Shouldn't you include some sort of personal message?" asked Knight.

"Like what?"

"Tell them not to harm Alice."

"That's not how it works in a kidnapping. They're only interested in one thing."

Gabriel clicked the SEND icon, and the computer emitted a *whoosh*.

"What now?" asked Knight.

"We wait."

"How long will it take?"

"Several hours, perhaps even a day. But don't worry, we're going to put the time to good use."

"How?"

"You're going to tell me all about your business. The properties you own, your partners, where you get your money."

"Out of the question. That information is strictly private."

"There's no such thing as privacy," said Gabriel. "Not in a kidnapping."

Edward Knight, only child of a headmaster and an NHS nurse, graduate of a second-tier redbrick university, had been toiling on the bond desk of a minor London house of finance when he noticed an emerging glut of distressed commercial properties on the British real estate market, especially in the Docklands area of the East End. With money borrowed from his parents, the Knight Group, as he called his nascent company, made its first acquisition—a tumbledown warehouse on the Isle of Dogs. Six months later, with a loan supplied by his firm, he purchased a second derelict warehouse, this time in neighboring Canary Wharf.

He sold the properties to a developer just eighteen months later and used the proceeds to snap up a terrace of cottages in Whitechapel. Next he ventured across the Thames to Southwark and Battersea, where he added still more residential assets to his portfolio. Other acquisitions followed in quick succession—in Earl's Court, Paddington, Notting Hill, and Chelsea, where he bought two commercial properties along the King's Road. He bought his first London hotel in 2000 and his first shopping center a year later, in the Thames Estuary town of Gravesend. He now held controlling stakes in more than a dozen hotels, several of which were located on the European mainland, and was the largest owner of shopping centers in the British Isles.

"I'm told you also own most of Sussex," said Gabriel.

"Told by whom?"

"My dinner companion at the Wickham House fundraiser."

"The countess? Silly old cow."

Because the Knight Group was entirely private, its founder was under no obligation to reveal the true scale of his current real estate empire, including his holdings in the former Kingdom of Sussex in southeast England. The document that Knight showed Gabriel revealed that they were extensive. Still, they were only the tip of the iceberg. All totaled, the Knight Group's current portfolio was worth an estimated eight and a half billion pounds.

"How's your debt?" asked Gabriel.

"A manageable five billion."

"Where do you get your financing?"

"Most of it comes from HSBC."

"And the rest?"

"Private investors."

"I'll need their names."

Knight frowned irritably. "How is this remotely relevant to Alice's abduction?"

"I'm wondering whether you have any enemies. Someone you wronged along the way. Someone you cheated." Gabriel paused. "Someone with the wherewithal to hire a crew of professional criminals to kidnap your wife."

"The real estate business is full of sharp elbows, Allon. It is not for the faint of heart."

"Can you think of anyone who might wish you harm?"

"Too many to count."

"I'll need their names as well."

Knight tossed out the names of a few potential enemies, none of whom Gabriel recognized, along with the names of his primary investors. All were British and of reasonable repute, with the exception of the sexually disgraced former Duke of York.

"The ass," groused Knight. "What on earth was he thinking, getting mixed up with a creature like that?"

Gabriel jotted down each of the names, then spent the remainder of the afternoon reviewing the property portfolio while Higgins saw to the burner phones and SIM cards, and Edward Knight paced and chain-smoked.

"Perhaps you should try to get some rest," suggested Gabriel. "Those cigarettes are doing you no good."

"I'll rest when Alice is home."

"It's going to be a while."

"Not if I have anything to do with it."

"You mustn't even consider agreeing to their initial demand."

"Whyever not?"

"Because they will conclude they asked for too little, and they will come back for more."

"I know how to negotiate a deal, Allon."

"Not when a life is on the line, you don't."

By seven that evening the phone had yet to ring, so Knight sent Higgins out to fetch some dinner. He returned forty-five minutes later with several bags from Lilibet's. They ate at the conference room table with the wall-mounted television flickering silently. The Russians had unleashed the largest missile barrage on Ukraine since the start of the war. Kyiv was burning.

Knight stared at the screen, disconsolate. "Damn dreadful war. Sometimes it feels as though the world is spinning out of control." He pushed his food away, lit another cigarette, and stared at the phone. "Ring, damn it!"

"Try to be patient," said Gabriel.

"You might feel differently if it was your wife sitting alone in some darkened room."

"I might," he agreed.

Knight turned to Higgins. "Call the bloody number. Make certain it's working."

"It's working, Mr. Knight."

"Humor me."

Higgins drew his phone and punched in the number. The landline phone rang instantly.

"That settles that," said Knight.

Higgins tapped END, but the phone on the conference table continued to ring. Gabriel snapped a photo of the caller ID screen, then reached for the receiver.

14

Berkeley Square

Do everything we say, or the woman dies."

The voice was female and fully automated. It was like listening to the voice of an answerphone.

"Look here now," replied Gabriel agreeably, "there's no need for melodrama, and no one is going to die. We both know what this is about, so let's get down to business, shall we?"

There was silence. It sounded to Gabriel as though they had muted the call. Edward Knight's eyes were wide and unblinking. Sotto voce he said, "What the hell is going on?"

Gabriel ignored the question. The automated voice had come on the line again.

"We want to speak to her husband," it said.

"I'm sure you would, but I'm afraid you're going to have to deal with me. Rest assured, I've done this sort of thing a time or two. You're in very good hands."

A long moment crawled by before the automated voice issued another threat. "Put the husband on the phone, or we'll kill her right now."

"No, you won't. You see, that would be a rather poor business decision on your part."

"Put him on the phone. Last chance."

"Sorry, gentlemen. But that's not going to happen."

Knight was crimson. "Damn it, Allon! What in God's name are you playing at?"

Gabriel shot him a dark look across the conference table. The phone at the other end of the connection was unmuted. Someone was typing a response.

It came a few seconds later. "We want to give him our demands."

"He has no interest in hearing your demands," replied Gabriel. "And neither do I. Not until I know that Ms. Winter is alive and well. It's a very basic concept in my line of work. We call it proof of life."

There was more typing on the open line, then, "You have to trust us."

"That's not going to happen either. But here's what I'd like you to do. You're going to take a photograph of Ms. Winter holding the current issue of *The Economist.* You can find it at any reputable newsstand. A bit on the expensive side, I realize, but not to worry. If you play by the rules, you will soon have all the money you need."

They muted the call again. Edward Knight ignited another cigarette and resumed his restless pacing. "You're pushing them too hard, Allon."

"Trust me, that was nothing more than a gentle nudge."

The automated voice returned. "How do we contact you?"

Knight, relieved, expelled a cloud of smoke. Gabriel recited the number of one of the burner phones, then said, "You have twenty-four hours. Otherwise we go to the police and sever all contact. Is that clear?"

The connection died without a response. Gabriel replaced the receiver, then marked the time. It was 9:05 P.M. "All in all," he said,

"I think that went rather well." He paused, then added, "With one minor exception."

"What's that?" asked Knight.

"You told them my name."

The Knight Group owned a number of commercial and residential properties in Mayfair, including the building in which its offices were located and a spacious mews house in Adams Row. Gabriel toppled into the bed in the master suite at midnight and fell into a dreamless sleep. The harsh ringtone of a mobile phone awakened him with a start shortly before seven the next morning. Regrettably it was not the burner.

"Mind telling me where you are?" inquired Chiara.

Gabriel swung his feet to the floor and wandered over to the window. Parting the curtain, he peered into the empty street below. "It appears as though I'm in London."

"Doing what, exactly?"

He explained.

"An unexpected turn of events," remarked Chiara.

"Not entirely. It was obvious to me from the start that she wasn't murdered in a botched robbery."

"It's still possible, you know."

"Which is why I insisted on proof of life before entertaining a demand for ransom."

"And how will you determine whether the proof of life photo is genuine and not a deepfake?"

"At the risk of sounding immodest, I have a rather good eye."

"For Raphaels and Leonardos, perhaps, but not for deepfake

images. You need someone who knows a thing or two about digital forensics to tell the difference."

"Any other helpful advice?"

"Don't even think about serving as the bagman."

There was no food in the apartment, so Gabriel walked to Popina for coffee. When he returned to the mews house, two blue-suited security guards were standing watch at the door and Edward Knight was wandering the sitting room. His suit was freshly pressed and his shirt was clean, but he looked dreadful nevertheless.

"Did you manage to get any sleep?" asked Gabriel.

"Not a minute." Knight cast a glance at his wristwatch. "I don't suppose you've heard from them yet."

"You would have been the first to know. But try not to worry, it's still early."

"There are only twelve hours left before your deadline."

"And you can be sure they'll use every minute of it. That's the way the game is played."

"And if they refuse to supply a photograph?"

"Then you'll have no choice but to cut off negotiations."

Knight lowered himself heavily into an armchair. "You left something in my office last night, a leather attaché case filled with a considerable amount of cash. I don't imagine that was an accident on your part."

"It wasn't."

"I was under the impression that Higgins told you the unspent money was yours to keep."

"Something tells me you're going to need it more than I do."

"A lousy five hundred thousand?"

"Not quite."

"Yes," said Knight. "I noticed that several thousand euros were missing."

"I gave the money to a young Spanish woman who works at a beach café where Alice bumped into an old friend. With the woman's help, we were able to identify him."

"Why did you give her so much?"

Gabriel explained.

"I see," said Knight. "And the friend Alice bumped into?"

"His name is Peter Hoffmann. He works for—"

"Bank Josef Bänzinger & Company in Zurich. Peter and Alice were at Cambridge together."

"Did she tell you that she ran into him?"

"Actually she didn't mention it."

"If my wife ran into an old friend from her university days, I'm certain she would tell me."

"I trust Alice where Peter is concerned."

"And why is that?"

"Peter looks after a substantial share of my personal fortune." Knight drew a packet of cigarettes from the breast pocket of his suit jacket. "Do you mind?"

"No," replied Gabriel with a frown. "Not in the least."

Under the terms of his formal separation agreement from his old service, Gabriel had been allowed to retain possession of a fully updatable copy of Proteus, the world's most formidable cell phone hacking malware. Its most insidious feature was that it required no blunder on the part of the target, no unwise software update or click of an innocent-looking photograph or advertisement. All Gabriel had to do was enter the target's phone number into the application, and within minutes the device would be under his complete control. He could read the target's emails and text messages, review the target's browsing history and telephone metadata, and monitor the target's physical movements with the GPS location services. Perhaps most important, he could activate the phone's microphone and camera and thus turn the device into a full-time instrument of surveillance.

He waited until Knight had left the mews house to unleash Proteus on the phone that the kidnappers had used to make contact the previous evening. Forty-five minutes elapsed before the malware informed him that repeated attempts to connect with the device had proven unsuccessful. Gabriel reckoned it had been switched off or placed in a signal-blocking Faraday pouch—or that it was lying on the bottom of a lake or a river. He nevertheless instructed Proteus to continue its labors. Professional criminals, like spies and master terrorists, sometimes made mistakes.

He passed the remainder of the afternoon stretched out on the couch in the sitting room with the burner phone resting on his chest. Shortly before six he shaved and showered and changed into clean clothing. Knight and Higgins arrived with a takeaway dinner at seven, this time from Socca. They ate without appetite at the dining room table, the phone resting between them. It rang at 8:05 P.M., an hour before the expiration of Gabriel's deadline. He accepted the call and raised the phone to his ear. "Good evening, Mr. Allon," said the automated female voice. "Now, listen carefully."

15

Parc de Bruxelles

It was one thing to dispatch a few lines of text via email, quite another to transmit undeniable photographic evidence that one's hostage was alive and well. This the kidnappers steadfastly refused to do. They were far too disciplined to make a mistake like that, too professional. Nor would they agree to leave the proof-of-life photo somewhere in London, with its Orwellian network of surveillance cameras. Brussels was as close as they would get.

The Bombardier Challenger made retrieval of the image a bit less arduous. Gabriel boarded the luxurious private jet at London City Airport shortly before the 10:30 P.M. curfew and was on the ground in Brussels an hour later. Thirty minutes after that, at 1:00 A.M. local time, a chauffeured Mercedes sedan delivered him to the Parc de Bruxelles. He slipped through an open gate on the Rue Ducale and then made his way along a cobbled footpath toward the octagonal ornamental pond at the center of the park. Along the left side of the walkway, nestled amid a stand of trees, was a café called the Woodpecker, an establishment he had frequented in a previous life.

The service windows of the small wooden hut were tightly shuttered, and the surrounding picnic tables were deserted and dripping with the remnants of a recent rain. He illuminated the underside of one of the tables—the one indicated by the automated female voice—and spotted a length of opaque masking tape holding a small object in place. With his thumbnail he pried away a corner of the tape and tugged gently. The object, a USB flash drive left by one of the kidnappers, dropped into his palm.

He walked back to the car, and the driver took him to the Hotel Brussels. It was located on the Avenue Louise, in an unsightly tower that looked like something the Soviets might have thrown up in East Berlin during the darkest days of the Cold War. Higgins had reserved a suite on an upper floor. Inside, Gabriel placed his laptop on the desk and with some trepidation inserted the USB flash drive. It contained a single file. He clicked the touchpad twice, and a photograph blossomed onto the screen.

She was wearing the same white blouse she had worn the day of her disappearance. Her pale hair hung limp and lifeless, and there were dark semicircles beneath her eyes. The faded contusion on her left cheek appeared genuine, as did the magazine she held in her hands. It was the current issue of *The Economist.* The cover story concerned the perilous state of American democracy.

The wall behind her was gray cinder block—a cellar, thought Gabriel, or perhaps an industrial room of some sort. He enlarged the photograph and searched for evidence of manipulation. Her skin tone, the shape of her nose and mouth, the curl of her fingers around the edges of the magazine, the consistency of the lighting. Harsh and white, like the light of the halogen work lamps in Gabriel's studio, it shone from Alice's left. The shadows fell to the left throughout the image, without deviation.

Indeed, to Gabriel's restorer's eye, the image appeared authentic. That did not mean, however, that it had not been fabricated with the help of artificial intelligence. Chiara was right; he required the services of a skilled cyber professional, someone who could subject the image to sophisticated digital analysis.

The ringing of his mobile phone shattered the silence in the hotel room. Gabriel saw the number and his heart sank. He was not looking forward to this conversation.

He accepted the call and heard the voice of Edward Knight. "Was it there?" he asked.

"I'm afraid so."

"Send it to me."

"I'd rather you not see it."

"She's my wife, Allon."

He dispatched the photograph by email.

"Dear God," said Knight a moment later. "Look what they've done to my beautiful Alice."

"Are you sure it's really her?"

"Who else would it be?"

"A computer-generated image of Alice."

"I know my wife, Allon. That's definitely her."

"I'd still like to have it examined before we proceed with the negotiations."

"Time is of the essence."

"For them, but not for us. This is only the beginning."

Knight exhaled heavily. "Do you have anyone in mind for the job?"

"One of the best in the business."

"And what business is that?"

"Cybersecurity."

"I insist you send me the bill."

"Don't worry, there won't be one."

Gabriel rang off and immediately dialed a number from his contacts. The woman who answered spoke English with a pronounced Danish accent.

"Do you have any idea what time it is?"

"Late," answered Gabriel.

"Is it urgent, or can it wait until morning?"

"It can't, I'm afraid."

"Another missing painting?"

"Missing girl, actually."

"When and where?" was all she said.

She claimed she was visiting a friend in Luxembourg, but Gabriel never knew quite what to believe where Ingrid Johansen was concerned. The more likely story was that she had ventured to the small but exceedingly wealthy country for professional reasons. Poor Ingrid suffered from a lifelong compulsion to acquire objects that did not belong to her. Gabriel had made her acquaintance while searching for a long-lost Vermeer, which Ingrid had pinched from the Amalfi Coast villa of a corrupt South African shipper. Sometime later, at the request of a colleague from the Central Intelligence Agency, he had sent her to Moscow to steal a secret Kremlin plan to wage nuclear war in Ukraine. The operation had ended at the Finnish border. Ingrid had only a vague memory of how she had managed to survive. Gabriel, for his part, recalled every awful detail.

Lately Ingrid had provided him with services of a different sort, namely her ability to penetrate even the most well-defended computer network as though she were walking through an open door. Her most recent hack involved an ethically challenged bank in Lugano, which collapsed as a result of the scandal she had helped to bring about. Attempting to determine the authenticity of a photograph was beneath her. At the very least it could be done remotely. Gabriel nevertheless prevailed upon Ingrid to join him in London. He had a feeling he would need her again before this was over.

He was back at the Adams Row mews house by half past ten the following morning. Ingrid arrived an hour later, dressed in black jeans, a black pullover, and a stylish houndstooth check jacket. Her shoulder-length hair was the color of toffee and streaked with blond. Parted in the middle, it framed a face of straight, even features. There was nothing out of place, not a line or mark.

They embraced in the entrance hall, then Gabriel automatically patted the front of his jacket to make certain he was still in possession of his billfold. His old friend Ingrid had the best pair of hands he had ever seen.

"You have something for me?" she asked.

He showed her the USB flash drive.

"Please tell me you didn't stick that thing into your computer."

"I didn't really have a choice in the matter."

She plucked the flash drive from his grasp and surveyed the interior of the mews house. "Nice."

"It can be yours for a mere fifteen million."

"Rental?"

"Borrowed."

"From whom?"

"The Knight Group Limited of Berkeley Square."

"Is he watching us, your friend Mr. Knight?"

"He's my client, not my friend. And he swore he wouldn't."

"Do you believe him?"

"Not quite."

She tugged a laptop from her luggage and hacked her way onto the Wi-Fi network. Then, after checking the upload and download speeds, she inserted the flash drive and clicked on the icon. Her expression darkened as she contemplated the image on the screen.

"Hello, Alice," she said quietly.

"Are you sure about that?"

"First impressions are important." She glanced at Gabriel over the top of the screen. "Wouldn't you agree, Mr. Allon?"

"And what was yours?"

"The photograph is genuine."

"But can you prove it?"

"Digitally?" She shook her head. "I'm afraid that's no longer possible. You see, there's an arms race underway in the cyber industry, a race between our ability to generate deepfakes and our ability to detect them."

"Which side is going to win?"

"The fakers, of course." Ingrid looked down at the screen again and began to type. "In the very near future it will no longer be possible to tell the difference between AI-generated images and those captured by a camera. Needless to say, the implications for our already turbulent world are too awful to contemplate. An authoritarian ruler, for example, will have the power to create his own reality. With a deepfake video he will be able to discredit his political opponents. Who knows? If he's ruthless enough, he might use deepfakes to throw his opponents in prison or even to start a war."

"I'm about to go to war with Alice Winter's kidnappers, and I need to know whether she's really alive."

"When does this war start?"

"Nine o'clock tonight."

"What happens at nine?"

"Ransom," said Gabriel.

"How much do you suppose she's worth?"

"Alice? Could be nine figures."

Ingrid ceased her typing and turned the computer in Gabriel's direction. On the screen was a photograph of a weary-looking woman holding a magazine. It was the current issue of *Paris Match*. The woman was Ingrid.

"And what about her?" she asked. "How much is she worth?"

"She's priceless," said Gabriel. "Now, get to work."

She began with a basic reverse-image search, which produced no results. If nothing else, it was proof that the kidnappers had not taken an existing photograph of Alice from the Internet and manipulated it to their ends.

Next she analyzed the photograph with several commercial-grade deepfake detectors, none of which found any reason to question its authenticity. She then turned to professional-grade products and products that were circulating among the worldwide community of hackers and cybersecurity professionals, including a deepfake detector that analyzed skin pigment for evidence of inconsistency. They too found no fault with the photo.

She conducted the final phase of her analysis with Gabriel at her side. Slowly, meticulously, they scoured the length and breadth of the image for something, anything, that looked distorted, out of alignment, or out of place. They were in agreement that every aspect of the photograph appeared genuine, especially the look of fear in Alice Winter's wide blue eyes.

By then it was approaching six in the evening. Gabriel rang Edward Knight and gave him the news. The kidnappers had delivered authentic proof of life, the ransom negotiations could begin. Knight sounded relieved, elated, even. He suggested that Gabriel come to the office in Berkeley Square at half past seven. They could have a spot of dinner before the nine o'clock call.

"And bring your cyber specialist," said Knight before ringing off. "I'd love to meet him."

16

New Bond Street

It was a two-minute walk from the mews house to Edward Knight's office, but Gabriel and Ingrid had an hour to kill so they wandered over to New Bond Street. Ingrid slowed to a stop outside a Chanel boutique and scrutinized the long-limbed mannequin posed in the window.

"I absolutely adore that jacket," she declared.

"I like the one you're wearing better," replied Gabriel.

"This little rag?" She tugged at the sleeve. "It's nothing."

"Let's have a look at the label."

She opened the front of the blazer.

"Givenchy? That little nothing cost you four thousand euros, at least."

"Actually it was complimentary."

"Ingrid . . ."

"I know, I know," she said with a theatrical sigh. "But it was just hanging there."

"I thought you'd managed to get a handle on your little problem."

"So did I. But it seems the spell that crazy Corsican witch doctor cast on me has finally worn off."

The Corsican in question was not a witch doctor. She was a *signadora*, a healer of those afflicted with the *occhju*, the evil eye.

"Perhaps we should pay her another visit," suggested Gabriel.

"I still haven't recovered from my last one. Besides, I've always enjoyed my little affliction. It's made me rather well off, which in turn has allowed me to contribute greatly to those in need."

Ingrid was like one of those characters one saw in films or read about in novels. She stole from the rich and gave to the poor, keeping only what she needed to finance her comfortable lifestyle. She was a true gentleman thief.

Gabriel nudged her along the pavement. "Is that why you were in Luxembourg?" he asked. "To raise funds for your charitable endeavors?"

"I told you, I was visiting a friend."

"What kind of friend?"

"You're not attempting to pry into my personal affairs, are you?"

"I wouldn't dream of it."

It occurred to Gabriel, not for the first time, that he knew next to nothing about Ingrid's private life, or the extent to which she even had one. She lived alone in a cottage overlooking the North Sea in Denmark and owned a large villa on the Greek island of Mykonos. The Danish government had rewarded her heroics in Russia by granting her official absolution for her past misdeeds—and by turning a blind eye to the substantial fortune she had stashed away at Banca Privada d'Andorra. She led a charmed though somewhat solitary existence. With the exception of Gabriel and his wife and children, Ingrid preferred the pleasure of her own company.

She paused next outside the Montblanc boutique. "Can I get you something? A nice fountain pen, perhaps?"

"Thank you, no."

"What about a lovely leather documents case?"

"I have one."

"How about another? After all, variety is the spice of life."

"My life is spicy enough as it is."

She checked the time on her wristwatch. It was a beautiful Cartier tank with a shiny black crocodile band. She noticed the cold glint of suspicion in Gabriel's eye.

"Oh, for heaven's sake, Mr. Allon. *Really.*"

It was approaching seven o'clock. They ducked into the bar at Claridge's for a drink, then walked down Davies Street to Berkeley Square. Liam Higgins was standing on the pavement outside the Knight Group's building, talking to a young woman wearing jeans and a King's College hoodie. She was gone before Gabriel and Ingrid arrived.

"A friend of yours?" asked Gabriel.

"A visitor to our fair city. She was looking for Hyde Park."

"She doesn't know how to use Google?"

"Apparently not." Higgins glanced at Ingrid. "Your cyber consultant?"

Gabriel smiled but said nothing.

Upstairs, Edward Knight sat alone at the head of the polished wooden table in his conference room, dressed in a blazer and a regimental tie. Like Higgins before him, he regarded Ingrid with puzzlement. "You're not what I was expecting." He rose and offered his hand. "I'm Edward Knight."

"Erika Carlsen," said Ingrid.

"Danish?"

"I'm afraid so."

"Mr. Allon assures me that you're the best in the business."

"In my experience," replied Ingrid, "Mr. Allon is a man of his word."

Gabriel placed the burner phone on the table and marked the time.

It was 7:42 P.M.

The promised dinner was arrayed on the credenza, but no one touched a thing. Knight managed to remain in his seat until eight fifteen. Then he lit a cigarette and stalked the room as the clock slowly advanced. Desperate for a distraction, he peppered Ingrid with questions about her life in Denmark. Her answers, delivered in a cool and level voice, bore no resemblance to the truth. Gabriel, for his part, enjoyed the performance. He never tired of watching Ingrid at work.

But by eight forty-five even Ingrid was beginning to show the strain. She helped herself to one of Knight's cigarettes, then to two fingers of his single malt whisky. Knight poured a generous measure for himself and dropped once more into the chair at the head of the table.

"And you're sure the photograph is genuine?" he asked.

"As sure as I can be," she replied, and then explained the current contest between the deepfakers and the deepfake detectors. She did so at considerable length—seven long minutes, by Gabriel's watch. Knight was engrossed. The next time he checked the time it was 8:52 P.M.

"You're very clever, aren't you, Ms. Carlsen?"

She helped herself to another cigarette and touched the end to the slender blue flame of Knight's lighter. She held on to the lighter afterward, twirling it between her fingers like a card sharp. Knight watched her with fascination, then turned to Gabriel.

"Where on earth did you find her?"

Gabriel, ignoring the question, checked the time.

8:54 . . .

"How much do you suppose they'll demand?" asked Knight.

"It doesn't matter how much. They're not going to get it."

"I was asking for an estimate, Allon. Not a lecture on negotiating tactics."

"We'll know soon enough."

"Unless they don't call."

"Don't worry, they will. That's the only way they'll get their money."

Two more minutes crawled past. Knight closed his eyes, Ingrid smoked and twirled the lighter. Gabriel, still as a statue, stared at the burner. It rang with the suddenness of a fire alarm at 8:57, three minutes ahead of schedule. He lifted the phone to his ear and heard the same automated female voice. She bade him a pleasant evening, then issued a detailed set of demands and instructions. Gabriel didn't bother to write anything down; there was no point. The only thing that mattered was the time of the next phone call. It would take place at six o'clock the following evening.

He killed the connection and laid the phone on the tabletop.

"How much?" asked Edward Knight.

"A billion," answered Gabriel.

Knight appeared strangely relieved. "Is that all? I was certain it was going to be more."

17

Adams Row

It would be twelve days from start to finish. Twelve days of waiting and worrying, of burner phones ringing at all hours, of numbers and deadlines—the size of the ransom payment, the length of time Alice had to live if Gabriel didn't agree to their demands. The automated female voice at the other end of the line was unfailingly courteous, even when she was issuing the direst of warnings. She never raised her voice, never uttered a profane word, never lost her cool. Her emotionless, staccato delivery lent an air of unreality to the proceedings. Gabriel grew fond of her and on several occasions attempted to engage her in small talk, but she was far too disciplined for that. Each call lasted three minutes, and not a minute more.

He spent the first forty-eight hours of the negotiations attempting to convince his adversary that Edward Knight, while wealthy, did not have a billion dollars to spend on ransom. The automated voice, however, was having none of it. Knight, she insisted, had more than enough money to meet their demands.

"I'm afraid you've been misled," Gabriel explained during one of the calls. "Mr. Knight simply doesn't have that kind of cash on hand."

"One billion dollars," repeated the voice cordially. "Otherwise his wife dies."

"Will you at least hear my counteroffer?"

"We're not interested."

"All right, I'll see what I can do. What time should I expect your next call?"

"Ten o'clock tomorrow morning."

"Noon would be better."

"Noon it is. Sleep well, Mr. Allon."

It was a tactic Gabriel employed at every turn of the negotiations, to delay the next contact, even by only an hour or two. Time, he explained to Ingrid, was his ally. Yes, the kidnappers had Edward Knight's wife, but Gabriel had Edward Knight's money—and that was what the kidnappers wanted. He would not allow himself to be swayed by empty threats.

"But how can you tell the difference between an empty threat and a real one?"

"Experience."

"And when they're serious about killing her?"

"We make a deal."

The price of that deal, in the end, would not be a billion dollars—of that much, at least, Gabriel was certain. Still, he needed to know how much Edward Knight was willing to hand over to ensure his wife's safe return. They hashed it out together, just the two of them, in the Knight Group's Berkeley Square office. The property magnate, as Gabriel suspected, did not have a billion dollars in cash at his disposal.

"Maybe four hundred million," he said. "But anything more would require me to unwind a few investments."

"How long will it take?"

"That is a question for my man at Bank Josef Bänzinger & Company in Zurich."

"Peter Hoffmann?"

Knight nodded, then asked, "But how exactly does one make a

nine-figure ransom payment? Not in cash, surely. It would take a lorry to hold that kind of money."

"Two lorries, at least. But we haven't broached that subject yet."

"Perhaps you should."

"We're not there yet."

"Get there," said Knight. "I can't take much more of this."

Gabriel advised his client to concentrate on his work, at least publicly. Knight responded by announcing the acquisition of a luxury hotel and golf resort in the Republic of Ireland. Looking none the worse for wear, he told a television interviewer that his wife, the prominent British socialite Alice Winter, would play a role in managing the property. Needless to say, he made no mention of the fact that Ms. Winter had vanished without a trace during a recent holiday on Ibiza. Her abductors phoned Gabriel, as scheduled, at two that afternoon. The automated female voice, for the first time, expressed a willingness to entertain a counteroffer.

"Ten million," said Gabriel.

The silence lasted nearly a minute. Then the voice said, "Don't insult us, Mr. Allon. It won't end well, I assure you."

"Your turn," he said. "Give me a number. Something I can work with."

Another long delay, then, "We will accept nine hundred million."

"I told you, he doesn't have it."

"He just bought an Irish hotel."

"With borrowed money."

"Tell him to borrow some more," said the voice, and the connection died.

That evening Gabriel and Ingrid attended a breathtaking performance of Beethoven's Violin Concerto in D Major by Nicola Bennedetti and the London Symphony Orchestra. They were back at the apartment at ten thirty, and the burner phone rang promptly at midnight. As always the automated female voice greeted Gabriel affably by name.

"I'm sorry," he informed her, "but nine hundred million is simply out of the question. You and your friends have to be reasonable."

"We've been more than reasonable, Mr. Allon. And our patience is growing thin."

It was music to Gabriel's ear. He was beginning to wear them down. "Let's get this done, shall we?"

"Yes, let's."

"I had a long heart-to-heart with my client this evening and managed to convince him to sweeten his offer."

"How sweet?"

"Twenty-five million."

"Ha, ha, ha," said the voice humorlessly.

"It's an enormous sum of money."

"Not for a woman like Alice."

She was right about that. "Give me a number," said Gabriel. "A *real* number."

At length the voice said, "Eight hundred and fifty million."

"The eight hundred part is never going to happen, but I might be able to swing fifty."

"Eight hundred and fifty is as low as we're willing to go. You have until nine o'clock tomorrow morning to give us an answer."

"Or what?"

"Good night, Mr. Allon."

At Gabriel's insistence the next conversation took place at ten the following morning rather than nine and was so productive it required four separate three-minute phone calls on the part of the kidnappers, each from a different device. By the time the automated voice bade him a cheerful farewell, he had managed to whittle down the ransom demand to $750 million. His counteroffer now stood at $100 million. It was an astonishing number and they were still miles apart, but they were moving in the right direction.

The next call, however, was full of threats and rancor, as was the call that took place the following morning. But the evening session once again required four calls from the kidnappers from four different phones. In a gesture of goodwill, as they described it, they reduced the ransom demand to $700 million, leaving Gabriel no choice but to increase his counteroffer to $150 million.

"I'm afraid a hundred and fifty won't do, Mr. Allon."

"Have a nice long think about it. And while you're at it, send me a photograph of Ms. Winter with the new issue of *The Economist.*"

"We already have."

The flash drive was taped to the trunk of a horse chestnut tree in the Bois de Boulogne. Gabriel and Ingrid retrieved it the following morning—same pose, same unwashed hair and bruised cheek, different issue of *The Economist*—and were back in London in time for the next call from the kidnappers. It was scheduled to take place at 6:00 P.M., but they rang at six fifteen instead. The automated female voice apologized for the delay, then asked, "Are we good, Mr. Allon?"

"I wouldn't go that far. She looks dreadful."

"Yes, I know. But you alone have the power to end her suffering."

"I'm prepared to offer two hundred million."

"Nice try."

"Can we do this again at midnight?"

"Can't wait," said the voice as her three minutes expired.

She rang, this time, at the appointed hour. The conversation went well—three calls, three different phones—and resulted in a narrowing of their differences. The kidnappers' automated spokeswoman indicated she might be willing to settle for a mere $650 million. Gabriel countered with an offer of $200 million. He advised the kidnappers to thank their lucky stars and take the deal. It was, he suggested, the best they were going to get.

"In that case," said the voice flatly, "the next time you see Alice she'll have a bullet hole in the center of her forehead."

The threat turned out to be as empty as its predecessors, as evidenced by the reduced ransom demand the kidnappers placed on the table at three the following afternoon. At $625 million it was still out of the question. Gabriel nevertheless raised his counteroffer to a quarter billion. The kidnappers rang him unexpectedly at nine that evening with a counteroffer of their own.

"Six hundred million," said the voice.

"Better than a billion," replied Gabriel. "But it's still never going to happen."

"I would advise you, Mr. Allon, to make it happen."

He informed his adversaries that he would put their demand to Edward Knight, though in truth he did nothing of the sort. The subsequent five calls came and went with no further progress—and with numerous threats of violence. Ingrid feared they were approaching the point of no return. Gabriel, for the first time, wondered the same thing. Reluctantly he raised his offer to $300 million and counseled the kidnappers to take the money and run. They held fast at $600 million instead.

"Sorry," said Gabriel. "No can do."

"Where would you like us to leave the photograph of Alice with a bullet hole in her head?"

"Why don't you deliver it personally to me here in London?"

"Six hundred million, Mr. Allon. Going once, going twice . . ."

"The offer is three hundred million." He paused, then added, "Take it or leave it."

"Unwise move," said the voice.

"I'll wait to hear from you."

But for the next forty-eight hours he heard nothing at all. Fearful he had overplayed his hand, he rang the old numbers the kidnappers had used but received no answer. Finally, at three o'clock in the morning of the twelfth day of the negotiations, the burner phone rang. Gabriel let it ring several more times before accepting the call. This time the female voice he heard was not automated.

"Help me, Mr. Allon," she said. "Please, you must help me."

18

Adams Row

Gabriel sat up with a start, switched on the bedside lamp, checked the time. It was 3:04 A.M. He pressed the burner phone to his ear. At the other end of the connection he could hear breathing, faint and shallow.

"Who is this?" he demanded to know.

"It's me, Mr. Allon. It's Alice."

"I need you to answer a few questions."

"Proof of Alice?"

"Exactly."

"I'm all yours."

"Where were you staying when you were kidnapped?"

"A very large estate on Ibiza."

"Who were you with?"

"Three old friends from Cambridge."

"Their names, please."

"Sophie Maxwell, Ella Burns, and Phoebe Chadwick."

"Which one left the island early?"

"It was darling Pheebs."

Gabriel eased his grip on the phone. "How are you holding up?" he asked.

"As well as can be expected."

"Are they taking good care of you?"

"I wouldn't put it that way. In fact, I think they've had quite their fill of me at this point."

"How many are there?"

"I wouldn't know."

"You're blindfolded?"

"Always. With the exception of the two times they took my photograph," she added. "I suppose those were for you. I must have looked dreadful."

"Quite the opposite."

"Did Edward see them?"

"Only the first one. This has been very hard on him."

"And what about you, Mr. Allon?"

"Suffice to say, I've done this sort of thing a time or two."

"Imagine my surprise when my captors told me that I would be speaking to the famous Gabriel Allon. I'm only sorry our first conversation didn't take place at the fundraiser."

"So am I. It was a wonderful evening."

"Was I missed?"

"Your guests spoke of nothing else."

She laughed quietly. "You're very charming, Mr. Allon. I hope to see you soon."

"We're almost there, Alice."

The connection failed before she could respond; it seemed their allotted three minutes was up. Gabriel pulled on a shirt and a pair of trousers and padded barefoot into the kitchen. He filled the electric kettle and took down a box of tea from the cupboard. The phone rang again as the water began to boil.

"Where were we?" asked Alice.

"I was about to tell you that you'll be home soon."

"How long has it been? I've lost track of time."

"We're trying our best."

"Please try harder. I'll die soon if you don't."

"No one's going to die."

Ingrid crept into the kitchen, silent as a housecat, a bewildered expression on her face. Gabriel placed the burner phone in speaker mode. "Is it money they want?" Alice was saying.

"A great deal of money," answered Gabriel.

"Why hasn't Edward paid them?"

"It's not as simple as that."

"It is to me, Mr. Allon. My captors tell me the negotiations have reached an impasse."

"We've hit a rough patch, but we're close."

"Please tell Edward to pay them whatever they want." Her voice broke. "I can't take much more of this. I want to come home."

"I know it's hard, but try not to cry in front of them."

"Too late for that, I'm afraid. It turns out that I'm not cut out for the hostage life."

"You're stronger than you realize."

"I'm spoiled rotten, if you must know." She laughed in spite of herself. "My captors just gave me a nudge. It appears I have to run. It was a pleasure almost meeting you, Mr. Allon. And please give my love to—"

The connection died before she could finish the thought. Gabriel placed the phone on the kitchen counter. Ingrid picked it up and dialed the most recent number in the directory of incoming calls. It went straight to voicemail.

"Why now?" she asked.

"They're at the end of their tether."

"So is Alice."

"She can hold out a few more days."

"You've pushed them far enough, Mr. Allon. It's time to make a deal."

The phone rang before Gabriel could reply.

"Well?" asked the automated female voice.

Gabriel hesitated, then said, "Five hundred million."

"Take it or leave it?"

"Yes."

"Done," said the voice.

Gabriel waited until 6:00 A.M. to break the news to Edward Knight. The billionaire businessman was at his mansion in Hans Place. He responded with a flash of dark humor.

"It must be some sort of record, don't you think?"

"Must be," answered Gabriel in the same mordant tone.

"It sounds to me as though they had their hearts set on a half billion from the beginning."

Gabriel didn't disagree.

"How is the money to be delivered?" asked Knight.

"Wire transfer. They'll give us the account and routing numbers when it's time to make the exchange."

"What are the rules of the road for this sort of thing?"

"The final exchange? There are none," said Gabriel. "Which means you should prepare yourself for the likelihood that things won't go smoothly."

"If you'd like to bow out . . ."

"We couldn't possibly make a change now. For better or worse, the kidnappers seem to trust me." Gabriel paused. "And so does your wife."

"That leaves the money," said Knight. "How quickly can you leave for Zurich?"

"Are you sure you want me to handle it?"

"Why wouldn't I?"

"I'm not exactly beloved by Swiss bankers."

"So I've heard," said Knight, and hung up the phone.

19

Bahnhofstrasse

Higgins booked a pair of suites for them at the Baur au Lac Hotel. They stopped there long enough to check in and shed their luggage and then set off along the graceful curve of the Bahnhofstrasse, Zurich's main artery of commerce and luxury. The headquarters of Bank Josef Bänzinger & Co. were located at Number 42. Gabriel deposited Ingrid at the café next door and headed inside.

A thirtyish woman wearing a dark pencil skirt and matching jacket met him in the lobby and with Swiss discretion escorted him upstairs. Heads turned as they crossed the firm's trading floor. It was no secret, it seemed, that the bête noire of the Swiss banking industry was in the building.

Peter Hoffmann's spacious office overlooked the Bahnhofstrasse. He was holding a phone to his ear as Gabriel entered. He bade the person at the other end of the call a hasty farewell and rose to his feet.

"I must admit, Mr. Allon, you're the last person in the world I expected to see today."

"Likewise," replied Gabriel, and grasped Peter Hoffmann's outstretched hand. The Swiss banker had aged slightly in the time since he had posed for his passport photo but radiated good health. His suit was gray, his necktie silver. Gabriel would not have been surprised to learn that he wore the same attire every day.

"Coffee?" he asked.

"Thank you, no," said Gabriel, and lowered himself uninvited into a stylish Barcelona chair. Peter Hoffmann remained standing a moment longer. He was tall and trim, with a narrow waist and square shoulders. He looked good on his feet, and knew it.

He placed a forefinger to his lips and eyed Gabriel speculatively through his rimless spectacles. "Five hundred million?" he asked at last.

"Dollars," added Gabriel.

"And what exactly are we going to do with it?"

"We're going to transfer it to another bank."

"Which bank?"

"That has yet to be determined."

Hoffmann was slow in taking his seat. "I can't send the money to just *any* bank, Mr. Allon. Swiss anti-money-laundering laws require me to know my customer."

"Your customer," said Gabriel, "is Edward Knight."

"Is he dissatisfied with the way I'm handling his portfolio?"

"Not at all."

"Then why is he withdrawing the bulk of his money?"

"That's his business, Herr Hoffmann. Not yours."

Gabriel had spoken in German. The banker responded in the same language. "And what is the nature of your relationship with Mr. Knight, if you don't mind my asking?"

"I'm restoring a painting for him."

"Not the Bellotto?"

"He mentioned it?"

"I handled the payment. It seemed a bit high for a Bellotto, if you ask me, but Edward was insistent." Peter Hoffmann swiveled round in his chair and watched a Number 11 tram slithering silently along the Bahnhofstrasse. "He's not in some sort of trouble, is he?"

"Edward? Not at all."

"His business appears to be thriving."

"Firing on all cylinders," Gabriel chimed in.

"So why is he converting his portfolio to cash?"

"I'm afraid that's—"

"None of my affair?"

Gabriel was silent.

"I've been handling Edward's money for more than ten years," said Peter Hoffmann, his tone indignant. "And if the truth be told, I've done very well by him."

Gabriel decided to probe a bit. "He tells me that you attended Cambridge with his wife."

"That's correct. Alice is the one who convinced Edward to hire me."

"Seen her lately?"

"As a matter of fact, I bumped into her quite by chance on Ibiza a few days ago. She was there with a few of our old friends from Cambridge. It's an annual thing."

"What's that?"

"A summer holiday together. Alice apparently rented the biggest house on the island."

Gabriel returned to the topic at hand—the exact amount of cash in Edward Knight's accounts at Bank Josef Bänzinger & Co.

"Three hundred and ninety million dollars," replied Peter Hoffmann. "Give or take. The rest of the portfolio is locked up in bonds, equities, and other complex financial instruments."

"Mr. Knight's time is in short supply."

"When does he need the money?"

"Close of business today." Gabriel rose from the chair, signaling the meeting had come to an end. "And don't even think about leaving the office until you hear from me."

"I'm afraid I have an engagement this evening."

"Cancel it," said Gabriel, and walked out.

The kidnappers had promised to make contact again at six that evening. Gabriel and Ingrid waited them out in their adjoining suites at the Baur au Lac. They nibbled on a room service lunch, they watched a dreadful British police drama on television, they stalked and paced and stared at the blue waters of the Zürichsee. Ingrid tried to assure Gabriel that the end was near, that Alice would soon be free. Gabriel, who refused to be mollified, told Ingrid about the last abduction case he had handled. The victim, he explained, was a young girl, the daughter of an immensely rich and powerful man. The kidnappers had strapped a bomb to her before the handover. It had blown her to pieces before Gabriel and her father could reach her.

"Dear God," whispered Ingrid.

"I assure you, God had nothing to do with it."

"But why did they kill her?"

"They were using her as a weapon in an assassination attempt. Her father was the primary target." Gabriel lowered his voice. "I was the icing on the cake."

"Is there a moral to this dreadful story?"

"The last act of any abduction case is always the most unpredictable. Which is why the negotiator must stand his ground until the final curtain falls."

"No Alice, no money?"

Gabriel nodded.

"And if they refuse?"

"We have no choice but to walk away."

"If we do that, they'll kill her."

"They have five hundred million reasons not to."

"Not yet, they don't."

Gabriel checked the time. It was only half past three, not quite close of business, but he rang Peter Hoffmann nonetheless. The Swiss banker kept him on hold for five minutes before taking the call.

"Sorry, Mr. Allon. I was on the phone to New York."

"How much cash do we have?"

"Only four hundred and twenty million."

"What's the holdup?"

"A rather large pile of derivatives that I'm having trouble unloading."

"You have exactly two and a half hours to come up with the rest of the money."

"Call me in an hour."

It limped slowly by, step by agonizing step. Ingrid passed the time with her laptop, Gabriel with his memories. He was kneeling on a rutted, unpaved track in a remote corner of southwest France, drenched in the blood of a child, his face lifted to a baleful black sky. The girl's father, dazed by the force of the blast wave, was frantically gathering up her severed limbs. No, thought Gabriel, there would be no mistakes tonight, no compromises or last-minute exceptions. No Alice, no money. Those would be the terms of the deal.

He was aware of Ingrid staring at him. "You look as though you're going to be sick," she said.

"It must have been the room service."

"You barely touched it."

It was true; the very thought of food had made his stomach turn. He checked the time. It was ten minutes past four. He allowed another twenty minutes to pass before ringing Peter Hoffmann. The

Swiss banker informed him that he had raised $504 million in cash on behalf of his client Edward Knight.

"All I need now is a letter signed by Mr. Knight, granting you the authority to transfer the money." Gabriel protested, but Hoffmann held firm. "Sorry, Mr. Allon, but I need that document. Otherwise the money can't leave this bank."

Gabriel dialed Edward Knight in London and explained the situation. Knight was unconcerned. "Don't worry, Allon, I'll personally authorize the transfer when the time comes."

Gabriel would have preferred to maintain control of the ransom payment, but he could hear in Knight's tone that there was no point in trying to change his mind.

"The money goes when I say it goes," insisted Gabriel. "Are we clear?"

"I'll wait to hear from you," replied Knight, and then hung up the phone.

It was the first unexpected turn of the evening, but Gabriel was certain it would not be the last. It therefore came as no surprise that the promised 6:00 P.M. call from the kidnappers did not come through until half past.

"Do you have the money?" asked the automated female voice.

"We have it," answered Gabriel. "All we need is the name of the bank and the account and routing numbers."

"The bank is CyproBank of Nicosia."

Gabriel knew it well. It was one of the world's least reputable financial firms. "And the account and routing numbers?"

The automated female recited them. Gabriel jotted the numbers on a piece of hotel stationery, then read them aloud.

"Correct and correct," said the voice.

"When would you like us to send the money?"

"Immediately."

"No Alice, no money," said Gabriel, and killed the connection. Then he looked at Ingrid and asked, "Do you think you can hack CyproBank of Nicosia?"

She opened her laptop and went to work.

20

Baur au Lac Hotel

The kidnappers waited only twenty minutes before calling again. The automated female voice repeated her demand that Gabriel transfer the $500 million at once, and for a second time he refused. The voice responded by issuing yet another threat to kill the captive, but even she seemed to realize her words rang hollow. The entire episode had been nothing more than a ploy on the part of the kidnappers to short-circuit the customary procedures of making the final exchange of ransom for victim. Gabriel had used their ill-advised gambit to his advantage. Ingrid was already knocking on the door of CyproBank's data network.

"Where are you now?" asked the voice after a silence of nearly a minute.

"You mean you don't know?"

"We aren't following you, Mr. Allon."

"You really should be, you know. That's the way it usually works."

She repeated her original question, and this time Gabriel informed her that he was in Zurich, where he had spent the better part of the day assembling a half billion dollars in cash. "All of which can be yours," he added, "if you play your cards right."

The connection died suddenly. Their three minutes had elapsed.

Ingrid looked up from her laptop. "Do you believe them?"

"That they don't know where we are?" Gabriel shook his head. "I have a feeling they've been watching me since the first time I walked into Edward Knight's office in London."

Ingrid returned to work on her laptop.

"How much time do you need?" asked Gabriel.

"In a perfect world . . . forty-eight hours."

"You have exactly *four* hours."

The burner phone was ringing again. Gabriel waited a few seconds longer before answering. The automated voice tonelessly issued her instructions.

"There's a train for Munich leaving Zurich at seven thirty-three. It's the last Munich-bound train of the night, so we would advise you to hurry. You'll hear from us again when you arrive."

"I'm not terribly fond of Munich, if you must know."

"Hurry, Mr. Allon," the voice replied, and then the connection went dead.

It was approaching 7:00 P.M. when he stepped from the hotel's entrance. During the twenty-minute walk to the Hauptbahnhof he saw nothing to suggest he was being followed. The train for Munich was already boarding by the time he arrived. He purchased a ticket at one of the windows and headed downstairs to the assigned track. Five other passengers followed him into the first-class carriage. None of them struck Gabriel as potential accessories to a kidnapping.

The train rolled out of the station at the stroke of 7:33. Edward Knight rang ten minutes later. The billionaire's voice sounded razor-sharp with tension.

"Where in God's name are you, Allon?"

Gabriel, phone to ear, hand over his mouth, described the events of the previous hour. As part of the briefing he disclosed that he had duped the kidnappers into surrendering the name of the bank where they wanted the ransom payment deposited, along with the account and routing numbers. His associate, he added, was now attempting to penetrate the bank's computer network, with the goal of rerouting the money before it disappeared forever.

Knight was apoplectic nonetheless. "You should have sent the money when they asked," he snapped.

"That's how kidnappings become murders. I know the waiting is hard, but you have to trust me."

"Do you really think your Danish friend can hack into that bank?"

"She can do it in her sleep. But she needs time."

"I'm not prepared to wait much longer. In fact, I'd feel better if you gave me the account and routing numbers."

"I'm afraid I can't do that."

"Why not?"

"Because those numbers are my guarantee that you're not going to do something stupid tonight."

"I insist you give them to me, Allon."

"I'm sorry," replied Gabriel, "but we just entered a tunnel. Can you say that again?"

"The numbers," shouted Knight. "Send me those bloody numbers."

Gabriel terminated the call and gazed at the postcard-perfect Swiss meadow flashing past his window. The memory of that night in France returned unexpectedly. He concealed it beneath a layer of obliterating paint, then absently checked the time. He considered calling Chiara and the children but decided against it. One untruth was all he could manage for now.

Darkness had fallen by the time they crossed the German border, and it was a few minutes after eleven when the train arrived at Munich Central Station. The kidnappers rang as Gabriel was stepping onto the platform. "Where to next?" he said by way of greeting, and the automated female voice replied, "Salzburg."

The evening's last train departed at 11:54. Gabriel purchased a first-class ticket, then went to a café in the departure hall and ordered coffee and a sandwich. Edward Knight rang at eleven thirty. Gabriel dispatched him to voicemail and phoned Ingrid instead.

"How's it going?" he asked.

"Until a moment ago, it was going quite well. What about you?"

"It seems I'm on my way to Salzburg."

"What time do you get in?"

"One twenty-eight, which means you have at least two more hours."

"It's not nearly enough time."

Edward Knight was calling again. This time Gabriel reluctantly answered.

"A tunnel? That was beneath you, Allon."

"You're right. The next time you make an outrageous demand, I'll simply hang up."

Knight's anger abated. "I just got off the phone with Peter Hoffmann. He was asking for an update."

"I would advise him to get a few hours' sleep. You too."

"Where are you off to next?"

Gabriel answered.

"Could they have smuggled Alice into Austria?" asked Knight.

"Quite easily."

"You will be careful, won't you?"

"I'm going to hang up now," answered Gabriel, and killed the call.

The empty ticket hall echoed with a boarding announcement for the Salzburg train. Gabriel finished the last of the sandwich, then headed downstairs to the platform. There were no other passengers in the first-class carriage, so he closed his eyes and slept. The ringing of the burner phone woke him at 1:28 A.M.

"Good morning, Mr. Allon," said the automated voice. "Welcome back to Austria."

21

Salzburg

Outside, Gabriel walked through the deserted streets of Salzburg to the Hotel Scherer, a modest establishment that catered to discount travelers. The kidnappers had left a Volkswagen sedan on the opposite side of the street. He ran a hand beneath the rear bumper and found the key. It was taped there in the same manner with which they had adhered the flash drive to the bottom of the table in Brussels. He tugged it loose, then switched on the flashlight function of his phone and searched the undercarriage of the car for a bomb.

Seeing nothing out of the ordinary, he unlocked the doors and dropped behind the wheel. The burner phone rang the instant he started the engine.

"How well do you know your way around Austria?" asked the voice.

"Better than you, I imagine."

"Head south on the A10. You'll hear from us again soon. But only if we determine that you are alone."

"You know I am."

"For Alice's sake," said the voice, "I hope that's true."

The A10, better known as the Tauren Autobahn, stretched southward from Salzburg to the Italian border. Near the ancient salt mining town of Hallein, Gabriel became aware of a pair of headlamps suspended a half kilometer or so in his wake. The burner phone rang as he was approaching Tenneck, a small village wedged between two soaring Alpine peaks. The automated voice instructed him to take the next exit.

It deposited him onto a two-lane road that ran along the western bank of the Salzach River. The burner phone rang again as he drove through a sleeping market town. The voice informed him that he was approaching a traffic circle.

"Take the first exit, then head west toward Mühlbach."

"We're taking the scenic route, are we?"

The road wound its way along the base of the Hochkönig, the highest peak in the Berchtesgaden Alps. There was no oncoming traffic at that hour, and no sign of the car that had followed him from Salzburg. He reckoned he was getting close to his destination, though, because the kidnappers remained on the line even after their three minutes had elapsed.

"You are approaching a turnout," the voice said at last. "Pull over and switch off the engine."

Gabriel spotted the turnout a moment later. He slowed to a stop, doused the headlamps, killed the engine.

"Well done, Mr. Allon. Now leave the key and your phones on the passenger seat and get into the trunk."

"Is this really necessary?"

"I'm afraid so."

Gabriel placed the key on the seat next to him, along with the burner phone and his iPhone. Then he pressed the internal trunk release and went to the back of the car. The compartment was not particularly roomy, requiring him to contort his modest frame into something resembling a fetal position. As he lay in pitch darkness he chided himself for not having switched on the hazard lights. He only hoped the kidnappers arrived before some fool rear-ended him. A less dignified end he could scarcely imagine.

At length he heard a car coming up the road from the floor of the valley. It pulled up behind the Jetta and a single occupant emerged. The leaden footfalls on the tarmac indicated he was a large chap, as did the way the Jetta sagged to the left when he settled behind the wheel. Then the engine started and the car shot forward as though it had been fired from a gun. No hurry at all, thought Gabriel as he braced himself against the interior of the trunk. Take all the time you need.

The secret to surviving confinement in a claustrophobic space, Gabriel reminded himself, was to place one's thoughts elsewhere. Some detainees sought refuge in their past but Gabriel's was filled with nights of blood and fire, so he took up an imaginary pad and pencil instead and mentally sketched a detailed map of western Austria—the mountain peaks and river valleys, the towns and villages, the network of well-maintained autobahns and roads connecting them all. Somewhere there was a villa, by no means large or ostentatious, but isolated. It was the sort of place where a group of outsiders would not attract attention. In all likelihood their hostage was locked in a room in the cellar, blindfolded and bound, frightened out of her mind.

But how had they managed to clandestinely transport her to Austria from the island of Ibiza? That had been the easy part. They had placed her aboard a motor yacht anchored off the island's coast and then spirited her to the mainland, probably at a spot along the

French coast. Gabriel knew of several suitable locations, places he had used himself. She had likely passed the long drive to Austria zipped into a nylon duffel and dosed with ketamine to keep her quiet. Gabriel had done that sort of thing too, more often than he cared to remember. He had always known that one day his past might catch up with him. Perhaps, he thought, tonight was the night.

In the absolute darkness of the trunk his wristwatch, with its non-luminous hands and face, was of no use. It was no matter; his internal clock, as accurate as any Swiss timepiece, told him it was 3:25 A.M. when the car made an abrupt left turn onto a gravel track. The upward tilt of the vehicle was eight or nine degrees. The man at the wheel made no attempt to give Gabriel a smooth ride.

Another two minutes passed before the car finally drew to a stop and the engine died. A second vehicle drew up behind them, and a moment later the trunk lid swung slowly upward, revealing the presence of two men wearing balaclava masks. One of the men pulled a hood over Gabriel's head. Then, together, they hoisted him from the trunk and propped him upright on his feet.

His right leg buckled instantly; it was numb from lack of circulation. The two men took hold of his arms and marched him along the paving stones of a walkway as if leading him to the place of his execution. The air, he noted, was colder here. They must have gained several hundred meters in altitude during the drive.

He managed to scale a flight of four stone steps. Then they passed through an open doorway, into the sudden warmth of the kidnappers' lair. The wooden floor beneath Gabriel's feet was rough-hewn. The air smelled of cigarettes and, curiously, freshly baked bread.

They nudged him to the left, and blindly he placed one foot in front of the other. After twelve paces exactly, the hands gripping his arms jerked him to a stop. Then a chair scraped across the floorboards and pressed against the back of his knees. The hands lowered him into it with unexpected care.

A long silence ensued. Gabriel attempted to execute a mental sketch of his surroundings, but the tableau eluded him. He was certain only that there was another person present, perhaps two.

At last he heard the clicking of a keyboard, followed by the toneless automated voice.

"Pleasant trip, Mr. Allon?"

"No," he answered truthfully.

More typing, then, "If you had sent the money, you would be home with your family by now."

"Let's leave my family out of this, shall we? The sooner you let me see Alice, the sooner we can all be on our way."

A hand pulled the hood from Gabriel's head, and the tableau around him came into view. He was seated at a rectangular table in a rustic kitchen, flanked by his two handlers, one of whom, as he had surmised, was built like a rugby player. Two other men sat opposite, both wearing balaclavas, dark woolen pullovers, and gloves. The one behind the laptop had the watchful brown eyes of a predatory animal. He laid his gloved fingers on the keyboard and typed. The automated voice read aloud the words he had composed.

"Call Peter Hoffmann in Zurich and instruct him to wire the money."

"How do you know that I was dealing with Peter Hoffmann?"

The hands typed, then, "How do you think we know?"

Alice . . .

"Bring her up here so I can have a look at her," said Gabriel.

"She's sleeping and wishes not to be disturbed," the voice said after a few seconds of typing.

"I'm sure she won't mind if you wake her."

The man shook his head.

"We had a deal," said Gabriel calmly. "No Alice, no money."

He typed his response. "The terms of the deal have changed, Mr. Allon."

The one built like a rugby player handed Gabriel his iPhone while his colleague on the opposite side of the table typed.

"Call Herr Hoffmann in Zurich," said the automated voice. "Tell him to wire the money."

"Not a chance."

The man replied by drawing a SIG Sauer pistol from the small of his back and leveling it at Gabriel's head.

"Nice gun," he said with a disarming smile. "But why don't you put it away before someone gets hurt."

"Call him," the man said aloud.

Gabriel treated him to another smile. "It's nice to finally hear your real voice. You can be sure I'll never forget it."

What happened next unfolded with the suddenness of an automobile accident. One minute Gabriel was upright in the chair, the next he was sprawled on the floorboards, with three of the kidnappers assaulting him like a pack of wolves. When they had finished pummeling him into submission, they bound his hands, knees, and ankles with silver duct tape. The last swath they placed over his mouth, leaving him incapable of complaint. Then, somehow, they managed to return him to his original seated position. The one behind the laptop eyed Gabriel through the slits of his balaclava mask, then went to work at the keyboard. The message was longer than his previous communiqués. When it was complete he took up a mobile phone and tapped the screen once. The call was answered instantly. The voice sounded desperate. It belonged to Edward Knight.

"Allon? Is that you? Have you got her?"

The man with the vigilant brown eyes placed the phone next to the laptop and played the message he had just composed. It was delivered by the same toneless yet unfailingly polite female voice.

"Good evening, Mr. Knight. You have exactly one hour to transfer five hundred million dollars to CyproBank of Nicosia. If the money does not arrive, we will have no choice but to kill your wife and your friend Mr. Allon. The time for games is over. This is your last warning."

The message concluded with the account and routing numbers. Gabriel attempted to warn Knight not to send the money, but with the metallic duct tape covering his mouth he could manage nothing more than a muffled lament. Knight, frantic, begged the kidnappers to repeat the two lengthy numbers, and the automated female voice obliged him. There was no need for her to issue another threat. Knight had already capitulated.

"You'll have the money within the hour. And whatever you do, please don't harm my wife."

The man behind the mask terminated the call, then regarded Gabriel across the tabletop. His brown eyes shone with mirth. He typed a final message, and the automated female voice read it aloud.

"Did you happen to notice that Edward Knight didn't ask us not to kill you?"

Gabriel, incapable of a response, stared at the masked figure until the hood was returned to his head and all was dark. Then two pairs of hands hauled him to his feet and carried him outside to the trunk of the Volkswagen. Before closing the lid they gave him a shot of ketamine and down he went, into the frigid black waters of an Alpine lake. His past, he thought, had indeed caught up with him. Sixty minutes was all the time he had left. Sixty minutes, then he would be dead.

Part Two

Proof of Death

22

Lower Austria

It was Babette, Karl Gruber's usually sensible daughter, who had insisted on the damn dog. He had arrived at that precarious stage in life, she informed him, alone and on the very doorstep of senility and incontinence, when he required a companion. Because she lived with her husband in an elegant district of Vienna, and he resided in the dreary Lower Austrian town of Falkenstein, another life form would have to fill the role—a German pinscher, deer red in color and malevolent in mood and aspect, whom she christened Oscar. They had taken an instant dislike to one another, dog and man, that five long years of living beneath the same roof had done nothing to diminish. If anything, their relationship had grown more strained with time. It was now characterized by resentment, especially on the part of the man. He had provided Oscar with a comfortable home and looked after his bodily needs and emissions without complaint. And yet the beast barely tolerated his presence, only occasionally allowing himself to be stroked or scratched. As for the notion of companionship, Karl Gruber had long ago reached the unsettling conclusion that it was he who was the companion of the canine, and not the other way around.

The cottage they reluctantly shared was on the northern end of Falkenstein, not far from the ruins of the medieval castle. At half past seven that morning its ramparts wore a fine gray cloak of fog. Oscar, having moved his bowels in a vineyard of Grüner Veltliner grapes, was straining resentfully at his leash. Though he had undergone rigorous training, he refused to walk at the heel of his owner, preferring instead to lead the way, as if he were the one in charge. His ears were cocked and alert, his banana-shaped tail erect. Pinschers, as Karl Gruber had discovered, much to his dismay, were ratters by breeding and instinct, which left them prone to bite. Oscar was never more contented than when sinking his teeth into the outstretched hand of a stranger. And no morning constitutional was complete unless it included the murder of an innocent rodent.

Beyond the castle lay a dense green wood cut with footpaths and bisected by a single two-lane road known as the L23. Oscar, with a glance over his shoulder, demanded to be freed from his leash, and Karl Gruber, though it was forbidden by local edict, happily complied. The thirty minutes that his canine companion spent roaming the woods in search of prey were the most pleasant of his day. Lately he had lost the ability to separate one from the other. In his mind they were distinguished only by the weather, the obsession of the aged. Babette was right, he was standing at the edge of the abyss. He could no longer summon the face of his parents or siblings from the cold soup of his memory, and even Lotte, his late wife, was slipping away. A part of him looked forward to the day he could no longer recall Oscar's name. The dog would become Babette's problem. Revenge, he thought to himself with a smile, would be his.

With a heavy heart he called out Oscar's name now, for it had been a long time since he had seen hide or hair of his dreaded companion. Not surprisingly his summons went unanswered; Oscar obeyed instructions only when it pleased him. But when another ten minutes or so went by with no sign of him, Karl Gruber allowed himself to consider the possibility that some unspeakable tragedy had befallen the beast. Then he heard the familiar sound of Oscar's bark, knife-edged and distant, and he realized with profound sadness that his most fervent prayers had not been answered after all.

The barking persisted, then grew irate. Karl Gruber followed the sound westward across the wood, and eventually he discovered Oscar gnawing on an object lying along the grassy verge of the L23. At first Karl Gruber thought it was the carcass of an animal or a sack of something that had fallen from a passing lorry. But upon closer inspection he realized that the object was not a dead animal or fallen debris but a rather well-attired man who was hooded and bound with silver duct tape. Oscar had latched onto the poor fellow's ankle. Karl Gruber, with considerable difficulty, managed to pull the dog away. Then he removed the hood from the man's head and found himself gazing into the greenest eyes he had ever seen.

The man's mouth was covered by duct tape as well. Karl Gruber removed it carefully, and the man addressed him calmly in German, with the accent of a native Berliner.

"Where am I?" he asked.

"Falkenstein."

"Lower Austria?"

"Yes, that's right."

The man absorbed this information, then asked, "Are you carrying a phone, by any chance?"

"Yes, of course." Karl Gruber dug the device from his pocket. "I'll ring the Bundespolizei right away."

"Please don't," the man replied in the same unruffled tone. "There's no need to involve the police in this matter." Then he recited the number he wanted Karl Gruber to dial. He entered it with his thumb while holding Oscar at bay, then placed the phone in speaker mode and held it near the man's mouth. A few seconds elapsed before the device at the other end of the connection began to ring. It was answered at once by a man who spoke English with a British accent. His tone was one of desperation.

"Where in God's name is my wife? You promised to release her if I wired the money."

Karl Gruber, who possessed more than a passing familiarity with the English language, shot a startled look at the green-eyed man lying helpless on the side of the road.

"Sorry, Edward," the man said. "It's only me."

The dog's razor-sharp teeth had sliced through Gabriel's gabardine trousers and carved four gashes in his lower leg. The creature's owner, perhaps fearing legal repercussions, suggested a visit to the nearby hospital for treatment, but Gabriel politely declined. All he needed, he insisted, was a bit of antibacterial ointment and a few plasters, and he would be as good as new.

The first order of business, though, was cutting away the duct tape that had left him defenseless in the face of the canine's assault. Fortunately the dog's owner was in the habit of carrying a pocketknife, a large Swiss Army model with many helpful tools and implements, including a pair of scissors. Herr Gruber carefully freed Gabriel's limbs and appendages, inflicting no new wounds in the process. Then they all three set off along the tree-lined road—Gabriel and Herr Gruber and Herr Gruber's dog. They were, he thought, a motley trio if there ever was one.

"We really should call the police," said the elderly Austrian.

"Probably," agreed Gabriel. "But we're not going to."

"You're not a criminal, are you?"

"Do I look like a criminal?"

"You do, actually."

It was a walk of nearly a kilometer to Herr Gruber's neat little cottage in Falkenstein. Inside, it smelled of dog and mothballs. He fetched a first aid kit, and Gabriel, after rolling up the left leg of his ruined trousers, applied the antibiotic ointment and the field dressing. Then he borrowed Herr Gruber's phone a second time and rang a local taxi company.

The car soon appeared, driven by a woman who spoke without cease during the hour-long journey to Vienna. Gabriel paid the fare in cash—the kidnappers had allowed him to retain possession of his billfold and passport—and then made his way to the Kärntnerstrasse, Vienna's famed pedestrian shopping street, where he purchased toiletries, a change of clothing, and a new iPhone. The first call he placed was to Edward Knight in London.

"Anything?" he asked.

"No," replied Knight. "Nothing at all."

"Are you sure they received the money?"

"They said they did, but perhaps you should have a word with your cyber specialist."

She was still at the Baur au Lac Hotel in Zurich, where she had spent a sleepless night attempting without success to penetrate the data network of CyproBank of Nicosia. Gabriel gave her a quick update, then instructed her to pack her bags.

"Where should I go?" she asked.

"I'm told Mykonos is lovely this time of year."

"What about Alice?"

"There is no Alice," he answered. "Not yet, at least."

There was a small hotel near St. Stephen's Cathedral where Gabriel, in another lifetime, had passed a tense Friday afternoon before killing two Hezbollah suicide bombers outside Vienna's main synagogue. Shopping bags in hand, he checked into the same hotel and, as misfortune would have it, was assigned to his old room. He stayed there long enough to shower and change and book a seat on the next British Airways flight to London. Then, after informing Chiara of his whereabouts and travel plans, he checked out of the hotel and, bidding the doorman a pleasant morning, went into the street.

The flight was scheduled to depart at half past two, leaving Gabriel with an hour to kill. He should have headed straight to Schwechat Airport, but against all better judgment he decided to lead himself on a walking tour of the Innere Stadt instead. Everywhere he turned there were reminders of his past. There was the famous coffeehouse where he had once come face-to-face with Erich Radek, colleague of Adolf Eichmann and tormentor of Gabriel's mother. And the little café where each afternoon, when he had finished work on the painting he was restoring in the cathedral, he used to take his young son for gelato. And the popular Italian restaurant where the child had eaten a last meal of buttered spaghetti while his mother, distracted by the television behind the bar, watched Iraqi Scud missiles falling on Tel Aviv.

Gabriel's last stop was the small square in the Jewish quarter where their car had been parked that night. He had strapped the child into his seat, he had kissed his wife. *One last kiss . . .* Even now he could taste the wine on her lips and hear the hesitation of the starter when she turned the key. Then, in a flash of brilliant white light, she and the child were lost to him forever. Somehow, he thought, the kidnappers of Alice Winter had known this.

Good morning, Mr. Allon. Welcome back to Austria . . .

Unshed tears blurred his vision as he left the square and went in search of a taxi. He found one on the Rotenturmstrasse and instructed the driver to take him to the airport. His flight departed on schedule and touched down at Heathrow at four o'clock, leaving him just enough time to make the 4:32 train from Heathrow Central to Exeter. Chiara and the children were waiting outside in the Range Rover when he emerged from the station. He slid into the passenger seat, pressed his lips to Chiara's cheek, then telephoned Edward Knight.

"Nothing," said the billionaire, and rang off.

23

Gwennap Head

It began, like most things these days, with a few pithy words on a social media platform controlled by a reactionary billionaire. The culprit was a gadfly British podcaster who specialized in celebrity gossip and scandal. She had discovered, thanks to her reputedly impeccable sources, that Alice Winter, the dazzling wife of real estate mogul Edward Knight, had vanished while on holiday on the island of Ibiza. The brief item caught the attention of a reporter from one of the lesser London tabloids, and with a single phone call to the Policía Nacional he confirmed its accuracy. His story appeared on the paper's website shortly before seven the following morning, and by lunchtime it was all anyone in Britain was talking about.

Attempts to reach Edward Knight would prove unsuccessful, but at half past four that afternoon he was spotted entering New Scotland Yard, headquarters of the Metropolitan Police, accompanied by a team of high-priced lawyers. The Met's press spokeswoman declined to characterize the nature of the discussions, saying only that Knight had been fully cooperative. No, she added pointedly, the billionaire was not considered a suspect in his wife's disappearance.

But what, precisely, had happened to Alice Winter? And why was her disappearance coming to light only now, some three weeks after the fact? It emerged the next day, thanks to an unauthorized press leak from Scotland Yard, that she had been abducted during her Ibizan holiday—and that her husband, like many exceedingly wealthy men before him, had decided to quietly meet the demands of the kidnappers rather than involve the authorities. A prominent figure in London's private security industry theorized that the billionaire had likely retained the services of an experienced kidnap-and-ransom specialist to negotiate the terms of the deal. Another expert suggested that the ransom payment might well have exceeded the $17 million demanded by the kidnappers of John Paul Getty III, grandson of the oil tycoon and art collector.

Edward Knight, for his part, had nothing to say on the subject of ransom, or much else, for that matter. Holed up in his mansion in Hans Place in Knightsbridge, he issued a single written statement, pleading with the kidnappers to release his wife at once. But when three additional days passed with no sign of her, friends and associates of the billionaire feared the worst. So too did authorities in Spain, where kidnappings by Basque separatists had once been commonplace. The payment of ransom, said one former counterterrorism official, did not guarantee the release of the hostage. Indeed, in some instances, it placed the hostage in even greater danger. The Metropolitan Police spokeswoman, while refusing to confirm that a ransom had in fact been paid, gently criticized the official's remarks as "unhelpful."

Britain would awaken the following morning to a report in the same lesser tabloid that Alice Winter had been found wandering dazed and disoriented through the streets of Barcelona. A hasty retraction soon followed. Yes, a British woman had been discovered in Barcelona, but her condition was the result of nothing more perilous than a night of heavy drinking. The Madrid newspaper *El País* published a lengthy follow-up story replete with harrowing anecdotes of English debauchery on Spanish soil. The leader of the British far right responded by calling on his fellow countrymen to cancel their summer holidays in Spain and remain in England instead. The leader of Spain's growing anti-tourism movement declared it a fine idea.

Lost in the unseemly Anglo-Spanish spat was the fact that a human life was at stake, a life that the British press placed under a microscope—her middle-class suburban upbringing, her years at Cambridge, her short-lived career in journalism, the extramarital affair that ended Edward Knight's first marriage. The billionaire issued another statement, this time asking for privacy. The press responded by turning their sights on Knight's opaque real estate empire and his repeated brushes with His Majesty's Revenue and Customs. A loose-cannon legal analyst on the American airwaves wondered whether Knight might have played a role in his wife's disappearance, a theory that quickly gained traction on social media. When a wife vanished, the thinking went, the husband was usually to blame.

The scrutiny relented, though, when a respected investigative reporter from *The Guardian* revealed that a large ransom had indeed been paid and that the kidnappers, as was often the case, had not lived up to their end of the bargain. The Metropolitan Police, according to the story, now feared that Alice Winter had been murdered by her captors, a fear shared by her husband. On the evening the story appeared on *The Guardian*'s website, he conducted an impromptu news conference on the doorstep of his home in Hans Place. Several reporters present made note of his ashen, haggard appearance. He looked, they said, like a man who believed he would never see his wife again.

Missing from *The Guardian*'s otherwise authoritative account were several crucial details, including the enormous size of the ransom payment, the manner in which the money had been paid, and the identity of the man who had negotiated the terms of the deal. He was not, as some had speculated, connected to London's lucrative K&R trade, but he was an expert nonetheless and had the scars to prove it. The newest were the four deep lacerations above his left ankle, a parting gift from a malevolent, deer-red German pinscher named Oscar.

It was by no means the gravest injury he had ever suffered, even as a result of an encounter with an angry canine, but it was surely among the most humiliating. He spared Irene and Raphael the shameful details—they were under the impression he had merely turned an ankle during his brief visit to Ibiza—but he told Chiara the unvarnished truth. She reacted, as he anticipated she would, by reminding him of her unambiguous warning about serving as the bagman. His ill-considered response—that he was not, technically speaking, the bagman because there had been no actual bag—did little to mollify her anger. He was lucky, she said, that the kidnappers hadn't left him on the side of that Lower Austrian road with a bullet in his head. For reasons he failed to disclose, he did not dispute the point.

He allowed himself, during the first seventy-two hours after his return to Cornwall, to entertain the hope that Alice Winter would likewise turn up along some remote stretch of European roadway. His hopes faded, though, as the days slid by with no sign of her. He was confident he had taken every measure possible to bring her out of captivity alive, including the extraordinary step of placing himself in the hands of her abductors. The mistake, he told Chiara one evening as she prepared their dinner, had been Edward Knight's.

"He never should have authorized the transfer of the money without a final demonstration of proof of life. It was a violation of the most basic rules of the kidnap-and-ransom game."

"What would you have done if you were in Edward's shoes?"

"I would have hired someone like me and let him do his job."

"And if I was the one who had been kidnapped?" she asked.

"I wouldn't be standing on the doorstep of my Knightsbridge mansion making tearful appeals."

The second of the two proof-of-life photos, the one the kidnappers had left in the Bois de Boulogne in Paris, somehow found its way onto the front page of *The Daily Mirror*. Gabriel feared that the next photograph to appear in the British papers would be his—and that the Metropolitan Police would soon be knocking on his door. He was, after all, the only person other than Alice to have laid eyes on the kidnappers. For some reason they had allowed him to live. It was, he thought, their only mistake.

There was one more false sighting—a beach in Biarritz, a fortyish woman from Leeds who had had too much to drink—but after that the trail appeared to go well and truly cold. By the second week of July even the tabloid press was beginning to lose interest in the story. Gabriel, his lower leg sufficiently healed, resumed work on the Bellotto. On a windblown Wednesday afternoon he was retouching the prow of a traghetto crossing the Grand Canal when he heard a car coming up the long drive. It was a Volvo ES90, a model frequently used by plainclothes officers of the Metropolitan Police. He was relieved, therefore, when the driver's-side door opened and Edward Knight stepped into view.

This time they set off eastward along the clifftops toward Penzance. Their pace was unhurried, contemplative, in part because Gabriel was favoring his left ankle.

"And where," inquired Edward Knight, "did this unfortunate incident take place?"

"In the woods outside a Lower Austrian town called Falkenstein."

"And when the police arrived?"

"There were no police."

"How did you manage that?"

"Practice."

Knight smiled briefly in spite of himself. "Can you ever forgive me, Allon?"

"Whatever for?"

"Getting you involved in this mess. You were a damn fool to place yourself in the hands of the kidnappers." Knight lowered his voice. "And damn brave as well. Imagine my surprise when the phone rang and that awful voice told me that they were going to kill you if I didn't send the money."

"You shouldn't have listened to them."

"And what if they weren't bluffing? What if they had killed the great Gabriel Allon? I couldn't have lived with that on my conscience," said Knight. "I rang Peter Hoffmann and ordered him to initiate the wire transfer."

"At what time?"

"Shortly after six A.M. Zurich time. The kidnappers called me a few minutes later to say that CyproBank had received the money and that you and Alice would be released unharmed. Obviously that turned out not to be the case." They slowed to a stop and stood shoulder to shoulder atop the cliffs near Porthchapel Beach. "Would you mind, Allon, if I asked you a difficult question?"

"You want to know why the kidnappers released me and not Alice."

Knight nodded.

"Once you wired the money, they had no incentive to release her."

"They promised they would."

"They're kidnappers, Edward. They say a lot of things that aren't true. Which means there's a distinct possibility that you will soon receive yet another demand for money."

"I'm afraid DCI Douglas Chapel of the Metropolitan Police told me the same thing. He also said it's possible the kidnappers never intended to release Alice because she might be able to identify them."

"It sounds to me as though DCI Chapel knows a thing or two about the K&R game."

"He seems to."

"Did you tell him the name of your negotiator?"

"I'm afraid I had no other choice. Needless to say, he'd like a word with you."

"Unfortunately I have no plans to travel to London at this time."

"Sorry to be the bearer of bad news, Allon, but you're expected at New Scotland Yard at eleven o'clock tomorrow morning."

Gabriel turned to face Edward Knight. "Shall I bring along my solicitor?"

"You're not a suspect, if that's what you're suggesting. DCI Chapel would simply like your assistance in clearing up one or two details."

"Such as?"

"I should probably let him explain," said Knight. "I wouldn't want anything to get lost in translation."

24

New Scotland Yard

When Gabriel last visited the headquarters of the Metropolitan Police, they were located in a glass-and-steel high-rise at 10 Broadway. They had since moved to the historic Curtis Green Building on the Victoria Embankment, which, like its predecessor, had been designated New Scotland Yard. DCI Douglas Chapel, in a dark suit and a restrained necktie, waited in the lobby. Gabriel reckoned he was about fifty-five, perhaps a year or two older. Once upon a time he would have been put out to pasture, but the Met had done away with mandatory retirement, provided officers maintained basic fitness standards. DCI Chapel looked as though he began each morning with a six-mile run and monitored his heart rate throughout the day.

Gabriel strolled through a magnetometer without setting off the alarm and followed Chapel into a waiting lift. It bore them to the fourth floor, where they proceeded to an interview room. There were video cameras overhead, an audio recording device, and a window of one-way glass. Stacked on the table were several thick files.

"The sum total of your exploits on British soil," explained DCI Chapel.

"Not even close."

Chapel switched on the recorder, then recited the date, the time, and the name of the subject he was about to interview.

"Shouldn't you caution me before we begin?" asked Gabriel.

"It's not warranted under these circumstances."

"Perhaps we should clear them up before we proceed. The circumstances, that is."

"I'm going to ask you a few questions," said Chapel, "and you're going to answer them. Because I haven't cautioned you, nothing you say can be used against you at trial. Therefore you should feel free to tell me everything you know about Alice Winter's abduction and your unsuccessful attempt to secure her release."

"I'm not going to tell you anything until you switch off that recorder."

Chapel pressed the stop button, then said, "The fundraiser at Edward Knight's estate in Devon."

Gabriel sighed. "I never would have been there if it wasn't for Julian Isherwood."

They went through it once, then, because DCI Chapel was taking nothing for granted, they went through it a second time. Gabriel's account was for the most part accurate, though somewhat incomplete. Chapel filled in at least one of the missing pieces.

"Mr. Knight mentioned a Danish cyber specialist."

"I asked her to determine the authenticity of the proof-of-life photos," replied Gabriel while smothering a yawn.

"Mr. Knight also said that she attempted to hack into CyproBank with a mind to rerouting the ransom payment."

"That's correct."

"Was she successful?"

"She wasn't."

"Are you sure about that?"

"Are you wondering whether she might have stolen the ransom money?"

"I might be," replied Chapel.

"She didn't."

"I'll need to speak with her nonetheless."

"Good luck with that."

Chapel moved on. "And it was Mr. Knight who authorized the transfer of the money, not you?"

"That's correct. I refused to wire the ransom until the kidnappers showed me Alice."

"Even after they threatened to kill you?"

Gabriel said nothing.

"And there were four, you say?"

"There were four that I saw," replied Gabriel. "It's possible there were more."

"Might you be able to recognize them again?"

"One of them, perhaps."

"Which one?"

"The one who pointed a loaded gun at my head."

Chapel sat back in his chair. "And what if I were to offer you a chance to find him?"

"If I were interested in finding him, I wouldn't need the approval of New Scotland Yard."

Chapel permitted himself a brief smile. "Will you allow me to ask the question another way?"

"My answer will be the same. Besides," added Gabriel, "the most obvious way to find the kidnappers is to follow the money."

"We asked our counterparts in Cyprus for permission to question the CEO of that bank. And what do you suppose they told us?"

"Permission denied."

Chapel nodded. "The money is gone. And so, it seems, is Alice Winter. We'd like you to find her too—or at least find out what happened to her."

"Isn't that your job?" asked Gabriel dryly.

"Actually the Spaniards have jurisdiction in this matter. But at this point you know a good deal more than they do." Chapel paused, then added, "And more than Scotland Yard as well."

"And if I refuse?"

"I will have no choice but to appeal to your sense of decency and fair play."

"Neither of which will help me find Alice Winter or the men who kidnapped her."

Chapel made no reply. Like all good detectives he knew the power of silence.

"Surely you must have a suspect by now," said Gabriel.

"We have a theory. And you happen to be uniquely positioned to help us determine whether that theory is correct."

"How so?"

"Our prime suspect in the disappearance and presumed death of Alice Winter is the man who hired you to find her."

"Edward Knight? You can't be serious."

The expression on the detective's face made clear that he was.

"I seem to recall Scotland Yard saying that he wasn't a suspect."

"I'm sure this won't come as a surprise to you, Mr. Allon, but Scotland Yard doesn't always tell the truth."

"I've spent a great deal of time with him, and he doesn't strike me as the sort to kidnap and murder his own wife."

"Our inquiries have led us to conclude that his marriage was deeply troubled and that they were headed for a nasty divorce. Mr. Knight therefore had a financial incentive to make the problem go away."

"But why kidnap her? Why not a nice, tidy murder instead?"

"Because he's smart enough to know that he would have been our prime suspect. As it stands now, he's the grieving husband who moved heaven and earth to get his wife back. And in the process, he managed to make a half billion dollars disappear into thin air."

"The ransom payment was a way to move money offshore?"

"That is our suspicion," said Chapel.

"Rather diabolical, don't you think?"

"I deal with diabolical on a daily basis, Mr. Allon. And so did you, once upon a time."

"Still do, as it turns out. But how do you explain the proof-of-life photos?"

"Our tech specialists think they're genuine."

"And the woman on the phone?"

"It was undoubtedly Alice Winter."

"Which means that I might have been one of the last people to speak to her."

"Other than her friends from Cambridge, of course."

"You've questioned them, I assume."

"We took detailed statements from all three women. Needless to say, we were troubled by the length of time Sophie Maxwell and Ella Burns waited to report Alice missing. Even so, we eliminated them as suspects in Alice's disappearance."

"What about Phoebe Chadwick?"

"She remains a person of interest."

"Any particular reason?"

Chapel handed Gabriel a printout of a two-day-old story from *The Times* concerning a number of unusually large anonymous donations to British relief and human rights organizations. The largest donation had been made to Global Relief UK, the organization where Phoebe Chadwick worked.

"Forgive me," said Gabriel, "but I'm afraid I don't see the connection."

"We think the anonymous donor could be Edward Knight."

"Phoebe Chadwick loathes Knight."

"He told us the same thing," said Chapel. "But the timing is interesting, to say the least."

"He was attempting to get in Phoebe's good graces?"

"Or silence her."

"Why?"

"We believe she might know why Mr. Knight had motive to kill his wife."

"Have you asked her?"

"Not in so many words. As for Mr. Knight," added Chapel, "his solicitor has made it clear that he will have nothing further to say to the police regarding his wife's disappearance."

"Which is why you need me."

Another strategic silence.

"Who else would know?" asked Gabriel.

"The commissioner of the Met, the home secretary, and your friend the prime minister. But I'll need to assign an officer to work with you."

"Trust me, DCI Chapel, that's the last thing you want."

"I'm afraid it's nonnegotiable."

Gabriel held out his hand. "Your notebook, please."

Chapel pushed it across the tabletop. Gabriel turned to the first clean page and wrote the name of the one British policeman with whom he would agree to work.

Chapel was incredulous. "But he's only a lowly DI from a county police force."

"Two counties, actually. And he's the one who cracked the Lennox case."

"The Chopper?" Chapel was clearly impressed. "A fine piece of detective work, that was."

Gabriel smiled. "I thought so too."

The officer in question, Detective Inspector Timothy Peel of the Devon and Cornwall Police, was at that same moment conducting door-to-doors in the former Cornish mining village of Sticker. They were, as a general proposition, one of the least appealing aspects of his job, posing the same questions over and over in the hope of unearthing some nugget of information, a sighting of a stranger, a rumor, a noise in the middle of the night, that might break a case. For two hours he had been interviewing the inhabitants of Cotswold Avenue, none of whom had any clue as to how one of their neighbors, a forty-year-old carpenter named Gareth Wright, ended up in a shallow grave in the woods near the Meadow Lakes caravan park, having first been bludgeoned to death with a hammer, which his killer had left at the scene.

Shortly before noon Peel was inhaling the smoke emitted by the cigarette of a dressing-gowned housewife when his mobile vibrated. Ordinarily he ignored calls during interviews, but this one, like all the others, was going nowhere, and the caller was none other than his chief constable. Much to Peel's astonishment she instructed him to drop what he was doing and proceed without delay to New Scotland Yard, where he was to report to a DCI Douglas Chapel.

"Why?" asked Peel.

"He didn't go into the details, but evidently he was quite impressed with your work on the Lennox case."

"How could he possibly know that I was the one who made the arrest?"

"Never mind how he knows," said the chief constable in that edgy voice of hers. "Just pack some kit and get on the next train."

DI Peel did just that and arrived at London's Paddington Station at half past five. He traveled by Tube to Westminster, then made the short walk up the Victoria Embankment to New Scotland Yard. The iconic three-sided sign, symbol of the Met's constant vigilance, rotated slowly outside the entrance. Peel went into the lobby and displayed his credentials to the barrel-shaped sergeant at the security checkpoint.

"You're a long way from home, Detective Inspector. Looking for a lost cat?"

"DCI Douglas Chapel, actually."

He received Peel upstairs in his office. By way of greeting he asked, "How old are you, Detective Inspector?"

"Thirty-six, sir."

He looked Peel up and down. "You look thirty at most."

"Must be the Cornish air."

"A sense of humor will get you nowhere around here, Peel."

"Of course not, sir."

"Spend much time in London?" inquired Chapel.

"I was born here, actually."

"How did you end up in Cornwall?"

"Family drama, sir."

"Ever think about coming back?"

"To London? Not really."

"Enjoy the country life, do you?"

"It has its charms."

"Well, DI Peel, this is your chance to play in the Premier League. If you perform your assignment with distinction, we might be able to find a place for you here at the Met. One cock-up, though, and I'll make certain you spend the rest of your career wearing the uniform of a lowly PC."

"And what exactly is my assignment?"

"I need you to keep an eye on someone."

"A surveillance job?"

"More or less."

"And the subject?" asked Peel.

25

Victoria

"You could have chosen someone else, you realize."

"There is no one else," said Gabriel. "You happen to be the only British police officer I know."

Peel gave this unlikely proposition further reflection as he wheeled his luggage along the Victoria Embankment. The grand buildings on the opposite bank of the Thames were awash in twilight. Cornwall seemed suddenly quaint by comparison.

"Surely," he said, "you must know *some*one at the Met after all these years."

"Not a soul, thank goodness."

"You know the director of the Secret Intelligence Service," Peel pointed out.

"And the director of MI5 as well," added Gabriel. "Not to mention the prime minister."

"What about that detective super who questioned you after the Covent Garden incident?"

"For the life of me, I can't recall his name. And it wasn't a terribly pleasant conversation."

"It sounds to me," said Peel, "as though you and DCI Chapel got on rather well."

"That's because the detective chief inspector wanted something from me."

"Investigate one of the richest men in the United Kingdom on suspicion of murder?"

"Not just murder," said Gabriel. "Money laundering and tax evasion as well."

"There are easier ways to evade taxes than killing one's wife and staging a kidnapping."

"It was two birds with one stone. At least that's the working theory at New Scotland Yard."

"Knight gets rid of his wife and his tax problem at the same time?"

"Exactly."

"But why would he want to kill a woman like Alice Winter?"

"Why does any husband kill his wife?"

"In Cornwall it usually involves alcohol."

"But in Belgravia and Knightsbridge, money is more often the motive."

Peel sidestepped a tourist snapping a photograph of the London Eye. "Do you believe it?"

"I'm not quite there yet. But it would explain why Edward Knight was so eager to meet the initial billion-dollar ransom demand—and why he wanted to personally authorize the wire transfer to that bank in Cyprus. It would also explain why his wife is still missing."

"But if he was involved in a conspiracy, why would he ask for help from someone like you?"

"A good question."

"And the answer?"

"I conferred a sense of legitimacy on the entire undertaking. And remember, on the evening that Knight supposedly learned that Alice was missing, he was surrounded by several hundred people. I happened to be one of them."

"The fundraiser at his estate in Devon?"

Gabriel nodded.

"It's a perfect alibi," said Peel.

"For a perfect murder."

"There's no such thing, you know. Every killer makes a mistake."

"DCI Chapel seems to think Edward Knight made a rather expensive one. By the way, we're having drinks with her later."

"How did you manage that?"

"I rang her, Timothy." Gabriel shook his head slowly. "Didn't they teach you anything at detective school?"

Oxfam, founded by a group of Quakers, social activists, and academics during the darkest days of World War II, had received the first contribution. It was one hundred thousand pounds, enough to move the needle but not quite noteworthy. Nor was it considered unusual that the donor wished to remain anonymous. There were many philanthropists, especially those of unimaginable wealth, who did their giving while protected by a veil of secrecy.

But just three days later the British arm of Médecins Sans Frontières received an identical contribution—one hundred thousand pounds, anonymous donor. Next it was the British Red Cross and Action Against Hunger, though each received a quarter million pounds, a not insignificant sum. Human Rights Watch received the same figure, as did Amnesty International and the Refugee Council. The venerable Save the Children, which had been in the business of caring for the young and destitute since 1919, received a half million.

It was at this point that a group email began to circulate inside the close-knit community of relief professionals and fundraisers, the topic of which concerned the origin of the donations. All were in agreement that the money had likely come from the same source, perhaps an individual, perhaps a charitable trust. As luck would have it, one of the emails landed in the in-box of a reporter from *The Times*, who decided to make some inquiries of her own. The first person she rang was a friend who worked for Global Relief UK, the newest, smallest, and neediest of the British-based international aid organizations. The friend, whose name was Phoebe Chadwick, was the coordinator of Global Relief's Africa program. It took a bit of cajoling, but eventually Phoebe admitted that GRUK, the group's unfortunate acronym, had received a large unsolicited donation as well.

"How much?"

"I couldn't possibly say."

"How about a hint?"

"It might have been in the neighborhood of a million quid. But you mustn't quote me."

"Global Relief sources?"

"Why not?"

"What else can you tell me?"

"The donor stipulated that the money was to be used exclusively for famine relief in Sudan."

"So it's all yours, then?"

"It might be, yes."

When the story appeared, Phoebe was besieged with phone calls and texts from friends and colleagues. The attention, she had to admit, had proved a welcome distraction. It was the first time in more than a month that Alice had not been at the forefront of her thoughts.

But forty-eight hours after the story's publication, Alice once again intruded. Not Alice herself, mind you—by all accounts she was lying in a shallow grave somewhere—but a man who claimed to be investigating her disappearance on behalf of the Metropolitan Police. Phoebe, for any number of reasons, was suspicious. In the first place, the man did not sound like the typical Met officer, or even a British subject. He spoke English with the faintest trace of a Continental accent that Phoebe couldn't quite put her finger on. It might have been Italian, she reckoned, but there was a dollop of German and a dash of French. All in all, he struck her as an altogether shady character.

"You work at Scotland Yard?" she asked.

"Not exactly."

"What does that mean?"

"It would probably be better if we spoke in person."

"At least tell me your name."

"It's Gabriel."

"Do you have a surname, Gabriel? Or do you just go by one name, like Madonna and Sting?"

"It's Allon."

Phoebe entered the name into her search engine and several thousand results spilled onto the screen. The most recent item was a story in *ARTnews* magazine concerning his appearance at a fundraiser hosted by Edward Knight. He was *that* Gabriel Allon.

"I thought I recognized your name," she said.

"Does that mean you'll agree to see me."

She had to admit, she was intrigued. "How about half past seven?"

"Perfect."

"Bloomsbury Tavern," she said, and rang off.

The offices of Global Relief UK were located in Great Russell Street, not far from the British Museum. Phoebe remained at her desk, reading about the exploits of the man she would soon be meeting, until twenty minutes past seven, when she bade her coworkers a pleasant evening and headed downstairs. The historic Bloomsbury Tavern was on the ground floor of a pie-shaped building at the intersection of Shaftesbury Avenue and West Central Street. Seated at a table in the back of the pub, lit by the dishwater-gray light streaming through a leaded window, was the legendary art restorer and erstwhile spy Gabriel Allon. Next to him was an attractive man of perhaps thirty-five. The evening, thought Phoebe, was looking better by the minute.

She walked over to the table and stared into the greenest eyes she had ever seen. "Are you him?" she asked.

"I'm afraid so."

She turned to his companion. "And what about you?"

"Detective Inspector Timothy Peel."

"Scotland Yard?"

"Devon and Cornwall Police."

"You're a long way from home, DI Peel."

"So I've been told," he said.

26

Bloomsbury Tavern

She was dressed in a pair of jeans and an oxford button-down shirt, the sort of attire she might have worn while on assignment in the Horn of Africa. She was not someone, thought Gabriel, who spent much time fretting about her appearance. She had mouths to feed, lives to save. Not for the first time, he wondered why she was friends with someone like Alice Winter.

Peel went over to the bar to fetch the drinks, leaving them alone for a moment. Phoebe Chadwick regarded him across the table. "Why you, of all people, Mr. Allon?"

"It would take all evening to explain."

"Try."

He gave her an abridged version of the story—that he had agreed to a request from Edward Knight to quietly investigate his wife's mysterious disappearance, that he had tried and failed to secure her release, that he was now working with the Metropolitan Police to determine what had happened to her.

"In that case," asked Phoebe, "why is your assistant a country policeman from the southwest of England?"

"I'm afraid that would take even longer to explain."

Peel returned to the table with three pints of Guinness. Phoebe took a draught from hers, then asked, "How much do you know about me?"

"I know that you and Alice were at Cambridge together, and that each summer you go on a week's holiday with two other university friends, Sophie Maxwell and Ella Burns. In case you were wondering, it was Edward who footed the bill for that enormous place on the northern coast of Ibiza."

"That's Edward's lot in life," replied Phoebe. "But please go on."

"On the fifth evening of your stay, the Tuesday, you and Alice quarreled during dinner at a restaurant called La Casita. You dined alone at the villa on Wednesday evening and returned to London the next day aboard a commercial flight."

"All true," she replied.

"When did you learn that Alice was missing?"

"The Saturday morning."

"Who told you?"

She lifted her gaze toward the ceiling in thought. "I believe it was Sophie."

"She's the solicitor?"

"Correct."

"How did she sound?"

"Quite matter-of-fact, if you must know."

"Do you recall your reaction?"

"Truth be told, I wasn't terribly worried either."

"You assumed that she'd spent the night with someone else?"

"It wouldn't have been the first time."

"She had lovers?"

Phoebe smiled at him over the rim of her glass. "You make her sound as though she's a character in a Victorian novel, Mr. Allon. I can assure you, love had very little to do with Alice's occasional extracurricular activities."

"Was she involved with one of your classmates from Cambridge, a Swiss banker named Peter Hoffmann?"

"Peter? Heavens no. But why do you ask?"

"They bumped into one another at a beach café the day after you and Alice had your quarrel."

"She didn't mention it. But then again we weren't on speaking terms."

A silence descended over the table. Phoebe's gaze lingered for a moment on Peel, who took the opportunity to pose his first question. "Did you know that Alice had an auto accident not long ago?"

"She told me that a tree leapt from the forest near Wickham House and hurled itself in front of her brand-new Aston Martin roadster. Why Edward bought it for her is beyond me. Alice was an absolute terror behind the wheel of a car."

"Did she happen to tell you *why* she was behind the wheel of a car at two fifteen in the morning?"

"Evidently she and Edward had a terrible row."

"About what?"

"She wouldn't say. But I had the impression it was serious."

"Why?"

"Because after the accident, Alice became very distant. I'm afraid our falling-out was a long time coming. The fight over the bill at that restaurant was the last straw."

"Edward was under the impression it had to do with Alice's social media habit."

"That was round two. But the fight started when I attempted to pay for our dinner. Alice wouldn't hear of it."

"She always paid?"

Phoebe nodded. "It could be annoying at times, but I couldn't afford to live in her world. As you probably know, Mr. Allon, relief work isn't exactly lucrative. We survive on the kindness of strangers."

"Donors, you mean?"

"Yes."

Gabriel handed her the story from *The Times*. "Like the one who gave you a million pounds?"

"The largest single donation in the history of Global Relief UK," she said.

"How was it delivered?"

"The Secret Sharer. It's an anonymous donor platform based in The Hague. The donor transfers the money to the platform, and the platform forwards it to us."

"And if I were to ask the Secret Sharer to reveal the identity of the donor?"

"In all likelihood they don't know it. Most anonymous donors act through an attorney or some other go-between."

"And what about the large donations that were made to the other relief organizations?"

"They all came through the Secret Sharer."

"Same donor?"

"That's the theory, but no one knows for sure."

"And you have no idea who it was?"

"None whatsoever."

"Why do you suppose your organization received the largest donation?"

"Trust me, Mr. Allon, I've been asking myself the same question." She shot a glance at her wristwatch, then rose to her feet. "I'm sorry, but I have to be going. If there's anything else you need, don't hesitate to call." She fixed her gaze on Peel and added, "The same goes for you, Detective Inspector."

And with that she was gone.

"Is it my imagination," asked Gabriel, "or does Phoebe Chadwick have a thing for you?"

"It's your imagination," replied Peel.

"Is she telling us the truth?"

"About not knowing the identity of the donor? Absolutely."

"Her friends Sophie Maxwell and Ella Burns didn't seem terribly concerned about Alice's disappearance, did they?"

"If it were my investigation, they would be sitting in an interview room with the recorder rolling."

"I suggest we follow the money instead."

"The ransom money?"

"The donations," said Gabriel.

"You think there's a connection?"

"Why did Britain's smallest relief agency receive the largest contribution? And why did all of the money go to Phoebe's Africa programs?"

"There's one way to find out."

"The Secret Sharer?"

Peel nodded.

"Since they're in the business of protecting the anonymity of their clients, it is highly unlikely they will betray one to the likes of us."

"I suppose we'll have to find a workaround." Peel smiled, then said, "The kind they don't teach you in detective school."

"You're a quick study, aren't you?"

"I learned from the best," replied Peel, and went to the bar to fetch two more beers.

27

Raamstraat

The European headquarters of the Secret Sharer silent donor service were located in an old brick house on the Raamstraat in the historic center of The Hague. Gabriel and Timothy Peel arrived there at eleven fifteen the next morning, having caught the early train from St. Pancras. In the gloom of the Channel Tunnel they decided that Peel was best suited to appear on the organization's doorstep unannounced. He was, after all, the one with the credentials and the actual job. Gabriel, for his part, was something of a minister without portfolio. He also happened to be cursed with a name and a face that sometimes attracted unwanted attention.

He took refuge in a café at the end of the street while Peel, an active phone tucked into the breast pocket of his jacket, presented himself at the entrance of the old brick house and, pressing the call button on the intercom, requested admittance. There followed a brief interrogation regarding the purpose of his visit, but eventually a buzzer sounded and a dead bolt snapped. The foyer was hung with black-and-white photographs of the wretched of the earth. Seated behind a small desk was a woman of perhaps twenty-five with magenta-colored hair and more earrings than Peel could count. He displayed his Met credentials, and the woman scrutinized them with manifest distaste.

"You realize, I hope, that we cannot disclose the identity of our donors."

"I do," said Peel.

"Then what, may I ask, is the purpose of your visit?"

"Background information only."

She gave him a skeptical look, then indicated an empty chair. "Have a seat, Detective Inspector."

She swiped a keycard through a reader and disappeared through a doorway. For several minutes there was no sign of her, long enough for Peel to entertain the possibility that she might never return. Finally the door opened and together they climbed a flight of crooked stairs to the second floor, where four twentysomethings sat staring at computers in cramped cubicles. The book-lined office of Dr. Rutger Timmerman, the organization's longtime executive director, overlooked the Raamstraat. Gray and professorial, he wore crumpled corduroy trousers and a cardigan sweater with shiny patches on the elbows. He smelled of pipe smoke and faintly of curry.

He shook Peel's hand warily. "Inspector Peel, is it?"

"Close enough," he said with a disarming smile.

Timmerman looked at the woman, who was still standing in the doorway. "That will be all, Greet. Thank you."

The woman withdrew, closing the door behind her, and Timmerman appraised Peel over a pair of half-moon reading glasses. "What seems to be the problem?"

"We're hoping there isn't one."

"I can assure you there isn't." Timmerman sat down behind his desk. "But how can I be of help?"

"It concerns the rather large donations that were made recently to a number of British-based relief and human rights organizations."

"Nearly three million pounds in all," said Timmerman. "A remarkable sum of money that will make life a little better for those who have nothing. But since when is generosity a crime in the eyes of the British police?"

"When it involves corrupt actors with corrupt intentions."

Dr. Timmerman offered Peel a condescending smile. "In my experience, Inspector, such individuals tend to spend their money on themselves rather than on others."

"Do you know the identity of the individual who made the donations?"

"Who says it was an individual? And even if it was only one person, which is not necessarily the case, I have no intention of divulging his name to you."

Peel took note of Timmerman's use of the male personal pronoun. "So it was a man, was it?"

"I don't know who the donor was, Inspector. Nor do I know whether the donor was a man or a woman. I dealt exclusively with an intermediary."

"I'd like the intermediary's name, please."

"I'm sure you would. But you're not going to get it. Oh, I suppose you could attempt to obtain a warrant from the Dutch Ministry of Justice, but I'm quite confident you won't get one. The minister is a good friend of our organization and knows that we are completely above reproach."

"But surely you must have done some sort of background check before accepting the money."

"We always do."

Peel adopted a confiding tone. "It didn't come from some dicey banking center, did it?"

"Like London, you mean?" Timmerman gave a wry smile. "No, Inspector Peel, there were no obvious red flags."

"And you maintain records for each transaction?"

"Yes, of course. We have copies of the paperwork for every anonymous donation we've ever facilitated."

"And how are they stored, if you don't mind my asking?"

"Digitally, of course. This is the twenty-first century, after all."

With that Peel wished Rutger Timmerman a pleasant day, and the magenta-haired girl happily saw him into the Raamstraat. He walked to the café at the end of the street and sat down at Gabriel's table.

"How did I do?" he asked.

"For a moment," said Gabriel, "I thought you were going to ask him for the password to the computer system. Otherwise I thought you handled yourself rather well for a country policeman on his first overseas assignment."

"He definitely knows the name of the donor's intermediary."

"He knows *a* name," said Gabriel. "Whether it's the name of the donor's intermediary is an open question. What we need are the bank records."

"The original wire transfer from the donor's bank to the Secret Sharer's account here in The Hague?"

"Exactly."

"He'll never let us see those. Not without a search warrant."

"What are the odds that you can obtain one from the Dutch?"

"Slim to none. Besides, it would take forever and a day."

"In that case," said Gabriel, "I'm afraid we have no choice but to spend a few days on Mykonos."

"What's on Mykonos?"

"A workaround, Timothy."

The first direct flight from Amsterdam to Athens departed at nine o'clock that evening. They spent the remainder of the day roaming the galleries of the Rijksmuseum and the Van Gogh Museum. Then, after an early dinner at a restaurant near the Bloemenmarkt, they took a taxi to Schiphol Airport. They arrived to find it surrounded by a sea of flashing blue emergency lights.

Gabriel checked the airport's website. "Looks like we're not going anywhere. Not tonight, at least. All departing flights have been grounded, and incoming planes are being diverted to other airfields."

"Why?" asked Peel.

"It doesn't say. But obviously this is not a drill."

The taxi dropped them at the airport Hilton, where they grabbed the last two available rooms and then headed for the bar. It was crowded with stranded passengers, all of whom were staring mystified at the televisions. One was tuned to the BBC, the other to CNN. Both networks were covering the same story.

"Drones?" asked Peel.

"Several drones, evidently. And they're circling Schiphol as we speak."

"Let's hope one of them doesn't crash into the Hilton."

"Yes, let's," agreed Gabriel.

"Any idea who might be behind it?"

"It's either a bored kid or the Russians. I'm betting it's the latter."

Peel fetched a couple of Heinekens from the bar while Gabriel pounced on an empty table. And there they remained until 2:00 A.M., watching the news with a hundred other marooned members of the twenty-first-century traveling public, until the Dutch prime minister announced that all of the intruders had departed Holland's airspace. Gabriel and Peel repaired to their rooms and reconvened at breakfast. The airport was scheduled to reopen at 8:00 A.M. There were two seats available on a Lufthansa flight departing at ten.

"It will require an extra stop," said Gabriel. "But we'll be in Mykonos in time for dinner."

"Unless, of course, the Russians launch a drone attack on Frankfurt Airport."

It was nearly eleven o'clock before the Lufthansa flight departed, but Frankfurt Airport was operating normally and they arrived in Athens in time to make their connection to Mykonos. As they stepped from the terminal, an all-electric BMW i4 sedan, midnight-blue in color, rolled to a stop at the curb. Gabriel dropped into the passenger seat, and Peel crawled into the back. Ingrid eyed the young British detective warily in the rearview mirror.

"Well, well," she said finally. "If it isn't my old friend, Inspector Dalgliesh."

28

Psarou Beach

Ingrid's house on the cliffs above Psarou Beach was smaller than the lavish *finca* on Ibiza where Alice Winter and her three friends from Cambridge had stayed before her disappearance, but only barely. White as a sugar cube, it had two soaring great rooms, four large bedroom suites, a fitness center, a billiards room, and a hacker's paradise of an office filled with computers and servers. They dined that evening on her multilevel terrace beneath a canopy of diamond-white stars. She listened with interest as Gabriel recounted the story of their twenty-four-hour journey from Amsterdam to Athens, brought about by a swarm of drones circling Schiphol Airport.

"What do you suppose they're up to?" she asked.

"Our Russian friends? The same thing they've been up to for the past two decades. Subversion, sabotage, election interference, and sophisticated information operations, all designed to sow discord and undermine the West. Once upon a time, the KGB referred to such tactics as active measures, and they were incredibly good at it. The new Russians call it hybrid warfare. And they're rather good at it too."

"But why drones?" asked Peel.

"It's not the first time a European airport has been shut down by drones. Remember, the airport in Copenhagen closed for several hours not long ago because of a drone sighting. So did Oslo Airport and Berlin Brandenburg. Imagine for a moment if those drones had been armed with high explosives."

"The Russians would never dare."

"Whyever not?"

"Because the West would retaliate."

"How?"

"With economic and political sanctions, at the very least."

"We've sanctioned the Russians repeatedly over the invasion of Ukraine. And what good has it done? There's nothing left in the West's quiver other than a military response."

"War with Russia? That will never happen."

"I agree. But if the Russians were to carry out an attack on a NATO country without triggering a response, it might well spell the end of the alliance. The Kremlin would like nothing more."

The talk of Russia had set Ingrid on edge, and she appeared relieved, at least temporarily, when Gabriel explained that he was now working for a certain DCI Douglas Chapel of the Metropolitan Police. Hearing this news, she smiled coolly and in German said, "That would explain why you brought a policeman into my home."

Gabriel, in the same language, replied, "I'm afraid it couldn't be helped."

"Really?"

"DCI Chapel insisted on placing a police officer at my side. Timothy was the solution. By the way, DCI Chapel would like a word with you."

"About what?"

"He seems to think you might have pocketed the five hundred million."

Ingrid reverted to English for Peel's benefit. "The money was long gone by the time I was able to hack into that bank."

"I don't suppose you were able to determine where it went?"

"It was moved from the original account into twenty-five other accounts and then transferred to twenty-five new accounts and cryptocurrency wallets around the world. You can be certain the money has been transferred many times since then and is now hidden in anonymous shell companies and layered trusts. It would take months for the US Treasury Department to track it down. For someone like me it would be next to impossible."

"How about something a bit less demanding?"

"What did you have in mind?"

"An organization in The Hague that facilitates anonymous philanthropic activity."

"Not the Secret Sharer?"

"You know it?"

"I'm a client. A secret client, of course. My banker in Andorra acts as my go-between."

"I'd like to know the source of several large donations to Oxfam, Save the Children, and Global Relief UK, to name a few."

"Your wish is my command." She directed her gaze toward Peel. In German she asked, "But did you really have to bring him here?"

"He saved your life once, as I recall."

"Yes," said Ingrid. "Never a dull moment."

She launched her opening salvo against the Secret Sharer early the next morning. Gabriel and Peel, who were capable of offering nothing more than moral support, spent the day relaxing by her pool. DCI Chapel rang sometime around three o'clock, but Peel allowed the call to go to voicemail. He listened to the message while drinking an ice-cold Peroni.

"He's wondering where we are and what we're doing."

"Perhaps you should tell him," replied Gabriel from the shade of a parasol.

"But we're not *doing* anything."

"Men of lofty genius sometimes accomplish the most when they work the least."

"The lofty genius," replied Peel, "is now locked in her office."

"Trust me, it's better that way."

"How on earth did she pay for this place?"

"Ingrid comes from a wealthy family."

"What sort of work does her father do?"

"He's a schoolteacher, I believe."

"They make a lot of money, Danish schoolteachers?"

"Evidently."

She made her first appearance at half past four, in a one-piece swimsuit that clung to her taut, athletic body. She plunged wordlessly into the pool and swam twenty laps, seemingly without effort, then performed a perfect handstand on the sun-drowned terrace. On her way back to her office she announced over her shoulder that the kitchen was closed and that her houseguests would have to see to their own supper. They dined that evening at a beachfront taverna in the windswept village of Ornos. Returning to the villa, Gabriel left a bag of takeaway outside Ingrid's office. It was still there when he awakened the following morning.

The ensuing day was a repeat of the previous one, though Gabriel and Peel spent part of the morning touring the island in Ingrid's BMW. She was still hard at work when they returned to the villa so they once again repaired to the pool. It was approaching five o'clock when she took her swim, this time in a stunning two-piece suit. Peel was sorry to see her go.

“Is she seeing anyone?” he asked.

“I thought we’d covered this ground.”

“Refresh my memory.”

“She’s not your type. Besides, it’s never wise to mix business and pleasure.”

Peel pried the cap from another bottle of Peroni. “What do you call this?”

“We’re pacing ourselves.”

Ingrid, however, worked without a break—and without offering Gabriel a clue as to her progress. It was no matter; having watched her hack the computer network of the Geneva Freeport, one of the world’s most secure storage facilities for art and other valuables, he was more than confident of a successful outcome. And so he passed the following day as he had the previous two, relaxing with his old friend Detective Inspector Timothy Peel at the luxurious Greek villa owned by a professional thief. The sun was dangling low over the Aegean when she finally appeared, in a pair of jeans and a cotton pullover against the encroaching evening chill.

“How was your day?” she asked.

“Brutal,” answered Gabriel. “Yours?”

“Quite productive,” she said, and opened her laptop.

29

Psarou Beach

As it turned out, Ingrid's illicit cyber activities extended far beyond a single silent donor service based in the Dutch capital. She also breached the data networks of a number of dubious financial services firms, all located in or around the Caribbean Basin, along with the records departments of two prestigious British institutions of higher learning. Based on material gathered during these digital raids, she could say with certainty that the recent charitable donations to a number of UK-based relief and human rights organizations had all been made by a shell company called Regency Holdings.

"It's a subsidiary of a shell company called Trident Resources," she explained. "And Trident Resources is a subsidiary of something called Pavilion Capital."

"And the beneficial owner of these companies?" asked Gabriel.

"Impossible to say. They're Bahamian-registered and as opaque as can be."

"And where, pray tell, do they do their banking?"

"The Cayman Islands, Mr. Allon. Where else?"

He considered this. "It could be exactly what it appears to be."

"A wealthy individual who hides money offshore displaying a sudden streak of generosity?"

"Something like that," he answered without conviction.

"I picked up one or two other tidbits as well."

"Such as?"

"Until recently all three companies were empty vessels. Bone-dry, in fact. But interestingly enough, they received a large infusion of capital just seventy-two hours after Edward Knight approved the payment of the ransom money."

"How large?"

"Four hundred and seventy-five million dollars, give or take. But one of the companies, Trident Resources, if I'm not mistaken, immediately transferred twenty-five million dollars to a company called RPH Investments. By the way, RPH does its banking in beautiful Belize."

Gabriel reflected upon this as well while watching the last of the sun slip below the horizon. "The question is," he said at length, "is that money the ransom payment that Edward Knight transferred to the bank in Cyprus?"

"I'm afraid I can't answer that. But I have a feeling I know someone who can."

"Who?"

Ingrid smiled and said, "RPH."

She was most intrigued, she continued, not by the size of the payment but by the company's initials—the second and third initials, to be precise, the *P* and *H*. They were, she pointed out, the same initials as Peter Hoffmann, chief of wealth management at Bank Josef Bänzinger & Co. in Zurich.

"What about the *R*?" inquired Gabriel.

"I asked myself the same question."

"And?"

"His curriculum vitae on the bank's website refers to him as Peter, and he was known as Peter during his time at Cambridge. But it turns out that Peter is his *second* given name."

"And his first?"

"Reinhardt."

"How did you determine that?"

"Rather easily, actually. You see, Peter Hoffmann was known as Reinhardt Hoffmann until he headed off to Cambridge. That's when he started calling himself Peter, probably because it sounded a bit less, well, Swiss."

"You're sure?"

"I can show you his official transcripts, if you like. He was quite a student," she added. "One wonders how he ended up at a bank like Josef Bänzinger. Do you remember that Wikileaks dump of confidential emails? They revealed that Bänzinger was laundering money through its affiliate in the Cayman Islands. And then there was that exposé in *The New Yorker* about Bänzinger stealing money from its clients. The CEO swore it wasn't true a few days before hanging himself from the doorknob in his private bathroom."

"That said, you have no proof that RPH Investments is linked to Reinhardt Peter Hoffmann."

"I also have no proof the sun will rise tomorrow, but based on the available facts, I can reasonably deduce that it will."

"Perhaps we should review them." Gabriel indicated Peel, then said, "For the benefit of the detective inspector."

"British socialite Alice Winter goes missing while on holiday on Ibiza," Ingrid began.

"A fine start," said Gabriel. "Please continue."

"Edward Knight, her wealthy and seemingly desperate husband, hires the renowned art conservator and retired spy Gabriel Allon to find her. Several days after her disappearance, Knight receives a ransom demand for one billion dollars. Gabriel Allon, now acting as Knight's negotiator, whittles it down to a half billion. Knight transfers the money to CyproBank of Nicosia before Allon can determine whether Alice Winter is still alive. Allon is dumped by the side of a road. Alice, however, is nowhere to be found."

"Why not?"

"That calls for a certain amount of speculation on my part."

"Speculate away."

"British socialite Alice Winter was abducted by men hired by her husband, Edward Knight. Knight retained you to find her, knowing that your involvement would suggest he was innocent of any wrongdoing. When the ransom negotiations began, you drove a hard bargain. But what you didn't realize was that the men at the other end of the line were working for your client."

"Were the proof-of-life photographs real?"

"I believe they were."

"Which means that Alice was alive then."

Ingrid made no reply.

"When was she killed?"

"If I had to guess, not long after the money arrived at that bank in Cyprus."

"In cold blood?"

"All contract killers murder their victims in cold blood, Mr. Allon. Why would Alice deserve better?"

"You were in the room with Knight when we received the initial ransom demand," Gabriel reminded her.

"I remember it well."

"Did he strike you as the sort of man who was about to have his wife murdered?"

"You could have played the role of the desperate husband, Mr. Allon. And I certainly could have played the role of a desperate wife."

"That's because we're both professional deceivers."

"Perhaps Edward Knight is too. Many wealthy businessmen are."

Gabriel didn't dispute the point. "That leaves Reinhardt Peter Hoffmann."

"Chief of wealth management at Bank Josef Bänzinger & Company, a firm with a rather dubious track record that includes laundering and concealing money on behalf of its clients."

"Hoffmann was in on it from the beginning?"

"Absolutely."

"If that was the case, why did he pretend to bump into Alice on Ibiza?"

"For the life of me," replied Ingrid, "I can't figure that one out."

"A rather large hole in your scenario, don't you think?"

"Unless Edward Knight had nothing to do with his wife's disappearance."

"Then who was behind it?"

"Reinhardt Peter Hoffmann."

With a movement of his hand, Gabriel instructed Ingrid to proceed.

"Peter Hoffmann hires a crew of highly professional operatives to kidnap his old friend Alice Winter during her Ibizan holiday in order to extort five hundred million dollars from her husband, who happened to be his client. He pays off the kidnappers with a portion of the ransom, not to mention the Cypriot banker, and buries the rest of the money offshore."

"Where's Alice?"

"Under this scenario, Alice is quite dead."

"Who killed her?"

"The highly professional operatives."

"Why would they do a thing like that?"

"They must have had a slip-up while she was in captivity. Or maybe that's just the way they roll."

It was entirely plausible, thought Gabriel. And it would explain Peter Hoffmann's presence on Ibiza and Alice's continued absence. There was, however, one flaw in Ingrid's premise.

"But why would Peter Hoffmann give away nearly three million pounds of his hard-earned loot?"

"The donations," admitted Ingrid, "are harder to explain."

30

Zollikon

On the website of Bank Josef Bänzinger & Co., Gabriel found a number for Peter Hoffmann's mobile phone. He attacked the device with the hacking malware Proteus at eight o'clock that evening and by midnight was reviewing the banker's emails, text messages, browsing history, photographs, geolocation data, and telephone metadata. There was nothing in the material to suggest that Hoffmann had been in contact with the Secret Sharer silent donor service. Nor was there any reference to the anonymous shell companies Regency Holdings, Trident Resources, Pavilion Capital, or RPH Investments. He had been in frequent contact of late—phone calls and text messages—with his client Edward Knight, but it had been six months since his last text exchange with his friend and Cambridge classmate Alice Winter. Hoffmann was in London at the time, at Bänzinger's office in Fleet Street. He met Alice for drinks that evening at the Connaught. The geolocation data indicated that Hoffmann had stayed for ninety minutes.

The rest of the phone's GPS data portrayed an orderly life befitting a gnome of Zurich. He arrived at his office no later than nine o'clock each morning and departed at the stroke of half past six. He dwelled along the shore of the Zürichsee in the toney Gold Coast suburb of Küsnacht with his wife, Ursula, and their two young daughters. Geolocation dots crisscrossing the lake in all directions, as well as numerous photos, suggested he owned a rather decent sailboat. Other data indicated he was a skilled climber. One photo showed him standing triumphantly atop the Lagginhorn, a four-thousand-meter peak in the Pennine Alps.

There was no suitable lodging to be found in exclusive Küsnacht, but Ingrid acquired a spacious three-bedroom holiday rental a kilometer up the road in the suburb of Zollikon. They settled into the apartment at six the following evening after an arduous day of travel and were sharing a bottle of Swiss white wine on the terrace when Peter Hoffmann sped past the building in his black Audi A8 sedan. He was on the phone at the time, talking to a client in America. He terminated the call as he turned through the gate of his lakeside villa, but the phone was acting as a transmitter when he greeted his wife. She asked him, indifferently, about his day. He informed her it had been uneventful save for a minor scrape with another senior executive. "Not Konrad again?" she asked, and Hoffmann replied, "Who else?"

They saw the same black Audi sedan at half past eight the following morning, but this time it was headed in the opposite direction. Ingrid and Peel followed the car up the lakeshore in a rented Mitsubishi SUV and spent the remainder of the morning window-shopping along the Bahnhofstrasse. Gabriel, for his part, passed the morning monitoring the audio and video feeds from Peter Hoffmann's compromised phone. Together they sat through a succession of meetings, each duller than the last. Gabriel lunched alone at the apartment, but Hoffmann dined with a female colleague at Restaurant Lumière, one of central Zurich's better French eateries. He didn't seem to notice the young British policeman and beautiful professional thief sitting at a nearby table.

The policeman and the thief followed the banker and his colleague back to Bänzinger HQ, then drove back to Zollikon. They couldn't bear the thought of spending the afternoon in the apartment, so Gabriel rented a Chris-Craft Bowrider and they did their eavesdropping while cruising the Zürichsee. At seven o'clock they were approximately two hundred meters due west of Peter Hoffmann's villa. He arrived there at seven fifteen, a few minutes behind schedule, and exchanged the same bland pleasantries with his wife. Then, drink in hand, he crossed his green lawn and walked to the end of his dock. And there he stood, still as a statue, watching the sun dipping behind the mountains on the opposite shore of the lake.

"What do you suppose he's thinking about?" asked Peel.

"Money," answered Ingrid, who was reclining at the vessel's prow.

"And what money is that?" asked Gabriel.

"The rather large fortune he has hidden in the Cayman Islands and Belize."

"There's nothing on his phone to indicate that the money is his," replied Gabriel. "Or that it was the ransom payment."

"Which would suggest," said Ingrid pedantically, "that he uses burner phones to conduct his illicit dealings." She smiled, then added, "Most criminals do."

"For the moment, at least, he looks like just another Zurich moneyman."

"I rest my case."

The Zurich moneyman was now holding something to his ear. Gabriel checked his laptop. Hoffmann's usual phone was powered on but inactive, no incoming or outgoing call. Furthermore its current position was approximately twenty meters from the shore of the lake, which would place it inside the villa.

"It appears," said Peel, "as though Herr Hoffmann has a burner."

"Who do you suppose he's talking to?" asked Gabriel.

"The possibilities," replied Ingrid, "are endless."

The subsequent three days were spent in the pursuit of Peter Hoffmann's second mobile phone. Not the device itself, at least not initially, but merely a number that Gabriel could enter into the hacking malware Proteus. They searched for it in the only source they had—the digital debris of his public-facing device. They isolated seventy-eight possible candidates and dialed each of the numbers from a prepaid device they purchased from a shop in Zurich Hauptbahnhof. Twenty-two of the phones were answered by women, thirty-eight by men other than Peter Hoffmann, and three by young girls. The remaining phones repeatedly went straight to voicemail. Gabriel fed the numbers into Proteus and in short order determined that none of the devices were in the possession of a banker from Zurich.

It was at this point, on the Thursday morning of that week, that Gabriel reached the unsettling conclusion they had no choice but to illicitly acquire the phone itself. He ruled out breaking into the Hoffmann villa in Küsnacht. It was undoubtedly protected by a high-quality security system, and finding the device would be akin to searching for the proverbial needle in a haystack. The only alternative, he submitted, was to remove the device from the owner's pocket.

"We would need a professional pickpocket," said Peel.

"We have one," replied Gabriel.

He was the first to acknowledge, though, that the plan was not perfect—far from it, in fact. The target only set foot outside the insular world of his bank at lunchtime, which meant the theft would have to occur on the Bahnhofstrasse or an adjacent street. Moreover there was no guarantee the target would be carrying his second phone when he left the office—or that the thief would necessarily be able to discern one device from the other. It was quite possible, he admitted, that she might steal the wrong phone.

"Which would leave us in the dark," said Peel.

"Until he gets a new phone," answered Gabriel.

They had seen enough of Peter Hoffmann to know that he was right-handed and carried his phone in the left breast pocket of his suit jacket. It followed, therefore, that he would carry a second device in the opposite pocket, the right. It was, Ingrid explained, the easier of the two pockets for her to pick, for she was right-handed as well. Her preferred method involved pleating the pocket lining to make the valuable easier to obtain. She demonstrated the technique on Peel during a rehearsal in the apartment in Zollikon. He admitted, much to his dismay, that he had felt neither the elusive touch of her hand nor the phone leaving his pocket.

He steadfastly refused, however, to serve as Ingrid's accomplice, only her chauffeur. They left the apartment at eleven thirty and made the short drive up the lakeshore to the Bahnhofstrasse. Ingrid did a bit of shopping, and at twelve forty-five, bags in hand, she was admiring the silver and gold trinkets displayed in the window of the luxury jewelry boutique located on the ground floor of Bänzinger HQ. Peter Hoffmann stepped from the door of the building two minutes later, bound for a business lunch at Restaurant Kronenhalle, his phone to his ear. Ingrid chose that instant to conclude her examination of the jewelry and, as misfortune would have it, a minor collision occurred. Peter Hofffmann, like Timothy Peel before him, never felt the touch of her hand. The breast pocket it probed was empty.

"Forgive me," she said in German. "I'm hopelessly clumsy."

"The pleasure was mine," said Peter Hoffmann with a smile, and walked away.

Which left them one final bite at the apple before the weekend. Because the target had got a good look at the thief, she would have to make a drastic change to her appearance. The second collision occurred at 1:07 P.M. Friday outside a popular Zurich restaurant specializing in the cuisine of Tuscany. The other party to the incident was a small, strikingly handsome man in his mid-thirties, or so it appeared to the target. Once again he failed to notice the hand that slipped inside his suit jacket. This time, however, it discovered a mobile phone resting on the bottom of the right breast pocket.

Polite apologies were exchanged, and the two went their separate ways. Within minutes, though, each would make a startling discovery. The banker discovered that his mobile phone was missing. The thief, much to her dismay, realized that it was the banker's primary device.

Leaving his office that evening, he walked to a nearby Apple store and, with a British detective looking on from a safe distance, purchased a replacement phone for the one that was now lying on the bottom of the Zürichsee. By the time he arrived home in Küsnacht, the hacking malware Proteus had seized control of the phone's operating system, and the device was acting as an audio and video transmitter. He passed a quiet evening with his wife and children, and early the following morning loaded a quantity of climbing gear into the trunk of his Audi sedan. It was a few minutes after seven o'clock when he sped past a small apartment house in the neighboring suburb of Zollikon. A rented Mitsubishi SUV eased from the curb and followed after him.

31

Bernese Oberland

He skirted the northern shore of the lake, plunged into the Uetliberg Tunnel, then headed south on the A4 toward Lucerne. His new iPhone was resting on the Audi's center console, and the car's superb Bang & Olufsen audio system was tuned to Radio Swiss Jazz. For that much, at least, Gabriel was grateful. At present he was slouched in the passenger seat of the Mitsubishi, laptop balanced on his knees. Ingrid was stretched out in the back seat, eyes closed. Peel was handling the driving.

"Where do you suppose he's going?" he asked.

It was Ingrid who answered. "To the mountains, Inspector Dalgliesh. Where else?"

"And when he arrives? What then?"

"Someone," said Gabriel, "will have to make the climb with him."

"Since I've spent the entirety of my life at sea level, it will have to be someone other than me."

"I couldn't possibly do it. My back is giving me fits today."

"That leaves your friend." Peel lowered his voice. "The one who stole the wrong bloody phone."

"It was an understandable mistake, Timothy. Anyone could have made it."

"Anyone?" Peel shook his head. "There aren't more than a handful of pickpockets in the world who could pull off a move like hers. I've never seen anything like it."

"You should see her with a pool cue in her hands."

"Where did she learn her craft?"

"Billiards?"

"Theft," said Peel.

"She's self-taught, I believe."

"A professional, is she?"

"It's more of a hobby."

"Now I know how she got the money to buy that villa on Mykonos."

"Trust me, Detective Inspector, you don't know the half of it."

Peter Hoffmann received his first phone call of the day as they were approaching the border between Canton Zurich and Canton Zug. The man at the other end of the connection was a wealthy Lebanese businessman who had entrusted Hoffmann with several hundred million dollars and was unhappy with the performance of his investments. By the time the conversation ended the banker was approaching the eminently climbable mountain inhabited, according to ancient Christian legend, by the deathless soul of Pontius Pilate. He sped past the peak and continued to the picturesque resort town of Interlaken. A few kilometers to the south were some of the highest mountains in the Bernese Alps. After making a brief stop for coffee, Peter Hoffmann headed straight for them.

"Something tells me we're getting warmer," said Gabriel.

"Or colder," said Peel, his eyes on the snowcapped peaks.

"It's summer, Timothy."

"Not up there, it isn't."

They were approaching the turnoff for Grindelwald. A climber's paradise, the town was surrounded by three of the most famous mountains in the Bernese Oberland: the Mönch, the Jungfrau, and the Eiger. Of the three, the Mönch was the most accessible, the Eiger the most treacherous. None were of interest to Peter Hoffmann, it seemed, for he sped past the turnoff without slowing.

"He must be going to Lauterbrunnen," said Gabriel.

"Lederhosen?" asked Ingrid playfully.

"You've never been?"

"To Lauterbrunnen? It's not really my style."

Gabriel interpreted the remark for Peel. "Your friend Ingrid prefers places like Zermatt and Gstaad."

"And St. Moritz," she added. "I positively adore the Badrutt's Palace Hotel."

"And why is that?" asked Peel.

"Use your imagination," answered Gabriel.

Lauterbrunnen, widely regarded as Switzerland's most beautiful village, lay at the bottom of a U-shaped glacial valley with thousand-meter walls, over which spilled numerous waterfalls. The most famous, the Staubbach Falls, was on the western side of the valley. Beyond it stretched the village high street, at the end of which stood a small rail station. On the opposite side of the valley, perched on a sloping green meadow, was a colony of handsome timbered chalets.

One of the chalets, the grandest of the lot, stood slightly apart from the others. It was the one where Peter Hoffmann, two hours and fifteen minutes after leaving his home, finally stopped. He parked the Audi next to a BMW X5. Then, after fetching a nylon duffel from the boot, he unlocked the front door of the chalet and disappeared inside. He left his phone on the car's center console, its camera staring into space, its microphone listening to a deep and abiding silence.

It was not the sort of place where three strangers sitting in a parked SUV would go unnoticed for long, so they retreated to the village high street and had breakfast at the Hotel Oberland. Gabriel brought along his laptop so he could monitor the feed from Peter Hoffmann's phone. Its position hadn't changed by the time the waitress cleared their plates.

"Something tells me Peter isn't going climbing today," said Peel.

"You think?" replied Ingrid archly.

Peel looked at Gabriel. "Is she always like this?"

"Don't take it personally, Timothy. She just has issues."

"Besides kleptomania?"

"She prefers the term impulse control."

"A rose by any other name," said Peel.

Leaving the hotel, they took a leisurely walk down the high street to the base of the Staubbach Falls. In the crystalline Alpine air they could see the large chalet on the other side of the valley—and the black Audi A8 parked outside. The car was still there at two o'clock when they sat down for a late lunch at the Hotel Silberhorn, and it hadn't budged when, at half past three, they departed. Ingrid had the waiter's all-in-one corkscrew in her coat pocket.

"What now?" she asked.

"Take a stroll across the valley," said Gabriel. "Have a closer look at that chalet."

She rented a bike instead, from a shop next door to the hotel, and for an additional charge of five Swiss francs they gave her a helmet that rendered her all but unrecognizable. She pedaled past the large chalet twice, then led herself on a pleasant tour of the valley. It was approaching five when she returned the bike to the shop. Gabriel and Peel were at the coffee bar on the opposite side of the street, the open laptop resting on the table between them. Ingrid sat down and delivered her findings.

"The shades were drawn tight. I couldn't see a thing."

"He's definitely not sitting there alone," said Peel.

"He might be," replied Gabriel.

"Doing what, exactly?"

"Give me a minute, Timothy. I'll think of something."

But just thirty seconds later the compromised iPhone resting on the center console of Peter Hoffmann's Audi transmitted the distinctive sound of a well-made car door opening and closing. Then the engine turned over and the winking blue geolocation light on Gabriel's laptop was suddenly in motion. At 5:07 P.M. the Audi flashed past the coffee bar on the high street of Lauterbrunnen. Peter Hoffmann was on the phone to his wife, Ursula. His climb had gone well, he told her. He would be home at seven fifteen at the latest.

"Shouldn't we follow him?" asked Peel.

"No," replied Gabriel. "We should acquire lodging here in beautiful Lauterbrunnen."

Ingrid sighed. "I only wish we were in St. Moritz."

After reviewing the available options, they rented a rustic holiday cottage located not far from the rail station. It had few amenities save for an unobstructed view of the large chalet on the opposite side of the valley. At ten o'clock that evening, as night fell over the Bernese Oberland, lights burned behind the tightly drawn shades of the chalet's windows.

"They could be on a timer," suggested Peel.

"And how would you explain that?" asked Gabriel as a figure, indistinguishable in the darkness, stepped onto the chalet's veranda.

"Man or woman?" was Peel's only reply.

"Impossible to tell."

Given the circumstances, an overnight watch was warranted.

Gabriel volunteered to take the first shift and somehow managed to remain awake until seven, when Peel relieved him. He roused Ingrid and together they drove down the valley to Interlaken, where they purchased a pair of Zeiss night vision binoculars and enough outdoor clothing to make them appear as though they were ordinary tourists. Returning to the cottage, they found Peel slouched in a chair in the window, eyes on the chalet on the opposite side of the valley.

"Anything?" asked Gabriel.

Peel shook his head.

Gabriel removed the Zeiss binoculars from their packaging and trained them on the chalet. Drawn shades, closed doors, a BMW X5 parked in the drive. He handed the glasses to Ingrid, who raised them to her eyes.

"What are you looking at?" he asked.

"Could be nothing more than a love shack," she answered.

"Peter Hoffmann has a little something stashed away here in lovely Lauterbrunnen?"

"It would certainly explain why he lied to his wife."

Gabriel reclaimed the binoculars and aimed them toward the chalet. "But what if Peter Hoffmann has something else stashed away here in lovely Lauterbrunnen?"

"Such as?"

"A hostage."

"That would explain why the shades are always closed," said Ingrid.

"And the single figure we saw standing watchfully on the balcony last night." Gabriel scrutinized the chalet window by window. He thought he saw movement behind one of the drawn shades but couldn't be sure. "I'm wondering whether it's time to borrow a cup of sugar."

"Forgive me, Mr. Allon, but you don't look like the cup-of-sugar type."

"I enjoy baking as much as the next person." He snatched up the key to the Mitsubishi and handed the binoculars to Peel. "Keep an eye on me."

"Don't worry, I will."

Gabriel slipped out of the cottage and made the short drive across the valley. He parked next to the BMW, climbed out, crossed the tidy front garden, rang the bell. Receiving no answer, he rang the bell a second time, with the same result. He was about to make a third attempt when suddenly the door was flung wide and he found himself staring into a pair of liquid blue eyes.

"Hello, Mr. Allon," said Alice Winter. "I was hoping it would be you." She stepped to one side. "Won't you please come in? I was just about to make a pot of tea."

32

Lauterbrunnen

The interior of the chalet was a work in progress. The walls were freshly painted, the wooden floors newly refinished, but there was little in the way of furniture and, with the exception of a half dozen novels piled on the low coffee table, even fewer personal touches. It looked to Gabriel as though she had been reading John Banville when he presented himself unannounced at her door. If nothing else, he admired her taste in literature.

At length she returned to the sitting room bearing a silver tray laden with a pot of tea and the usual accoutrements, including an unopened package of English digestive biscuits. She placed the tray on the table and sat down. Gabriel, still on his feet, regarded her for a long moment, a hand to his chin, his head tilted slightly to one side.

"Who are you supposed to be?" he asked at last.

"Marlena Brunner."

"Nice."

"I thought so too. But I didn't choose it."

"Who did?"

Ignoring his question, she poured a cup of tea. "Biscuit?" she asked cordially.

"They're a dead giveaway, you know."

"The McVitie's? Marlena Brunner is half English. In fact, she spent most of her life living in the United Kingdom."

"Does she speak German?"

"She can order in a restaurant, but otherwise she's quite hopeless."

"That would explain the stack of English-language novels."

"She's read them all twice. If you have anything good lying around, she would love to borrow it."

"I'm sure the Metropolitan Police will find something for her to read when she gets back to London."

"Come now, Mr. Allon. There's no need for dramatics." Despite her unruffled outward demeanor, the hand that poured the next cup of tea was no longer steady. "Nor is there any need to involve the police."

"I'm afraid it's too late for that. The police have been involved from the beginning. That's what happens when the wife of a British real estate mogul goes missing."

"And the British real estate mogul asked you, of all people, to get her back." Quietly she added, "Just my luck."

"Mine too, as it turned out."

"Edward paid you well, I assume."

"Unlike you, Alice, I wasn't in it for the money."

"Is that why you think I did it?" She gave him a shrewd smile. "Perhaps I overestimated you, Mr. Allon. I thought you were more intelligent than that."

"Obviously not. How else to explain that I risked my life trying to save the likes of you?"

"In point of fact you were never in any danger."

"The four blokes at that house in Austria gave me quite a thrashing."

"They were only trying to appear convincing."

"But the bruises they left were quite real. So was the ketamine they pumped into me. They're lucky they didn't kill me."

"If it's more money you want—"

"I don't want your money," said Gabriel, cutting her off. "I want to know why you did what you did."

She sat back in her chair. "It will cost you, I'm afraid."

"I'm shocked to hear that. What do you want?"

"Your forgiveness."

"You're not going to get it."

"I would reserve judgment, if I were you. After all, you haven't heard my side of the story."

He couldn't help but admire her icy calm. "Surely you want more than that."

"Surely," she agreed.

"Here are the terms of the deal, Alice. Are you ready?"

"I find showdowns a bore, Mr. Allon. But please continue."

"You're going to tell me everything you did and everything you know. And if I find your story remotely plausible, I will consider our options. If not, I'm going to call the police, and you and your accomplice Peter Hoffmann will spend the next several years in a Swiss jail. Which is undoubtedly where you both belong."

"Peter wasn't my accomplice," she replied.

"How would you describe him?"

"He was my friend and financial adviser."

"Is Peter the one who provided you with a Swiss identity?"

"No," said Alice. "That was Sentry Global."

It was, she explained, a corporate security firm headquartered in the Wiedikon district of Zurich. Its clients included some of the biggest financial services firms in Switzerland, including Bank Josef Bänzinger & Co. Most of the services offered by Sentry were legitimate, but it had a secret division that provided tailored solutions to intractable problems.

"The sort of solutions," said Alice, "that Sentry never mentions on its website."

"Such as staged kidnappings?"

"Evidently I wasn't the first."

"Whose idea was it?"

"It was entirely mine, I admit. But Peter handled all the arrangements on my behalf."

"He came to see you while you were on Ibiza. You pretended to bump into one another on the beach at Cala d'Hort. I suppose that photograph of Es Vedrà that you posted on your social media was a signal that you wanted a word."

"Very good, Mr. Allon."

"Why did you want to see him?"

"My abduction was scheduled to take place in two days' time, and I was having second thoughts. We worked out a simple way for me to signal him that I wanted to go ahead with it."

"The white hat you purchased at Louis Vuitton."

She smiled but said nothing.

"Why the withdrawal from the ATM?"

"I was running low on cash, if you must know. Silly me, but I ended up being a few minutes late for my own abduction."

"The kidnappers were Sentry operatives?"

She nodded.

"How did it go down?"

"There were no fireworks, if that's what you're asking. I simply got out of my car and got into theirs. Then they rolled my car into the ravine and we left."

"The sandal you left behind on the beach was a lovely touch."

"You think so? I was worried it was a tad over the top."

"I suppose there was a motor yacht waiting offshore."

"It was on the small side because we had to crew it ourselves. We were at sea for a couple of days. Then we put in at a marina along the Côte d'Azur and settled into a villa in the Luberon."

"They locked you in a cellar, did they? Bread-and-water rations?"

"Hardly. But I did keep a low profile. After all, I had just vanished without a trace."

"You must have been surprised by the fact that it never became public."

"Not really. You see, I happen to be married to one of the world's most secretive men. We were, however, quite startled when Edward blurted out your name during our first phone call."

"You weren't alone."

"I must say, you were a worthy opponent."

"And you were quite the actress. That was an impressive performance you gave on the telephone. You clearly missed your calling."

"I was in the Dramatic Club at Cambridge."

"Congratulations," said Gabriel.

She frowned at him over her tea. "Bitterness doesn't suit you, Mr. Allon."

"Where were you that night?"

"The night of our phone call? Still in the Luberon. I came to Switzerland a few days after Peter wired the money to that bank in Cyprus."

"I suppose he's done business with CyproBank in the past."

"You would have to ask Peter about that."

"What was his cut?"

"Twenty-five million."

"Sounds a bit steep to me."

"I chose the number, not him."

"And Sentry Global?"

"Another ten million," said Alice. "But it included a Swiss passport."

"Which left you a mere four hundred and sixty-five million dollars."

"Four hundred and sixty, actually. This chalet cost me a pretty penny."

"And then there was the nearly three million pounds you donated anonymously to charity," said Gabriel. "Including the one million pounds you gave to the international relief organization where your friend Phoebe Chadwick works."

"Is that how you found me?"

"That's how I found Peter," said Gabriel. "And Peter led me to you."

"He warned me not to give Phoebe that money, but I thought we'd covered our tracks with the other contributions."

"Why did you do it?"

"I wanted to make amends for what happened between us."

"Perhaps you should have done that before she left Ibiza."

"I couldn't. My *real* accomplices and I wanted her off the island before my disappearance."

"Sophie Maxwell and Ella Burns?"

She nodded.

"A solicitor who works for the Magic Circle law firm that represents your husband's company," Gabriel pointed out. "And an executive at the British bank where he gets his financing."

"You're wrong about that, I'm afraid. HSBC stopped doing business with Edward years ago."

"In that case, where has he been getting his money?"

"In Moscow, Mr. Allon. Where else?"

33

Lauterbrunnen

The trouble began in the dreary winter of 2009, when the recklessness of Wall Street's investment banks plunged Britain's economy into the worst recession since World War II. Hardest hit was the property market, with the average British home losing twenty percent of its value, almost overnight. The declines in the commercial real estate sector were even more severe. One closely watched index plunged a catastrophic forty-six percent.

Edward Knight weathered the storm with only minor losses, or so he claimed. In truth the Knight Group was hemorrhaging cash. Twelve months into the crisis, the company was on the verge of bankruptcy. A sale of existing assets was not an option, for there were no buyers and prices were at rock bottom. Knight asked his man at HSBC for an additional line of credit and a restructuring of his current debt, and was denied both. Having nowhere else to turn he sought a private solution to his problems. He found one in the form of a billionaire Russian oligarch living grandly in London.

"Which one?" asked Gabriel.

"Dmitri Savin."

"The name rings a distant bell."

"Made a mountain of money in Russian chemicals," said Alice.

"Fertilizers, if I'm not mistaken. Poor Dmitri found himself at the wrong end of sanctions after Russia invaded Ukraine and was forced to return to Moscow, leaving a couple billion in frozen assets behind in the West, including his enormous mansion in Prince of Wales Terrace. It has since fallen into a state of disrepair, much to the dismay of Dmitri's former neighbors."

"An art collector, isn't he?"

"Aren't they all? Bloody Russians," she murmured.

"They're not all bad, you know."

"Name one good Russian, Mr. Allon."

"I've always been rather fond of Tchaikovsky."

"What about Pasternak?" she asked.

He quoted a line from *Zhivago*. "'And remember, you must never, under any circumstances, despair.'"

She finished the passage for him. "'To hope and to act, these are our duties in misfortune.'"

Gabriel regarded her for a moment, then asked, "Why on earth were you always posting all those silly photos of yourself online?"

"It wasn't me, Mr. Allon. It was just a role I was playing. Dazzling Alice Winter, glamorous wife of a billionaire. But it turns out that Edward would have gone under if Dmitri Savin hadn't thrown him a lifeline."

"How much money are we talking about?"

"Difficult to say. But if I were to hazard a guess, it would have been in the neighborhood of two billion pounds. Once Edward accepted Dmitri's money, the Knight Group was little more than a Russian subsidiary."

But all that, Alice added quickly, was long before she came on the scene. In the winter of 2009, as Edward's business was crumbling, she was a recent graduate of Cambridge looking for work as a journalist. In her mind's eye she saw herself as a muckraker and crusader, a defender of the poor and dispossessed, an exposer of corruption, a righter of wrongs. And yet even with her vaunted Cambridge education she found it difficult to land a job in an industry that had been cast into disarray by the rise of the Internet. Eventually she found work at a magazine that catered to the posh set. After spending a few years writing about restaurants and dim-witted pop stars, she landed an interview with a notoriously publicity-shy real estate investor named Edward Knight.

"And the rest, as they say, is history."

"It was love at first sight?"

"Not exactly. Edward hated my story and told me so in no uncertain terms. He rang a few days later to apologize and asked whether I might have dinner with him. I felt obliged to accept."

"You began an affair?"

"That very night."

"He was married at the time."

"To Mildred," said Alice. "Or Mildew, as I used to refer to her. It wasn't one of my finest hours. But if it hadn't been me, it would have been someone else."

"The divorce was rather costly."

"Which was the reason Edward insisted I sign a prenuptial agreement. The terms were draconian."

"But you signed it nevertheless."

"I was in love."

"Were you really?"

"Close enough," she admitted.

"There was a sizable age difference."

"And how old is your wife, Mr. Allon?"

"No comment."

"Rascal," she hissed.

"I've been called worse."

"I find that difficult to believe."

"Wait until you get to know me a little better."

"Any chance of that?"

"That depends on the rest of your story."

It was the kind of story, she said, that used to grace the pages of her old magazine—the mansions in Knightsbridge and Devon, the private jet, the yacht, the celebrity friends. She and Edward were much in demand and were seen in all the right places, with all the right people. She began to chronicle their remarkable life on social media, and her notoriety grew. Edward did not discourage her habit, quite the contrary. Dazzling Alice was good for Edward's business.

But by then he was already ensnared in a relationship with a Kremlin-connected oligarch from which he could not extract himself. Alice knew nothing of Edward's ties to Dmitri Savin—that is, until Dmitri met a beautiful young Russian model and decided to divorce his wife of twenty-eight years. The wife, who was called Masha, retained a powerhouse London law firm to represent her and came to the first meeting armed with a trove of documents she had downloaded from her husband's computer.

"Those documents painted a true picture of Dmitri's enormous net worth. They also contained a list of companies in which he held a controlling stake. One of the companies was the British real estate firm known as the Knight Group."

"Oh dear," said Gabriel.

"I'm afraid it gets better. You see, the law firm that Masha chose to represent her is the same firm where my friend Sophie Maxwell practices. In fact, dearest Sophie was assigned to Masha's legal team."

"She saw the documents?"

Alice nodded.

"And then she told you about them?"

"That would have been unethical, Mr. Allon. But let's just say that

I was made aware of Dmitri Savin's relationship with my husband. Never mind how."

"And your reaction?"

"I rang my friend Ella Burns. And what do you suppose Ella told me?"

"That HSBC stopped doing business with your husband in 2009."

Alice placed a forefinger against the end of her nose.

"Did she have documents as well?"

"Chapter and verse."

"And where are those documents now?"

"Stored on a carefully hidden external hard drive, along with Dmitri Savin's treasure trove. And they can be yours if you can somehow get me out of this mess."

"We're not there yet, Alice. In fact, we're not even close."

"You want to know why I staged my own abduction in order to embezzle a half billion dollars from my husband?"

Gabriel didn't bother with a reply.

"For a start," said Alice, "there was the prenuptial agreement."

"How much would you have received?"

"I'd rather not say."

"I'd rather you did."

"A lousy ten million."

"You would have been practically penniless," said Gabriel acidly.

"It's not easy to be poor after you've been rich."

"Ten million isn't exactly poor, Alice."

"It would have been a nest egg, nothing more. But there was another reason why I did what I did, Mr. Allon. A much more important reason."

Which brought them, at long last, to the early-morning hours of the twelfth of February, when Alice Winter, having had far too much to drink, and in a state of profound emotional distress, wrapped her Aston Martin roadster around a tree a mile from her husband's grand estate in the English county of Devon.

34

Lauterbrunnen

She had spent the evening alone with Edward at Wickham House, which was unusual. Even in rural Devon, the endless merry-go-round of their social life rarely stopped. They had a quiet dinner together, then Edward retreated to his office and Alice traipsed upstairs with a glass of Bordeaux and switched on the television. Around half past ten her glass was empty so she went downstairs for a refill, enough to get her through the next episode of *Shetland*. As she was leaving the kitchen she wandered over to Edward's wing of the house and heard him shouting at someone over the telephone behind the closed door of his office.

"This too was unusual, Mr. Allon. Edward occasionally puts on a booming boardroom voice when he wants to sound impressive, but he's not the sort to lose his temper."

"I don't suppose you went back upstairs to watch *Shetland*."

"Heavens no. I did what every other wife would have done in that situation."

"You picked up an extension?"

"The one in the kitchen."

"And what did you hear?"

"The voice of Dmitri Savin."

They had slipped out of the chalet and were walking side by side along a footpath on Alice's side of the valley. With her short dark hair and oversize sunglasses she was all but unrecognizable.

"And you're absolutely sure it was Dmitri?"

"Edward referred to him by name. Called him a lot of other things as well, none of them flattering."

"And the topic of conversation?"

"Edward informed Dmitri that he was terminating their relationship. He also said he had no intention of repaying the money Dmitri had invested in the Knight Group because Dmitri was under sanction and unable to conduct business in the West. That was when things got really ugly."

"How so?"

"Dmitri threatened to terminate Edward, or words to that effect. And then he threatened to kill me as well. As you might imagine, it was the last straw. Somehow I managed to wait until the call had ended before barging into Edward's office. We went at it hammer and tongs until two in the morning, when I climbed into my lovely Aston Martin and set off for London. Regrettably I'd had another glass of wine or two during our lengthy quarrel."

"And to make matters worse," said Gabriel, "a tree leapt out of the woods and hurled itself in front of your car."

"It's possible I said those exact words to the constables who pulled me out of the wreckage. It was little wonder they took me straight to the A&E ward in Exeter. Edward and his lawyer showed up soon after."

"They refused to allow the investigating officer to talk to you."

"Now you know why."

They had reached the fringes of the village. They turned onto the high street and strolled past a parade of shops. "And when you were out of the hospital?" asked Gabriel.

"Edward was sweetness and light. He waited on me hand and foot. It was quite pathetic."

"Did it work?"

"Edward thought so. But I had no intention of remaining married to a man who was doing business with the bloody Russians in the middle of the war in Ukraine."

"You had drinks with Peter Hoffmann at the Connaught not long after the accident."

"That's where the conspiracy was hatched," said Alice. "In the bar of the Connaught Hotel. We agreed that I would disappear during my annual summer holiday with my Cambridge chums. Darling Pheebs thought we should go to Iceland this year, but I overruled her. Ibiza was the perfect spot for an abduction."

"When did you tell Sophie and Ella of your plans?"

"A week or so before our departure."

"Why not Phoebe?"

"Because she's the most honest person I've ever known. I was certain she would fold under police interrogation."

"So you intentionally picked a fight with her and drove her away."

"Poor Pheebs was voted off the island," replied Alice with a sigh. "After that everything went according to plan—until Edward asked you to find me, of course. And to think it was all because of that fundraiser."

"You have something against Botticelli?"

"Not at all. They make wonderful shoes." She gave him a sidelong glance. "I'm joking, Mr. Allon. I went to Cambridge, after all. And I adore Botticelli's paintings."

"Do you have a favorite?"

"I go weak in the knees while standing before *Primavera*."

"Perhaps there's hope for you, after all."

"Is there?" She paused outside a hair salon and gazed at the woman reflected in the glass as though she were a stranger. "What are you going to do with her, Mr. Allon? Hand her over to the Swiss authorities? Forget you ever met her?"

"Actually," replied Gabriel, "I was thinking about committing a major felony myself."

"What sort?"

"Aiding and abetting a fugitive."

"That would make you an accessory after the fact."

"Not for the first time."

"You've committed crimes before?"

"It's possible I've planned one or two in the bar of the Connaught."

Her smile was reflected in the glass. "Where are you planning to take her?"

"Back to Britain."

"And then?"

"I wouldn't want to spoil the surprise."

"She's not terribly fond of them, if you must know. Edward learned that lesson the hard way on the occasion of her thirty-fifth birthday." She ran a hand through her short, dark hair. "I don't suppose I can get a wash and a blow-dry before we leave. I wouldn't want to arrive at Heathrow looking like something the cat dragged in."

"You look fine. Besides, your return to Britain will be entirely secret."

"No police?" she asked.

"Not exactly."

"What does that mean?"

Gabriel took her by the arm. "Do you remember the detective who was at the hospital the night of your accident? Nice-looking chap. Speaks with a Cornish accent . . ."

35

Wiltons

It was inevitable, perhaps even fated, that the bar of Wiltons would serve as the backdrop for what unfolded next. It was the usual scene that evening, with the usual cast of characters arrayed upon the stage—tweedy Jeremy Crabbe from Bonhams, suntanned Simon Mendenhall from Christie's, slick Nicky Lovegrove, art adviser to the vastly rich. Roddy Hutchinson, universally regarded as the most unscrupulous dealer in all of St. James's, was arguing politics with Niles Dunham, an unapologetic supporter of the Labour Party, warts and all. Julian Isherwood had once again drawn the short straw and was stuck with Oliver Dimbleby. Tubby Oliver was delivering a homily about the current Turner and Constable exhibit at the Tate Modern. Julian was peering into his Chablis as though contemplating suicide.

Sarah Bancroft, for her part, was seated at her usual table in the corner, drinking her usual Belvedere martini, three olives, Saharan dry, Siberian cold. Amelia March, with her insatiable need for art world gossip, had joined her uninvited. Amelia was drinking Campari and soda, a fine concoction, surely, but Sarah had never really seen the point.

Heads turned as Olivia Watson made her entrance. Amelia eyed her enviously. "It's really not fair, is it?"

"It won't last forever."

"I'm not so sure about that. She seems to be getting more beautiful by the day." Amelia leaned across the table and adopted a conspiratorial tone. "I don't mean to bring up a sore subject, but I was wondering whether—"

"The delicious rumor you heard about Olivia and my husband was true?"

"It was the talk of the Wickham House fundraiser."

"I was afraid of that," said Sarah morosely.

"Well?"

"I won't dignify your question with a response."

"There was another rumor making the rounds as well," said Amelia. "It involved you and a rather well-known art conservator."

"Oh, for heaven's sake."

"A classic nondenial denial. Your second of the evening, in fact."

"It isn't true."

"The rumor was started by the well-known art conservator's lovely wife. Which begs the question," said Amelia leadingly.

"And which question is that?"

"Are you or aren't you?"

Sarah raised her martini to her lips. "Are you asking whether I once worked for the Central Intelligence Agency?"

"He's a former spy, and you were once madly in love with him. The connection seems obvious."

"To you, perhaps." Sarah was spared an additional response by the ringing of her mobile. The name of the caller was displayed on the screen.

"Speak of the devil," said Amelia, and rose to her feet. "Do give him my best."

Sarah accepted the call and placed the phone to her ear. "Your timing," she murmured, "is impeccable as always."

"I'm not interrupting anything important, I hope."

"Amelia March was just wondering whether I was once madly in love with you. Having seen my caller ID, she's now absolutely certain I was."

"You really need to change my name in your contacts."

"I'm doing so as we speak, Mr. Mud. But how can I be of service?"

"I need to borrow your husband."

"You can't have him."

"Why not?"

"Because he just returned to London, and I was planning to spend the next several days doing unspeakable things to his body."

"I wouldn't ask if it wasn't important."

She sighed. "Where are you this time?"

"Back in Switzerland."

"You're not planning to rob another Mafia-controlled bank, are you?"

"Something better."

"Hard to imagine."

"Just tell that husband of yours to get to Bern as quickly as possible," said Gabriel before ringing off. "I promise he won't be disappointed. And neither will his friends from the Firm."

The Firm was how insiders sometimes referred to His Majesty's Secret Intelligence Service. Sarah's husband was known there, and everywhere else in the overt world, as Peter Marlowe. She had never cared for the name—it sounded like something invented by a novelist—and privately she referred to him only by the name bestowed upon him at birth, which was Christopher. His surname was Keller, a remnant of his family's German roots. Sarah, though she was an American by birth, was English to the core—more English than her British husband. His superiors at SIS, who were never thrilled with his decision to wed a retired officer from another service, even a friendly one, were of the opinion that Sarah should make it official and acquire a UK passport. For now, at least, she intended to remain exclusively an American.

The maisonette they shared was located in Queen's Gate Terrace in Kensington. Sarah arrived there at half past six to find Christopher taking down a bottle of Johnnie Walker from the kitchen cabinet. He wore an elegant gray suit by Richard Green of Savile Row and a shirt and tie by Turnbull & Asser. His hair was sun-bleached, his skin was taut and dark, his eyes were bright blue. The notch in the center of his chin looked as though it had been cleaved with a chisel. His mouth seemed permanently fixed in an ironic half smile.

He loosened the cap on the bottle and poured three fingers of the whisky into a cut-glass Baccarat tumbler, a wedding gift from an old friend on the island of Corsica. His packet of Marlboro cigarettes was lying on the countertop. Sarah pinched one, then told her husband about her phone conversation with their mutual friend Gabriel Allon.

"I wonder what it could be this time."

"Knowing Gabriel," replied Sarah, "it could be anything."

"What's he been up to lately?"

"He's supposed to be restoring a Bellotto for me."

"Riveting stuff." Christopher returned the bottle of whisky to the cabinet. "Anything else?"

Having spent the better part of the summer in eastern Ukraine, Christopher was in desperate need of a few days of down time in London. But after hearing his wife's answer, he reserved a seat on the morning's first flight from Heathrow to Geneva. From there it was a pleasant two hours by train to Bern. Gabriel was waiting outside the station in a Mitsubishi SUV. Christopher dropped into the passenger seat and ignited a cigarette.

"Must you?" asked Gabriel.

"I'm afraid so, old love."

"This is a nonsmoking car."

"Not anymore, it isn't."

Gabriel lowered his window to vent the smoke and pulled away from the station.

"Mind telling me where we're going?" asked Christopher.

"The Bernese Oberland."

"I wish you would have told me. I would have packed some kit."

Despite a lifelong addiction to tobacco, Christopher was a world-class climber who had already bagged most of Switzerland's toughest mountains, including the Matterhorn and the North Face of the Eiger. The first mountain he ever climbed was the Pen y Fan in South Wales. He had done so while carrying a fifty-five-pound rucksack and a ten-pound assault rifle provided to him by his instructors at the Special Air Service, Britain's elite commando regiment. He had come to the Secret Intelligence Service later in life than most, and with a closet full of skeletons that would have sunk an ordinary recruit. It was Gabriel who had vouched for him.

"How much did Sarah tell you?" he asked.

"Not much. But then you weren't terribly forthcoming when you spoke to her."

"I said as much as I could over an insecure phone."

"Who were you worried about?"

Gabriel inclined his head toward the east.

"You have my full attention."

"I have a source for you and your service," said Gabriel.

"Russian?"

"British, actually."

"Not another wayward SIS officer, I hope."

"She's wayward, all right, but she has no connection to Vauxhall Cross."

"She?"

"You heard me correctly."

No, thought Christopher. It wasn't possible. "What sort of work does our wayward girl do?"

"She used to do a bit of journalism. Now she doesn't do much of anything."

"And what exactly do you want SIS to do with her?"

"Exfiltrate her back into Britain and stash her away somewhere nice and remote."

"Any particular reason?"

"Because she's dead, Christopher. And she needs to stay that way for a while."

He smoked in silence for moment. "You were dead once, as I recall. You died in that car bombing on the Brompton Road."

"Yes," said Gabriel darkly. "Good times."

During the drive up the valley, Christopher regaled Gabriel with tales of mountaineering derring-do. The Eiger, he said, had been a snooze. He scaled the North Face in just under eighteen hours, then repaired to the outdoor bar at Kleine Scheidegg and drank himself stiff on lager. His nearest brush with death had occurred on Mont Blanc's Goûter Pass. The culprit was a rockslide, which missed him only by a meter or two. Four other climbers were not so fortunate. Christopher had carried one of the bodies down to Chamonix.

"What on earth were you doing on that mountain in the first place?"

"I was climbing it, you idiot. What do you think?"

"Do you know how many people die on Mont Blanc each year?"

"More than on Everest."

"Far more."

Christopher only shrugged in reply.

"Perhaps you should take up another hobby," suggested Gabriel.

"Like what?"

"Sailing is a fine pastime."

"No one ever dies sailing," quipped Christopher.

An hour after leaving the rail station in Bern they arrived in Lauterbrunnen. Gabriel made for the eastern side of the valley and rolled to a stop outside the largest chalet in sight.

"Nice crib," said Christopher. "How much did she pay for it?"

"Too much." Gabriel indicated the BMW. "That's hers too. Given her driving record, it's a miracle the thing is still in one piece."

"We should probably lose it somewhere." Christopher opened his door. "How much does she know about me?"

"It's possible she heard about your torrid affair with Olivia Watson, but otherwise you're a blank canvas."

"Let's keep it that way, shall we?"

Christopher followed Gabriel across the garden to the entrance of the chalet. Inside, DI Timothy Peel of the Devon and Cornwall Police was playing a game of Scrabble with Britain's most famous missing woman. Ingrid was hunched over her laptop.

"What's she doing?" asked Christopher.

"Downloading the entire database of the Knight Group Limited."

Christopher looked at Alice Winter, who was placing lettered tiles upon the board. "Does Mr. Knight's wife know?"

Gabriel smiled. "Where do you think Ingrid got Mr. Knight's password?"

36

Bern–Dartmoor

After hearing the story for himself, Christopher agreed with Gabriel's conclusion that secure communications were in order, so he commandeered Alice's BMW and drove it dangerously fast down the valley to the British Embassy in Bern. There, in a safe-speech room inside the SIS station, he rang the European operations desk at Vauxhall Cross and requested private air travel from Bern to Britain for himself and four other passengers. Their arrival, he explained, would need to be pitch black, with no passport checks and no ground personnel of any kind near the aircraft. One of the passengers, he added, would require safe lodging for the foreseeable future.

"It's not another Russian defector, I hope," said the desk officer. "We're still cleaning up the mess from the last one."

"Not to worry. She's housebroken."

"Name?"

"Alice Winter."

"I beg your pardon?"

"You heard me right."

"Why is this a matter for SIS?"

"You'll know soon enough."

Because British budgets were tight, even at the Secret Intelligence Service, the desk officer required the approval of higher authority before he could authorize the expenditure for a private plane. Christopher cooled his heels in the Head of Station's office for nearly an hour before the desk officer finally rang him back.

"The plane's in the air. It should be on the ground in Bern in two hours' time."

"What about a safe house?"

"The staff at Wormwood Cottage are eagerly awaiting your arrival. So is the chief, by the way."

"Is there any chance he can join us for dinner? An old friend of his will be on the flight."

"Which one?"

Christopher said the name.

"That explains everything," said the desk officer, and the connection went dead.

The Head of Station had listened in on the call from an extension. "What would you like us to do about her car?" he asked.

"Have one of your officers leave it in a dodgy quarter of Lyon with the key on the passenger seat. It will be gone in no time."

With that Christopher rang Gabriel and told him they were a go. Then he repaired to the embassy canteen for a bite to eat. A few diplomats and clerks were huddled around the television. A swarm of drones had once again halted traffic at a European airport, this time in Helsinki. Finnish authorities had yet to identify the culprit, but the television analysts were all but certain it was Finland's belligerent neighbor to the east.

There were no delays, however, at Bern's small airport. Christopher traveled there by taxi and arrived at Alpine Sky Jets, the airport's fixed-base operator, to find his four traveling companions relaxing in the executive lounge. Their Gulfstream was taking on fuel outside on the tarmac. Christopher sat down next to Gabriel, who was typing something on his mobile phone.

"I'm just trying to save my marriage," he explained.

"Thanks to you, I'm rather in the same boat." Christopher looked at Alice Winter. "She's not having second thoughts about going home, is she?"

"She doesn't have a choice in the matter."

"Are you sure that fake Swiss passport of hers is going to work?"

"It better. Otherwise we're not going anywhere."

It was another twenty minutes before the FBO's ground staff informed them that they had a departure slot. A Swiss Border Guard waited at the foot of the airstair, electronic passport reader in hand. He swiped the travel documents of the four pesky foreigners—Christopher and Gabriel, Peel and Ingrid—but waved Alice onto the aircraft with scarcely a glance at her Swiss passport.

"Is there any chance of a preflight drink?" she asked after settling into her seat. "I'm not sure I can face this sober."

There was no cabin attendant, but the galley was provisioned with plenty of food and drink, including four bottles of decent French champagne. Alice remained in good spirits for most of the flight, but her mood darkened as they settled onto the runway at Luton Airport. In a distant corner of the airfield was a Sikorsky executive helicopter, and next to the Sikorsky was an unmarked SIS van with blacked-out windows. Five minutes later both were headed west. The helicopter contained four passengers, the van only one—a detective inspector from the Devon and Cornwall Police who, for the moment, at least, had outlived his usefulness. His phone rang as the van was approaching Slough. It was DCI Douglas Chapel of the Metropolitan Police. He slid the device into his pocket and let it ring.

The road had no name and appeared on no map. Viewed from space, it looked like a scratch in the moorland, perhaps the remnant of a brook that had run over the land in the days when men erected circles of stone. At its entrance was a sign, weathered and rusted, warning that the road was private. And at its end was a gate that whispered quiet authority.

The grounds beyond the gate were barren and bleak, an acquired taste. The man who built the cottage there had made his money in shipping. He had bequeathed it to his only son, and the son, who had no heirs, had entrusted it to the Secret Intelligence Service, where he had worked for the better part of a half century. He had served in many distant corners of the empire, under many different names, but mainly he was known as Wormwood. The service named the cottage in his honor. Those who stayed there found the name appropriate.

It stood atop a swell in the land and was fashioned of Devon stone that had darkened with age and neglect. Behind it, across a broken courtyard, was a converted barn with offices and living quarters for the staff. When Wormwood Cottage was unoccupied, a single caretaker called Parish kept watch over it. Parish was old service, old enough to have worked with some of the greats, including the father of the current director-general.

It was Nigel Whitcombe, the DG's eternally boyish factotum and cupbearer, who informed Parish that a party of four—in the lexicon of the cottage, they were referred to as "company"—was headed his way. Two members of the party were return visitors, and the third was a Danish national who had pulled a black bag job in Moscow a couple of years ago that had spared the world a nuclear calamity.

"And the fourth?" asked Parish.

"She's the guest of honor."

"How shall we refer to her?"

"Miss Nobody."

"Anticipated time of arrival?" inquired Parish as blandly as possible.

"Early evening. And by the way," added Whitcombe, "they're traveling by helicopter."

A rarity, thought Parish, even for high-level company. He asked whether Miss Coventry, the staff cook, should prepare dinner.

"For five, please," replied Whitcombe.

"I assume the chief will be joining them?"

"You assume correctly."

Wormwood Cottage, like the Secret Intelligence Service itself, was a place of time-honored traditions, and Parish, as was his custom, was waiting in the forecourt when the helicopter settled onto the grounds. The cabin door opened and a ruggedly handsome SIS officer who went by the work name Peter Marlowe came bounding down the stairs, followed by the legendary former chief of Israeli intelligence and a petite woman with toffee-colored hair—the Dane, no doubt.

The last to emerge was the guest of honor, Miss Nobody. She was on the tallish side, late thirties, attractive, with short dark hair that in Parish's opinion didn't suit her. He had a strange feeling he had seen her somewhere before, but for the life of him he couldn't remember where it had been. It would come to him eventually. Parish had been a watcher in his day. He never forgot a face.

Mr. Marlowe was now marching toward him across the forecourt, an arm raised in greeting. "Parish, you old scoundrel," he called out. "What a sight for sore eyes, you are."

"As are you, Mr. Marlowe." Parish turned toward Mr. Marlowe's old friend and occasional partner in crime. "It's a pleasure to see you again as well, Mr. Allon. I'd heard a terrible rumor that you'd left the game."

"You know what they say about old spies, Parish." He gestured in the general direction of the Danish woman. "This is my dear friend Ingrid. If any valuables happen to go missing during our stay, you'll know where to find them."

"I'll bear that in mind." Parish turned finally to Miss Nobody. "If there's anything we can do to make your stay more comfortable, please don't hesitate to ask."

The woman smiled without parting her lips but said nothing. Parish was once again gripped by the nagging sense that he had met her in the recent past.

There were a number of rules and regulations at Wormwood Cottage, none more inviolable than those forbidding the use of mobile phones and computers. Mr. Marlowe and his friend Gabriel Allon handed over their devices without protest, but Parish had to well-nigh pry the phone and laptop from the grasp of their Danish companion. As for Miss Nobody, she had no devices to surrender.

"She left her phone on the plane," explained Mr. Marlowe on the woman's behalf.

A likely story, thought Parish. He couldn't remember the last time someone had showed up at Wormwood Cottage without a phone.

"Cocktails at seven," he said. "Dinner at eight."

"Cottage pie?" asked Mr. Marlowe hopefully.

"Lamb, I'm afraid."

Mr. Marlowe turned without another word and set off toward the entrance of the cottage, trailed by the legendary Gabriel Allon, a temperamental Scandinavian called Ingrid, and a mute woman without a name or a phone. Parish went to his office in the converted barn and sat down at his computer, the only computer at Wormwood Cottage with an Internet connection. He entered two words into his search engine, a given name and a surname, and a torrent of results appeared on the screen, including several photographs. In one of the images the subject was staring directly into the camera while holding a copy of *The Economist.* The hair was different, but the face was the same one Parish had seen a moment ago—in the forecourt of Wormwood Cottage, of all places. But why was she about to have a dinner with the chief of His Majesty's Secret Intelligence Service? If nothing else, he thought, it promised to be a most interesting evening. Gabriel Allon was never one to disappoint.

37

Wormwood Cottage

It was hardly the way Graham Seymour, director-general of the Secret Intelligence Service, had intended to spend his afternoon. His busy schedule included a meeting of his section chiefs at Vauxhall Cross, a briefing for Prime Minister Jonathan Lancaster at Downing Street, and drinks with Amanda Wallace, his counterpart at MI5, at her office in Thames House. But after learning of Christoper Keller's unusual request for a private aircraft, he abruptly cleared his calendar. He told only the prime minister the reason why. He placed the call from the back seat of his official car while headed west on the M4. Lancaster was in his private study at Number 10.

"Is it really her?" he asked.

"She looks different, and somehow she got herself a Swiss passport. But there's no question it's her."

"I suppose it was our friend Gabriel Allon who found her."

"It was, Prime Minister. But how on earth did you know that?"

"Because the Metropolitan Police prevailed upon him to look into her disappearance."

"Is there some reason why no one bothered to tell SIS?"

"It was a matter for the Home Office, not Vauxhall Cross. Besides, Graham, you have quite enough on your plate at the moment."

Which was indeed the case. The Secret Intelligence Service was desperately trying to prevent a Russian conquest of Ukraine and the collapse of the NATO alliance, all at a time when Britain's economy was reeling and its public finances were in disarray. To make matters worse, the Americans were pressuring the Kyiv government to accept a peace agreement on Russia's terms. Graham steadfastly opposed allowing the Kremlin to redraw Europe's map by force, as did the prime minister. Together with the French president, Germany's chancellor, and Denmark's prime minister, Jonathan Lancaster was the leader of what was once fondly known as the free world. It was a role he relished. No one loathed the Russians more than Jonathan Lancaster—and with good reason.

"The question is," he asked, "why in the name of all that is holy would she do such a thing?"

"Evidently it had something do with her husband's business. The details are somewhat murky, but it appears he got himself entangled with one of the Russian oligarchs."

"Which one?"

"Dmitri Savin."

"A nasty piece of work," remarked Lancaster.

"Quite."

"A member of the Russian president's inner circle, is he not?"

"As inner as it gets," replied Graham. "Which was only one of the reasons why we seized his British-based assets and sent him back to Moscow after the Russian invasion of Ukraine."

"And the other?"

"He has long-standing ties to Russia's intelligence services, the GRU in particular."

"What sort of ties?"

"Financial, Prime Minister. We have reason to believe that Dmitri

Savin has been clandestinely bankrolling the GRU's activities here in Europe."

"You don't think he was using Edward Knight to—"

"It certainly sounds like that might be the case."

"Not that it matters," said Lancaster, "but Edward is a major donor to the Conservative Party. That said, I never cared for the man."

"Neither does his wife, it seems."

"Met her once. Lovely woman."

"I'm told she has the receipts."

"About her husband's involvement with Dmitri Savin?"

"Apparently so."

"Tread carefully, Graham. The last thing we need is another scandal."

He had one last cancellation to make, a small dinner party that his wife, Helen, was hosting that evening at their home in Belgravia. He did so with a modicum of guilt and no small amount of relief, for Helen was a passionate but dreadful cook. Having done the deed and endured the usual recriminations, he silenced his secure phone and dug a weighty document from his attaché case. It was an assessment he planned to deliver to the Joint Intelligence Committee, the bureaucratic overseers of SIS and the rest of Britain's security and defense community. Stark in tone, it warned that Britain was obligated to commence preparations for war with Russia. Ukraine, it argued, was only the beginning. Once the country had been turned into a Russian vassal, the Kremlin would proceed to its next target, in all likelihood one of the Baltic states or perhaps even Poland. And on it would go until Moscow had reconstituted the old Soviet Union and established its dominance over Europe. As far as SIS was concerned, Britain and its European allies had no choice but to fight—for the simple reason that Russia was already at war with them.

By the time Graham finally looked up from the document, his car was speeding across the northern reaches of Dartmoor. About a mile past the old Warren House Inn was the turnoff for Wormwood Cottage. He arrived there to find the forecourt deserted. It seemed Parish the caretaker had other matters to attend to besides welcoming his director-general to SIS's most secure safe house.

Graham locked his phone in his attaché case—a product of Q Division, it was impenetrable to any and all electronic signals—and entered the cottage empty-handed. Miss Coventry, powdered and churchy and vaguely formidable, stood before the AGA stove, wooden spoon in hand, an apron tied around her ample waist. Once upon a time she was one of the service's best listeners. She spoke several languages fluently, including Russian.

Graham opened the oven door and inhaled the savor of roasting lamb. "You've outdone yourself, Miss Coventry."

"Mr. Marlowe is miffed we're not having cottage pie."

"He'll get over it, I'm sure." Graham closed the oven. "Where's Parish? Under the weather?"

"In the drawing room with the company."

"That's not like him."

"Could be the guest of honor," said Miss Coventry knowingly.

"Has he figured out who she is?"

"In about two seconds flat." She removed the lid from a pot and gave the contents a stir. "How long will she be staying with us?"

"Is there a problem?"

"She's not happy with her room. Nor is she pleased that she has to share a bathroom with the others." Miss Coventry replaced the lid. "Wormwood is a safe house, not a five-star resort or a mansion in Knightsbridge. I'm afraid she's used to a level of luxury that we simply cannot provide."

"I'll have a word with her."

"And while you're at it, you might make it clear that we cook with butter here at Wormwood, not avocado oil."

"The more butter the better."

"Say that five times quickly. Now, go away, sir. Otherwise you and your friends will be having a midnight supper."

Graham headed off to the drawing room, wondering what he might find there. Tread carefully, he heard his prime minister say. The last thing he needed was another scandal.

Graham had no desire to spoil Alice Winter's first meal at Wormwood Cottage, so he waited until Miss Coventry had cleared the plates and poured the coffee to get down to brass tacks. Several times Gabriel and Christopher tried to answer on her behalf, but Graham was having none of it; he wanted to hear it from her mouth, not theirs. By the time he had posed his last question, he was certain that Edward Knight's ties to Russia went far beyond a single oligarch. It was possible they were criminal in nature, but this was of no concern to Graham. He was not a policeman, he was a spy. And Edward Knight's sins, whatever they were, had presented him with a golden opportunity.

None of which he shared with the missing British socialite who had fallen quite unexpectedly into his lap. At the conclusion of the meal he bade her a pleasant evening and asked Gabriel and Christopher whether they might accompany him on an after-dinner walk around the grounds. Outside, the three-quarter moon hanging low in the cloudless sky was luminous enough to throw shadows. Christopher took out his cigarettes and ignited one with his old Dunhill lighter. Then he offered the packet to Graham, who did the same.

"A compelling story," he said. "But is she telling the truth?"

"I've heard it three times now," replied Gabriel, "and it hasn't changed."

"But that doesn't make it true, does it? Perhaps our Alice is nothing more than a clever schemer who concocted this admittedly compelling tale after you showed up at her door in Lauterbrunnen."

"You give her too much credit, Graham."

"And you seem to be forgetting that together with her Swiss banker she pulled off a half-billion-dollar heist and stashed the money offshore. And what about that tearful phone conversation she had with you while she was supposedly in captivity?" Graham shook his head slowly. "Bloody Cate Blanchett."

"All valid points," conceded Gabriel. "But she does have a substantial number of documents to back up her story. And we've managed to obtain a few of our own."

"The documents your Danish friend stole from the Knight Group's database? For the record," said Graham, "that was a crime under British law."

"Mea culpa, mea culpa, mea maxima culpa."

"Never mind the apologies. Just bring me proof that the Knight Group is controlled by Dmitri Savin. I want to know where the money is coming from and, more important, where it's going."

"It can't be good."

Graham dropped his cigarette to the footpath and ground it out with the toe of his oxford. "Did you happen to see the news from Helsinki today? Yet another European airport shut down by drones. A few days before that, saboteurs attempted to blow up a Polish train carrying relief supplies bound for Ukraine. And then there was the recent fire at a shopping center in Vilnius."

"What about the incident involving the plane carrying the president of the European Commission?" asked Gabriel. "The navigation system failed midflight. The pilots were forced to use paper maps to get the plane on the ground again."

"Vauxhall Cross concluded it was a blatant assassination attempt," said Graham, "ordered by the Kremlin and carried out by Unit 29155 of the GRU. Its sole mission is to sow division and discord in the West through disinformation and acts of sabotage and violence. For years it operated in Europe with virtual impunity, largely because its personnel were able to travel on false passports. They were rather sloppy as a result. But all that changed after the invasion of Ukraine, when we expelled Russian diplomats en masse and imposed travel restrictions on ordinary Russian citizens. The GRU had no choice but to clean up its act. It now has an entire unit dedicated solely to creating a network of illegals, and we have reason to believe that those illegals are the ones orchestrating the attacks here in Europe."

"Illegals cost money, Graham. Lots of money."

"And so do their operations. What's more, the money has to be laundered so that it can't be traced back to Moscow. Otherwise the entire network would be in jeopardy."

"Find the money, find the illegals."

"Precisely. Which is why I've created a special unit of my own. It has but one task as well, to identify and burn all the illegals the GRU has managed to place in the West, preferably before they launch a major sabotage operation here in Britain. We know they would love nothing more," added Graham. "The PM is a thorn in the Kremlin's side. And so am I, for that matter."

"I'm not exactly beloved in Moscow myself," said Gabriel. "And neither is Christopher."

"But Christopher is obliged to obey my directives. You, on the other hand, have a wife and two children waiting for you in Cornwall."

Graham pointed absently toward the west. “It’s two hours by car in that direction.”

“I’m not going anywhere. Besides,” said Gabriel, “who better to confront Edward Knight than the fool he hired to track down his wife?”

Christopher laughed. “He *does* have a point.”

38

Wormwood Cottage

The trouble began immediately after breakfast. Not surprisingly the Danish woman called Ingrid was to blame. The problem was her computer. She required it, she declared, in order to review certain sensitive documents stored on an external hard drive. Her entreaties, while passionate, left Parish unmoved; it was strictly forbidden by Wormwood Cottage rules. When informed of this, the Danish woman demanded to see the actual rule book, but once again Parish demurred. This too, he explained, was prohibited.

She took her case to Mr. Marlowe, and Mr. Marlowe had a go at Parish on her behalf. "Look here, old sport," he began in that clubby West End voice of his. "Surely we can find some sort of elegant solution to our little problem."

"It's not *our* problem," was Parish's riposte. "It's hers."

"And mine too, you see. Because we need to review those documents *tout de suite*."

"I'd be happy to print them for her."

"There's enough material on that disk to fill a warehouse. Now, give me the damn computer."

Parish surrendered it after first compelling the woman to affix her signature to a memorandum of understanding regarding the use of the computer. It could be operated, the document made glaringly clear, only in an offline mode. Any attempt to connect the device to the Internet would leave the user liable to criminal prosecution under the Official Secrets Act. Never mind that she was a Danish citizen and as such was not subject to the OSA; Parish would find some way to punish her. He was as wicked as the rest of them and didn't take kindly to being crossed.

They worked in the drawing room—Mr. Marlowe and Mr. Allon, the petite Danish woman called Ingrid, and the beautiful Englishwoman who was pretending not to be the socialite who was missing and presumed dead. Precisely what they were doing was a mystery to Parish and Miss Coventry, though the confines of the cottage were such that they couldn't help but overhear at least a portion of the proceedings—especially Miss Coventry, a listener by trade who missed nothing.

"It involves her husband," she informed Parish on the afternoon of the first day. "Evidently he's in business with a Russian oligarch, the one who used to live in that enormous place in Prince of Wales Terrace."

"Not Dmitri Savin?"

"Yes, that's the one."

Parish absorbed this information in thoughtful silence. They were seated in the kitchen's cozy little nook, partaking of their afternoon tea. Mr. Marlowe had challenged the Danish woman to a footrace in the wilds of Dartmoor. Mr. Allon and Ms. Winter were still hard at work in the drawing room.

"Do you remember the last time he was here?" asked Parish.

"It was the Rebecca Manning case, wasn't it?" Miss Coventry sipped her tea. "A scandal for the ages, that one. Imagine, the daughter of none other than Kim Philby . . ."

"He found her too, as I recall."

"He certainly has a knack for it." She smiled. "And always the perfect guest. Such beautiful manners."

"Unlike his little friend from Denmark."

"Here she comes now."

Parish peered out the nook's leaded window and saw the Danish woman bounding across the moor. Mr. Marlowe was nowhere to be seen.

"Where do you suppose he could be?"

"I'm sure he'll turn up soon enough. After all," said Miss Coventry, "we're having cottage pie for dinner."

It would be another twenty minutes before he staggered into the forecourt. Exhausted and soaked with sweat, he slipped into the cottage without a word and headed off to his room with his tail between his legs to dress for dinner. It was a relaxed affair, noisy and filled with laughter, most of it at Mr. Marlowe's expense. The Danish woman offered him a rematch, with a five-minute head start. Wisely he declined.

After breakfast the following morning they were back at work. Parish and Miss Coventry overheard several exchanges—through absolutely no fault of their own, mind you—that led them to believe that Ms. Winter's husband was not nearly as wealthy as he had made himself out to be. Indeed it sounded as though Edward Knight was entirely beholden to the aforementioned Dmitri Savin, a relationship he had taken great pains to conceal from HMRC, otherwise known as His Majesty's Revenue and Customs. It appeared as though the Russian oligarch had plowed money into Knight's firm through a number of dodgy offshore shell companies, the kind with three-letter names like ABC Holdings and XYZ Capital. Knight in turn had paid the Russian a handsome return on his investment, somewhere in the neighborhood of twenty-five percent, which had been funneled into an entirely different set of offshore front companies—including something called Landmark Ventures, a Bahamian-registered shell corporation that did its banking in Nassau.

"It sounds to me," said Miss Coventry, "as though Landmark holds the key."

"To what, exactly?" asked Parish.

"Mr. Marlowe seems to think that Landmark is controlled by the GRU."

"A band of thugs," declared Parish with an uncharacteristic flash of vehemence. "Always the mailed fist, never the delicate touch. Give me a good old-fashioned Moscow Center hood any day of the week. They were worthy opponents in their day, weren't they, Miss Coventry?"

They overheard other things as the day wore on—snippets of conversations, announcements of interesting discoveries, even the odd exchange of a harsh word—that indicated the unlikely team of burrowers toiling away in the drawing room were closing in on their target. Parish received additional supporting evidence of this theory when the young Danish woman, having forgone her afternoon training run, requested permission to attach her laptop computer to the Internet via a mobile hotspot. Parish, aghast, put his foot down.

"Not now, not ever. World without end, Amen."

A quarrel ensued, one that all parties would later regret. Voices were raised, threats issued. Even Mr. Allon, he of the impeccable manners, joined the fray. Parish, seeking a way out of the morass, reluctantly offered the Danish woman use of the computer in his office. That, said Mr. Allon, was the worst idea he had heard since Brexit. Eventually, however, the parties reached a compromise, one that permitted the Danish woman to remove the ethernet cable from Parish's computer and attach it to hers. She did so at 7:20 P.M., with Parish looking warily on. "Leave," was all she said.

He ate a late dinner with Miss Coventry and then retired to his rooms to watch a little something on the telly. The door to his office, which was just down the corridor, was tightly closed, though it did little to dampen the relentless machine-gun clatter of her typing. Worse still was her strange music, meandering notes on a piano interspersed with the dissonant wailing of a saxophone. Parish, a devotee of Haydn and Mozart, had never heard such drivel.

She was still at it at dawn when Parish, after a sleepless night, staggered from his bed—and at 1:00 P.M., when the others sat down to an al fresco lunch in the garden. She finally emerged from the office at half past four, with the laptop tucked under one arm. She delivered her findings to Mr. Allon, who in turn had a quiet word with Mr. Marlowe, who rang Vauxhall Cross from the secure phone in Parish's office. The helicopter set down on the grounds of Wormwood Cottage a few minutes after six o'clock. Much to Parish's disappointment, it took on only two passengers.

39

Number 10

Downing Street was deserted save for the enormous tabby cat sitting on his haunches outside Number 10. The feline eyed Gabriel and Christopher malevolently as they approached the famous black door. It swung slowly open to reveal Geoffrey Sloane, the prime minister's chief of staff. No introductions were necessary. They were all three well acquainted.

"The PM is upstairs in the White Drawing Room," said Sloane. "I believe you know the way."

The understated quality of Number 10's entrance hall concealed what the eighteenth-century prime minister William Pitt described as "my vast, awkward house." In truth it was not one house but three—a redbrick mansion overlooking St. James's Park, a cottage, and a town house on Downing Street that supplied the residence its iconic address. Constructed on marshy soil, the dwelling was prone to sinking and, consequently, soon became a hazardous place in which to live. Floors buckled, staircases and chimneys sagged, woodwork turned to sawdust with dry rot. So weakened were Number 10's bearing walls that by the middle of the twentieth century admission to the upper floors was strictly limited for fear the house might collapse.

Two painstaking reconstructions—not to mention extensive repairs made after an IRA mortar attack in February 1991 that nearly killed Prime Minister John Major and his Cabinet—had stabilized Number 10. Still, successive British leaders had found it lacking, including Jonathan Lancaster, who had personally financed a complete renovation of Number 10's private living quarters during his first premiership. The Conservative Party had unexpectedly returned him to power after the scandal involving Home Secretary Hugh Graves and his wife, Lucinda—a scandal that Gabriel, with help from Christopher, had brought about. Much of the British public regarded Lancaster merely as a caretaker. Indeed, if the polls were correct, he would soon preside over the worst Tory electoral defeat in nearly a century.

Like many of his predecessors, Lancaster used the Cabinet Room as his office but conducted most informal meetings upstairs in one of Number 10's state drawing rooms. The White Drawing Room was the smallest and most intimate of the three. Gabriel and Christopher arrived to find Graham Seymour admiring the view of the Horse Guards Parade. The prime minister was standing at the sideboard, filling two tumblers with whisky. Spotting Christopher, he automatically filled a third. Then he looked at Gabriel and asked, "What about you?"

"It's a bit early in the day for me, Prime Minister."

"It's gone eight o'clock." Lancaster filled another glass and handed it over. "I think you'll find this to your liking. It's Macallan."

"What's the occasion?"

"Your long-overdue return to Downing Street."

"I'd rather drink to yours instead."

"Hardly what I had in mind at this late stage of my career," said Lancaster. "But then I have you to thank for that."

"The country needed you," said Gabriel. "You were the right man at the right time."

"A time of more emerging threats to Britain's security than I can count, none greater than the threat posed by Russia. But our cousins in America seem to think the Russians, after attempting to wipe Ukraine from the map, can somehow be rehabilitated and reintegrated into the global economy. Never mind that the only thing the Kremlin is interested in exporting these days is chaos."

"It appears," said Gabriel, "that they've found a business partner here in Britain."

"Edward Knight?"

Gabriel nodded.

"Can you prove it?"

"Not in a court of law, Prime Minister."

"And what about in a dark room somewhere?"

"I'd like my chances."

Graham Seymour spoke for the first time. "Edward Knight is a prominent British subject, Prime Minister. Which means there are no dark rooms in his future."

"Are there really no exceptions?" asked Lancaster mischievously.

"I'll pretend I didn't hear that."

"And what if Gabriel were to handle the dirty work for us?"

"We'd all go down together."

Lancaster sighed. "It's not as if the four of us have never done anything naughty before. Do you remember the time we duped the Russians into poisoning—"

"That was different," said Graham, cutting him off.

"So we play it by the book?"

Graham nodded. "But only if the case against Edward Knight is strong enough for us to proceed."

"And who makes that determination?"

"You do, Prime Minister."

Lancaster lowered himself into one of the room's white armchairs and looked at Gabriel. "Court is in session, Mr. Allon. You may proceed with your opening statement."

There was, for a start, Edward Knight's initial dalliance with the Russian oligarch Dmitri Savin during the depths of the real estate crisis in 2009. That much, said Gabriel, was beyond dispute. Knight was in desperate need of cash, and Savin willingly provided it. In all, the Russian businessman poured more than two billion pounds into the Knight Group, which allowed the company not only to weather the storm but also to significantly increase the size of its holdings. In return, Savin earned hundreds of millions of pounds in fees and interest payments.

"Can you prove it?" asked the prime minister.

"I can show you the documents."

"You will do no such thing," murmured Graham Seymour from his outpost at the window.

The nature of the relationship, Gabriel continued, deepened sometime in 2016, the same year Russia's intelligence services embarked on a sweeping and unprecedented attempt to influence the outcome of an American presidential election. Savin poured still more money into the Knight Group, and Edward Knight, for his part, dumped the fees and interest payments into a number of different anonymous offshore holding companies, including a Nassau-based shell corporation called Landmark Ventures.

"And who controls Landmark?" asked Lancaster.

"An undercover GRU officer based in the Russian Embassy in Mexico City."

"And how exactly were you able to determine that?"

"We hacked the bank in Nassau where Landmark does its business."

"That's the spirit." Lancaster went to the sideboard to freshen his drink. "But as of now I've heard nothing that sounds like clear and convincing proof that Edward Knight knew that he was in business with Russian intelligence."

"I'm sure he'll be able to clear up any lingering confusion."

"You would be wise not to underestimate him," said the prime minister. "He'll ring his lawyers the minute he gets a whiff of trouble."

"We're hoping it won't come to that."

"How do you intend to handle it? Appeal to his patriotism? His sense of decency?" Lancaster took a pull at his drink. "Anyone who was in business with the likes of Dmitri Savin after the Russian invasion of Ukraine has none."

"We have no choice but to make a deal with him. It's the only language he understands."

"And if he agrees to talk? What then?"

It was Graham Seymour who answered. "We use Edward Knight to help us roll up the GRU's illegal sabotage network."

"I rather like that," said Lancaster. "But what do we do about his wife?"

"At some point she's going to need a new identity."

"What about the money she embezzled from her husband?"

"Obviously," said Graham, "we cannot allow her to keep any of the proceeds of her little scheme."

"Perhaps we should place the money in an escrow account here in London," suggested Lancaster. "Given the many complexities of the case, I imagine it might be frozen for some time." He raised his glass to his lips. "Several years, in fact."

"We have reason to believe Revenue and Customs will want a substantial chunk of it."

"Are you suggesting that Edward Knight failed to pay sufficient taxes on his income?"

"Not even close," said Graham.

"Well, well," said Jonathan Lancaster. "This truly is a special occasion."

40

Hans Place

Where once Edward Knight was a fixture on the London social scene, he was now a prisoner of his redbrick mansion in Hans Place, a recluse, a hermit king. He ran the Knight Group by phone and email and avoided calls from old friends. It had been weeks since he set foot in Annabel's, his exclusive Berkeley Square club, and his gray-blond locks were now borderline Branson, for he hadn't summoned the nerve to show his face at Taylor Taylor. The tabloids, he thought, would crucify him.

Showered and dressed, he headed downstairs to the kitchen, where Liam Higgins, his sole remaining companion, was preparing his breakfast. The menu never varied. An egg-white omelet, a single slice of whole-grain toast, fresh fruit with nonfat yogurt. The morning papers were arrayed on the table. Knight started, as always, with *The Financial Times.*

Higgins placed a cappuccino at his elbow. "Good morning, Mr. Knight."

"We'll see about that."

"Any news, sir?"

"The pound is taking a beating." Knight looked up from the paper. "And no, Higgins, there's no news about Alice. Not real news, at least."

Higgins laid a plate in front of Knight. As he was tucking into his omelet, the doorbell tolled solemnly. "Who in the world could that be?"

"I'm sure it's only a reporter, Mr. Knight. I think I saw one or two milling about when I arrived this morning."

"In that case, don't answer it." The bell tolled a second time. "Oh, for heaven's sake."

"I'll get rid of them," said Higgins, and went out. He was gone only a few seconds. "It's not a reporter, Mr. Knight."

"Who is it?"

"An associate of Mr. Allon. Apparently it's urgent."

Knight shot to his feet and hastened down the corridor to the entrance hall. The man waiting there wore a dour gray suit and the benevolent smile of a country parson.

"Who the bloody hell are you?"

"I'm Whitcombe," replied the man. "Nigel Whitcombe."

"Where's Allon?"

"Here in London."

"He has news?"

"Important news."

"Why didn't he contact me himself?"

"You'll have to ask him that question." He gestured toward the car parked curbside. It was a Mini Cooper, neon blue in color. "Shall we, Mr. Knight? We really mustn't keep him waiting."

Knight followed the man out the door and squeezed into the car's cramped passenger seat. They rounded Hans Place in a blur and a moment later were racing westward along the Brompton Road. Knight maintained a tight grip on the armrest.

"Where are you taking me?" he asked.

"To see Mr. Allon, of course."

"Has he found her?"

The man blew through a red light without lifting his foot from the throttle. "Found who, Mr. Knight?"

Their destination turned out to be a cottage in St. Luke's Mews—Number 7, to be precise. Like the rest of the dwellings on the cobbled street it had once been a garage. The door was opened by the pretty Danish cyber specialist, the one with the nimble fingers of a card sharp. Her greeting was solicitous, compassionate, even. Her hand lingered soothingly on Knight's upper arm as she spoke—or was it the front of his sport jacket? He was so enchanted by the empathetic glow in her pale blue eyes that he couldn't say for certain.

She led him into a small, sparsely furnished sitting room and then disappeared from view. Gabriel was seated in a modular armchair, legs crossed, hands bunched reflectively beneath his chin. In the chair next to him sat a man wearing the formal charcoal-gray suit of a Whitehall mandarin. A third man—blond hair, deeply tanned skin, a notch in the center of his chin—was pacing the room as though awaiting the arrival of a long-delayed train.

On the coffee table was a stack of documents, including one bearing the corporate logo of Edward Knight's company. Craning his neck, he read the first few lines. It was dated October 22, 2009, and concerned a ten-figure investment in his company.

"Where the hell did you get that?" he demanded to know.

Gabriel indicated an unoccupied chair. "Sit down, Edward."

He did so, then looked at the man sitting to Gabriel's right. "Friend of yours?"

"You don't recognize him?"

"Should I?"

"Once upon a time you would have never known his name. But all that changed in 1992, when Sir Colin McColl decided to tell the British people what he really did for a living."

Knight's eyes narrowed. "Graham Seymour? Chief of the Secret Intelligence Service?" Receiving no answer, Knight looked down at the documents. "That would explain how you acquired the confidential records of my company."

"In point of fact," said Graham, "the Secret Intelligence Service had absolutely nothing to do with it."

"Who did?"

"Me," said Gabriel.

"Why?"

He appeared to give considerable thought to his answer. "Do you remember when I came to your office in Berkeley Square the morning after Alice's kidnappers made contact with you?"

"It is not a day I will ever forget, Allon."

"Nor will I," he replied. "In fact, I have a very distinct memory of asking whether you had any enemies who might have wanted to harm your wife. I also asked you for a list of your investors and a portfolio of your current holdings. You gave me both and assured me they were accurate, which was not the case. The Knight Group's property empire is far larger than you let on. And it turns out that you're beholden to a single private investor, a Kremlin-connected Russian oligarch named Dmitri Savin."

Knight chose to respond with incredulity, hardly a novel tactic. "Have you taken leave of your senses, Allon?"

"Not at all. In fact, to hear Dmitri tell it, you're simply the manager of a company that he controls."

"Dmitri Savin never invested a pound in the Knight Group."

With a heavy sigh, Gabriel picked up a stack of documents. "These are only some of the business records that Dmitri's wife gave to her team of divorce lawyers at Ambler & Rose." He pulled one of the documents from the stack and handed it to Knight. "It's rather unambiguous when it comes to who has ultimate control of the company that bears your name."

Knight examined the document, then tossed it onto the coffee table and rose to his feet. "This conversation is over."

"This conversation," said Graham evenly, "is only just beginning."

"You have no legal right to question me like this."

"You can deal with me, or you can deal with DCI Douglas Chapel of the Metropolitan Police. He'd like to have a word with you, under caution, of course, about your role in Alice's disappearance."

"I had no role!" Knight roared.

"DCI Chapel isn't so sure about that."

Knight reached into the front of his jacket and frowned.

"Something wrong?" asked Gabriel.

"I seem to have rushed out of the house without my phone."

"Who were you planning to call?"

"My lawyer."

"You'll only make your situation worse," said Graham.

"How much worse could it possibly get?"

"Based on the documents I've seen, a great deal worse. But if you want a lawyer, be my guest."

Knight looked at Gabriel. "May I borrow yours?"

"My phone?" He shook his head. "No, Edward."

Knight's gaze settled on Graham. "Surely you jest," said the SIS chief with a wintry smile.

Knight turned finally to the third man in the room, saw that no phone was in the offing, and sat down again. Gabriel was leafing through the documents, a look of consternation on his face. "There's something else you neglected to tell me," he said after a moment. Then, wordlessly, he tossed a file onto the coffee table. It was a copy of a report, filed by DI Timothy Peel of the Devon and Cornwall Police.

"Those records were supposed to have been destroyed," said Knight.

"A single copy somehow survived the purge. It makes clear that the investigating officer thought Alice was under the influence when she crashed her car into that tree. But that's not the reason you were so interested in making sure she was never interviewed by that detective, was it, Edward? You were far more concerned she might tell the police about the phone call she overhead that evening."

Knight was pale with rage. "There's only one other person in the world who knows about that, Allon."

"And who would that be?"

"My wife."

"Which means she must have told someone else about it. After all, no one has seen Alice since her abduction." Gabriel was silent for a moment. "Or perhaps she put it in writing and gave a copy to a lawyer friend in the event something untoward were to happen to her." He handed over one more document. It was a copy of a sworn affidavit—signed, dated, and notarized—made by one Alice Winter in the presence of Sophie Maxwell, solicitor at the law firm of Ambler & Rose. "I don't suppose you mentioned any of this to the Metropolitan Police, did you, Edward?"

He made no reply.

"I'm not a lawyer," said Gabriel. "But I've watched enough British detective dramas to know that DCI Chapel might conclude that you were attempting to obstruct his investigation."

"I didn't think it was relevant."

"We'll let Scotland Yard be the judge of that. And I imagine

Revenue and Customs, and the Financial Conduct Authority, will want to take a long, hard look at some of your offshore banking. It appears to us like a rather glaring example of tax evasion."

"It wasn't."

"How would you describe it?"

"It was a matter of life and death," said Edward Knight, and then he told them everything.

41

St. Luke's Mews

It might never have come to pass, Knight began, if he hadn't popped into Annabel's for a drink early one evening in May 2009 and found Dmitri Savin sitting alone at a corner table in the Elephant Room. Dmitri had bought his way into London's most exclusive club—as had Knight, for that matter—and rarely missed an opportunity to show his face there. Knight, having spent a thoroughly unpleasant day with his suddenly tightfisted bankers at HSBC, was in no mood for company and settled into a table of his own with a very large glass of whisky and that week's edition of *The Spectator*. He was lost in a lengthy article about a recent scandal involving MPs and their expenses when a shadow fell across his page. Lifting his eyes, he saw a smooth Russian face leering down at him. Then a hand appeared, smallish, white as bone, and the smooth Russian introduced himself.

"Asked if he could join me," said Knight. "Sat down before I had a chance to answer."

They exchanged the sort of small talk typical of the crowd at Annabel's before embarking on a prolonged discussion of the current financial crisis. Dmitri implied that, all things considered, the collapse of global markets had been good for his business. Knight engaged in no such pretense. Everyone in London knew that developers and real estate investors were taking a drubbing.

They ordered another round of drinks, and the discussion turned more pointed. Dmitri said he had several billion sitting on the sidelines and was eager to invest in real estate while prices were still at rock bottom. His personal portfolio included several luxury homes, including his mansion in Prince of Wales Terrace, but he wanted to expand into commercial and residential property.

"By investing in your company?" asked Gabriel.

Knight nodded. "Said he had a check for two hundred and fifty million in his pocket. Said the check had my name on it."

"How did you respond?"

"I said I didn't want his money. And what do you suppose Dmitri told me?"

"I imagine he told you that he knew you were on the verge of insolvency and were in desperate need of cash."

"Words to that effect," muttered Knight.

The two hundred and fifty million pounds, he continued, went some way to stabilizing the Knight Group, but as the financial crisis turned into the Great Recession, the company's finances grew steadily worse. Knight delivered this blunt assessment to Dmitri Savin, once again over drinks at Annabel's, and Savin responded by giving Knight a billion pounds. The money righted the ship but left the tiller in the hand of a ruthless Russian oligarch closely associated with the country's kleptocratic ruler. Knight knew enough about Russian business tactics to realize that the relationship was unlikely to end well, that one day his newfound partner would demand something in return. The debt came due in the autumn of 2015, when Dmitri Savin prevailed upon Knight to invest in a real estate holding company called Landmark Ventures.

"And the terms of the deal?" asked Gabriel.

"Landmark required a steady stream of capital, ten or twenty million a month. In return the company was willing to put up nothing in collateral. Nor did it provide any assurances that I would receive repayment or a share of future profits."

"Sweet deal."

"That's one way of putting it."

"And you, of course, turned Dmitri down flat."

"That option wasn't available to me."

"Because by then you were little more than Dmitri's pawn."

Knight was silent.

"I don't suppose you asked Dmitri what Landmark Ventures intended to do with the money?"

"Never."

"Why not?"

"Because a part of me didn't want to hear the answer."

"Surely you must have suspected that you were being used to launder money for a Russian intelligence network."

"I'm not an idiot, Allon." Knight lowered his voice. "Not a complete idiot, at least."

"In that case," said Graham Seymour, "why didn't you come to us?"

Knight seemed to find the suggestion laughable. "And how exactly does one come to the Secret Intelligence Service? Ring the bell at that fortress of yours at Vauxhall Cross? Ask to speak to someone in the Russia department?"

"There are rather more subtle ways for men in your position to make contact with us."

"And what would have happened if Dmitri found out that I was talking to you?" Knight answered his own question. "I would have ended up like that poor chap Litvinenko. I calculated it was better for my health and peace of mind to simply pretend that I was making legitimate investments in a legitimate company."

"Those investments," said Gabriel, "increased substantially after the Russian invasion of Ukraine."

"Fifty million a month."

"At Dmitri's request?"

"Who else?"

"But he was in Moscow by then, along with the rest of the pro-Kremlin oligarchs."

"The relationship continued as though nothing had changed."

"How did you communicate?"

"Encrypted text messages."

"And if you missed a payment?"

"If I was so much as a day late," replied Knight, "Dmitri would send a guided missile my way."

"Shortly before midnight on the twelfth of February, he rang you at Wickham House."

Knight nodded.

"What was the occasion?"

"I was nearly two weeks late with my monthly *investment* in Landmark Ventures."

"And you told Dmitri the check was in the mail?"

"I told him I wanted out."

"He reacted badly, I take it."

"That's one way of putting it."

"Which is why you agreed to keep the money flowing."

"What would you have done in my position?"

Gabriel ignored the question. "And what if you were to have another go at Dmitri?" he asked.

"What sort of *go*?"

"Divorce proceedings."

"On what grounds?"

"Irreconcilable differences, I imagine."

"And the settlement?"

"Not another penny."

"If I were to terminate the marriage," said Knight, "I imagine Dmitri and his friends in the Kremlin would do their very best to kill me."

Gabriel smiled. "We can only hope."

"What the hell are you playing at, Allon?"

Graham answered for him. "He's not playing at anything, Edward. What he's doing is offering you a chance at redemption. I would advise you to take it."

"All I want," said Knight, slumping in his chair, "is my wife."

"Sorry, Edward," said Gabriel. "But I'm afraid Alice is gone for good."

The room was less than half the size of her walk-in closet at Wickham House. There was space enough for a double bed and a laminated chest of drawers—bright white, of course—but not much else. It was, she thought, a glimpse into the drastically reduced circumstances of her future. Or perhaps not. Notting Hill cottages like this one were hideously expensive these days, thanks in no small part to the greed of real estate investors like her husband.

The sound of his voice was seeping through the floorboards. Poor Edward, it had not been a pleasant conversation. A part of her pitied him; his soiled laundry was now hanging on the line for all to see. She only hoped that he was wise enough to accept their offer. Edward had a stubborn streak, especially when he felt cornered. It was one of his least attractive qualities. But then again she could think of not a single one she admired. Not for the first time she wondered why she had married him. Because he was rich, she told herself coldly. She had to face the fact she was one of those girls.

The bed, while small, was moderately comfortable. She was seated on the left side, Edward's side, with her back against the headboard and her legs crossed at the ankle. Ingrid was next to her, identically posed. Edward's phone, its distinctive ringtone silenced, lay between them. At present it was pulsating with an incoming call. The screen read LIAM HIGGINS.

"Edward's personal assistant," explained Alice.

"We've met," replied Ingrid.

"Really? Where?"

"Your husband's office in Berkeley Square. It was the evening you issued your ransom demand."

Liam Higgins rang off without leaving a voicemail. Alice took a stab at unlocking the phone, then tossed it aside. "How did you learn to pick pockets like that?"

"I watched a couple of videos. It's really quite easy once you get the hang of it."

"Perhaps you could give me a pointer or two. I'm going to need a source of income when this is over."

"Don't worry, they'll take good care of you."

"The Secret Intelligence Service? They'll lock me away in that awful little cottage with Parish and Miss Coventry and throw away the key. And for my penance I'll spend the rest of my days wandering Dartmoor like Jane Eyre."

Downstairs, the conversation had grown suddenly heated. Edward was shouting at the top of his lungs, hurling insults, issuing threats, all in the manner of one clad in a cape and clutching a drawn sword. Then things quieted down again, and a businesslike conversation ensued. It sounded as though Graham Seymour was doing most of the talking.

"What's happening now?" she asked Ingrid.

"Final terms, I imagine."

"Edward is going to work for the Secret Intelligence Service?"

"Something like that."

"Are they going to tell him that I'm alive?"

"At some point, perhaps. But not today."

"I'd rather just . . ." Her voice trailed off.

"Disappear?"

"Yes."

Ingrid smiled sadly. "I know how you feel."

Part Three

Irreconcilable Differences

42

London–Cornwall

They quibbled over the code name—eventually the undertaking would be christened Sapphire—but on one point they were in complete agreement. For reasons of operational security, Liam Higgins, Edward Knight's faithful if officious personal assistant, had to go. It was Knight himself who did the deed, using as his justification the state of his finances, which had been depleted by the half-billion-dollar ransom he had paid to the phantom kidnappers of his wife. He nevertheless offered Higgins a generous severance package before showing him the door. The Sapphire team, which monitored the proceedings via concealed cameras and microphones, declared the operation's modest opening act a rousing success.

A replacement for Higgins arrived at Hans Place early that evening in the form of Nigel Whitcombe, aide-de-camp of none other than SIS chief Graham Seymour. Whitcombe, after settling into his rooms, immediately laid down a few ground rules. His role, he told his ersatz employer, was one of physical surveillance, not perpetual servitude. There would be no preparation of meals, no running of errands, no answering of bells—unless, of course, there was an operational necessity. Knight, incensed, fired off a written complaint to Christopher Keller, Sapphire's nominal leader, and Christopher, after giving the document no consideration whatsoever, dropped it into his burn bag.

For the most part, though, Knight accepted the yoke of SIS discipline without complaint, even when Nigel Whitcombe demanded the password for his mobile phone and computer—and when Whitcombe declared that, henceforth, he would be reading all incoming and outgoing emails and text messages, and monitoring all calls and videoconferences. For good measure, the digital snoops at GCHQ, Britain's signals intelligence service, did the same. Like Whitcombe, they saw nothing to suggest that SIS's reluctant recruit had violated the terms of his agreement with His Majesty's Government.

They were spelled out in a draconian document drafted in secret by an SIS lawyer and signed by Knight in a somber evening ceremony at Hans Place. It was Christopher Keller who supplied the handsome gold pen and the soothing words of encouragement. He then gave his new recruit the first of several private lessons in basic tradecraft, though later he would concede that Edward Knight required little training in the art of deception. He was a spy by nature, and a rather gifted one at that. Had he attended Oxford or Cambridge instead of the University of Leeds, he undoubtedly would have received a quiet tap on the shoulder from an SIS talent spotter.

His debut as a newly minted SIS asset would take place only seventy-two hours after his formal enlistment and was occasioned by the receipt of a much-anticipated encrypted text message from the Russian oligarch Dmitri Savin, the subject of which concerned the failure of the Knight Group Ltd. to make its monthly investment in Landmark Ventures of Nassau, the Bahamas. At Christopher's direction, Knight waited another forty-eight hours before informing his Russian business partner that no additional investments in Landmark would be forthcoming, though in point of fact it was Nigel

Whitcombe who composed the text and tapped the SEND icon. A laser-guided missile of a response arrived from Moscow a few minutes later, and Knight, after yet another lengthy delay, suggested they speak by telephone at Dmitri's convenience. The Russian oligarch said he was looking forward to it.

So too was the Sapphire team, the Financial Conduct Authority, the Serious Fraud Office, the National Crime Agency, and HM's Revenue and Customs, all of which were poring over the Knight Group's ledgers and bank records. A select interagency delegation was permitted to listen in on the call, which was initiated by Dmitri Savin at 6:20 P.M. London time, 9:20 P.M. in Moscow. Dmitri, who sounded as though he'd had a drink or two that evening, skipped the pleasantries and got straight to the point. But much to the Russian oligarch's dismay, Edward Knight stood his ground. His wife's kidnapping, he declared, reading from Christopher's carefully worded script, had laid waste to his personal finances. The well was dry.

"You'll regret this, Edward," came the reply from distant Moscow.

"Sorry, Dmitri. But I'm afraid it's over."

At which point the conversation descended into a replay of the one some six months earlier that had precipitated the unraveling of Edward Knight's marriage. Dmitri Savin made it clear that only he could end the relationship, that Knight had until the close of business on Friday to wire the money to Landmark Ventures, that failure to do so would prove fatal, in so many words. He didn't bother to issue a threat against the British tycoon's wife. As far as Dmitri Savin knew, Alice Winter was already dead and buried.

The delegation from British law enforcement was under the same mistaken impression, and after monitoring the tense phone call, they feared that Edward Knight might soon meet with the same fate. Therefore they would have been shocked to learn that their cunning counterparts from the Secret Intelligence Service wanted nothing more—not Knight's assassination, of course, but a serious attempt on his life, carried out by an operative of GRU Unit 29155. Such an outcome, after all, had been the point of the entire charade.

But how to arrange the circumstances whereby the Russians might try to make good on Dmitri Savin's threat? This aspect of Sapphire they left in the hands of their silent partner, the one who had brought them Edward Knight and his wife in the first place—the one with the matchless operational touch. He drew up a proposal and forwarded it to Graham Seymour and Christopher Keller at Vauxhall Cross. It would have to be something splashy, he told them, perhaps a touch over the top. The art world bash of the season.

Gabriel chose Olivia Watson, of all people, to set his gambit in motion. As instructed, she let it slip to Nicky Lovegrove over lunch at Franco's, and Nicky, perhaps hoping for a piece of the action, promptly told Simon Mendenhall of Christie's. Simon being Simon, he kept it under wraps for twenty-four hours while making repeated attempts to contact the collector in question—the real estate mogul Edward Knight, he of the long-missing spouse. Receiving no response, Simon mentioned it seemingly in passing to Julian Isherwood, from whom Knight had purchased several paintings in the past. Julian, as was often the case of late, professed complete and total ignorance. Sarah Bancroft, his beautiful American-born partner, was only marginally more forthcoming.

"Don't quote me on this," she murmured over her martini at Wiltons that evening, "but I hear Edward's going in a different direction."

"And which direction is that?" probed Simon.

Her eyes settled briefly on tweedy Jeremy Crabbe.

"Bonhams?" asked Simon, aghast.

Sarah smiled over her drink. "If you snooze, you lose, darling."

The talk soon spread from the insular art world of St. James's to the palaces of high finance in Mayfair and the City of London, until finally it reached the ears of Amelia March of *ARTnews*. She too made several attempts to contact Knight, but like Simon Mendenhall she received no response. She nibbled around the periphery, though—the periphery being Sarah's corner table at Wiltons—and twenty-four hours later she posted a lengthy story on the *ARTnews* website. Edward Knight, having no other recourse, or so it seemed to the uninitiated, issued a statement through the real estate investment firm that bore his name, confirming the story's accuracy.

Needless to say, Amelia's account made no mention of Knight's connections to the much-sanctioned Russian oligarch Dmitri Savin or the Secret Intelligence Service, only that after careful reflection he had decided to dispose of a portion of his collection of museum-quality Old Master paintings. There was intense speculation in the London art world, the story went on to say, that Knight had consigned the paintings to Bonhams, which quickly issued a press release of its own. The auction, it said, would be held in just ten days' time, not at the firm's New Bond Street salesroom but at Knight's grand manor house near the coast of Devon. The proceeds would be donated to organizations dedicated to combating violence against women in all its forms, with Bonhams receiving a fraction of its usual commission. Edward Knight, the statement read in conclusion, planned to attend.

A furious battle soon commenced on social media, and in the less high-minded press, as to Knight's motives. His legion of detractors, which now included the gadfly podcaster who had originally broken the story of his wife's disappearance, saw a rather transparent attempt to repair an irreparably damaged image. The opposing camp, led by friends and associates of the billionaire, was far more magnanimous. Losing Alice, they said, had left Knight a changed man—and for the better.

And yet none of those friends and associates, including his employees in Berkeley Square, had laid eyes on Edward Knight in ages. Indeed the first verified sighting occurred on the Wednesday afternoon of that week, when Knight was spotted at Taylor Taylor hair salon in Regent Street. His glamorous wife, missing and presumed dead, was at that same moment trudging across the windswept hills of Dartmoor, accompanied by two SIS minders. Knight dined that evening at his Hans Place mansion, she at Wormwood Cottage. Miss Coventry prepared a mixed green salad, lightly dressed with a lemon vinaigrette, followed by grilled haddock and a medley of steamed vegetables. Parish complained bitterly throughout the meal. Tomorrow evening, he declared while helping Miss Coventry with the dishes, they were having steak and kidney pie.

"With butter," he added. "The more butter the better."

There was a bit of grousing, but then that was to be expected. After all, the auction had been scheduled for the first week of August, a time when most of the London art world decamped to the south of France or Tuscany, and so flights had to be rebooked and hotel reservations revised. No one was more put out than Nicky Lovegrove, who had to delay his departure for New Zealand in order to attend. Niles Dunham happily threw away three nonrefundable nights at a villa he had rented in the Loire Valley. The last gathering at Edward Knight's Devon manor house had been the most fun he'd had in years.

The inconvenient timing of the auction notwithstanding, there was no shortage of those wishing to attend, if only to catch a glimpse of the billionaire whose wife had disappeared from the face of the earth. In the first twenty-four hours alone, some two hundred art world figures and assorted hangers-on requested admission to the event. Not surprisingly media interest was high. The BBC asked Bonhams whether it could send a camera crew, as did CNN's London bureau. Jeremy Crabbe put it to Edward Knight's personal assistant, a certain Nigel Whitcombe, and Whitcombe ran it past the Sapphire team. The request rattled around the upper floors of Vauxhall Cross for a day or two before receiving the stamp of approval. Television camera crews were welcome, the more the merrier.

In all, some sixteen paintings would go under the gavel, which would be wielded by Jeremy Crabbe himself. High-resolution photographs soon appeared on Bonhams's website, along with a detailed provenance for each work. Five days before the auction a select group of dealers, curators, and consultants were allowed to view the paintings at Wickham House. One work, however, was not yet on display, for it was still propped on a pair of easels in a studio in deepest West Cornwall.

Gabriel believed that the craft of restoration was a bit like making love, that it was best done slowly and with painstaking attention to detail, with occasional breaks for rest and refreshment. But in a pinch, if the craftsman and his subject matter were adequately acquainted, it could be done at extraordinary speed, with more or less the same result. The primary challenge of the Bellotto was its scale; at 136 by 242 centimeters it was the size of a barn door. Still, the losses were far from catastrophic. He repaired them swiftly, with his trademark invisible touch. Even Bellotto himself would have been hard-pressed to discern his original brushstrokes from Gabriel's inpainting.

He worked each day from dawn until dusk, isolated from those around him. Only Raphael dared to enter his studio. He lay on the floor at Gabriel's feet, with the tip of his Faber-Castell pencil scratching against an open Strathmore Series 300 sketchpad. Occasionally Gabriel looked down and was astonished by what he saw there. He had no doubt that his gifted son, should he choose to study art, would one day find fame and fortune as a painter.

The boy's incorrigible twin sister, her career path seemingly determined, spent those days contentedly in the company of Ingrid, whom she adored. They hiked the Coast Path, they sunned themselves on the sands of Sennen Beach, they attended a small but spirited protest in Penzance sponsored by the Climate Coalition. Radio Cornwall reported that there had been five arrests. Gabriel was relieved to learn his daughter had not been among those taken into custody.

He checked in with Christopher at least once a day using a secure phone provided to him by Vauxhall Cross, usually while standing before the easel in his studio, where for some mysterious reason the cell reception was the best. During one such call, he received an update on the latest news from Moscow, courtesy of GCHQ.

"Our friend Dmitri got picked up on a hot mic, as it were."

"The hot mic being his compromised mobile phone?"

"I'm not at liberty to say."

"To whom was Dmitri speaking?" asked Gabriel.

"The director of the GRU. Evidently they go way back."

"And?"

"The director is concerned that Edward Knight might spill the beans to British intelligence."

"The train has left the station on that one."

"Not as far as the Russians are concerned."

"Sounds to me as though Edward has a target on his back."

"Dead man walking," agreed Christopher.

Once upon a time the GRU's operatives and assassins moved in and out of the United Kingdom at will on ordinary Russian passports. But the war in Ukraine, with its accompanying sanctions and expulsions and travel bans, had made that impossible. A GRU officer attempting to enter Britain now would have no choice but to pose as a citizen of another country. More than one hundred thousand foreign visitors entered the UK each day—by air, by rail, and by passenger ferry. Christopher and the Sapphire team, with the help of their colleagues from MI5, scrutinized each new visitor, including the one hundred or so refugees who washed ashore each day in inflatable rafts. It was their abiding hope that one of the foreign visitors planned to attend an art auction in Devon and kill Edward Knight.

Gabriel's contribution to Sapphire seemed inconsequential by comparison; he had only to complete the restoration of a large Venetian canal scene by Bernardo Bellotto. He did so with only twenty-four hours to spare, and at four o'clock the following afternoon, after entrusting his children to the care of Cecily Newton of Sennen Cove, he set off for Devon, accompanied by Chiara and Ingrid. This time, he thought, he had no one to blame but himself.

43

Wickham House

For the second time that summer the art world in all its glory came rolling through the gate of Edward Knight's estate in Devon. The official guest list had some four hundred and fifty names, but an untold number simply showed up at Knight's door uninvited like revelers drawn to Gatsby's house in West Egg. Smiling young girls from Bonhams granted them admission regardless, the evening's host having decreed that no one was to be turned away. Once inside the grand entrance hall they ran a gauntlet of dark-suited private security types with earpieces and wrist mics and handheld magnetometers. Some of the attendees bristled at the intrusive searches, but most opened their bags and blazers without complaint. Edward Knight, they told themselves, had good reason to be concerned about security.

So dense was the throng that most of the attendees never caught so much as a glimpse of him. Fifteen minutes before the scheduled start of the auction he was circulating through the crowd outside on the terrace, casually but smartly attired, surrounded by no fewer than six bodyguards. "I'll get her back," he was overheard telling one well-wisher after ignoring the man's outstretched hand. "I know she's out there somewhere." No one had the courage to tell him that his faith was misplaced. "Poor Edward," said the heiress to a British supermarket fortune who, if the tabloids were to be believed, had once tried to murder her philandering husband with a butcher knife. "He doesn't seem to realize that dazzling Alice is never coming back."

But even the supermarket heiress, whose eye was keener than most, had no sense that something might be afoot. For a start, the bodyguards surrounding Edward Knight were not employees of a private security firm; they were in actual fact officers of Her Majesty's Secret Intelligence Service. The same was true of the two figures hovering vigilantly at the billionaire's side. One was a ruggedly handsome man with sun-bleached blond hair, the other a boyish-looking bloke with the aspect and manner of a vicar. Someone in the know said the younger of the two men, the one who looked as though he belonged in a pulpit, was Knight's new personal assistant. "Poor lamb," said the heiress. "I don't envy him."

In the far corner of the terrace was an oddball assembly of London art world figures, including the former fashion model who now ran a contemporary art gallery in King Street. She was whispering something into the ear of a reporter from *ARTnews*, who in turn was attempting to console the inconsolable chief auctioneer from Christie's. A petite Scandinavian woman in a Givenchy jacket was gently fending off the advances of a corpulent art dealer with pink cheeks, much to the bemusement of the general manager of the most prominent restoration company in Venice. Her husband, the world-renowned art conservator who had spoken at the last Wickham House gathering, was searching the crowd with those unusually green eyes of his, as though trying to locate an old friend. Sarah Bancroft, who was standing at his side, raised a martini glass to her lips and said, "A perfect night for an assassination, don't you think?"

"All we need now," replied Gabriel, "is our assassin."

"Any candidates?" asked Sarah.

He nodded toward a man who bore a striking resemblance to Russia's foreign minister.

"That's James Hargrave, you dolt. The shipping baron."

Gabriel indicated another prospective candidate.

"Roger Gordon," said Sarah. "Construction equipment."

"I suppose that leaves him," said Gabriel, and directed his gaze toward Christopher.

"Perhaps you should ring him."

Gabriel took out his secure SIS phone and dialed. Christopher, on the opposite side of the terrace, answered at once. "If you're wondering whether I've spotted the guest of honor," he said, "the answer is no. In my professional opinion it's a thoroughly British crowd. My colleagues are of a similar mind."

"I think we should wait a few more minutes before starting the auction. Our guests seem to be enjoying the champagne and canapés." Gabriel rang off and turned to Chiara. "Let's mingle, shall we?"

She glanced at Ingrid, who had yet to extract herself from the clutches of Oliver Dimbleby. "What about her?"

"She can look after herself."

"That's what I'm worried about." Chiara threaded her arm through Gabriel's and they set off across the broad terrace. "No sign of him?" she asked.

"Or her," replied Gabriel. He took two glasses of champagne from the tray of a waiter and handed one to Chiara. In the process he scrutinized a man who was eyeing her from the garden below.

"Well?" she asked.

"Just one of your many admirers." They carried their champagne through a pair of open French doors into a congested drawing room.

Gabriel's eyes moved left and right. "I can barely breathe in here. Let's see if the next room is a little less crowded."

It wasn't. Nor was there any sign of a Russian assassin. The supermarket heiress caught Gabriel's eye and summoned him with the wave of her jeweled left hand. In her right she held the remnants of a Beefeater and tonic.

"How lovely to see you again, Mr. Allon. What brings you to our little soirée?"

"You, of course."

She made a skeptical face. "Has anyone ever told you that you're a terrible liar?"

"Never," he answered truthfully.

She directed her gaze toward Edward Knight. "What do you think? Did he do it?"

"Murder his wife? Come now," said Gabriel.

"He's as guilty as the day is long. Everyone says so."

"As I recall, they said the same about you."

"It happened to be true." A chime sounded, signaling that the auction was about to begin. "Have you a favorite?" she asked.

"The Bellotto is quite fine."

"How much should I pay for it?"

"Twelve million. Not a pound more."

The chime sounded a second time, and the pretty girls from Bonhams began prodding the crowd toward the great hall, which had been transformed into a replica of the auction house's New Bond Street salesroom, complete with a rostrum, a video wall, cameras, and a bank of phones for remote bids. Edward Knight sat down in the first row, with Christopher on one side and Nigel Whitcombe on the other. Gabriel and Chiara settled into their reserved seats in the fourth row. Sarah and Ingrid joined them a moment later.

"You might have warned me," said Ingrid.

"About Oliver?" asked Gabriel. "He's really quite harmless."

"But I'm not," she replied, and handed over a gold Longines wristwatch. Gabriel in turn gave the timepiece to Chiara, who slipped it into her handbag.

"We can't take her anywhere," she said.

The first painting to go under the gavel was the luminous landscape by Claude Lorrain that for many years had hung in the exhibition room of Isherwood Fine Arts. Jeremy Crabbe, a mere art world bureaucrat, conducted the proceedings with a matador-like flair that impressed even Simon Mendenhall, universally regarded as the most dashing auctioneer in the business. Oliver Dimbleby put a toe in the water at three and a half million but appeared to develop a sudden case of paralysis in his right arm when a telephone bidder went to four. Nicky Lovegrove, bidding on behalf of one of his clients, pushed the price to four and a quarter but retreated to safer ground when the supermarket heiress tossed her hat into the ring. She went three rounds with the telephone bidder before throwing in the towel.

"The bid is now six point two with Clarissa on the telephone. Fair warning now. Last chance." Jeremy cast his eyes around the room, then brought down the gavel for the first time. "Sold to Clarissa's bidder for six point two million pounds, which represents a record price for Claude at auction."

It was, everyone agreed, a fine start to the evening.

The next painting was another landscape, this one by Rubens. As two Bonhams employees placed it upon the display pedestal, a dozen or so late arrivals, none of whom looked to Gabriel like a Russian assassin, took their seats in the makeshift salesroom. And ten minutes later, after Nicky Lovegrove bagged the Rubens for one of his clients, four additional attendees were granted admission. One was a bespectacled man with a full head of gray hair and a neatly trimmed gray beard. He was six feet tall at least, wore a three-piece bespoke suit, and walked with the aid of an ebony cane, which he held in his right hand. The seat into which he lowered himself with some difficulty gave him an unobstructed view of Edward Knight. He cast a glance around the room, then watched as the next painting, a portrait by Frans Hals, was placed on the display pedestal.

"What do you think?" asked Ingrid.

"It could go for as much as two and a half," replied Gabriel.

"I was talking about the chap who just arrived."

"I have a feeling he doesn't need that cane."

"Oldest trick in the book," she agreed.

Gabriel pointed out the man to Christopher via text message as Jeremy Crabbe opened the bidding for the Frans Hals. Christopher phoned Gabriel five minutes later, after the Hals had fetched two point seven in the room.

"He showed up without an invitation. The Bonhams girls, as instructed, welcomed him with open arms."

"Did they happen to get a name?"

"Walter Klein."

"Accent?"

"Maybe German."

"He had a good long look at your client after taking his seat."

"Trust me, it didn't go unnoticed."

"He's not carrying a gun, is he?"

"Only that walking stick."

"I'm not crazy about it."

"That makes two of us."

The fourth painting of the auction was now on the display pedestal. "An absolutely stunning portrait of Princess Mary by Sir Anthony van Dyck," purred Jeremy Crabbe. "Do I have one million?"

The first bidder signaled his intentions by holding aloft a handsome ebony cane.

"One million with the gentleman to my right. Do I have any interest at one and a quarter?"

He bowed out when the bidding shot past two million, then waged a valiant campaign for the Bronzino, only to step from the field of play late in the contest. After sitting out the Cavallino, he fought tooth and nail for a striking Roman tavern scene by Valentin de Boulogne, once again in a losing effort.

"Are you sensing a pattern?" asked Ingrid.

Gabriel nodded. "He's a bidder, not a buyer."

"I wonder why."

"Perhaps he came here for another reason."

The final lot of the auction was the Bellotto. During his introduction, Jeremy Crabbe made certain to mention the name of the conservator who had carried out the painting's recent restoration. The gray-haired man used his handsome ebony cane to cast three bids but once again capitulated as the contest grew heated and the price soared beyond expectations. In the end it went to the supermarket heiress for fourteen million pounds.

"I know, I know," she told Gabriel in the excited scrum that follows any auction, large or small. "But when I heard that you were the one who restored it, I couldn't let it slip through my fingers."

"I'm honored," he replied, one eye on the well-turned-out man with the ebony walking stick. He was having a word with Niles Dunham. Edward Knight, flanked by bodyguards, was granting a post-auction interview to the crew from CNN. Julian Isherwood, a hopeless romantic, was flirting with Clarissa the telephone girl.

"Who do you suppose he is?" asked the heiress.

"I'm sorry?"

"The one who made a vast show of bidding, only to get a case of cold feet at the altar."

"I haven't the foggiest."

"Whoever he is, he's definitely disreputable."

"Isn't everyone in the art world?"

"Everyone but you, Mr. Allon."

The CNN crew now had its lights and cameras trained on Olivia Watson. Clarissa the telephone girl was laughing at something Julian had said, and Simon Mendenhall was graciously congratulating Jeremy Crabbe on a job well done. Gabriel, after bidding the heiress a pleasant evening, rejoined Chiara and Ingrid. Together they watched the gray-haired man advancing laboriously across the room toward Edward Knight, each step an effort, or so it appeared.

"Spare me," said Ingrid.

"He could be disabled, you know."

"Have I ever been wrong about anything?"

Gabriel nodded toward Oliver Dimbleby, who was staring mystified at his left wrist. The gray-haired man was making slow but steady progress toward Edward Knight, who was accepting the condolences of the well-preserved countess from Kent.

"Do you remember the Georgi Markov case?" asked Gabriel.

"Can't say that I do," replied Ingrid.

It was Chiara who explained. "Markov was a dissident Bulgarian playwright who worked for the BBC in London. He was waiting for a bus near the Waterloo Bridge one morning when he felt a sharp sting in his right thigh. Four days later he was dead."

"Of what?"

"The sting," said Gabriel, "was a small pellet of ricin entering his leg. It was no larger than the head of a pin."

"How was it administered?"

"An umbrella."

They all three stared at the man with the ebony walking stick. "Perhaps Edward should take his leave now," suggested Chiara.

Gabriel shook his head. "We have to let the guest of honor sign his name first."

"At least warn Christopher."

It wasn't necessary; he had already unbuttoned his suit jacket, thus making it easier to access his concealed Heckler & Koch nine-millimeter pistol. The rest of the security detail was on high alert as well. Knight, smiling, was having a quiet word with fellow billionaire Roger Gordon, unaware of the approaching Russian assassin. He was shouldering his way through the crowd that had convened around Knight and his entourage. There was no sign of the previous leg ailment. He held the ebony walking stick not in his left hand but in his right.

"Seen enough?" asked Chiara.

"More than enough," replied Gabriel.

And so had Christopher. He raised his wrist to his lips, and the six-man SIS detail closed around Edward Knight and frog-marched him from the room, much to the astonishment of the knot of attendees gathered around him. It happened so quickly, so thoroughly, that one startled onlooker wondered aloud whether the billionaire had just met with the same fate as his wife.

Gradually the small crowd dispersed, leaving only Christopher and the Russian assassin behind. The two men eyed one another for a moment, cordially, it seemed. Then the Russian gave a small, stiff bow and joined the parade of attendees filing out of the room. His limp had returned, his ebony cane was once again in his left hand. It was, thought Gabriel, a fine end to the evening.

44

Devon–Lisbon

Sapphire's official record, which would never see the light of day, would state that the suspected Russian assassin departed Wickham House at 9:48 P.M. In point of fact it was closer to ten o'clock. By then his vehicle, a Mercedes sedan rented earlier that day at the Hertz outlet near Marble Arch in London, had been fitted with a limpet tracking device, courtesy of SIS's Tech-Ops branch. The car reached Bristol shortly after midnight. From there it headed north to Birmingham and Liverpool, then west to Holyhead, where it rolled into the belly of an early-morning ferry bound for Dublin. Vauxhall Cross arranged for two teams of watchers to make the voyage as well, each in a separate vehicle. The four officers followed their target upstairs to one of the cafés on the main passenger deck, a trek he made without the aid of his ebony walking stick.

Because he was not a citizen of the United Kingdom or Ireland, he had been required to display a valid passport during the boarding process. In his case it was a Spanish passport bearing the name Felix Serrano, the same passport he had produced the previous day at the Gare du Nord in Paris before boarding a Eurostar train bound for London's St. Pancras International. Exactly how he came by the passport in the first place was established with the help of Spanish intelligence officials in Madrid. It seemed a Felix Serrano from Venezuela had applied for one under a program that allowed those of Spanish descent to claim citizenship in their ancestral homeland. The desk officers at Vauxhall Cross didn't have the heart to tell their Spanish allies that they had undoubtedly bestowed citizenship on an illegal Russian intelligence operative, thus allowing him to roam the countries of the European Union, and much of the world, at will.

Officers on SIS's Russia operations desk, otherwise known as the Russia House, were doing some digging of their own. Namely they were attempting to determine the true identity of the holder of the Spanish and Venezuelan passports. Their task was made easier by the fact they now had his photograph. When a simple reverse-image search yielded nothing of interest, they scoured old yearbooks of known GRU training academies. They found someone who looked a good deal like "Felix Serrano" in a yearbook from the GRU's Military-Diplomatic Academy in Moscow—and in a photograph of several Spetsnaz GRU officers taken in war-ravaged Grozny during the so-called Second Chechnya War.

Next they ran the two photos through sophisticated facial recognition software, and the software declared conclusively that they were the same man. When they added a third photograph to the mix—the one in the passport granted by the government of Spain—the results were once again beyond dispute. Felix Serrano was in truth Captain Yuri Ivanov, forty-eight years of age, formerly of the GRU's elite 14th Brigade, now an illegal operative assigned to Unit 29155. It was the assumption of the Russia House that Ivanov was no ordinary secret foot soldier. He was, in their estimation, a very big fish indeed.

All this they determined before the ferry had reached Ireland. It did so a few minutes ahead of schedule, and at seven fifteen, having dropped his car at the Hertz outlet at Dublin Airport, Captain Yuri

Ivanov boarded an Aer Lingus flight in Terminal 2. Three hours and five minutes later, when the plane arrived at its destination, four officers from the local station were waiting. They followed Captain Ivanov to his door, then dispatched a message to the Sapphire team at Vauxhall Cross. The big fish had landed in Lisbon.

The street was a cobbled pedestrian lane in the quarter of Lisbon known as the Alfama. At one end a woman sat at a folding table for several hours each day, selling shots of Portuguese cherry liqueur to anyone who happened by. At the opposite end, where the street turned to a flight of steps, was a trellised court with a restaurant that catered mainly to a local clientele. Captain Yuri Ivanov of the GRU dined there often, for he lived in the building next door.

His apartment was on the second floor. It had a small balcony where he took his coffee in the morning and something a little stronger in the evening, when the heat of the day finally abated and the street came alive. He took careful note of all those who passed beneath him. Those who caught his eye he photographed, always while pretending to be reading something on his mobile phone.

On his application for a Spanish passport, Ivanov had listed his occupation as "businessman." In Lisbon, though, he conducted himself in the manner of a flaneur. He was an urban explorer of the highest order, a true connoisseur of the street, an observer of life and its many spectacles. He moved about the city on foot, never in a motorcar, and never with the aid of an ebony walking stick. He was particularly fond of Lisbon's coffeehouses—his favorite seemed to be Paleio Café on the Rua da Madalena—and of its bookstores, especially Ler Devagar, with its towering shelves. His lunches were long and leisurely and always included a pricey bottle of local wine. He never paid his bill with a credit card, only with cash.

For the better part of the next week he was observed during his daily excursions by a rotating cast of watchers from the Secret Intelligence Service. He impressed them with the quality of his tradecraft. He was, they wagered, of a higher caliber than the other GRU operatives they had followed. His wanderings were not wanderings at all but carefully choreographed maneuvers designed to expose surveillance. Never once, though, did they fall into the trap he set for them, for they were of a higher caliber too.

But he seemed entirely oblivious to the fact that the three occupants of the apartment on the opposite side of the street were photographing him as well. He was to be forgiven for this lapse, for they kept their shades and windows closed, even during the blast-furnace heat of the afternoon. The two male occupants of the apartment never set foot outside the building—one had a face that would not allow it, and the other had been nose-to-nose with Captain Ivanov at a recent art auction in Devon—but their female companion roamed Lisbon at will, always with a markedly different appearance, sometimes, even, a different gender. During one outing she requested permission to pluck the phone from the breast pocket of Ivanov's sport jacket. Her two associates, while sorely tempted, instructed her to take a pass.

They shared her desire, however, to have a closer look at Ivanov's Lisbon pied-à-terre, but their overlords at Vauxhall Cross expressly forbade it. In their opinion, the chances of breaking into the apartment without detection were slim. Better a proverbial bird in the hand, they reasoned, than no bird at all. Better to watch and wait than to risk losing the match with a costly own goal.

And so the Lisbon game, as they had taken to calling it, entered a second week. Captain Yuri Ivanov of the GRU passed the next three days as he had passed the previous seven, an urban nomad, a connoisseur of everything the enchanted city had to offer. On the fourth day of that week he took his late-morning coffee at Curva on the Rua Damasceno Monteiro. As was often the case at the popular café, a number of patrons were working remotely on laptops. One, an angular-cheeked woman in her mid-thirties, was leaving as Yuri Ivanov was looking for a place to sit. After laying claim to her now empty table, he deftly collected the scrap of paper the woman had adhered to the bottom of the chair. An SIS watcher who witnessed the move thought it the best piece of old-school tradecraft he had seen in some time.

The angular-cheeked woman, after leaving the popular coffeehouse, engaged in a few basic countersurveillance moves before taking a taxi to the airport. A watcher followed her into the terminal and snapped a photo of her checking in for a flight to Belgrade—Serbia being one of the few European countries where Russians were still welcome. As a consequence, SIS's Belgrade Station was staffed with a number of capable officers, two of whom tailed the woman from the airport to the St. Regis Hotel, where she was seen having drinks with a Russian businessman whom Vauxhall Cross had previously identified as an undercover GRU officer, thus putting to rest any lingering questions as to her real nationality and occupation.

The Lisbon game, it seemed, had borne its first fruit. They now had two birds in the hand, including an apparent courier for the GRU's network of illegals. But they had a problem as well, a newly unearthed piece of intelligence so alarming, so sensitive, it compelled Graham Seymour to forsake his lair in London and travel clandestinely to Portugal to have a quiet word with his Lisbon team, such as it was. There was no need for the operations desk to arrange a safe house. Graham had one in his back pocket.

45

Costa de Prata

The villa stood a mile from the sea near the medieval town of Óbidos, flanked on one side by a grove of olive trees and on the other by a coppice of cork oak. Graham Seymour had acquired it as he was nearing the end of a sometimes tumultuous career at MI5. His plan, to the extent he had one, was to paint dreadful watercolors while Helen attempted to poison him with her exotic cooking. But all that fell by the wayside when Prime Minister Jonathan Lancaster chose him to be the sixteenth director-general of the Secret Intelligence Service. He had now been in the post longer than anyone since Stuart Menzies, who had led SIS during World War II and the early years of the Cold War. There were some in Whitehall who thought Graham had overstayed his welcome, that it was time for him to go quietly into the night, but he was in no hurry to step from the stage. Indeed, at moments like these, he dared to think of himself as irreplaceable.

He had traveled from London to Lisbon on a discount commercial flight, with a false British passport in his pocket and two plainclothes Metropolitan Police protection officers at his side. They arrived at the villa in the glare of the early afternoon, in a rented Renault. The air inside the house was stale, unbreathed. Graham threw open the doors and windows, then went into the kitchen in search of something to serve his guests. There were a few tins of soup, a jar of tomato sauce, and a half-drunk bottle of single malt, but otherwise the cupboard was bare. He supposed the whisky would have to do.

He took down the bottle and three cut-glass tumblers and carried them into the great room. He scarcely recognized the furnishings—or the view of the mutinous garden and the blue swimming pool, its surface covered in fallen leaves. Indeed he had the strange sensation he had wandered into someone else's Portuguese retreat by mistake. The sound of a car crunching over the gravel drive dispelled that notion, as did the comforting sight of Christopher Keller and Gabriel Allon striding through the front door. They were accompanied by Harry Wilson, a sapling from Lisbon Station.

Christopher, seeing the expression on Graham's face, placed a hand on Wilson's shoulder. "Why don't you make yourself scarce so the grown-ups can have a word in private?"

Wilson joined the two Met protection officers in the forecourt, and Graham poured two glasses of the whisky, one for himself and the other for Christopher. Then he displayed the bottle to Gabriel and said, "I don't suppose I can interest you in a drop or two of this stuff."

"I'm observing dry January."

"It's August."

"Already?" Gabriel surveyed the unlived-in room around him. "I love what you've done with the place, Graham."

"I don't get here often."

"When was your last visit?"

"The summer before the Russian invasion of Ukraine."

"And what brings us here today?"

"The recent drone incidents at airports across Europe," said Graham. "It turns out they all have one important factor in common."

"And what's that?"

Graham took up his glass. "Captain Yuri Ivanov."

Helsinki was the most aggressive of the lot. Eight drones in all were involved, eight drones that relentlessly circled the airport for nearly two hours. Seven of the drones eventually departed Finnish airspace, but the eighth did not.

"It was lying in pieces near the end of the airport's main runway," explained Graham. "Apparently it got caught up in the wash of an inbound Lufthansa flight."

"If memory serves," said Gabriel, "the Finnish president said that none of the drones were recovered."

"That's because the Finnish president was lying through his teeth. Rather well, I might add. By the time he issued that statement, the wreckage of the drone was already in the hands of a team of technical analysts at the Finnish security service. And they came to a rather startling conclusion."

"Which was?"

"That it was no ordinary over-the-counter commercial drone."

"Military-grade?"

"Without question."

"Russian?"

"The drone's provenance," said Graham, "could not be established with any degree of certainty. It was an FPV drone with a high-resolution camera and satellite connectivity, which means it was probably operated by someone sitting at a computer terminal. What's more, it was powerful enough to carry a significant payload."

"A kamikaze drone?" asked Christopher.

"That was the conclusion of our friends in Finland. They believe the Kremlin was trying to send them a clear signal to mind their own business when it comes to Ukraine. They're also convinced the Russians used the incursion to probe Finnish air defenses. The Dutch reached the same conclusion after the incident in Amsterdam. But unlike the Finns, the Dutch actually tried to prove it."

"How?" asked Gabriel.

"As you no doubt recall, the Dutch intelligence service punches well above its weight. They were the ones who hacked the GRU when it was meddling in the 2016 American presidential election. They burrowed their way right into the room at GRU headquarters in downtown Moscow where the Russian hackers were working and recorded everything they were doing. It was a remarkable achievement."

"Am I to understand the Dutch have made a return visit?"

"They're inside GRU headquarters as we speak."

"Have they seen anything interesting?"

"A room with twelve stations for Russian drone operators, or so it would appear. They've also been reviewing CCTV video recorded in Amsterdam at the time of the attack. And you'll never guess who they found."

"Yuri Ivanov?"

Graham opened his attaché case and removed a large manila envelope. Inside were a dozen still images of the Russian intelligence officer. "The Finns have confirmed that he was in Helsinki too. It seems that wherever Yuri goes, the drones are sure to follow."

"Perhaps we should ask Yuri where he's planning to travel next."

"The Russia House believes he was given his marching orders at that coffee shop in Lisbon yesterday. That said, we are inclined to leave him in circulation for the time being. The same goes for another Russian illegal we've identified," added Graham. "She goes by the name Chloé Lamont."

"Where did you find her?"

"London," replied Graham. "Using CCTV and other surveillance tools, we reconstructed Yuri Ivanov's movements the day before the art auction. He bumped into her in Leicester Square. In case you're wondering, the real Chloé Lamont died in 2003 at the age of seven. But that didn't stop the Canadians from issuing this Chloé Lamont a passport when she applied for one."

"It can't be that bloody easy," groaned Christopher.

"It is," replied Gabriel knowingly.

"I'm afraid it gets worse," said Graham. "Ms. Lamont earned her undergraduate degree at McGill University in Montreal and is now pursuing a PhD at King's College London. Russian history, if you can believe that."

"Sounds like a future SIS officer to me."

"Evidently the thought has crossed our mind."

"Don't tell me . . ."

"Our talent spotter at King's thought rather highly of her and passed along her name to Personnel."

"I don't suppose you vetted her."

"Fortunately it never got that far. For the moment, at least, Chloé Lamont is MI5's problem. And Yuri Ivanov is ours." Graham checked the time, then rose to his feet. "Sorry to be leaving so soon, but my prime minister needs me."

"Bridge night at Number Ten?" asked Christopher.

"The Ukrainian president is coming to London for a meeting at Downing Street. The French, German, and Danish leaders are attending as well. If everything goes according to plan, they will announce a new multibillion-euro military and economic aid package for Ukraine. Needless to say, it's going to be one of the most important meetings at Number Ten in years."

"The Russians," said Christopher, "will go positively apeshit."

"So will the Americans, which is why we will make no announcement until the morning of the meeting." Graham finished the last of his drink, then took a final look around the room. "Helen did a lovely job with it, don't you think?"

"Perhaps the two of you should spend some time here," said Gabriel.

"I'll come back when the war is over or when they show me the door at Vauxhall Cross, whichever comes first."

Graham placed his empty glass on the coffee table and drew his mobile phone from the breast pocket of his blazer. A few seconds later Christopher did the same. The two men pondered their devices in silence for a moment, each wearing the same grave expression.

"Is there a problem?" asked Gabriel.

Christopher handed over his phone. On the screen was a message from Lisbon Station via Vauxhall Cross. It appeared as though Captain Yuri Ivanov was on the move again. And wherever Yuri went, thought Gabriel, the drones were sure to follow.

46

The Borgen

The Kingdom of Denmark, a nation of just six million inhabitants with a gross domestic product of $450 billion annually, was arguably the West's staunchest defender of Ukraine. In perhaps its most dramatic show of support, Denmark had provided the Ukrainians with nearly all of its available weaponry. It had also declared its intention to acquire long-range missiles capable of striking deep inside Russia, a move that raised tensions with the Kremlin to the boiling point. The drones appeared in Danish skies soon after. Copenhagen Airport was not the only target. Smaller airports around the country saw drone incursions as well, as did several Danish airbases and other military installations.

At the sharp end of Denmark's shadow war with Russia was Lars Mortensen, director-general of the PET, the country's small but capable security and intelligence service. Shortly before three o'clock that afternoon he learned, much to his alarm, that an illegal Russian intelligence operative linked to previous European drone incursions was headed his way. Even more troubling was the fact that this news had been delivered by none other than Gabriel Allon. Mortensen had worked with the legendary spy several times in the past, most recently on an operation in Moscow involving a Danish national named Ingrid Johansen.

"How is he traveling?" inquired the Danish spymaster.

"TAP Air Portugal."

"Name?"

"Felix Serrano."

"Portuguese passport?"

"Spanish, actually."

"Real name?"

"Yuri Ivanov."

"Affiliation?"

"GRU Unit 29155."

Mortensen swore softly.

"Sorry to be the bearer of bad news, Lars."

"I'm used to it by now. But why am I hearing it from you?"

"I'll explain everything when I get to town."

"Is there anything else you can tell me?"

"Don't even think about letting him out of your sight."

Much was left unsaid during that brief phone call, including the fact that it nearly didn't happen at all. The debate that preceded it was tense and unwieldy, for the participants were scattered from Vauxhall Cross to the Costa de Prata. There was one camp, led by a hard-liner in the Russia House, who condemned it as heresy. Yuri Ivanov, he insisted, had been bought and paid for by SIS, and therefore his very existence was not to be disclosed to another service, even one as friendly as Denmark's PET. There were others, though, who insisted they had an absolute duty to warn, regardless of the consequences. In the end it was a close-run thing, with the deciding vote cast by Graham Seymour. He wisely asked Gabriel to serve as his messenger. He and Mortensen were as close as two old spies could be.

Gabriel had placed the call from the back seat of an SIS car, with Christopher at his side and young Harry Wilson behind the wheel.

They stopped at the apartment in the Alfama long enough to collect Ingrid, then headed to Lisbon Airport. By the time they arrived, Yuri Ivanov was already airborne. They caught the 5:00 P.M. Scandinavian Air flight and were on the ground in Copenhagen by ten o'clock. A PET reception committee met them at the end of the jetway and placed them in an official sedan bound, they assumed, for PET headquarters in the northwestern suburb of Søborg. It delivered them instead to the Christiansborg Palace, the fortresslike government compound in central Copenhagen that Danes referred to colloquially as the Borgen. Lars Mortensen waited in the central courtyard.

"The prime minister," he informed Gabriel, "would like a word."

"In that case, Lars, you probably shouldn't keep her waiting."

Mortensen placed a hand on Gabriel's shoulder. "I'm not the one she wants to see."

Little about Kalla Eriksen's life and career had prepared her for the role in which she had been cast. A committed environmentalist and proponent of human rights, she had earned a master's degree in African studies from the University of Copenhagen and had worked briefly as a trade unionist before being elected to Parliament. A decade later she was the leader of the Social Democratic Party. During her first term as prime minister, her skillful management of the COVID-19 pandemic resulted in Denmark recording one of the world's lowest rates of illness and death. Her second term had been dominated by the war in Ukraine and the threat posed to Western Europe by Russia. To make matters worse, she was contending with an erstwhile ally in Washington that had declared its willingness to use military force to annex Greenland, the strategic Arctic island that had been a Danish territory for more than three centuries. Tiny Denmark was now caught in a vise between two global superpowers, an unenviable place to be.

Despite the late hour she was still at her desk. Dressed in a businesslike pantsuit, with her hair pulled into a careful chignon, she radiated seriousness and resolve. "Mr. Allon," she said, looking up from a stack of paperwork. "It's a pleasure to finally meet you." She came out from behind the desk and offered Gabriel her hand. "Lars has told me so much about you."

"I was afraid you were going to say that."

She smiled, then turned to Christopher. "And you must be Mr. Marlowe."

"Guilty as charged, Prime Minister."

"Secret Intelligence Service?"

"On my good days."

The prime minister greeted Ingrid quietly in Danish, then led them to the seating area and poured five cups of coffee. Lars Mortensen removed a photograph from his attaché case and handed it to Gabriel. It was Captain Yuri Ivanov, emerging through the doorway of Gate 19 at Copenhagen Airport.

"Is that your man?"

"One version of him," replied Gabriel.

Mortensen handed over another photograph—Captain Yuri Ivanov gliding through passport control. "We ran the name Felix Serrano through our immigration records. He was definitely in the country during the first wave of drone incursions. He arrived two days before they began and left the morning after the last one."

"Where is he now?"

"He picked up a Škoda hatchback at the airport and went straight to his hotel. He's staying at the Scandic Palace on the Rådhuspladsen.

But if the prime minister has her way," added Mortensen, "he won't be there long."

Gabriel turned to Kalla Eriksen. "Don't do it, Prime Minister."

"Whyever not?" she asked.

"Because you would be making a dreadful mistake."

"It wouldn't be my first, I assure you."

"We have that in common, you and I."

"But I'm the prime minister of Denmark, Mr. Allon. Which means that I'm responsible for the security of my citizens. Some of my countrymen have taken issue with the fact that I didn't order our armed forces to shoot down the drones that entered our airspace last autumn. I won't make that mistake again. Nor will I allow Captain Yuri Ivanov to slip through my fingers."

"Arresting him tonight won't make Denmark any safer."

"But it *will* prevent the Russians from launching those drones."

"Possibly," Gabriel conceded. "But it will also rob you of an invaluable opportunity to gather intelligence that might help you defend Denmark in a future conflict. They're probing you, and you have to probe them in return."

"The future is already here, Mr. Allon." With a glance at Ingrid she added, "I shouldn't think I need to explain that to you."

"You don't, Prime Minister."

"What exactly are you suggesting?"

"We watch and wait."

"Sit on our hands and do nothing?"

"I don't believe I said that."

She gave him a stern look over her cup. "Go on, Mr. Allon."

"Lars and his officers will watch Yuri Ivanov's every move. In the meantime you will place your air defenses on a heightened state of alert."

"And when the drones come?"

"You will have undeniable proof of Russian involvement."

"The Kremlin will deny it, which is what they always do."

"They won't be able to if one of their GRU officers is sitting in a Danish jail cell."

The image clearly appealed to her. She exchanged a look with her intelligence chief, then said, "Lars and I need to have a word in private."

Gabriel followed Christopher and Ingrid into the prime minister's anteroom. From inside the office there soon came the sound of a heated debate. "Poor Lars," said Ingrid. "I don't envy him." She looked at Gabriel and added, "Or you, for that matter."

"She wasn't impressed by my plan?"

"That's putting it mildly."

"Perhaps I should go back in there."

"I wouldn't advise it."

The argument grew increasingly contentious, though now it was Lars Mortensen who was on the offensive.

"The tide has definitely turned," said Ingrid.

"Not for long," murmured Christopher as the prime minister issued a sharp retort. "She has a touch of Mrs. Thatcher, doesn't she?"

"More than a touch," replied Gabriel. "She terrifies me."

Suddenly there was a silence from within the office, followed by a temperate final exchange.

"It appears," said Ingrid, "we have a resolution."

"Which way?"

The door swung open before she could answer and Lars Mortensen, his face red with exertion, stepped into the anteroom. "We have forty-eight hours. And God help us if anything goes wrong."

47

Rådhuspladsen

It fell to Christopher to hammer out the operational accord. Gabriel, who represented no service, and therefore had no official standing, was relegated largely to observer status, though occasionally he offered a few sage words of advice that brought the negotiations back from the brink. On one point, though, Lars Mortensen was unyielding—the surveillance of Captain Yuri Ivanov would last forty-eight hours and not a minute more. Christopher and Gabriel would be kept fully abreast of Ivanov's movements and were welcome in the PET's op center, day or night, but under no circumstances were they to operate themselves. This, added Mortensen, was strictly forbidden.

"That's never stopped us before," said Christopher.

"I realize that."

"And when the clock expires?"

"Ivanov will be arrested."

"He belongs to us."

"Not anymore he doesn't."

"And what happens if he attempts to leave Denmark before the end of regulation play?"

"You should assume," said Lars Mortensen, "that Captain Yuri Ivanov is never leaving Denmark."

Unlike the British, the Danes didn't bother with a code name. They merely went about their business calmly and quietly, in a very Danish sort of way. The first item on their to-do list was the installation of cameras and listening devices in Ivanov's room at the Scandic Palace. Two PET tech officers saw to it the following morning while Ivanov was downstairs partaking of the complimentary buffet breakfast, and all of the devices were transmitting normally when the Russian returned to his room at eight fifteen. He watched a Spanish-language newscast until nine o'clock. Then, after conducting two brief calls in Spanish on his mobile phone, he left the room a second time.

Outside, he reprised the role of the sophisticated urban explorer, this time for the surveillance artists of the PET. For the next three hours he led them on a merry chase from one end of Copenhagen to the other. Once again coffeehouses and bookstores were his preferred oases. He made and received several phone calls during his wanderings, but he met with no one, and the watchers saw nothing that looked like a brush pass or impersonal communication.

After a traditional Danish lunch at an outdoor café in Nyhavn, he returned to the Scandic Palace long enough to collect his rented Škoda, which by then had been fitted with a tracking device. He drove through the streets of central Copenhagen for the better part of an hour before heading to the southeastern suburb of Kastrup, where he ate a second lunch, this time at a small café adjacent to Copenhagen Airport. Leaving the café, he set off along the airport perimeter road, stopping now and again to snap a few photographs. The PET watchers managed to snap a few photos of him as well, and the airport's CCTV cameras recorded nearly a half hour of video. He was, in the lexicon of the intelligence game, blown to high heaven.

At seven that evening he was back in his hotel room, and Gabriel,

Christopher, and Ingrid, having been summoned by Prime Minister Kalla Eriksen, were once again inside the Borgen. Also present was Denmark's foreign minister, interior minister, and minister of defense. The mood in the room was tense. It was the assumption of everyone present, including Gabriel, that an incursion of Russian drones into Danish airspace was imminent. The prime minister again suggested taking Yuri Ivanov into custody. Though it took some doing, Lars Mortensen managed to talk her out of it.

By midnight it seemed apparent that tonight would not be the night, so the prime minister went home to her family, and Gabriel, Christopher, and Ingrid headed to the Hotel Sanders. Ingrid and Christopher made straight for the bar, and Gabriel, against all better judgment, joined them for a nightcap. While partaking of his usual Johnnie Walker Black Label, Christopher scrolled through the headlines on his phone.

"Bloody hell," he said suddenly.

"What is it now?" asked Gabriel.

"Have a look at *The New York Times.*"

Gabriel awakened his phone and opened the *Times* app. The lead story had been written by Peter Baker, the paper's chief White House correspondent. The headline read UKRAINE'S PRESIDENT, OTHER EUROPEAN LEADERS TO MEET AT DOWNING STREET SUMMIT.

"Exactly what we needed," said Gabriel.

"When it rains, it pours," added Christopher.

"Where do you suppose the leak came from?"

"I'm not an expert when it comes to the inner workings of Washington, but it looks to me as though it came from someone at the White House."

"Why do you suppose they would have done a thing like that?"

"Spite, I imagine. Whatever their motive, you can be sure Downing

Street is livid. After all, they were counting on the element of surprise to help secure the summit."

"So much for the special relationship," said Gabriel.

"There's no such thing. Not anymore, at least. Vauxhall Cross is withholding intelligence from our friends at Langley on a broad range of issues, including Russia. You can be sure the Americans know nothing about Yuri Ivanov."

"They will the minute the Danes put the cuffs on him."

Christopher glanced at his wristwatch. "By my calculation we have exactly twenty-four hours before his arrest. At which point the curtain will fall on Operation Sapphire."

"It was fun while it lasted."

"I'll say," said Christopher, and ordered another drink.

Captain Yuri Ivanov began his last day of freedom with a leisurely breakfast at the Scandic Palace. Then he set off on another walking tour of Copenhagen, tailed by no fewer than eight PET officers on foot and a dozen more in unmarked vehicles.

This time his wanderings took him farther afield to Assistens Cemetery, burial place of Denmark's most notable citizens, including the writer Hans Christian Andersen and the philosopher and theologian Søren Kierkegaard. While Ivanov was standing before the grave of the nineteenth-century Danish painter Christen Købke, a woman of perhaps forty went to his side and their hands briefly touched. Four members of the surveillance team, after witnessing what appeared to be a rather sloppy brush contact, gave up the chase of the primary target and followed the woman instead. She led them from the cemetery straight to the Russian Embassy.

At which point Prime Minister Kalla Eriksen and her senior ministers reconvened in emergency session, this time with no outside observers present. Christopher went to the British Embassy to have a secure word with Vauxhall Cross, but Gabriel hid out at the Sanders with Ingrid. By midafternoon they were both stir-crazy, so they slipped out of the hotel and wandered over to the Strøget, Copenhagen's pedestrian shopping street. Ingrid held Gabriel's arm as they walked.

"Are you afraid you're going to have a relapse?" he asked.

"Office doctrine, Mr. Allon. Remember?"

"A fancy hotel and a pretty girl?"

"Exactly. Besides, the Strøget is my home turf." She pointed to a CCTV camera. "And you can be sure our friends at PET headquarters are watching our every move."

Gabriel's phone rang suddenly.

"See what I mean," said Ingrid.

He drew the phone from his pocket and checked the caller ID. There was no name, but he recognized the number. It was the op center at PET headquarters.

He tapped ACCEPT and lifted the phone to his ear. "Drones?" he asked.

"No, Mr. Allon," said the voice at the other end of the connection. "But you and Ingrid need to get off the street immediately. Your friend from the GRU is headed straight for you."

Gabriel killed the connection, then explained the situation to Ingrid. She pointed toward a busy café and said, "Let's have a coffee, shall we?"

They went inside and were seated at a table against the window. Ingrid placed their order at once and then peered into the busy pedestrian street. Two minutes went by with no sign of Yuri Ivanov.

"I wonder what's keeping him."

"He must be doing a bit of shoplifting."

"I got my Givenchy blazer just up the street."

Gabriel shook his head with dismay. "Perhaps we should enjoy a moment or two of silence."

"An uncomfortable silence, you mean? Yes, let's." The waiter delivered their coffees. Ingrid added artificial sweetener to hers and resumed her contemplation of the street. "Oh, for heaven's sake. Go see what he's doing."

"So much for the uncomfortable silence."

"Pretend to walk out on me."

"With pleasure."

Gabriel tossed a banknote onto the table and went into the street. A crowd of about twenty people had gathered in a circle outside a nearby H&M boutique. He walked over at an unhurried pace, only to discover a man lying unconscious on the paving stones. A young woman was compressing the man's chest in a desperate attempt to restart his heart. As she lowered her mouth toward his, Gabriel forced his way through the crowd and pulled the woman away. "Don't!" he shouted. "Whatever you do, don't touch him."

48

Strøget

It was the appearance of the hazmat team of the Danish National Police that alerted the media to the incident on the Strøget. Clad in their lime-green protective suits, the specialists initially cordoned off only the area outside the popular H&M boutique. But just thirty minutes later, with no explanation to the public, they sealed the kilometer-long pedestrian street from end to end and ordered all the shops and restaurants to immediately discharge their customers and shutter their doors.

When at last the police issued a statement, it shed little light on the matter. A man they described only as "a Spanish national" had suffered a medical emergency while walking along the Strøget shortly after four in the afternoon. He had expired at Copenhagen University Hospital at 6:26 P.M. A second person, a woman who had attempted to resuscitate the victim, was receiving treatment at the same hospital, for what reason the police did not say. In the statement's only glaring falsehood, she was characterized as a Good Samaritan who had merely happened upon the scene. In truth she was a surveillance specialist from the Danish security and intelligence service who had been walking behind the victim when he collapsed.

The statement made no mention of a man, described by numerous witnesses, who had prevented the woman from rendering further aid to the victim, and by some miracle there was no cell phone video to confirm the witnesses' accounts. He too was taken to Copenhagen University Hospital, but only for observation, as he was experiencing no symptoms of illness. He finally signed himself out at 7:00 P.M. and, accompanied by an attractive Danish woman in her late thirties, traveled by motorcar to PET headquarters in Søborg. Lars Mortensen met them in the lobby.

"The two of you picked a fine time to go for a stroll along the Strøget."

"You're lucky we did," replied Gabriel. "Otherwise there would be more than one other person fighting for her life tonight."

"Her respiratory system is shutting down. They're not at all sure she's going to make it."

"She'd already be dead if she had tried to give Ivanov mouth-to-mouth."

"How did you know to stop her?"

"It was obvious to me that Ivanov had been poisoned with a nerve agent."

"We think it's Novichok."

"The likely candidate. The question is," said Gabriel, "where was it administered? And by whom?"

"Not by *whom*," replied Mortensen. "By *what*."

They headed down to the op center and found Christopher sitting in a chair in the back row. "Fancy meeting you here," he said to Gabriel. "You saved a lot of lives this afternoon."

"With one exception."

"Wait until you see this."

Lars Mortensen was still on his feet. "Let's start at the end, shall we?"

One of the techs punched a key on his computer, and a CCTV image appeared on the screen—Captain Yuri Ivanov lying on the paving stones of the Strøget, surrounded by a circle of some twenty people. A woman was kneeling beside him, hands on his chest, fingers interlaced.

The tech set the scene in motion, and a few seconds later Gabriel entered the image from the left side of the screen. His attempt to save the life of the surveillance specialist bordered on assault and battery. The onlookers were clearly startled by what they were witnessing.

"That video," said Gabriel, "must never see the light of day."

"Don't worry," replied Mortensen. "It won't. But here's what happened before you arrived."

The tech punched another key. The shot that appeared on the screen was from the same camera, but the time stamp was ninety seconds earlier. Yuri Ivanov entered the image from the right. His step was heavy, and he appeared disoriented. Then his legs buckled and he crashed to the pavement as though he had fallen from a third-floor window. The PET surveillance officer was there in less than ten seconds. The crowd gathered quicky around her.

"Her name is Freda Hansen," said Mortensen. "One of our best officers. She noticed something was wrong about a minute before he collapsed. Little did she know that she was standing not ten meters away from Ivanov when he was poisoned."

The tech switched to a new CCTV camera. Yuri Ivanov was standing outside the entrance of the redbrick Church of the Holy Spirit, one of the Strøget's most well-known landmarks. It was 4:00 P.M. exactly. In less than two minutes Ivanov would be lying unconscious in the street.

"Watch carefully," said Mortensen.

A few seconds into the video, at 16:00:13, Yuri Ivanov glanced at his phone. Then, nine seconds later, he waved a hand in front of his face, as though he were brushing away a cobweb.

"Did you see it?" asked Mortensen.

"No," admitted Gabriel.

"That's not surprising. Neither did he."

The tech rewound the video to the spot where Ivanov was checking his phone, then enlarged the image.

"Now do you see it?" asked Mortensen.

Gabriel rose and walked to the front of the room to have a closer look at the screen. It took him a moment to spot it, a misty smudge of something hovering near Ivanov's right ear.

"It's a mosquito drone," said Mortensen. "Probably no bigger than two or three centimeters. It sprayed the nerve agent in his face, then fled the scene of the crime."

The tech once again set the scene in motion. Yuri Ivanov, after casting another glance toward his phone, turned away from the door of the church and started across its small brick courtyard. Within a few seconds his step was noticeably slower. Then he turned to the left and set off in the direction of the H&M boutique. Freda Hansen and a male colleague followed after him, oblivious to the fact he was already dying.

"That's quite enough," said Mortensen. "We know what happens next. You just witnessed the first documented assassination carried out by a miniature drone. No political leader or opposition figure will ever be safe again. Welcome to a world gone mad."

The tech froze the image, and a heavy silence fell over the room. Gabriel was the first to speak. "It looked as though Ivanov was planning to meet someone at that church."

"He was," replied Mortensen. "At least he thought he was. He was sent there to die."

"By whom?"

"You tell me."

"The woman from the cemetery?"

Mortensen nodded. "Ivanov was still carrying the message she handed to him. Guess what it said."

"The Church of the Holy Spirit. Four o'clock."

"Words to that effect."

"But why would his own service want to kill him?"

"I was hoping you might be able to tell me."

"They generally reserve that sort of punishment for those they regard as traitors."

"The GRU thought that Ivanov was working for us?"

"Perhaps," said Gabriel. "But the more likely explanation is that they thought you were about to take him into custody. Either way, he had to go. Their weapon of choice was a drone the size of an insect. It was a perfect hit. With the exception of his phone, of course," said Gabriel. "He was carrying it when he collapsed. A real Russian assassin would never have left it behind."

"We're trying to unlock it as we speak."

"If you need any assistance—"

"We can handle it." Mortensen looked at Christopher. "And don't worry, the PET will forward a copy of the contents to your service."

"Much obliged, Lars. But in the meantime, Downing Street is wondering whether your prime minister is still planning to attend tomorrow's summit in London."

"Why wouldn't she?"

"The Russians just used a weapon of mass destruction in the middle of Copenhagen."

"All the more reason she'll be there. She will, however, address the Danish people at nine o'clock this evening from the Borgen."

"What is she planning to say?"

"Knowing the prime minister, she won't mince words. But she agreed to let me review the speech before she delivers it." Mortensen turned to Gabriel. "She'd like you to read it as well."

"I'm honored. But do you really think it's a good idea for me to be around her?"

"In case you haven't noticed," said Mortensen, "our prime minister doesn't frighten easily."

They listened to the breaking news coverage on Danish radio during the twenty-minute drive to the Borgen. The closure of Denmark's most famous shopping street had left the country decidedly on edge. Already there were accusations of a cover-up from the far right, and social media was awash with conspiracy theories, several of which were undoubtedly concocted at GRU headquarters in Moscow. Even with a reckless assassination of one of its own, Unit 29155 had somehow managed to sow discord and division in the West.

It was approaching half past eight when they were shown into the prime minister's office. Her closest aides were gathered around her desk, reviewing the final draft of the speech she was scheduled to deliver in just thirty minutes' time. Mortensen acquired a copy for Gabriel. It was in Danish, of course, but Ingrid provided a quick translation. The wording was unambiguous. "Russia is now at war with us," Prime Minister Kalla Eriksen would soon tell the people of Denmark. "It's a so-called hybrid war, but it's a war all the same. We have no choice but to defend ourselves."

Ten minutes before airtime she chased her aides from her office and, taking a compact from her handbag, quickly freshened her makeup. She directed a glance toward Gabriel while applying a new coat of lipstick. "Well, Mr. Allon?"

"It's rather detailed where Captain Ivanov is concerned."

"Have I betrayed any sources or methods?"

"Not quite."

"What does that mean?"

"The British have identified another Russian officer currently living in London. The minute you say Yuri Ivanov's name and occupation, she will know that she is in danger."

"Are the British watching her?"

"She's under round-the-clock surveillance."

"In that case, I will deliver the speech as written." The prime minister closed the compact with a snap. "How long are you planning to remain in Denmark?"

"We're returning to London in the morning."

"What a coincidence," said the prime minister. "I'm going there myself. You're welcome to fly to London with me, if you like."

"I wouldn't want to impose."

"If it were an imposition, Mr. Allon, I wouldn't have extended the offer." She rose to her feet. "We board at eight o'clock sharp. Don't be late."

49

Copenhagen–London

The speech was twelve minutes in duration but meteoric in its impact. Russia's military intelligence service, said the Danish prime minister, had conducted a reckless and barbaric assassination on Copenhagen's busiest shopping street using a miniature drone armed with the world's most lethal nerve agent. She identified the victim as Captain Yuri Ivanov of GRU Unit 29155, the same unit that had carried out numerous acts of sabotage and disruption in an attempt to destabilize and undermine the democracies of Western Europe. Any further action by Russia on Danish soil, the prime minister warned, would be met with a swift and forceful response. No options, she added ominously, would be off the table.

The Russian retort, delivered by the mendacious Kremlin spokesman Yevgeny Nazarov, appeared only minutes after the Danish premier had concluded her remarks, which led some in the press to speculate that his statement had been prepared in advance. It was a masterclass of mockery and misdirection, a truly bravura performance. As Yevgeny Nazarov saw it, it was the West that was trying to undermine Russia, not the other way around. GRU Unit 29155, he claimed, was nothing more than a clumsy piece of Western propaganda. If anyone was to blame for what had taken place in

Copenhagen, it was the Ukrainians. Or perhaps, he suggested, the Danish intelligence service had carried out the assassination to create a pretext to attack Russia.

But the most powerful rhetorical question in the Kremlin's arsenal was the question of why. Why would Russia's military intelligence service assassinate one of its own? The rented television experts had no good answer, and neither, admittedly, did Gabriel. He met Christopher and Ingrid downstairs in the lobby of the Hotel Sanders shortly after seven the following morning, and they crawled into a PET sedan for the drive to Copenhagen Airport. The prime minister's plane waited on the apron, surrounded by a formidable ring of protection officers. Lars Mortensen stood at the foot of the airstair.

He handed Christopher an external hard drive. "A little reading material for the flight to London."

"The contents of Yuri Ivanov's phone?"

"As promised," said Mortensen.

Ingrid led the way up the airstair, and they settled into their assigned seats. The prime minister boarded a few minutes before eight, along with a half-dozen aides. She looked at Gabriel and gave him a warm smile.

"Good morning, Mr. Allon. Sleep well?"

"Not a wink, Prime Minister. You?"

"Never better."

The cabin steward closed the forward door, and the engines whined. Christopher peered warily out his window. "It occurs to me," he said, "that now would be the perfect time for the Russians to shut down this airport with a swarm of drones. Or better yet, they might disable the plane's navigation system."

Gabriel frowned. "Why do you think I couldn't sleep last night?"

Only Ingrid had brought along a laptop. She waited until the plane was airborne before attaching the external hard drive and opening a folder labeled PET 9055-8337. Inside were several additional folders. Emails and text messages, browsing history, location data, telephone metadata, photographs. It was the lifeblood of an illegal Russian intelligence officer, his very operational soul. And it was theirs to explore at their leisure, all because the GRU had sent a miniature drone to kill Yuri Ivanov instead of a man with a gun.

Ingrid copied the contents of the phone onto a second external hard drive, then said, "Where would you like to start?"

"The emails," replied Gabriel.

There were some twenty-five thousand in all. The majority were of the encrypted variety, sent from a numeric Proton Mail address, but the rest were from an ordinary Gmail account bearing the name Felix Serrano. They appeared innocuous in nature, but when viewed through the proper prism, and with the benefit of hindsight, they bore the hallmarks of en clair communication between an undercover asset and his service. One of the incoming emails concerned an auction at the Devon estate of the British real estate baron Edward Knight. Attached was an article from *ARTnews* magazine, written by Amelia March.

They had only scratched the surface by the time the plane landed at RAF Northolt. The prime minister and her aides filed off first and boarded their motorcade for a high-speed ride to Downing Street. Her three unlikely traveling companions made the trip into central London in a neon-blue Mini Cooper piloted by Nigel Whitcombe.

"Shouldn't you be babysitting Edward Knight?" asked Christopher.

"I needed the morning off, and Mr. Knight was most accommodating."

"How is he holding up?"

"Better than I am," replied Whitcombe, and lowered his window to vent the smoke of Christopher's cigarette.

"Sorry, Nigel. But it was definitely a nonsmoking flight."

"The chief was rather impressed, I must say."

"Rest assured, I had nothing to do with it. For some reason, the Danish prime minister is rather fond of Gabriel, which proves there's no accounting for taste." Christopher had a look at the speedometer. Whitcombe was sailing along at eighty miles per hour. "Where's the bloody fire, Nigel?"

"The chief is at Downing Street with the prime minister. They'd like a word before the summit begins."

Christopher checked their speed again. Ninety and change.

They dropped Christopher at the rear entrance of Downing Street, then headed to his maisonette in Queen's Gate Terrace. Sarah was downstairs in the kitchen, eating a breakfast of coffee and yogurt. She was pleased to see Gabriel and Ingrid strolling through her door but disappointed her husband was not hard on their heels. When Gabriel explained Christopher's present whereabouts, Sarah directed her eyes toward the Bose radio resting on the countertop.

"It's all they're talking about on *Today*. The tense security around the summit, that is."

She put on a fresh pot of coffee, and they went upstairs to the drawing room to watch the BBC's special coverage. Prime Minister Jonathan Lancaster stood outside the open door of Number 10, posing for photographs with his counterpart from Denmark.

"Did you happen to catch her speech last night?" asked Sarah.

"As a matter of fact," replied Gabriel, "we were all inside the Borgen when she delivered it."

"Am I to assume that your visit to Copenhagen is somehow connected to yesterday's assassination?"

"I'm afraid that's classified," replied Gabriel.

"I'll take that as a yes."

With his silence, he confirmed it was so.

"I don't suppose Captain Yuri Ivanov of the GRU was the same chap who came to the auction at Wickham House?"

"I'm not at liberty to say."

"Another yes."

Sarah watched a limousine drawing up at Number 10. It was the German chancellor, tall and slender and bald, who emerged from the back seat. He pumped Jonathan Lancaster's hand as though trying to draw water from a well.

"You know," she said at length, "just because Christopher can't tell me anything about his work doesn't mean you have to abide by the same rules. After all, you're not actually an officer of the Secret Intelligence Service."

"Close enough," said Gabriel.

Sarah looked at Ingrid. "That leaves you."

With Gabriel's consent, she delivered a thorough briefing.

"With the exception of your regrettable exposure to Novichok," said Sarah, "it all sounds like a great deal of fun, especially the Lisbon game. Why wasn't I invited?"

"You have an art gallery to run."

The next limousine to arrive at Number 10 dispensed the president of France. In his tailored suit and dark necktie he looked as though he were arriving for a premiere at the Cannes Film Festival.

"Heaven knows I've been out of the game for a while now," said Sarah, "but once upon a time I was rather good at it. And I'm troubled by the fact the Russians killed one of their own."

"We all are."

"Theory of the case?"

Gabriel repeated the same two theories he had presented to Lars Mortensen the previous evening, that the GRU killed Captain Yuri Ivanov because they thought he was a traitor or that he was blown and about to be arrested.

"Rubbish," said Sarah.

"You have a better one?"

"Have you considered the possibility that Yuri Ivanov knew he was under surveillance in Lisbon?"

"If that were true, why would he go to Denmark to coordinate a drone attack against Copenhagen Airport?"

"Because his controllers in Moscow knew you would be watching."

"They *wanted* us to see him?"

"Yes, of course."

"Why?"

"I believe it's known as a feint." Just then another car rolled to a stop at the door of Number 10, and out popped the president of Ukraine. "The five most important politicians standing between Russia and its territorial ambitions," said Sarah. "And they're all gathered under the same leaky old roof."

"What if I were to tell you that we have the contents of Yuri Ivanov's mobile phone?"

"I would tell you that I have an art gallery to run."

"Any appointments today?"

"No," said Sarah. "Not a one."

50

Trafalgar Square

She noticed him for the first time in Moxon Street. She was standing in the queue at the Ginger Pig, maker of the finest sausage rolls in all of London, and he was seated at a sidewalk table across the street at Aubaine, accompanied by a plain woman of perhaps thirty. He too was unremarkable looking, with a face so dull and drab it defied description. His clothing was without style. His shoes were worn.

The queue at the Pig was long and slow that day, which allowed her to examine the dull man and his plain companion at considerable length. By all appearances they were a couple of some sort—their hands were entangled on the tabletop—but there was something forced about their manner, especially the way the woman threw back her head with laughter when the man uttered some witticism to their waiter, who by contrast was not amused.

By the time she left the Ginger Pig, the man and woman at Aubaine had yet to order anything more than water. She devoured the sausage roll while walking to the Baker Street Tube station, then boarded an anticlockwise Circle Line train. A lithe, slender man with caramel-colored skin stepped into the carriage a few seconds later, and they each clung to a yellow pole during the twenty-minute ride around central London to Temple. They left the carriage together but upstairs on the Victoria Embankment they went their separate ways, he in the direction of Waterloo Bridge, she toward King's College. There she attended a lecture on contemporary Russia delivered by a professor widely assumed by the student body to be a former officer of the British Secret Intelligence Service. He was under the impression that his gifted Canadian student named Chloé Lamont had come by her proficient Russian in a classroom, which was not the case. She had learned it on Kovenskiy Lane in Saint Petersburg, where she had lived as a child. Back then she was Zoya Danilova, but Zoya was no more; she had been erased, extinguished, by the GRU. Zoya was now Chloé Lamont from Toronto, a graduate of McGill University presently pursuing a PhD at King's College London. The last bit, at least, was true.

Indeed, in addition to her clandestine activities on behalf of Unit 29155, Chloé was hard at work on her doctoral dissertation, so when the lecture concluded she headed over to the Maughan Library in Chancery Lane for a few hours of research. Leaving the library, she received a text from a classmate, a daft American called Wade who had spent the better part of the last semester attempting to coax Chloé into his bed. Though she had done nothing to stoke his lust, she had skillfully played the role of friend and confidant, for daft Wade seemed destined for a career in government, quite possibly the US intelligence community. And so she accepted his invitation to meet for a drink at Tequila Mockingbird in Covent Garden and listened with genuine interest as he spoke of his future plans. She was distracted, though, by the two men drinking at the bar. The one nearest to her was the man she had spotted in Moxon Street, she was certain of it. He was wearing different clothing but had neglected to change his shoes. They were the shoes, she reckoned, of a man who spent a great deal of time on his feet. That was the instant she knew MI5 was onto her.

She spotted the plain woman from Aubaine the following day while walking along Oxford Street—and the slender, caramel-skinned man the day after that during an afternoon run in Regent's Park. The man with the face that defied description followed Chloé to the door of her building in Gloucester Place late that evening. That was the instant she knew she was in serious trouble.

Upstairs in her tiny flat, she told her handlers in Moscow as much in an en clair email sent to the digital equivalent of a dead letter box. Her handlers, in clear but coded language, pledged to bring her in from the cold—but only after she had carried out her assignment. In the chaos that would follow the event, she was to proceed to a remote safe house near Inverness in Scotland and await extraction. The property was owned by a GRU front company called Landmark Ventures and was well provisioned with food and other supplies. She could hide out there for a month or more, and no one would be the wiser.

On her final night in London, Chloé watched with alarm a speech delivered by the Danish prime minister about an incident that had taken place earlier that day in Copenhagen. She knew the victim—they had met recently in Leicester Square—and she could not fathom the reason why the GRU had killed him in so ruthless a manner. She considered approaching one of the MI5 watchers and requesting their protection but quickly ruled it out; there was no hiding from the long arm of the GRU. If she threw in her lot with the British, she would undoubtedly meet with the same fate as her colleague Captain Yuri Ivanov.

And so she rose early the following morning and put her things in order before showering and dressing in the most unremarkable outfit she could muster—dark jeans, a dark pullover, a pair of trainers.

In her King's College rucksack she stuffed a woolen jumper and cashmere beanie. She left her flat in Gloucester Place for the last time at nine fifteen and, tailed by two MI5 watchers, walked to the Ginger Pig for a final sausage roll, which she consumed on the way to the Baker Street Tube station. Once again she caught an anti-clockwise Circle Line train, but this time she got off at St. James's Park. She crossed the park from south to north, then followed Pall Mall to Trafalgar Square.

It was a turbulent sea of demonstrators of every stripe, including a noisy contingent of several hundred displaced Ukrainians waving the blue-and-yellow flags of their shattered homeland. Chloé plunged into the crowd and wandered the immense square for several minutes, from the steps of the National Gallery to Nelson's Column and, finally, to the church of St. Martin-in-the-Fields. When at last she left the square she was wearing the woolen jumper and cashmere beanie and had shed her King's College rucksack. She had also dropped her MI5 watchers. This time she crossed St. James's Park from north to south, then followed Birdcage Walk westward toward Belgravia. She was no longer Chloé Lamont from Toronto, she was Zoya Danilova from Kovenskiy Lane. And she was about to set the world ablaze.

Gatherings of world leaders in London were by nature a security nightmare. The Metropolitan Police shouldered most of the burden, but it was MI5 that provided the critical intelligence. On the morning of the Downing Street summit, MI5's analysts and field personnel were monitoring a constellation of potential threats emanating from the far right, the far left, the environmental movement, ISIS, Iranian sleeper cells, and even a band of unreconstructed Irish militants. The last thing Director-General Amanda Wallace needed that morning was a seemingly unrelated problem. But that was exactly what Miles Kent, MI5's deputy director for operations, brought her at 10:20 A.M., as Prime Minister Jonathan Lancaster and four other heads of government and state entered 10 Downing Street for a summit that might well determine the future of the civilized world.

"What do you mean, they *lost* her?" asked Amanda.

"Perhaps 'lost' is too strong a word," replied Kent.

"Choose another."

He hesitated, then said, "Misplaced."

Amanda gave him a withering look. "One misplaces one's reading glasses, Miles. One *loses* a Russian illegal who's working on her bloody PhD at King's College."

He made no reply.

"How did it happen?"

Miles Kent explained.

"Sounds deliberate to me."

"The A4 team had the same impression."

"Did they?"

The remark required no response, and Miles Kent did not provide one. He had spent more than a decade jousting with Amanda Wallace and knew the rewards of holding his tongue. Presently she was admiring the view of the river from her top-floor office, something she often did in moments of stress or indecision.

"The question is," she asked, "did Ms. Lamont know we were watching her, or was it merely a by-the-book countersurveillance move on her part?"

"She's never done anything like it before."

"We've only been watching her for a few days."

"True," said Kent. "But it looks to me as though she might be making a run for it."

“Why now?”

“Copenhagen,” suggested Kent.

“She knows she’s blown?”

“Possibly. Or perhaps Moscow ordered her home.”

Amanda cast a glance at her television monitors. All the major news networks were covering the same story. “But why today of all days?” she asked.

“Maybe our friends at GRU headquarters thought we would be distracted.”

She raised an eyebrow. “Were we?”

“She chose her spot well. But not to worry, we’ll find her. The CCTV cameras never blink.”

“In the meantime,” said Amanda, “I need to inform my counterpart from across the river that we’ve *misplaced* his girl.”

“I believe he’s at Downing Street.”

“What’s he doing there?”

“Ukraine is his account.”

“Cheeky bastard, isn’t he?” Amanda reached for her phone but, thinking better of it, headed for the door instead. “I won’t be gone long, Miles. And when I get back, I want you to tell me that you’ve found that woman.”

51

Number 10

Samantha Cooke, chief political correspondent for the Tory-tilting *Telegraph*, had a premonition of disaster within minutes of crawling from the warm embrace of her bed. There was, for a start, her failure to properly set the alarm on her phone, which resulted in her oversleeping by nearly an hour. And then there was the absence of anything clean to wear in her closet, the carton of spoiled milk in her refrigerator, and the mound of cat poo next to a perfectly clean litter box. It occurred to her, not for the first time, that she was hanging by a very slender thread. Such was the life of a print journalist in a world where no one could read anything longer than a Tweet and newspapers were going the way of dinosaurs. She would be better off looking for work as a lamplighter. The pay was better and the future brighter.

And yet, for all the precariousness of her existence, Samantha Cooke was without question the most celebrated political journalist in London. After all, she was the one who had brought down Hugh and Lucinda Graves—with considerable help from a trusted friend who had handed her the story on a silver platter. Since then, however, she had fallen into a rut, lots of stories of Westminster sound and fury signifying little if anything at all. She needed a scoop to get back on her game. She had a feeling, despite the dreadful start to her morning, that today might be the day. Prime Minister Jonathan Lancaster was hosting the most important summit at Downing Street in years, a meeting that might well determine the future of both NATO and Ukraine. Her editor wanted something to set *The Telegraph*'s coverage apart from its competitors, something more than the usual podium drivel.

But reaching Number 10 that morning proved a challenge; the security was the tightest Samantha had seen since the last G7 summit. She eventually negotiated the labyrinth of roadblocks and checkpoints and joined her colleagues in the Downing Street press pen in time to witness the arrival of the foreign dignitaries. She sat out the shouted questions, though; at this point they were beneath her, and the leaders would have nothing substantive to say until the conclusion of the meeting. It was far better to use her time productively by reaching out to her sources.

She rang two or three but got nothing but Whitehall mush. She was about to ring a fourth, an ancient flame who worked in the Foreign Office, but was distracted by the sight of another car drawing up outside the door of Number 10. She recognized the woman who emerged from the back seat. It was Amanda Wallace, the director-general of MI5. But why would the head of the Security Service be coming to Downing Street in the middle of a summit? Samantha, smelling a scoop, rang one of her best sources, a man to whom she spoke only when necessary. "Not a good time," said Miles Kent, MI5's deputy director for operations, and the connection went dead.

Geoffrey Sloane, the prime minister's chief of staff, met Amanda in the entrance hall and escorted her upstairs to the door of the White Drawing Room.

"Is there something I should know?" he asked.

"This won't be a pleasant conversation." Amanda opened the door and found Graham Seymour seated in one of the luminous white wing chairs. In the other sat Christopher Keller. "What's he doing here?" she asked.

"Actually," replied Graham, "I'm rather more interested in why you're here."

"We have a problem."

"What's that?"

"Chloé Lamont."

Graham's expression darkened. "What about her?"

"We seem to have . . ."

"Lost her?"

"Misplaced," said Amanda. "Temporarily, of course."

"How long has she been missing?"

Amanda checked the time. "Approximately forty-five minutes."

"Last known location?"

"Trafalgar Square."

"It is essential," said Graham, "that you locate her as quickly as possible."

"Don't worry, we will. But it might help matters if you told me how SIS managed to find Ms. Lamont in the first place."

"You know how we found her."

"Yuri Ivanov?"

"That's correct."

"But tell me something," said Amanda. "How *exactly* did you find Yuri?"

What followed was a long-overdue clearing of the air. Graham was selective in his memory, sharing only what he deemed necessary. Amanda was appalled nonetheless.

"When were you planning to tell me?"

"About Alice Winter? Probably never."

"Does her husband know?"

"For the moment, at least, Edward Knight believes his wife is dead."

"Monstrous," whispered Amanda.

"Ruthless, yes. But hardly monstrous."

"Do you know how many laws you've violated?"

"None, actually. We received the necessary approval from higher authority."

"Don't tell me you involved the PM in this."

"He just did," said Christopher.

Amanda threw him a black look, then turned to Graham. "We heard a rumor that Edward Knight had retained Gabriel Allon to find his wife."

"You heard correctly. Gabriel was the one who brought us Alice."

Amanda glanced at Chirstopher. "That would explain why you're here. The two of you are thick as thieves."

"If it wasn't for Gabriel Allon—"

Graham placed a restraining hand on Christopher's arm and attempted to lower the temperature. The leaders had gathered a short distance away in the Pillared Room, and the prime minister was addressing the press. A nasty intramural spat between the directors of SIS and MI5 would not play well in the morning papers.

"There will be plenty of time for the usual recriminations later," he said. "For now, it would be best if we focused on the problem at hand."

"Agreed," said Amanda evenly. "But if anything happens today, you can be sure that neither I nor my service will be blamed for it."

"I would have expected nothing less."

Amanda rose to her feet and looked at Christopher. "Where's your friend Gabriel Allon now?"

"On his way back to Cornwall, I believe."

"Tell him to stay there. Things tend to go off the rails whenever he's in town."

And with that she was gone.

"Did you just lie to the director of MI5?" asked Graham.

"It was a white lie," said Christopher with a smile. "Told in the White Drawing Room."

52

Zoetermeer

The headquarters of the AIVD, the Dutch General Intelligence and Security Service, were located a few kilometers west of The Hague in the drab suburb of Zoetermeer. Like every other security professional in western Europe that morning, Anton de Graaf, AIVD's director-general, had one eye on the Downing Street summit. A part of him was relieved it was Jonathan Lancaster who had convened the meeting and not the prime minister of the Netherlands. Russia's intelligence services, he feared, were no longer rational actors. Anything and everything was possible.

The brutal murder of Yuri Ivanov the previous evening in Copenhagen was proof of that. The first documented use of a killer miniature drone was an alarming development, to say the least. De Graaf had already assembled an AIVD working group to determine whether anything could be done to protect Holland's political leaders and senior government officials, short of locking them away in sealed rooms. His own opinion was that the Kremlin could now kill any leader, anywhere, at any time—unless, of course, intelligence professionals like De Graaf could provide the leaders with advance warning of an assassination plot.

The AIVD was better positioned than any other Western

intelligence service to meet the emerging threat, for it had once again managed to digitally breach the Aquarium, which was how ordinary Russians referred to the GRU's imposing headquarters in downtown Moscow. Anton de Graaf, who no longer trusted the Americans, had shared this information only with the director of Britain's Secret Intelligence Service. And yet even the British did not know the full extent to which their Dutch allies had penetrated the GRU. In the lexicon of the signals intelligence trade, the AIVD owned them. And so Anton de Graaf's heart seemed to skip a beat when, at 12:10 P.M. Central European Time, he lifted the receiver of his secure internal phone and heard the voice of Jaan Hendriks, the chief of the AIVD's cyber division.

"You'd better get down here," he said.

It was a walk of five full minutes from De Graaf's top-floor suite to the underground lair inhabited by the cyberwarriors, a realm of eternal darkness where the sun neither rose nor set. Jaan Hendriks stood before the video wall, eyes on the center screen.

De Graaf went to his side. "The drone room?" he asked.

Hendriks nodded.

"What are they up to?"

"We can't say for certain yet." Hendriks pointed to a stout figure with iron-gray hair. "But his presence would suggest that something big is in the works."

It was General Igor Karpov, commander of GRU Unit 29155.

"How long has he been there?" asked De Graaf.

"About fifteen minutes." Hendriks pointed toward the adjacent video screen. "That's Fancy Bear, the hacking unit. And the man standing over their shoulders is General Karpov's deputy."

Two rooms in downtown Moscow, two elite teams of Russian intelligence operatives, two senior officers, five leaders gathered beneath the same roof in London—it was more than enough to send

Anton de Graaf rushing back to his office. Upon arrival he phoned Graham Seymour in London. The call was answered by Nigel Whitcombe, Seymour's longtime private secretary.

"Where's your boss?" asked De Graaf, slightly out of breath.

"He's at Downing Street for the summit."

"I need to speak to him, Nigel. This minute."

Though Anton de Graaf did not know it, three teams of analysts were at that same moment scouring the contents of the late Yuri Ivanov's captured mobile phone—one at PET headquarters in the Copenhagen suburb of Søborg, another at SIS headquarters in London, and a third in a maisonette located at 18 Queen's Gate Terrace in Kensington. Of the three, the Kensington team was the smallest but arguably the most capable, for it included Ingrid Johansen, a master computer hacker who could have taught the cyberwarriors of the AIVD a trick or two.

She was perched atop a stool at the kitchen island, searching for patterns and nodes in Yuri Ivanov's telephone metadata. Sarah Bancroft, seated opposite, was reading the emails and text messages. Gabriel, having no laptop of his own, was scrutinizing Ivanov's photographs on the desktop computer upstairs in Christopher's office.

An hour into his work he checked the headlines and saw a brief item from his friend Samantha Cooke of *The Telegraph*. It seemed Amanda Wallace had just been spotted at Downing Street. Gabriel quickly rang Christopher, who explained why the director of MI5 had popped into Number 10 in the middle of a high-stakes summit.

"What do you mean, they lost her?" asked Gabriel.

"Evidently she gave them the slip in Trafalgar Square."

"Intentionally?"

"MI5 can't say for certain. Needless to say, they're using all the tools and resources at their disposal to locate her."

"Every square inch of Metropolitan London is covered by CCTV cameras. How hard can it be?"

"If memory serves, you evaded detection a time or two back in the day."

"That's because I was good."

"So is Chloé Lamont, it seems."

"May I give you a piece of advice?" asked Gabriel.

"By all means."

"Find her."

"You know," said Christopher before ringing off, "it's quick thinking like that that made you a legend."

Gabriel replaced the receiver with a frown and resumed his scrutiny of Yuri Ivanov's photographs. At 11:22 A.M. London time, he found what he was looking for.

The rapidly increasing concern of the various spymasters and security professionals notwithstanding, the mood inside Number 10 was all business. The five leaders seated around a table in the ornate Pillared Room made swift progress on a declaration of principles regarding the war in Ukraine. First and foremost was a rejection of the Kremlin's demand that, in exchange for peace, Ukraine surrender a large swath of territory in the eastern half of the country. The declaration was sure to ruffle feathers at the White House, as the territorial concessions were a key part of the American president's Ukraine peace plan—a plan dictated largely by the Kremlin.

Next the five leaders discussed additional military and financial support for Kyiv. During a particularly long-winded lecture by the French president, Geoffrey Sloane slipped into the room and presented Jonathan Lancaster with a handwritten note. The prime minister read it quickly, then said, "Not now, Geoffrey."

"He was quite insistent."

"He usually is."

"When shall I tell him to expect your call?"

"When our meeting is over, I imagine."

"I'll let him know," said Sloane with a smile, and withdrew. Lancaster looked at Prime Minister Kalla Eriksen, who was seated to his right. "The American president," he said sotto voce, "would like a word."

"If it's about Greenland," she whispered in reply, "tell him it belongs to Denmark."

"Don't worry, I already have."

"So have I," she said. "But he doesn't seem to get the message."

After reaching broad agreement on the aid package, the leaders turned to the thorny issue of seizing frozen Russian assets. Twenty minutes into the discussion, Geoffrey Sloane once again stole silently into the Pillared Room, note in hand.

"Is it really that serious?" asked Lancaster.

"Apparently so."

Lancaster rose to his feet and, with apologies to his four counterparts, followed his chief of staff into the White Drawing Room. Graham Seymour and Christopher Keller were waiting for him. The tension in the small chamber was palpable.

"This had better be good," said Lancaster.

"I'm afraid it isn't," replied Graham. "Quite the opposite, in fact."

53

Number 10

It was Graham Seymour's practice to provide his customers in the British government with the intelligence they needed to make critical decisions, but rarely did he divulge how that intelligence had been collected, especially when allied foreign services were involved. To that end, he had neglected to tell his primary customer, Prime Minister Jonathan Lancaster, that the Dutch intelligence service had digitally burrowed into what appeared to be a drone control room at GRU headquarters in Moscow. He did so now, as succinctly as possible. Then he informed the prime minister that cyberwarriors from the Dutch intelligence service were at that moment staring at ten drone operators sitting at their control stations.

Lancaster, always cool under fire, was unruffled. "And the Dutch are absolutely certain that they're drone operators?"

"Few things in the intelligence business are certain," replied Graham. "But I strongly suggest that we take additional measures to protect you and the other leaders."

"What more can we do?"

Graham answered without hesitation. "You need to leave, Prime Minister. All of you."

"Leave?"

"Evacuate," said Graham carefully.

"To where?"

"The Citadel." It was a secure underground command center located beneath the Cabinet Office. "You and your colleagues can make your way there through the Downing Street tunnel and continue the meeting in the COBRA room. And when the threat has passed, you can quietly return to Number Ten for the news conference."

"What do we tell the press?"

"Nothing."

"And when it leaks?"

"It won't."

"Don't be naive, Graham. It always leaks." Lancaster shook his head. "I will not go down in history as the prime minister who fled this house out of fear for his life."

"Now is not the time for heroics, Prime Minister."

"That's where you're wrong," replied Lancaster, and walked out of the room.

"Well," said Christopher, "that went about as well as could be expected."

"If I were in his shoes," admitted Graham, "I would have done the same thing."

"Does that mean we're not going back to Vauxhall Cross?"

"We're not going anywhere, Christopher."

He went to the window and searched the sky. "Do you remember the IRA mortar attack in ninety-one?"

"Like it was yesterday."

Christopher lowered his gaze toward the spot in Number 10's walled garden where the shell had landed. "They came damn close, didn't they? Thirty more yards and . . ."

He left the thought unfinished. Graham finished it for him.

"Thirty more yards, and John Major and his entire Cabinet might well have been killed."

"I always liked John Major."

"I'm sure he feels the same about you, Christopher."

He wandered over to the sideboard and removed the stopper from the crystal decanter.

"May I ask what you're doing?" inquired Graham.

"Helping myself to the prime minister's Macallan. What does it look like?"

"Perhaps you should do something a bit more productive."

"What did you have in mind?"

"Call your friend Gabriel," said Graham. "Tell him to find those bloody drones."

The lines had been drawn with care. There were ten in all, radiating outward like the hands of a clock from the same fixed point. Most of the lines—eight, to be precise—fell between the hours of two and four o'clock. One stretched toward five o'clock, another toward approximately nine fifteen. At the midway point of each of the lines was a handwritten number. The shortest line was labeled *849.78*, the longest *2574.95*. Gabriel enlarged the image and examined the numbers. They had been rendered, he reckoned, by the hand of a woman.

He printed a copy of the diagram and, downstairs, showed it to Sarah and Ingrid. They scrutinized it in silence for a moment, then Ingrid asked, "Where did you find this?"

"It was saved in Yuri's photo library."

Ingrid pushed her computer across the countertop, and Gabriel found the original image. Reclaiming the laptop, Ingrid ran a few diagnostics to determine its provenance.

"It wasn't taken by his phone," she said after a moment. "It was emailed to him about six months ago."

"By whom?"

"A user of Proton Mail."

Ingrid recited the anonymous numeric address and the date of transmission, and Sarah found a copy of the original email, complete with the attached photograph. The subject of the email was HELLO. The text was one sentence in length.

Thought you might find this interesting . . .

"Why would a GRU officer find lines on a page interesting?" asked Ingrid.

"It could have been a diagram for one of the recent airport drone incursions," replied Gabriel.

"Or?"

"It might be a future attack."

"Another airport?" asked Sarah.

"I doubt it."

"Why?"

Gabriel's phone rang before he could reply. He accepted the call and heard the voice of Christopher. He managed to speak only a few words before the connection was lost. Gabriel tried to ring him back, but the call wouldn't go through. He checked the signal meter on his phone. It read NO SERVICE.

Ingrid checked her phone as well, then said, "No service." Gabriel picked up the receiver of the kitchen's landline phone, but there was no dial tone. Sarah entered the address for the BBC into her web browser, but nothing happened.

"The Internet seems to be down," she said.

Gabriel looked at Ingrid. "What are the odds?"

"That London's phone and cellular system would crash in the middle of a summit? I would need a calculator."

"Could an individual have pulled it off?"

"The more likely explanation," said Ingrid, "is that it's a state actor."

"Any candidates?"

"Only one."

"The question is," said Gabriel, "why would they do it?"

"They might simply be attempting to show their displeasure over the fact that the Ukrainian president is in town."

"Possibly," replied Gabriel. "But I have feeling it's a prelude to something bigger."

"Like what?" asked Sarah.

"The director-general of the Dutch intelligence service rang Graham a few minutes ago with a rather dire warning. Christopher managed to relay only a part of it before the phones went down."

"And?"

"Evidently ten remote drone operators are sitting at ten drone stations at GRU headquarters in Moscow."

"And you just found a diagram on Yuri Ivanov's phone with ten lines," Sarah pointed out.

Gabriel contemplated the diagram for a moment, a hand to his chin, his head tilted slightly to one side. "You don't happen to have an offline London map, do you?"

"This is your lucky day."

"I wouldn't be so sure."

Gabriel opened the app on Sarah's laptop, adjusted the location and scale, and pressed the diagram to the screen. The light rendered the printer paper semitransparent.

"Dear God," she said.

Each of the ten lines ended at a London landmark: the Royal Albert Hall, Buckingham Palace, the US Embassy at Nine Elms, the headquarters of both MI5 and SIS, the Palace of Westminster, the Foreign Office, New Scotland Yard, the Ministry of Defense, and the official residence of the British prime minister at 10 Downing Street.

Which left only the center point where the ten lines converged. It was approximately one mile to the east of where they were now standing, in the central London district of Belgravia. If the crude diagram was in fact a schematic for a drone incursion, common sense suggested that this was the launching point.

Common sense also dictated that they should immediately alert someone in a position of authority. Sarah tried the landline, but there was still no dial tone. Gabriel checked his mobile.

NO SERVICE.

"Does your husband still have that peashooter of his?" he asked.

"The Walther PPK?"

"Yes, that one."

"It's upstairs in his dressing room," said Sarah. "Second drawer from the right."

54

Wilton Crescent

The keepers of London's telecommunications networks quickly determined that the unprecedented breakdown in phone and Internet service was no accident. Nor was it happenstance, they concluded, that Westminster, home of the British Parliament and most of HMG's ministries, had been targeted first. From there the outages had spread like wildfire, northward to Camden Town and Finsbury Park, southward to Battersea and Brixton, eastward to Canary Wharf, westward to Hounslow. The British government quickly switched over to its emergency backup system, but London's residents, not to mention tens of thousands of tourists and business travelers, were largely cut off from the rest of the world. Beneath London, some five hundred trains across eleven Underground lines rolled to a stop, stranding tens of thousands of passengers. Controllers at Heathrow Airport, the world's seventh busiest, suspended operations and diverted inbound flights to other destinations. At the London Stock Exchange, traders stared dumbfounded at black screens.

If there was one bright spot, it was the traffic signals, which were still functioning normally. Sarah nevertheless disregarded several red lights as she raced down Kensington Road in her husband's Bentley Continental. She made a harrowing right turn into Sloane Street, a reckless left into West Halkin, then proceeded to 27 Wilton Crescent, one of the most desirable addresses in London's poshest neighborhood.

"This can't possibly be right," she said.

"What did you expect?" asked Gabriel.

"Do you know how much this place is worth?"

"Fifty million, in the shade. But it's exactly where the ten lines meet."

The elegant Georgian house, like its neighbors to the right and left, was five floors in height, with a wrought-iron balustrade on the second level and a flight of steps leading to the basement entrance. The shades were tightly drawn, and there appeared to be no lights burning within. It was a common sight in Belgravia. Most of the homes were owned by wealthy foreigners and investors. At night it was one of London's darkest neighborhoods.

They climbed out of the car and approached the door. Gabriel laid his thumb on the bell push. There was no response from within.

"Try it again," suggested Sarah.

He jabbed the bell push a second time. Nothing. Next he tried the latch. As expected, it was locked.

"I don't suppose you brought along that magic key of yours," said Ingrid.

Gabriel drew a pair of slender lockpick tools he carried habitually in the breast pocket of his jacket and, crouching, went to work. Sarah watched a car roll slowly past in the street.

"Is this really a good idea?" she asked.

"Do you have a better one?"

"Someone's bound to call the police."

"They can't," Gabriel reminded her.

"Silly me," said Sarah. The phones weren't working.

They should have made quick work of it. After all, the subject had shed her team of A4 watchers not in some remote corner of the West Country but in Trafalgar Square, one of London's most heavily surveilled public spaces. Even so, for more than an hour after Amanda Wallace's return to MI5 headquarters, the subject's whereabouts remained a mystery. As was usually the case, Amanda took out her anger on her deputy Miles Kent, who had predicted a quick resolution to the matter, only to be proven wrong.

He remained confident, however, that the Russian illegal called Chloé Lamont had not vanished into thin air, that somewhere there was video of her, captured by CCTV. Despite the still-unexplained phone outage, live feeds and recorded video from all of Trafalgar Square's cameras were available to the team of surveillance specialists hard at work in MI5's Thames House op center. With Miles Kent looking over their shoulders, they subjected the video to the myriad scrubbing tools they had at their disposal, including two new behavioral programs utilizing artificial intelligence. The programs identified some twenty-five candidates, one of whom turned out to be the MP for Warrington North. None of the remaining twenty-four was the Russian intelligence operative for whom they were searching.

In the end it was a well-trained pair of human eyes that finally spotted her. They belonged to a young analyst who had spent countless hours monitoring the movements of known London-based jihadists and was personally responsible for preventing at least two acts of terrorism. It was the walk that had given the Russian woman away. She had dumped the rucksack and pulled on a jumper and a beanie, but neglected to alter her gait.

The analyst summoned Miles Kent and showed him the first

piece of video. It had been shot by a CCTV camera located near the Travellers Club in Pall Mall. The woman walked past the camera at 11:16 A.M. Thirty-five minutes later, after crossing St. James's Park, she arrived at her destination.

"Is she still there?" asked Miles Kent.

"As far as I know," replied the analyst.

"Anyone else?"

"Three other people just gained entry to the premises."

"Gained entry?"

The analyst played the video. All three subjects had their backs turned to the nearest CCTV camera. One was crouching.

"Who's the locksmith?"

The analyst showed Kent a still image of the three subjects emerging from a Bentley automobile.

"Is that who I think it is?"

"Yes, sir. Facial recognition left no room for doubt."

"And the other two?"

They were both women. The analyst pointed toward the taller of the two. "That's Sarah Bancroft. American citizen, former CIA officer, runs an art gallery in St. James's. Her MI5 file is rather extensive, to put it mildly."

"And the other one?"

"Ingrid Johansen. She's Danish," added the analyst. "Her name appears in our files as well."

"But why are they in the same house as a Russian illegal?"

"Actually there's someone else there too." The analyst displayed another still image. The subject was wearing a hat and sunglasses to conceal his appearance. "He arrived about fifteen minutes before the woman."

"Name?"

"Don't have one yet."

"Find out who he is."

"On it, sir."

Miles Kent snatched up a phone and rang Amanda Wallace. "We've got her," he said.

"Where is she?"

"Number Twenty-seven Wilton Crescent."

"Doing what?"

"Unclear," said Kent. "But you'll never guess who else just showed up."

It was a lock of superior quality, but after two minutes of diligent probing and manipulation Gabriel bent it to his will. Christopher's Walther PPK was wedged into the waistband of his trousers at the small of his back. He placed a hand on the gun's grip, then gave the brass knob a twist and swung into the entrance hall. It was in semi-darkness. There were no furnishings of any kind—no ornamental table on which to leave one's keys, no hook to hang one's coat. On the black-and-white chessboard floor was a pile of unopened post. It was addressed to someone called Leonard Crabtree.

Gabriel beckoned Ingrid and Sarah, and they stepped inside and closed the door behind them. Ingrid threw a light switch. Sarah moved the post around with the toe of her pump.

"Looks like we've come to the right place."

Gabriel placed a finger to his lips, then drew the Walther and advanced down the dark and silent center hall, pirouetting through open doorways with the weapon in his outstretched hands. Sarah and Ingrid walked a few paces behind him. The rooms along the corridor—the reception room, the dining room, the breakfast nook, the study—were unfurnished, as was the large drawing room at the back of the house.

"Perhaps poor Leonard Crabtree ran out of money," suggested Sarah.

"There is no Leonard Crabtree," replied Gabriel.

"But why buy a house on one of the world's most expensive streets and leave it empty?"

"Location, location, location."

Gabriel went into the kitchen. On the counter were two oversize mugs, each with the string of a teabag hanging over the rim. One of the mugs was half full. He dipped a forefinger into the brownish liquid. It was lukewarm.

"Someone was here recently."

Ingrid pointed to the smudge of lipstick on the rim of the second mug. "And he had female company."

"Who's to say they aren't still here?" asked Sarah.

Gabriel headed for the staircase. On the lower level of the house it was the same story—a gym without fitness equipment, a cinema without reclining chairs, a large service kitchen empty of pots and pans and cooking utensils. At the back of the house was a garage with two separate bays. One of the doors was open.

"Looks like our two visitors went out the back way," said Sarah. "But one wonders why they neglected to close the door."

"Perhaps," said Ingrid, "they were in a hurry."

Gabriel closed the door with a press of a button and headed once again for the stairs. On the uppermost floor of the house were two unfurnished bedrooms, an unfurnished sitting room, a library empty of books, and a door with two unsightly interior padlocks. The latch had a lock as well, openable only with a key.

“Where do you suppose it leads?” asked Sarah.

“There must be a roof terrace.”

She tugged at one of the padlocks. “How long will it take you to pick these?”

Gabriel placed the barrel of the Walther against the lock and pulled the trigger.

“One down,” said Sarah, rubbing her ear. “Two to go.”

55

Number 10

It took Amanda Wallace two excruciating minutes to get Graham Seymour on the line. First she tried his mobile number. Then, after receiving no answer, she rang Number 10's main switchboard on the emergency backup line, and an operator transferred the call to the phone in the White Drawing Room. The connection was not quite secure, but it would have to do.

"Wilton Crescent?" he asked.

Amanda responded by reciting the street address of the house in question.

"And you're sure it was Gabriel?"

"Positive," said Amanda. Then she added, "So much for him being on his way back to Cornwall. By the way, Christopher Keller's wife is with him. So is that Danish woman, the one who was involved in that messy business out in Somerset."

"There's only one reason the three of them would be there."

"I'm all ears, Graham."

"Not on this line, I'm afraid. We've said too much already."

"How shall I handle it?"

"Ring the commissioner of the Met immediately. Make sure he sends MO19. Tell them not to bother ringing the bell."

The line went dead. Graham replaced the receiver and looked at Christopher. He had heard only one end of the conversation, but it was more than enough.

"They must have found something on Ivanov's phone," he said.

"So it would appear."

Christopher rose to his feet. "Would you mind terribly if I wandered over to Wilton Crescent to check on my wife?"

"Actually," said Graham, "I need you here."

"Whatever for?"

"We need to get the five leaders out of the Pillared Room and into the Downing Street tunnel immediately."

"If I'm not mistaken, the PM has made his position clear on that question."

"But you're going to tell him that he has no other choice."

"Lucky me," said Christopher, and followed Graham out the door.

Neighbors and passersby would later offer conflicting accounts as to how many gunshots they heard emanating from inside the vast, empty house in Wilton Crescent. Some said it was three, others claimed it was five or even six. In point of fact, seven rounds were fired, the entire capacity of a subcompact Walther PPK. Gabriel ejected the spent magazine and inserted a backup. Then he leaned his shoulder hard against the ruined door and crashed onto the roof terrace.

The wail of approaching sirens filled the air. It sounded as though the entirety of the Metropolitan Police Service was headed their way. Gabriel sidestepped a vine-covered trellis and spotted the drones. There were ten in all. Each was the size of a small café table and had four rotors. Three had a payload of some sort, doubtless explosive in nature.

Gabriel took hold of the nearest armed drone and placed it topsy-turvy on its propellors, rendering it incapable of flight. It was an effort; the payload was fifty pounds at least. He reached for a second armed drone, but its propellors were suddenly spinning like buzz-saws, as were the propellors of the other eight drones. All nine leapt simultaneously from the roof an instant later and set off toward their assigned targets. One headed toward the Royal Albert Hall, one toward the US Embassy at Nine Elms, one toward Buckingham Palace, which was exactly 849.78 meters away. The two armed drones made straight for Downing Street.

Gabriel wheeled round and saw Sarah staring horrified at the London sky. "Not since the Blitz," she was saying. "We have to warn them somehow."

Gabriel crouched next to the disabled drone. It was a flying IED, he thought, capable of inflicting enormous damage and loss of life, all with a single keystroke by a remote operator in Moscow. The high-resolution camera was its most insidious feature. It gave the operator the ability to guide the device to its target and kill with precision. At present the operator was staring at the face of Gabriel Allon.

"We need to get off this roof," he said. "Now."

Graham and Christopher entered the Pillared Room to find it deserted save for a few junior aides who were tidying up the mess. "Where are they?" Christopher demanded to know, and one of the aides, a red-haired woman of perhaps twenty-five, answered nervously, "They're about to hold the press conference, sir."

By the time Graham and Christopher reached the reception area, the five leaders were filing out the famous black door. On the opposite side of Downing Street, behind a line of metal barricades, were some two hundred reporters and photographers. Lights flashed as Jonathan Lancaster stepped up to the modest wooden podium. Christopher didn't hear a word the prime minister spoke. He was listening only to the distant sound of sirens.

In hindsight Gabriel should have left the Walther behind. Fully loaded and charged, it was still in his right hand as he chased Ingrid and Sarah down the long staircase to the ground floor of the enormous house, inwardly counting the number of seconds that had passed since the Russians had seen his face. When at last they reached the entrance hall, the door came crashing open and a dozen officers of the Met's M019 Specialist Firearms Command poured through the breach.

One of the officers spotted the Walther pistol and pointed his Heckler & Koch submachine gun toward Gabriel's heart. He quickly dropped the gun to the marble floor and four of the officers dragged him from the house. A moment later he was lying face down on the pavement of Wilton Crescent with his hands behind his back and a knee on his neck, staring into the eyes of Ingrid, who was similarly posed. "Downing Street!" he shouted. "Russian drones are heading for Downing Street!" Then London shook with a thunderous explosion, followed a few seconds later by another. The third explosion was closer at hand. After that everything turned to black.

Part Four

The Dead Zone

56

Bloomsbury Tavern

The official committee of inquiry would later determine that the Protection Command of London's Metropolitan Police received only thirty-three seconds' warning that a swarm of drones was approaching Downing Street, though where the warning originated and how the information was obtained in the first place would never be determined to anyone's satisfaction. It was chief of staff Geoffrey Sloane who informed Prime Minister Jonathan Lancaster of the impending attack, and Lancaster who in turn told the four other leaders standing next to him outside Number 10's black door. Several Protection Command officers quickly escorted the visiting dignitaries into the Downing Street tunnel, but Lancaster refused to go. In one of the attack's most enduring images, he was seen calmly herding the press corps into the safety of the neighboring Foreign Office. Several journalists refused to heed his warning, including Samantha Cooke of *The Telegraph*, who used her smartphone to capture an iconic photo of the drones skimming across the treetops of St. James's Park.

As the drones passed low over Horse Guards Road on their final approach to Number 10, a man in a dark business suit was seen firing on the aircraft with a SIG MCX tactical rifle. The committee of inquiry would later identify him as a plainclothes Protection

Command officer, though some observers, including Samantha Cooke, would suggest he worked elsewhere. Regardless of his affiliation, the business-suited man with the tactical rifle managed to damage the rotors of one of the armed drones. It tumbled to earth in Mountbatten Green and detonated on impact. Because the area was closed to vehicular and pedestrian traffic, there were no casualties.

A second drone, also armed with an explosive payload, passed over the security gate at the western end of Downing Street and made straight for the door of Number 10. Samantha Cooke quickly sought cover in the Foreign Office, where, along with the prime minister and his chief of staff, they awaited impact and detonation. But much to everyone's surprise and relief, the drone sailed harmlessly over the gate at the opposite end of Downing Street, over the deserted pavements of Whitehall, over the car park between the Ministry of Defense and New Scotland Yard, over the Victoria Embankment and Westminster Pier, and into the steel-gray waters of the River Thames. Its detonation sent a towering geyser of water skyward. While precariously close to the London Eye observation wheel, the explosion resulted in no damage or injuries.

The same could not be said, however, for the third detonation. It took place not in a park or waterway but on the roof of 27 Wilton Crescent in Belgravia. The blast left the house and the two neighboring dwellings in ruins and injured twelve Metropolitan Police officers. Three other people sustained minor injuries as well, though for reasons never made clear their names were withheld from the public.

Seven remaining drones, all unarmed and presumably decoys, met with watery ends—one in Hyde Park's Round Pond, two in the Serpentine, a fourth in St. James's Park Lake, and three in the Thames. By midafternoon London's phones and Internet were once again working, and at 5:00 P.M. the prime minister returned to the podium outside the iconic black door of 10 Downing Street, this time to declare the incident over. He then headed straight to the COBRA room in the Citadel, where he would remain, huddled with his senior ministers and defense and intelligence chiefs, until nearly midnight.

By then the jihadist terror group ISIS had issued a claim of responsibility—as had a hitherto unknown environmental group and a long-forgotten Irish faction—but the television experts were certain Russia was to blame. The British government, however, refused to assign responsibility until the investigation was complete. That didn't prevent Kremlin spokesman Yevgeny Nazarov from issuing a preemptive denial, which one analyst likened to an unintended admission of guilt. A bellicose Russian television commentator known to reflect Kremlin thinking warned Britain not to retaliate. "Otherwise," he said with a smile, "the next munition aimed at Downing Street will be nuclear-tipped, and it won't miss."

But why had so many of the drones, eight in all, veered wildly off course and crashed? Once again the British government said it would withhold judgment until all the facts were known, but so-called well-informed sources told anyone who would listen that the aircraft had been knocked off course by signal jammers deployed around Downing Street. In truth, signal jamming had played no role whatsoever in the failure of the drones to strike their intended targets; it was a team of computer hackers from the Dutch intelligence service who had spared Britain a calamity. Sitting at terminals in their darkened lair in Zoetermeer, they had remotely seized control of the Russian drones and guided them harmlessly into the nearest body of water—all while their counterparts at GRU headquarters in Moscow, including the commanding general of Unit 29155, stared at their screens in disbelief.

Official London misled the press and the British public about other key aspects of the incident, including the events surrounding the third and final detonation in Wilton Crescent. *Why did the third drone fail to take flight?* Official London would have more to say at a later date. *What about the reports of gunfire inside the house?* Official London was looking into the matter. *Were the three injured civilians somehow connected to the case?* Official London declined comment.

Nor did official London have anything to say—at that early juncture, at least—about the female Russian intelligence operative who had entered the house in Wilton Crescent after expertly dropping a team of MI5 watchers in Trafalgar Square. She left the house through a rear garage door ten minutes before the start of the attack, accompanied by a man who was wearing a hat and sunglasses to conceal his appearance. It was the assumption of MI5 and the Secret Intelligence Service that the man was likewise an illegal Russian operative. Five days after the incident, both individuals remained unaccounted for, much to the dismay of official London.

Eventually the brick wall of official silence began to crumble, as such walls invariably did. It was *The Guardian*, quoting a slew of intelligence and security sources, that first pointed the finger of blame at Moscow and, more specifically, at GRU Unit 29155. The article appeared shortly before Jonathan Lancaster made his first post-attack appearance in the House of Commons. Conservative and Labour MPs alike gave him a hero's welcome, which prompted one commentator to say that Lancaster, with his act of courage after learning of the pending attack, had single-handedly restored his party's fortunes for the next election.

Away from the glare of the Commons, Lancaster and his Cabinet were considering an array of retaliatory measures against Russia, ranging from additional economic and diplomatic sanctions to a massive air strike on Russia's frontline forces in Ukraine. The prime minister's rage notwithstanding, his primary goal was to avoid a war with a vastly superior nuclear power—a war that Britain, in its current state, could ill afford. It was Graham Seymour, director-general of the Secret Intelligence Service, who suggested an alternative. It was time, he said, to take the gloves off—in the British tradition, with stealth and low cunning and, yes, a touch of wickedness. SIS would confront Russia's so-called hybrid war on the West with a hybrid war of its own, led by the same officer who, after draining two glasses of the PM's Macallan whisky, had calmly snatched a SIG MCX rifle from the Downing Street weapons room and shot down one of the two approaching Russian drones.

None of which the prime minister mentioned when, six days later, he appeared before the press to announce the results of Britain's initial investigation into the drone incident. He confirmed that GRU Unit 29155 had carried out the attack and announced a raft of new sanctions, including the expulsion of thirty-two diplomats from the Russian Embassy in London and the seizure of all Russian money held by British banks. Additionally British authorities issued arrest warrants for a GRU officer known as Chloé Lamont and her as yet unidentified male accomplice.

There were some on the traditional anti-Russian right who found Lancaster's response woefully inadequate, even cowardly, and others, especially in the press, who were sure they were getting only part of the story. Phoebe Chadwick, coordinator of the Africa program at Global Relief UK, fell into the second category. Like most relief workers and advocates for human rights, she maintained a healthy mistrust of the organs of state security. Still, she was relieved that Jonathan Lancaster had not gone off half-cocked. The last thing the world needed now, she thought, was yet another war.

The prime minister made his case to the Commons the following day, but by late afternoon all of Britain was consumed by lurid new revelations about the king's oversexed brother and his appalling friendship with an American pedophile and sex trafficker. Even Phoebe, a certifiably serious person who had largely averted her gaze from the unfolding scandal, found the story too shocking to ignore. Around half past five she checked her text messages and noticed that she had received an anonymous invitation for drinks at the Bloomsbury Tavern at six. The sender of the message would be seated in the corner table beneath the television. Phoebe was to come alone.

She was not in the habit of meeting strangers for drinks, but it was only the Bloomsbury Tavern, after all, and she had a sneaking suspicion the anonymous email had been sent by the famous art restorer and retired spy she had met there several weeks previously. She entered the pub at the stroke of six o'clock and made her way as instructed to the corner table. And there sat not the man she had been expecting but a woman in jeans and trainers and a stretched-out cotton pullover. Her face was hidden behind a pair of movie-starlet sunglasses. Her hair was short and dark.

Phoebe glanced around the interior of the pub.

"Looking for someone?" asked the woman in a sultry drawl.

"A friend of mine," said Phoebe. "Not a friend, actually. More like an acquaintance."

"Really? Who?"

"You wouldn't know him."

"Shortish chap? Eyes like jade?"

"Yes, that's the one. Did you happen to see him?"

"He just left, I'm afraid." There was something remotely familiar about the woman's voice. She nodded toward the chair opposite and said, "But why don't you have a drink with me instead?"

"I wouldn't want to intrude."

"I insist."

Phoebe sat down, extended her hand across the tabletop, and introduced herself. The woman frowned and said, "Yes, I know. We were at Cambridge together."

"Were we?"

"We had a terrible row one evening. You threatened to throw me off the Magdalen Bridge."

Phoebe stared at the woman for a long moment, then said, "Take off those glasses."

She lowered them a fraction of an inch, revealing a pair of liquid blue eyes, then returned them to their original position. "You really mustn't cry, my darling Pheebs," she said in that posh drawl of hers. "After all, it's only me."

57

Wiltons

By then it was September, and the start of the Italian school year was fast approaching. Irene and Raphael, after spending three months in a remote corner of West Cornwall, were eager to resume their life in Venice, an enchanted place where one never encountered motorcars or lorries—or sheep or bovines, for that matter—and where one walked to dinner, then, after a stop at Venchi in the Rialto for gelato and butter cookies, one walked home again. Their mother was likewise anxious to return to the city of her birth, for she had two new restoration projects requiring her immediate attention. She was mildly displeased, therefore, that the esteemed director of her paintings department, having ruined his summer holiday searching for a missing British socialite who wasn't really missing, had decided to remain in the United Kingdom for another week in order to tie up a few loose ends.

She was more annoyed, admittedly, that he had nearly been blown to bits by an exploding Russian drone along with his friends Sarah Bancroft and Ingrid Johansen. But this, she reminded herself yet again, was the man she had married. He was a restorer of all things—paintings, old sports cars, British socialites, even thieves and contract killers—who could never seem to leave well enough alone. Still, when all was said and done, he had come through his latest adventure in remarkably good condition, nothing more than a few scrapes and bruises and a nasty dog bite on his left ankle. Oscar was the perpetrator's name. Leave it to Gabriel Allon to be bitten by a deer-red German pinscher called Oscar.

On the last day of their summer holiday they rose before dawn and sailed the Beneteau to the Isles of Scilly. So rough was the return trip that Chiara, once safely ashore in Penzance, swore she would never again set foot on a boat—a vaporetto or water taxi, perhaps, but not a vessel powered by the wind. Next morning she helped the children pack their bags and loaded them into the Range Rover for the drive to Heathrow. Gabriel brought along a garment bag with a dark suit and a sober tie. He had an appointment with the committee of inquiry in the morning and wanted to look his best.

"And what exactly," said Chiara, "are you going to say to them?"

"As little as possible."

"And when the members of the committee of inquiry *inquire* as to how it was you got mixed up in this affair in the first place?"

"Alice Winter, you mean?"

"Yes."

"My SIS-appointed lawyer will intercede on my behalf and change the subject."

"So the truth will never come out?"

"Never," replied Gabriel.

"A shame, don't you think? After all, you and your friends Sarah and Ingrid were the ones who saved Number Ten."

"With help from Christopher," Gabriel pointed out.

"And the Dutch," added Chiara.

"Let's not forget Alice. If she hadn't arranged for her own abduction, we never would have known about her husband's involvement with the Russians."

"It was a crime, you know."

"Staging one's own abduction? A very serious crime."

"And yet for her punishment," said Chiara, "she will receive immunity from prosecution and a new British identity."

"But not housing. In fact, she's about to be evicted from Wormwood Cottage."

"Parish and Miss Coventry have finally had enough?"

"A new arrival," said Gabriel.

"Where are they going to put her?"

"They've offered her temporary use of another safe house, but it wasn't up to her standards."

"Balmoral wasn't available?"

"Apparently not."

"Perhaps she can go stay with her fellow criminal Ingrid in Denmark."

"Ingrid is back on Mykonos. And Alice doesn't have a valid passport yet."

"Well," said Chiara, "I'm sure the great minds of the Secret Intelligence Service will think of something."

"Yes," agreed Gabriel. "They always do."

Their flight departed Heathrow at half past four. Gabriel dropped them outside Terminal 5, then, after swearing that he would undertake no new assignments during their absence, bade them farewell. Alone, he drove into central London and settled into a corner table at the bar at Wiltons and watched the parade of art world figures traipsing through the door—tubby Oliver Dimbleby, tweedy Jeremy Crabbe, suntanned Simon Mendenhall, ravishing Olivia Watson, Amelia March of *ARTnews*, slick Nicky Lovegrove, art adviser to the vastly rich. Sarah and Julian arrived last. Julian took up his usual post at the end of the bar, and Sarah joined Gabriel at her usual table. A three-olive Belvedere martini, Saharan dry, Siberian cold, appeared as though it had been conjured out of thin air.

She raised the frosted glass to her lips. "Off safely, are they?"

"Venice bound," he replied.

"So, I have you all to myself?"

"What about your husband?"

"The one who shot down the Russian drone?"

"Yes, that one."

"He left London this morning. Evidently he'll be gone for ages."

"Mind if I crash at your place tonight?"

She raised an eyebrow provocatively. "I'd love nothing more."

"I have an early call in the morning."

"Your appointment before the inquisition? I don't envy you."

"You're welcome to join me."

"Thank you, no. I have enough problems as it is."

"What problems do you possibly have?"

She glanced at Olivia Watson.

"It was a long time ago, Sarah."

"Not as long as the two of us."

"I'll never forget the first time I laid eyes on you," said Gabriel. "You were walking along P Street near Dupont Circle."

"The dew was still on me." Smiling, she surveyed the art world figures lining the bar. "It's a wonderful way for our story to end, don't you think? A late-summer evening, a corner table at the bar at Wiltons, all our old friends."

"It's not over yet, Sarah."

"You promise?"

Gabriel smiled. "Cross my heart."

His appointment before the committee of inquiry was at 9:00 A.M. The setting was a safe-speech room deep within Vauxhall Cross. SIS's chief legal officer, a man called Drake, sat by his side throughout. The questions were polite in tone, respectful, even, and Gabriel answered them to the best of his ability, which was limited. Indeed, whenever the inquisitors strayed onto dangerous ground, Drake the legal officer would mumble something that sounded like an incantation, and the inquisitors would dutifully move on. Thus they learned nothing from their star witness that they did not already know—nothing about Alice Winter and her husband Edward Knight, nothing about Alice's Cambridge friends Sophie Maxwell and Ella Burns, nothing about the staged abduction or the half-billion-dollar ransom payment or the chalet in Switzerland or the dog that had taken a chunk out of Gabriel's ankle in Lower Austria.

Which left the inquisitors little choice but to focus their attention on the day of the attack itself. Why, they wanted to know, had Gabriel made forcible entry into the house in Wilton Crescent? And who were the two women who entered the home with him? A glance at Drake and a mumbled magic spell made both questions disappear. He was more forthcoming, though, about what he had found on the roof of the house—and how he had managed to disable one of the drones. The lead inquisitor wanted to know why the toppled drone had detonated. Gabriel answered with what amounted to informed speculation.

"It was an assassination attempt."

"Who was the target?" asked the inquisitor.

"I was."

When the session finally ended, Gabriel headed to the SIS's private bar for a quick drink with Graham Seymour and was behind the wheel of the Range Rover in time to beat the London evening rush. The sun was setting by the time he reached Dartmoor. About a mile past the old Warren House Inn was the turnoff for Wormwood Cottage. He stopped there long enough to collect a single passenger. Parish the caretaker and Miss Coventry the cook, for all their forbearance and decency, were not sorry to see her go. She was, they assured themselves, someone else's problem now.

58

Wickham House

Of the minor role played in the affair by Detective Inspector Timothy Peel, neither his colleagues at the Devon and Cornwall Police nor the broader British public would ever know a thing. He was a page torn from a tattered book—or a ghost note, he thought, recalling his torturous childhood piano lessons, a softly struck E-flat, scarcely heard and soon forgotten. Slow to anger or feelings of resentment, he was appalled at how quickly he had been cast aside. The long ride home to Exeter on the night they brought Alice Winter back to Britain had left him cold. He had watched the events that unfolded next—the murder of a Russian agent in Copenhagen, the attack on Downing Street—certain in the knowledge that his old friend Gabriel Allon was the thread that ran through it all. And Ingrid, of course. What a pair of hands she had. Plucked a phone from the jacket pocket of a Swiss banker as though she were picking a daisy. Too bad it was the wrong bloody phone. Still, it all seemed to have worked out in the end, though no thanks to DI Timothy Peel. He was not ashamed to admit that from time to time, in moments of boredom and Cornish loneliness, it left a bitter taste.

Upon his return to duty, he rejoined the team investigating the murder of Gareth Wright, the carpenter who ended up in a shallow grave near the old mining town of Sticker. In Peel's absence the case had gone cold as ice. Having been away for a few days—truth be told, it seemed more like a month—he took it upon himself to conduct a thorough review of his colleagues' work. He read the notes and transcripts from the door-to-doors, he scoured the forensics reports from the SOCOs, he ran down the owner or operator of every vehicle that had passed a plate-recognition camera on the B3287 around the time Gareth Wright was last reported alive.

It was the camera that led Peel to the doorstep of one Trevor Knox of the hamlet of Blackwater. Knox, it seemed, had dabbled in carpentry himself before embarking on a life of crime. He claimed not to know the victim, but interviews with friends and associates revealed that some years earlier Trevor Knox had worked with Gareth Wright on a couple of projects—apparently not with any proficiency or diligence. Furthermore his explanation as to why he was in Sticker on or about the night of the murder didn't hold a drop of water. Claimed he went there to see an old girlfriend, but the girlfriend said that if Trevor Knox ever showed up at her door, the D&C Police would have another murder to investigate. She was a bit of a wreck, the old girlfriend, but Peel couldn't help but admire her style.

He took his findings to DCI Tony Fletcher, and Fletcher, after a few choice words to the other members of the investigative team, granted Peel permission to place Trevor Knox under surveillance. He conducted much of it personally and after a fortnight was convinced that it was time to interview the subject again, this time at headquarters in Exeter with a recorder rolling.

On a cold and rainswept morning in early September he dispatched a half-dozen uniforms to rouse Knox from his Blackwater bed and bring him in. But Peel scarcely had time to caution his prime suspect when DCI Fletcher entered the room and brought the interview to an abrupt end. And so it was that Timothy Peel was thrust once more into the strange case of Edward Knight and the missing British socialite who was not really missing.

It had been two months since she last set foot in Wickham House, but all the old rules still applied, especially those regarding her bereaved husband's office door, which was never to be opened or even knocked upon when closed. Charlotte Rose, Wickham's chief housekeeper, had violated the rule early in her tenure and had received such a tongue lashing—first from Mr. Knight, then from his personal assistant, Mr. Higgins—that the thought of violating it a second time never crossed her mind. She got the worst of it from Higgins, or Hiccups as the late Alice Winter used to call him, not only behind his back but straight to his face. Alice had loathed Higgins, and Higgins had loathed her in return.

But Higgins, thankfully, was gone, as was his replacement, a lovely fellow called Nigel Whitcombe. Charlotte had been sorry to see Mr. Whitcombe go, though she was pleased that Mr. Knight had finally rid himself of the security men who sat in a parked car just inside the manor's front gate. Every morning they insisted on inspecting Charlotte's driving license as though they had never laid eyes on her before. She reckoned she would have had an easier time getting into Number 10 wearing a suicide vest.

On that morning, however, Charlotte Rose rolled unmolested through Wickham's grand gate in her dowdy little Vauxhall and parked in her usual spot in the rear courtyard. She entered the house through the flower room and headed to the kitchen, passing the door of Mr. Knight's office along the way. It was tightly closed, which was not unusual, as Mr. Knight was an early riser and a dogged worker.

What *was* unusual was the silence within. Mr. Knight had a booming telephone voice and typically watched the financial news at a wall-vibrating volume.

Ninety minutes later, long after Charlotte commenced her daily cleaning of the enormous manor, she made a return visit to Mr. Knight's wing of the house and saw that the situation had not changed. A closed door, silence within. Gently, soundlessly, she tried the door's latch and discovered it was locked. Next, after first calling Mr. Knight's name, she gave the door the tenderest of knocks, but there was no answer. Nor did she receive any answer when she dialed the number for Mr. Knight's mobile phone, though she could hear the device ringing inside the office, clear as a bell.

At which point, having lived through the drama of Ms. Winter's abduction, Charlotte Rose thought it best to telephone the Devon and Cornwall Police. Two fresh-faced PCs appeared at Wickham House a few minutes later and, after obtaining permission from higher authority, forced the lock on the office door, whereupon they discovered Edward Knight seated at his desk, with two bullet holes in his chest and a third in the center of his forehead.

The two fresh-faced constables rang DCI Fletcher, and DI Timothy Peel was soon flying along the A3052 in an unmarked car, siren howling, grille lights flashing. Arriving at Wickham House, he donned the requisite protective gear and took control of the crime scene. His first stop inside the house was the victim's office. He was troubled by the lack of evidence of a struggle, which suggested the victim knew his killer. He was more troubled, though, by the fact that the property's elaborate security system had been switched off, which implied the killer possessed knowledge of the manor's inner workings.

Fortunately the plate-recognition camera located approximately a mile from Wickham House was working just fine that morning, and at 6:07 A.M., which just so happened to coincide with the estimated time of death, the camera snapped a photo of a Ford Fiesta that had been reported stolen the previous evening in Swindon. A vehicle search undertaken at Peel's directive revealed that in the intervening two hours and fifteen minutes, the Ford had passed three more plate-recognition cameras—one west of Exeter, one in little Launceston, and a third near Truro.

It didn't take a genius to see that the driver of the vehicle, whoever he was, and for whatever reason, was headed straight for the western tip of the Cornish Peninsula. Peel requested a helicopter from the National Police Air Service and, in his capacity as a newly certified AFO, a Glock 19 pistol. Before boarding the helicopter he placed a last phone call, mobile to mobile. As was frequently the case, the call failed to connect. The cell service out there was for the birds.

59

Gwennap Head

The guest room was upstairs in what was once an attic. It lacked the opulence to which Alice was accustomed, but it was nicer than her old digs at Wormwood Cottage, and from the little window next to the double bed she could make out the towering Wolf Rock Lighthouse rising from the sea. She slept soundly for the first time in months and finally wandered downstairs to the kitchen around nine o'clock. Gabriel made her a breakfast of tea and toast and muesli. She declared it positively divine.

They had arrived at the cottage in the dead of night, and now, in the cold light of morning, she was able to consider it properly for the first time. The kitchen was a real kitchen, not some epicurean showplace ripped from the pages of a magazine, and the large drawing room was at once comfortable and yet refined in every way. There were paintings on the walls, monographs on the shelves, faded carpets on the rustic wood floor. It was quite obviously the home of an artist—a warrior poet, she thought. If only she had married someone like him instead of Edward. Her life might have looked like this.

"Who was your decorator?" she asked.

"My wife."

"She has exquisite taste."

"In most things," he said. "I was her one inexplicable mistake."

She gave him a disapproving look. "I'm sure you have countless lovers."

"Only one," he said, and pointed toward a large seated nude of a woman with riotous dark hair. She was intoxicatingly beautiful.

"Is that her?"

He nodded.

"And the artist?"

"Fortunately she only poses for me."

When she had finished her breakfast, he led her on a proper tour of the house. Like many old homes in the English countryside, he said, it seemed to have a mind of its own. He showed her which cabinets contained the pots and pans and which the dishes and glassware, where she could find clean bedding and bath towels, and where they kept the Wellies and the torches and the candles and the matches. He taught her how to set and disable the security alarm, gave her the password for the Wi-Fi network, and showed her the places in the house where the cellular service was the most reliable.

"As a general rule," he explained, "it's hit-and-miss out here in West Cornwall except for in the largest towns and villages. If I were you, I'd stay off the phone entirely. It will significantly reduce your chances of being found out."

"How long can I stay?"

"That depends on your tolerance for Cornish winters."

"You can't be serious."

"You can stay here as long as you like, Alice."

"And the rent?" she asked.

"A single peppercorn, payable at your convenience."

"Edward would be horrified."

"I'm not a terribly business-minded person."

"Neither was Edward, as it turned out."

Lastly he took her to his studio. It was the one part of the property he asked her to avoid. With the exception of his wife and children and two employees of London's most respected art shipping company, only one other person had set foot there.

"And who was that?" she asked.

"Your husband."

"Is this the part where you tell me how bereft and bereaved he was by my disappearance?"

"It was an unconscionable thing you did."

"And if I hadn't?"

"Downing Street might well be in ruins."

The weather forecast called for rain until late morning, so he drove her to the Morrisons in Long Rock for a bit of shopping. None of the other patrons gave her a second look as she loaded her cart with mounds of microwavable fare. She paid with a credit card bearing the name of her new British identity.

"I prefer your old name," said Gabriel as they started back to Gwennap Head.

"So do I, but that would rather defeat the purpose of an assumed identity." She stared gloomily out her rain-spattered window at the sands of Long Rock Beach. "It's not exactly Saint-Tropez, is it?"

"It will grow on you."

"I don't know about you, Mr. Allon, but I try to avoid things that grow on me."

The rain had ended by the time they returned to the cottage, but the weather was still blustery and cold. After loading the groceries into the pantry and fridge, Alice asked, "What now?"

"I keep a sailboat in Penzance Harbor."

"In this weather? Sounds a bit treacherous to me."

"How about a nice long walk along the cliffs instead?"

"A much better idea."

They pulled on oilskin coats and Wellington boots and set off across the sodden meadow. When they reached the Coast Path, Alice slowed to a stop.

"Which direction?" she asked.

"The choice is yours."

She debated for a moment, then turned to the right and started toward Land's End. Gabriel followed after her, unaware of the fact that Detective Inspector Timothy Peel of the Devon and Cornwall Police was at that same moment trying desperately to reach him.

The NPAS helicopter was an Airbus H130, with a never-exceed speed of 160 miles per hour. Forty-five minutes after leaving Exeter it was on the ground at Land's End Airport. A cruiser waited on the rain-dampened tarmac, driven by PC Elenore Tremayne. Peel had worked with PC Tremayne on one of the Chopper murders, a young woman from Great Torrington who was killed while walking home after a night of drinking with friends at the Black Horse pub. PC Tremayne had found the killer's shoeprints not far from the scene of the crime. While Peel was in the air over West Cornwall, she had found the stolen Ford Fiesta.

"It's in the Porthgwarra car park. We have four uniforms on the scene. The SOCOs are on their way."

"Did anyone happen to see the driver?"

"No, sir."

"I have a fair idea where he went next."

"And where is that, sir?"

"A rather large house about a quarter mile to the north."

"The one next to Charlie Twigg's place?"

"That's the one."

PC Tremayne switched on her lights and siren and pushed the throttle to the floor. It was a seven-mile drive, much of it along treacherous hedgerow-lined lanes, but she managed to cover the distance in just under ten minutes. As they turned through the gate, Peel spotted Gabriel's Range Rover parked in the forecourt. The door to his studio, which was never left unlocked, had been opened with the help of a firearm. So too had the door to the main house.

Peel drew his Glock 19 and searched the house from top to bottom. It was unoccupied and, with the exception of the front door, undamaged. Based on the number of breakfast dishes soaking in the kitchen sink, at least two people were currently in residence, one of whom was staying in the upstairs guest room. Peel, after inspecting the clothing in the guest's suitcase, was confident he knew who she was.

Outside, he dialed Gabriel's number but once again received no answer. Then, with the radio in PC Tremayne's cruiser, he raised DCI Fletcher in Exeter and gave him an update. Fletcher immediately asked the NPAS to get the helicopter back in the air, this time over the South West Coast Path between Gwennap Head and Land's End. By the time the helicopter was finally airborne, Peel was passing the National Coastwatch Institution observation point, Glock 19 in hand, running as fast as his legs could carry him.

60

Land's End

She pleaded with him to take her for a proper English tea at the Land's End Hotel, and when he refused, she agreed to settle for a pasty from the Cornish Pantry instead. By the time they set off for the return trip to Gwennap Head, the weather had taken a turn for the worse and a veil of mist hung over the Coast Path, limiting visibility to a few hundred yards at most. For a time it seemed like they were the only two people in the world, lone survivors of some cataclysm that had claimed the lives of others like them. Then the mist parted and a lone figure appeared. He was wearing ordinary street clothes rather than the outdoor attire worn by most hikers along the footpath. His head was lowered against the sharp wind blowing from the sea. His pace was brisk, as though he were running late for an appointment.

"No," said Alice suddenly. "It can't possibly be him."

"Who?"

"The man walking toward us. That's bloody Hiccups."

"I'm sorry?"

"Liam Higgins," she said. "Edward's old assistant."

Gabriel eyed the man marching toward them through the mist. "It has to be someone else."

"I'd recognize that walk anywhere. It's definitely him."

"But why on earth would he be here, of all places?"

"Edward must have sent him."

"Edward doesn't know where you are."

But Edward knew the location of Gabriel's remote Cornish retreat, and therefore so did his former assistant, Liam Higgins. After all, it was Higgins who had fetched Gabriel at Land's End Airport after he agreed to look into Alice's disappearance.

"Walk back to the hotel," he told her. "And while you're there, you should probably call nine-nine-nine."

"Why?"

Higgins was upon them before Gabriel could answer. He bore little resemblance to the pressed and polished figure who had whispered into the ear of Edward Knight the evening of the Wickham House fundraiser. His clothing looked slept in, his hair was uncombed, his cheeks were unshaven, his eyes were red and raw with fatigue. And bloodlust, thought Gabriel.

"Allon!" he called out with counterfeit astonishment as he slowed to a stop. "Fancy meeting you here." Then he looked at Alice and said, "You too, Ms. Winter. After all, aren't you supposed to be dead?"

Gabriel answered on Alice's behalf. "What's that you have under your jacket, Higgins?"

He drew the gun in reply, an ugly old Makarov with a suppressor screwed into the end of the barrel.

"A Russian gun for a Russian agent," said Gabriel. "So much for the GRU upping its game."

"I fooled you, though, didn't I?"

"You did," admitted Gabriel.

He smiled with what appeared to be genuine satisfaction. His forehead seemed more prominent, his cheekbones harder and more defined. Gabriel admonished himself for having missed what was now obvious.

"What's your real name?" he asked.

"It's not important."

"Don't I have the right to know the name of the man who's about to kill me?"

"My name," he answered in Russian-accented English, "is Valery Fedorov."

"I'm glad we cleared that up." Gabriel removed his eyes briefly from the Russian's face and glimpsed a distant figure loping along the Coast Path near Mill Bay. "And your GRU rank?" he asked.

"Colonel."

Which meant that he had outranked Yuri Ivanov. It was important to keep him talking. Flattery seemed the safest option.

"Why would they use an important man like you to do a wet job like this? Why not kill me with a miniature drone the way they killed Yuri Ivanov in Copenhagen?"

"It was determined that you should receive a proper Russian execution."

"*Vysshaya mera*?"

"I never realized you spoke our language."

"And who determined that I should receive the highest measure of punishment? The director of the GRU?"

"Oh no," said Colonel Valery Fedorov. "It was the Russian president himself who handed down your sentence."

"I suppose Edward Knight is next."

"Mr. Knight," said Fedorov with mock sadness, "is already dead."

"Did he know your real identity?"

"Of course not."

"How did you end up working for him?"

"My previous employer was expelled from the United Kingdom

after the beginning of the special military operation in Ukraine. He asked Mr. Knight to take me on, and Mr. Knight generously agreed."

"Your previous employer was Dmitri Savin?"

"Very good, Allon."

"And Dmitri, of course, knew your real identity."

"We spoke only Russian to one another."

Gabriel permitted himself a glance toward the approaching figure. "And when you've killed me?" he asked. "What then?"

"I shall return to the motherland."

"How are you going to manage that?"

"There's a boat waiting for me in Padstow." It was a little fishing village on Cornwall's northern coast. "I'll meet up with a cargo ship in the Irish Sea. It's part of our shadow fleet."

"That doesn't sound like much of a plan to me, Colonel Fedorov. In fact, as someone who knows these waters well, I rank your chances of survival at one in ten."

"Rest assured, Allon, your odds are much worse." He pointed the Makarov at Gabriel's face and spoke in the voice of Liam Higgins. "In all honesty, I'm a rather dreadful shot. But even I can't miss at this range."

Just then the air shuddered with the distant thump of a helicopter rotor. The man running along the Coast Path had closed to within about three hundred meters. He might have been nearer by now had he not been wearing a detective's dark suit and carrying a Glock 19 pistol, which weighed nearly two pounds when fully loaded. Gabriel needed to buy him another minute.

"Your superiors have sent you on a fool's errand," he told Colonel Valery Fedorov. "You'll never get out of Britain alive. Put the gun down, and I'll make sure my friends at the Secret Intelligence Service take good care of you."

"I'm not a traitor, Allon. And if you must know, I volunteered for the job of killing you. You should consider yourself lucky that I didn't do it sooner."

"What stopped you?"

"I had a more important assignment."

"You and your colleague Chloé Lamont were assembling ten drones at that house in Wilton Crescent. She was the one you were talking to that evening in Berkeley Square. I only wished you had introduced us. I would have enjoyed meeting her."

"Regrettably she was running late."

"Where is she now?"

"Safely back in Moscow."

"Her DNA is all over that house. And so is yours, for that matter."

"And yours," said Fedorov, "will soon be splattered along this path." He pointed the gun toward the cliff's edge. "Turn around and get on your knees."

"Not a chance."

He swung the gun toward Alice. "I'd be more than happy to kill her first, if you prefer."

Gabriel briefly considered attempting to disarm the Russian but calmly directed his gaze toward the northern sky instead. "Look there, Colonel Fedorov. That's not a sightseeing helicopter, not on a day like this. That will be the police."

He had a look at the helicopter for himself. It had the effect of diverting his attention away from Detective Inspector Timothy Peel of the Devon and Cornwall Police, who was approaching from the opposite direction. He was at least a hundred yards away. Even Gabriel would struggle to pull off a shot like that.

"It's over, Colonel Fedorov," he said, raising his voice to be heard over the sound of the helicopter. "Put down the gun and give yourself up. It's your only chance."

The Russian responded by grabbing a fistful of Alice's hair and screwing the barrel of the Makarov into her right temple. His face was white as a bedsheet, revealing the skull beneath his skin. "On your knees, Allon."

Gabriel rotated slowly to the right, granting himself one last look at Peel, then walked the five steps from the footpath to the cliff's edge and dropped to his knees. Colonel Valery Fedorov forced Alice to her knees at his side. She seized hold of Gabriel's hand and squeezed it so tightly he feared his fingers might snap. "Please forgive me," she was saying, but he was staring spellbound at the sea. There were, he assured himself, far worse places to die.

At last he felt the cold barrel of the Makarov pressing against the nape of his neck and an instant later heard a single deafening gunshot. He had expected to see a flash of blinding light, but instead there was only the sea, heaving itself silently against the rocks of Pordenack Point. He looked down and saw Alice lying next to him in a bed of purple thrift and red fescue, the left half of her face covered in blood. Surely, he thought, it was his blood, because he was the one who had been shot, not her, and he was the one who was now dead. "I'm sorry," she shouted over the thunderous roar of a helicopter. "None of this would have happened if it wasn't for me."

61

Cornwall–Venice

The chief constable issued her carefully worded statement at two fifteen that afternoon. It said that the real estate investor Edward Knight had been found shot to death inside his historic Devon manor shortly after 9:00 A.M., by all appearances the victim of a homicide. It offered no plausible motive, identified no possible suspects, made no promise of an imminent arrest. No, the chief constable said pointedly in response to a reporter's question, there appeared to be no link whatsoever between Edward Knight's murder and the recent abduction of his wife, the socialite Alice Winter.

Also absent from the chief constable's statement was any reference to the killing, later that same morning, of the billionaire's former personal assistant. The cause of death was a single gunshot to the left side of his head. The weapon was a Glock 19 nine-millimeter, the standard pistol carried by Authorized Firearms Officers of the Devon and Cornwall Police. The distance of the shot was approximately thirty-five yards, though this would never be determined with any degree of forensic certainty because elements of British intelligence, acting under the authority granted to them by the Official Secrets Act, laid claim to the decedent's corpse before a postmortem could be carried out. The remains went up in smoke forty-eight hours later at the Putney Vale Crematorium, and the ashes were scattered to the four winds. As for the billionaire's missing wife, she assumed her new identity and once again disappeared, this time for good.

The London papers followed the events surrounding Edward Knight's murder with intense interest, but for the most part Gabriel averted his gaze. With Timothy Peel's help, he replaced the two ruined doors at the Gwennap Head cottage with exact duplicates and repaired the shattered woodwork. Then, with a can of glossy white paint and a two-inch brush, he carried out one of the most important restorations of his long career. It was a bit heavy-handed, he judged, but masterful all the same. Not even his eagle-eyed wife would ever be able to tell the difference. Indeed the only clue as to what had transpired in her absence was the seascape he left on the easel in his studio, a view from the cliffs above Pordenack Point, painted from the depths of his memory.

He took the Beneteau out for a final sail, then instructed Ronnie Mills to put it up on the rack for the winter. The Range Rover he entrusted to Peel, provided he agree to shuttle Gabriel to Heathrow. He caught the four o'clock flight and arrived in Venice as the sun was setting on a perfect late-summer day. During the water taxi ride into the city he wondered whether any of it had really happened, whether it was only just a dream.

The driver dropped him at the Grand Canal entrance of the palazzo, and he climbed the stairs to the apartment. Irene was lying on the floor of the sitting room, a pencil in her hand, a tiny fist pressed to her porcelain brow. Her brother, having completed his schoolwork, was sketching away at something in a Strathmore pad.

Chiara was in the kitchen, singing along to the silly Italian pop song playing on the Bluetooth. She poured Gabriel a glass of bloodred Barbaresco and asked about his flight. It was fine, he assured her. Everything was fine.

Author's Note

Ransom is a work of entertainment and should be read as nothing more. The names, characters, places, and incidents portrayed in the story are the product of the author's imagination or have been used fictitiously. Any resemblance to actual persons, living or dead, businesses, companies, events, or locales is entirely coincidental.

There is indeed a large dwelling near Cornwall's Gwennap Head, but Gabriel Allon and his family do not spend their summers there. Visitors to the Lizard Peninsula hamlet of Gunwalloe should not expect to find the Corner Market or a bakery owned by the enchanting Vera Hobbs, for neither establishment exists. The rest of the remarkable region is, for the most part, accurately rendered. While it is true that cellular service can be spotty outside the larger towns, I granted myself a certain license to suit the needs of my story. Guests of the Land's End Hotel should have no problem making a phone call while dining in the restaurant, though barring an emergency they should simply enjoy the breathtaking view instead.

Sadly the dire financial condition of Britain's public art museums portrayed in *Ransom* is entirely accurate. The National Portrait Gallery did indeed rely largely on private contributions to carry out a recent renovation, and the names of large donors now grace the main courtyard and an important wing. The National Gallery, for its part, is attempting to raise £95 million to pay for renovations on its iconic building overlooking Trafalgar Square. When the museum resolved to add Orazio Gentileschi's *The Finding of Moses* to its collection, it had no choice but to undertake a yearslong slog to raise the necessary funds. The monumental painting now hangs in Room 31, along with works by Correggio, Tintoretto, Rubens, and Van Dyck.

The Venetian cityscape by Bernardo Bellotto depicted in *Ransom* is invented, but Bellotto made many paintings like it, including *View of Verona with the Ponte delle Navi*, which fetched £10.5 million in July 2021 at Christie's in London, a record price for the artist. Needless to say, the gavel was not wielded that evening by Simon Mendenhall because suntanned Simon, like the rest of the madcap menagerie of London art world figures who grace the pages of *Ransom*, is entirely fictitious. I once again offer profound apologies to the management of Wiltons restaurant. Rest assured, I have tried to convince Julian Isherwood and his friends to find another watering hole, but they regard the very idea as blasphemous. Besides, given their well-earned reputation for debauchery, I'm afraid no other reputable establishment would have them.

There are numerous real estate investment firms in the United Kingdom, but the Knight Group Ltd. of Berkeley Square is entirely fictitious, as is the conduct of its founder and his beautiful wife. There is no Magic Circle law firm known as Ambler & Rose, no London-based international aid organization known as Global Relief UK, and no silent donor service known as the Secret Sharer, a name I borrowed from Joseph Conrad. HSBC, the British bank that employs the fictitious Ella Burns, was fined a record $1.9 billion by US regulators in 2012 for laundering more than $881 million for Mexican and Colombian drug cartels. One should not attempt to open an account at Bank Josef Bänzinger & Co. on the Bahnhofstrasse in

Zurich because, thankfully, no such financial service firm exists. Nor is there a Swiss corporate security company known as Sentry Global, though there are others like it, including the outfit hired by Credit Suisse in 2019 to illegally surveil the head of its wealth management division. The ensuing scandal, which became known as Spygate, would play a key role in the bank's eventual collapse.

There is indeed a grand house on London's Prince of Wales Terrace that has fallen into disrepair, but the owner is not the fictitious Russian oligarch Dmitri Savin. Deepest apologies to tiny Luxembourg for using its beautiful embassy in Wilton Crescent as the setting for the novel's climactic sequence, but given the circumstances, a private residence wouldn't do. For the record, the sausage rolls at the Ginger Pig are consistently rated as among the finest in London. And yes, at the time of this writing there was a popular bar in Covent Garden called Tequila Mockingbird.

Devotees of the late P. D. James surely noticed that I borrowed elements of *The Black Tower* for the penultimate scene of the novel, an ending foreshadowed when Alice Winter thoughtlessly spoiled Phoebe Chadwick's poolside reading material. I also borrowed the title of *The Skull Beneath the Skin* in my description of Colonel Valery Fedorov's desperate appearance. Imagery from *The Great Gatsby* likewise found its way into my typescript, especially in my depictions of the art world gatherings at Wickham House. Sarah Bancroft, while reminiscing with Gabriel over drinks at Wiltons, borrowed a line from *Tender Is the Night*, as she often does.

The Amsterdam and Helsinki drone incidents portrayed in *Ransom* are fictitious, but Copenhagen Airport was the target of a major drone incursion on the evening of September 22, 2025, that resulted in continent-wide travel delays and disruption. In the days that followed there were drone sightings at three other Danish civilian airports and at Denmark's primary base for fighter aircraft. Prime Minister Mette Frederiksen placed the police and military on the highest state of readiness and reportedly considered activating military reservists. When European leaders convened in Copenhagen the following week for an emergency meeting, Danish security officials were so concerned about the possibility of a drone attack that they borrowed anti-drone kits and other assets from their European allies. French president Emmanuel Macron dispatched some thirty-five specialists to help secure the summit.

The Danish defense minister described the drone incursion as a "hybrid attack" carried out by a "professional actor" but stopped short of assigning blame. Still, the minister's carefully chosen words would suggest that he believed the perpetrator undoubtedly had a Moscow address—perhaps Khoroshevsky Highway 76, the headquarters of the Main Directorate of the General Staff of the Armed Forces of the Russian Federation, better known as the GRU. If that was indeed the case, it was in all likelihood the work of Unit 29155.

The very existence of the elite unit was first revealed in the autumn of 2019, when European security and intelligence officials reached the unsettling conclusion that Vladimir Putin's Russia was actively waging a clandestine shadow war against the West. In the lexicon of the Kremlin it was hybrid warfare, a blend of subversion, sabotage, assassinations, election interference, cyberattacks, and information and propaganda operations. The goal of this secret war is nothing less than the destruction of the NATO alliance and the liberal Western order, which Putin regards as a threat to Russia's very existence. GRU Unit 29155 has no other mission.

Lately Unit 29155 has been in the business of punishing western European countries that have provided military and economic assistance to Ukraine. The travel bans and sanctions imposed on Russian citizens after the onset of the so-called special military operation have indeed required Unit 29155 to change its tradecraft and tactics, but that has not slowed the tempo and audaciousness of its operations. A report prepared by the Center for Strategic and International Studies found that the number of Russian sabotage attacks against western Europe increased fourfold during the first year of the war in Ukraine, then tripled again during year two of the campaign. Most were directed against transportation targets, followed closely by attacks against industrial targets, pipelines, undersea cables, and other critical infrastructure. Many of the attacks have been carried out not by line GRU officers but proxies and criminals, who have proven less than reliable. Richard Moore, who served as the director-general of Britain's Secret Intelligence Service from 2020 to 2025, has said that Russia's intelligence services have "gone a bit feral, frankly, in some of their behavior."

In perhaps the most shocking incident, the GPS navigation system of the plane carrying EU president Ursula von der Leyen failed during a flight to Bulgaria, requiring the pilots to resort to paper maps to land the aircraft safely. EU officials wasted little time in pointing the finger of blame at Russia, which denied any involvement. Regardless of whether it was an assassination attempt, Vladimir Putin surely would not have shed a tear if the EU president, a steadfast supporter of Ukraine, had died in a mysterious plane crash.

It would be far easier, though, to murder a meddlesome political leader—or opposition figure or investigative journalist, for that matter—with a drone. It need not be a moth-sized microdrone armed with a lethal nerve agent; a small Black Hornet drone with an explosive payload would do just fine. The drone could kill a president or prime minister as she stepped from her official car or while she relaxed in the walled garden of her residence. If such an assassination were planned and executed skillfully, it would be difficult to determine conclusively who was responsible. In the words of my Danish spy chief Lars Mortensen: "Welcome to a world gone mad."

Western European intelligence officials and political leaders have watched the Russian sabotage activity with increasing alarm—and with the growing realization that Europe might soon find itself in something more than a shadow war with Russia. "Conflict is at our door," NATO secretary general Mark Rutte said in December 2025. "We must be prepared for the scale of war our grandparents or great-grandparents endured." Whether Europe would wage such a war with the help of the United States, NATO's most powerful member, remains an open question. After all, in January 2026 eight NATO countries deployed troops to Greenland to defend the Danish territory against a threatened invasion by another member, an ignoble first in the long history of the most successful military alliance the world has ever known.

In chapter 37 of *Ransom*, I describe the French president, the German chancellor, and the prime ministers of Denmark and the United Kingdom as the leaders "of what was once fondly known as the free world." It is fair to ask, though, whether "the free world," or even "the West," still exists. The collapse of the postwar liberal order was brought about by too many factors to list in this small space, but one element cannot be denied: For more than two decades a vengeful and revanchist Vladimir Putin, with the help of his intelligence services, has worked tirelessly to destroy the old order and replace it with one led by Moscow. Perhaps it is time, as my fictitious British spymaster Graham Seymour suggests, to take the gloves off and launch a hybrid war against Russia—with stealth and low cunning and, yes, a touch of wickedness. Turnabout, as the old saying goes, is fair play.

Acknowledgments

Maxwell L. Anderson, who has five times served as the director of a North American art museum, including the Whitney Museum of American Art in New York, gave me a tutorial on the rigors of staging special exhibitions and raising the necessary funds. Mark Hertling, the former commanding general of the United States Army Europe, advised me on drone technology, the activities of Russia's GRU, and the emerging threat facing western Europe. A former senior US intelligence official answered the questions he could, deflected the ones he couldn't, and never once failed to make me laugh.

My children, Lily and Nicholas, managed to find time in their busy schedules to provide me with moral and technical support, and my son-in-law, Kamil Sadik, an investment banker at Morgan Stanley, was an invaluable source of information on the world of international commercial real estate. My wife, Jamie Gangel, listened with admirable patience while I worked out the multilayered plot of *Ransom* and then skillfully edited the stack of paper I euphemistically refer to as my first draft, all while serving as special correspondent in CNN's Washington bureau. My debt to her is immeasurable, as is my love.

My Los Angeles superlawyer, Michael Gendler, was a source of wise counsel, legal and otherwise. Harper president and publisher Jonathan Burnham made countless improvements to *Ransom*, as did my dear friend Louis Toscano, who has been editing my copy since I was twenty-four. Kathy Crosby made certain the final galleys were free of typographical and grammatical errors, and David Koral and Brianna Cedrone shepherded the book through the production process on the tightest of schedules.

I consulted hundreds of newspaper and magazine articles while writing *Ransom*, far too many to cite here, but I owe a special debt to the reporters of *The New Yorker*, *The New York Times*, *The Wall Street Journal*, *The Guardian*, and the BBC for their remarkable coverage of Russia's clandestine war against the West.

Finally, a heartfelt thanks to the rest of the team at HarperCollins, especially Brian Murray, Liate Stehlik, Leah Wasielewski, Doug Jones, Leslie Cohen, Milan Bozic, Mark Ferguson, Robin Bilardello, Bonni Leon-Berman, Carolyn Bodkin, Chantal Restivo-Alessi, Julianna Wojcik, Mark Meneses, Beth Silfin, Catherine Barbosa-Ross, Lisa Erickson, and Amy Baker.

About the Author

Daniel Silva is the award-winning #1 *New York Times* bestselling author of twenty-eight previous novels. He is married to the television journalist Jamie Gangel. His books are critically acclaimed bestsellers around the world and have been translated into more than thirty languages.